Rory
IN A KILT

Other Books by Anna Durand

Lachlan in a Kilt (The Ballachulish Trilogy, Book One)
Aidan in a Kilt (The Ballachulish Trilogy, Book Two)
The American Wives Club (A Hot Brits/Hot Scots/Au Naturel Crossover Book)
Brit vs. Scot (A Hot Brits/Hot Scots/Au Naturel Crossover Book)
Dangerous in a Kilt (Hot Scots, Book One)
Wicked in a Kilt (Hot Scots, Book Two)
Scandalous in a Kilt (Hot Scots, Book Three)
The MacTaggart Brothers Trilogy (Hot Scots, Books 1-3)
Gift-Wrapped in a Kilt (Hot Scots, Book Four)
Notorious in a Kilt (Hot Scots, Book Five)
Insatiable in a Kilt (Hot Scots, Book Six)
Lethal in a Kilt (Hot Scots, Book Seven)
Irresistible in a Kilt (Hot Scots, Book Eight)
Devastating in a Kilt (Hot Scots, Book Nine)
Spellbound in a Kilt (Hot Scots, Book Ten)
Relentless in a Kilt (Hot Scots, Book Eleven)
One Hot Chance (Hot Brits, Book One)
One Hot Roomie (Hot Brits, Book Two)
One Hot Crush (Hot Brits, Book Three)
The Dixon Brothers Trilogy (Hot Brits, Books 1-3)
One Hot Escape (Hot Brits, Book Four)
One Hot Rumor (Hot Brits, Book Five)
One Hot Christmas (Hot Brits, Book Six)
Natural Passion (Au Naturel Trilogy, Book One)
Natural Impulse (Au Naturel Trilogy, Book Two)
Natural Satisfaction (Au Naturel Trilogy, Book Three)
Fired Up (a standalone romance)
Echo Power (Echo Power Trilogy, Book One)
The Mortal Falls (Undercover Elementals, Book One)
The Mortal Fires (Undercover Elementals, Book Two)
The Mortal Tempest (Undercover Elementals, Book Three)
The Janusite Trilogy (Undercover Elementals, Books 1-3)
Obsidian Hunger (Undercover Elementals, Book Four)
Unbidden Hunger (Undercover Elementals, Book Five)
Willpower (Psychic Crossroads, Book One)
Intuition (Psychic Crossroads, Book Two)
Kinetic (Psychic Crossroads, Book Three)
Passion Never Dies: The Complete Reborn Series

Rory IN A KILT

The Ballachulish Trilogy, Book Three

ANNA DURAND

JACOBSVILLE BOOKS ⬥ MARIETTA, OHIO

RORY IN A KILT

ISBN: 978-1-949406-77-1 (paperback)
ISBN: 978-1-949406-78-8 (ebook)
ISBN: 978-1-949406-79-5 (audiobook)

Manufactured in the United States.

Jacobsville Books
www.JacobsvilleBooks.com

Publisher's Cataloging-in-Publication Data
provided by Five Rainbows Cataloging Services

Names: Durand, Anna, author.
Title: Rory in a kilt / Anna Durand.
Description: Marietta, OH : Jacobsville Books, 2021. | Series: Ballachulish Trilogy, bk. 3.
Identifiers: ISBN 978-1-949406-77-1 (paperback) | ISBN 978-1-949406-78-8 (ebook) | ISBN 978-1-949406-79-5 (audiobook)
Subjects: LCSH: Man-woman relationships--Fiction. | Scots--Fiction. | Americans--Fiction. | Highlands (Scotland)--Fiction. | New Orleans (La.)--Fiction. | Marriage--Fiction. | Romance fiction. | BISAC: FICTION / Romance / Contemporary. | FICTION / Romance / Romantic Comedy. | GSAFD: Love stories.
Classification: LCC PS3604.U724 R67 2021 (print) | LCC PS3604.U724 (ebook) | DDC 813/.6—dc23.

Chapter One

I sweep my gaze around the main bar of Pat O'Brien's one last time, half hoping and half dreading I'll find a woman with a body made for slaking my lust. A one-night stand in New Orleans will hardly become the highlight of my first visit to America. The idea of studying this country's legal system had aroused my intellectual passion a few days ago when I'd suggested it to my mate, who's a lawyer here in New Orleans, and the trip had been my excuse to escape from my life. But none of the women I've come across in the past week aroused my sexual passions. Maybe I've grown jaded about sex, the way I have about love. My third and final fling, thirteen months ago, had put me off one-night stands. Sex without names, without sharing a bed for more than an hour, has lost its appeal.

What do I need? Or want? Got no bloody clue, MacTaggart, do you?

Swigging the last of my whisky, I pull a face at the subpar quality of the drink. American single malts can't compare to the genuine Scottish variety. I set down my glass and stride out of the main bar into the carriageway between the sections of Pat O'Brien's. A small group of people rushes past me, their laughter a bit too loud and their smiles a bit too exuberant. Buckled, they are. If I'd gotten intoxicated, maybe I would enjoy this night more.

Not likely.

The group ambles off down the carriageway, and I glimpse the doorway on the other side. Soft lighting and soft piano music emanate from the adjoining section of this establishment. I consider walking into the piano bar, but I've lost my enthusiasm for…everything. My thoughts travel back to Scotland, to my home in the Highlands and my family there, brothers and sisters, parents and uncles, cousins too. A pang aches in my chest. I should go back to my hotel room and ring the pilot to inform him to get my jet ready so we can head home tonight.

I start to turn away from the door, but movement snares my attention.

A blonde woman perches on a wooden stool, her curvaceous body twisting and turning as she strives for the perfect posture for a self-portrait. She holds a mobile above her head at arm's length, rotating and tipping the device until she seems satisfied with the angle. A broad, brilliant smile lights up her stunning face.

Have I found an angel in disguise? No, I'm not that fortunate.

No room in my life for an angel, anyway. No room for any woman, for longer than a night.

The blonde snaps a picture, then stuffs the mobile in the back pocket of her jeans.

I stare at the angel, frozen in my fascination with that lush body bound in jeans and a short-sleeve shirt.

She bites her lower lip and glances around the bar. Satisfied with whatever she sees or doesn't see, the lass shoves a hand inside her shirt to root about in her bra.

My lips begin to kink into a slight smile, but I flatten it out. Tilting my head to the side, I absorb the sight of this beautiful woman and her bizarre task. She peeks inside her shirt, where her hand remains lodged inside her bra, and then whisks her hand free. She pats her chest and clasps her delicate hands around a tall, curved glass that holds red liquid. The bonnie lass gulps down a long draft of the beverage.

A wistful smile curls her delicate mouth.

I march into the piano bar, headed straight for her.

What force compels me to move, I have no idea. Something about this woman lures me to her, inexorably, inescapably. Her pensive expression a moment ago seems a contradiction to her usual demeanor—or rather, the way she'd behaved for all but two seconds of the time since I first saw her. The lass possesses an inner light that streams out of her in every smile and glance, in the way she moves and in her complete disregard for decorum.

I've become mired in a need to control my emotions, my expressions, my behavior. And all for what? I want what this woman exudes from every pore of her enticing body. I want freedom.

For one night only. Aye, one night.

Perhaps if I bury myself inside that lithe body, I might absorb a hint of her…essence.

Ridiculous. I should walk out the door and head home as I'd planned. I shouldn't keep striding toward this woman. And I absolutely should not speak to her.

She has closed her eyes, relishing her drink. Her lips part slightly, and her head slants back a wee bit, accentuating her slender neck.

Turn around, man. Leave now.

I stop behind the empty stool adjacent to hers. "May I take this seat?"

The lass jumps, snapping upright, her eyes wide and blinking furiously. She raises a hand as if to touch her hair, then clamps both palms around the glass.

She is…exquisite. Her shirt clings to her full breasts and highlights the curve of her waist, drawing my gaze lower to her hips and those shapely legs. I can't see her erse, since she's sitting down, but I know it will be as delectable as the rest of her. When I finally settle my gaze on her face, I freeze. She looks so young. Should I, a man approaching forty, proposition a bairn? What if she's underage?

Dimly, I notice the words printed on her shirt—ComicCon. Whatever that means, I don't give a shit.

As she admires my body with unabashed interest, my cock pulses.

I want her with a scorching lust, but I need to make certain. "How old are you?"

She tears her focus away from my lower body. Her lips tick up at the corners. "You must not get lucky very often if you ask women that question."

A feisty one. I like it. Feisty women make the best lovers.

"You look young," I say, tilting my head left and right to appraise her, "but your manner is mature."

"Oh, I get it. You're worried I'm jailbait. Relax, I'm thirty-four." She lifts her glass. "Ask the bartender. He carded me."

"I'll take your word for it."

My cock won't let me wait for the bartender's confirmation or think about the ramifications of what I intend to do with this woman. To her. For as long as it takes to satiate this need for her incredible body. I've never reacted to a woman this fiercely in my entire life. It's more than her body, though, more than those breasts I long to knead and suckle or those hips I hunger to grasp and lift as I plunge inside her wet sheath. She has an indefinable air about her, one I can't understand or describe. Her pale hair shimmers in the muted lighting, like a halo around her beautiful face, and her hazel eyes spark with an inner fire whenever she smiles.

I ease between her stool and the vacant one. "Well, would you mind having me?"

Her eyes have gone soft, her pupils blown, and her breasts lift with every breath. Her voice grows breathless when she murmurs, "Have you?"

"As a neighbor," I explain, since she seems confused. Patting the empty stool, I give her the smile I reserve for seduction. "May I?"

"This is a free country. Be my guest."

I settle onto the stool, sliding in until my erse bumps the back, and lay an arm atop the copper bar. "Being the guest of a bonnie lass appeals to me."

Everything about her appeals to me. Once I've fed my lust with her pleasure, I can leave her without looking back. I'll have gotten her out of my system.

She tips her head to the side, studying me with keen interest, even as desire ignites in her eyes. "Are you Scottish?"

I rarely smile these days, except to seduce a woman into my bed, but her straightforward question coaxes another smile from me. "What gave me away?"

"Can't fool a college graduate." She leans forward to wrap her hands around her drink again. A natural blush tints her cheeks as she gives me a teasing smile. "You have a kilt and an accent. Even if I were stoned, I could've figured that one out."

My God, she is enthralling.

I slant forward a touch, my body seeming to crave her proximity. "College graduate, eh? I found an intellectual woman to bide my time with. What was your field of study?"

Stop asking stupid bloody questions. You don't need to read the woman's CV before you fuck her.

The American angel fixes me with an assessing look, then sits up straight and slaps her hands on her thighs. "Computer programming."

"Ah," I purr, captivated by her pale, golden eyes. "You expect me to be less than impressed."

"My occupation isn't the stuff of men's wet dreams, now is it?"

To my surprise, a throaty chuckle rumbles out of me. When was the last time a woman made me laugh? She's bonnie, aye, but also full of a fire I long to devour, even if it burns me to ash. "I prefer professional women. And anyway"—I bend closer to her, so close her breaths whisper over my lips—"you'll be featured in all my dreams tonight."

Her tongue slides across her lower lip, and her eyes turn glossy.

My mouth waters. I need to taste her, to ravish her with a kiss of raw, animal hunger. I need to strip her naked and consume her. I need to possess her.

She stares at my mouth, her lips parted, her tongue whisking along the bottoms of her top teeth.

Bod an Donais. All the blood in my body rushes to my groin.

"Tell me," I say, "what is a beautiful, intelligent woman doing all alone in a bar? You should have a horde of men slavering to do your bidding."

"I got into town this evening. Haven't had a chance to drum up a horde." She wiggles her lovely erse on her seat, swiveling toward me. Then she crosses her legs and drapes an arm on the bar while her other hand rests on her thigh. "Would you do my bidding?"

"Ah, lass," I say, fingering a lock of her hair. Our faces linger tantalizingly near each other, and her feminine scent drugs me. "For you, I'd go down on my knees and do whatever is necessary to make certain you feel nothing but satisfaction."

She aims her luminous eyes at me, her mouth open just far enough I could plunge my tongue between her lips.

I groan at the thought, shifting my mouth to her ear, that silky hair brushing my mouth. "I love your eyes. They sparkle like topaz dusted with emerald flecks. A man could drown in those eyes of yours, and he'd never want to come up for air."

When I slide my hand onto the back of her stool, she freezes.

Take her, have her, for one night only.

The scent of her hair and the way it grazes my skin drives me mad with a reckless hunger for her. "Let's go somewhere more…intimate."

"I'm not that easy." Her voice is low and sultry, decadent beyond belief.

And I chuckle, again. "I am."

"Telling me you're a man-whore is supposed to turn me on?"

"You are aroused," I say, my own voice turning husky. "I can see it. We're adults, and I willnae do anything without your consent."

"Damn straight you won't."

She can't see my smile. I have no power to contain it, faced with this fiery, sensual lass. In the back of my mind, a voice whispers to me. *You can have her for more than a night, for more than a week, for a lifetime.*

I do *not* want that.

Even if I do, in some deeply buried part of myself, I have no right to drag this sweet and sexy woman into the tangled web of my life.

One night only.

I nuzzle her throat, just below her ear, savoring the way her breaths quicken. "I want to kiss you."

She hesitates, swallowing visibly. "I'd like that."

"Good."

A ridiculous sort of relief floods through me. I need a good shag, that's all. This is nothing more than relief that my cock will soon be sated and cease throbbing every time I inhale this woman's scent. I skim my lips along her jaw, then drag them across her cheek to the corner of her mouth. My tongue flicks out to sample her skin.

She sucks in a sharp breath.

While I fight to keep my breaths even, I explore the seam of her lips with my tongue and then reposition my mouth over hers. I keep the barest distance between our lips, not quite touching her, though I'm desperate to claim her mouth and brand her with my kiss. Her lips ease apart, begging me to take her, and her body sags toward me. Her palms float up to my chest. The light pressure of her hands, the whispers of her breaths, all of it spins me down and down into a black hole of lust, and I am helpless to resist the gravity of her.

I skate my lips over hers.

She lets out a breathless moan.

A need seizes me, an irresistible impulse to take her moan into me. I press my mouth to hers, those lips soft and yielding.

She clenches my shirt in her fingers, opening her mouth as if pleading for more.

I lick at her tongue in delicate, teasing laps until I have the lass dissolving into me, our bodies stretched across the distance between our stools and our knees grazing each other. My free hand finds the elegant curve of her back and glides upward until my palm lands on her nape. A shudder ripples through her body. I push my fingers into her hair to cradle the back of her head.

No turning back. I will have her tonight, for hours and hours, until we've both satisfied our thirst for each other completely.

I plunge my tongue inside her mouth. The brazen lass meets my every thrust with matching swipes, our tongues tangling like we can't bear to sever the contact. When she moans into my mouth, I thrust my tongue harder and deeper. My balls pull back into my groin, a sign I'm far too aroused for a public venue. If I don't unhand this woman, right this instant, I'll *caith* right here in the middle of a crowded bar. I need to spirit her away to my hotel so I can come inside her body instead of all over my kilt.

I break the kiss, my gaze pinned to hers, my chest heaving. "How much have ye had to drink?"

"What? Two sips and one gulp of this one drink. Why?"

"Yer still thinking clearly, then." Thank heaven for that. I couldn't survive walking away from her now. Decision made, I ghost the backs of my fingers over her cheek. "Come with me to my hotel. Stay the night."

Her mouth falls open, tempting me to devour her again.

She meets my gaze head-on and sighs one word. "Yes."

A thrill shoots through me, electric and shocking. Aye, tonight I will have her.

Tomorrow…I'll be gone before the morning comes.

Chapter Two

The door to my room clicks shut behind us. It's a bloody enormous suite in the Ritz-Carlton, far too large for one man, but I'd meant to stay for a week or two and decided this would be my apartment while I'm away. Besides, I'm used to large spaces. My home in Scotland is rather…sizable. The lass and I stand in a short hallway, beyond which lies a spacious and luxurious living room. Other doorways open off the hall, leading into more rooms. I watch her face while she glances around at what she can see of the suite, her brows rising and her eyes widening, though only for a moment.

I settle my hands on her hips and back her into the wall, my gaze riveted to hers, my body tautening in anticipation of what's to come. During our taxi ride from the bar to the hotel, I'd kissed and fondled the lass until she was virtually melting in my arms. She tastes like nothing I've ever experienced before and feels so good that I want to savor every inch of her body. I roam my hands down to her erse to splay them over her flesh, like I'm branding her body as my property. Well, it does belong to me—for tonight. I mold my body to hers, my stiff cock crushed to her belly.

She cranes her neck back to gaze up at my face, her expression tender and lustful at the same time.

I search her face, wondering for the twentieth time if I should really do this. But I cannae stop now. I massage her erse and grind my hips into her. She rocks her hips forward as if she's craving contact as much as I am. I draw her earlobe into my mouth to suckle and nip at the tender skin, then trace a path down her throat with my lips and tongue.

"I haven't changed my mind," she says. "In case you were wondering."

"Mmmm," I murmur against her skin. "Ahmno doubting ye want me."

"Who are you?"

"Does it matter who I am?" I feather my lips over hers. "We'll have one night and only one night."

Why do I feel so excited by the prospect? I've shagged strangers before, but the thought of shagging this woman excites me more than anything I've ever done in my entire life.

I dive a hand under her T-shirt and sweep it up to close my palm over her breast. When I thumb her nipple, she arches her neck. *Bod an Donais,* I want her naked right now. Only a thin layer of fabric separates our bodies, but I need her skin on mine. I flick my thumb across her nipple, earning a wee gasp from her that makes my cock throb. I grasp her erse in both hands again while I seal my lips over hers and plow my tongue deep inside, ravishing her mouth with abandon. She moans, the sound muffled by our joined lips, and flings her arms up to encompass my neck, her fingers tunneling into my hair.

Lifting the lass onto her toes, I bring our faces closer and tear my mouth away from hers. A slight pinkness tinges her cheeks, and I'm sure mine look the same. "For you, ahmno rushing. Plan on savoring every moment with ye, my wicked little angel."

She is little compared to me. I tower over most women, which usually makes them uncomfortable. But this lass doesn't seem to mind at all.

I claim her mouth again, devouring it with ravenous swipes of my tongue while I knead her erse, pushing her forward into my waiting erection. She hooks a knee around my thigh, plastering her flesh to my groin. I rub my length into her cleft while the scent of her need overwhelms my senses with its musky, heady aroma. I need to be inside her, but her clothing still shields her body. So I dip my head to her breast and swallow the nipple through her clothing, sucking it hard and fast. She arches her back and clutches my head to her chest. I've saturated her shirt, but I donnae give a toss.

"More," she pleads, her voice throaty. "Oh God, please, more."

A raspy growl rumbles out of me, and I gather her in my arms, carrying the lass into the living room. With heavy-lidded eyes, she glances around the room at the pool table upholstered in crimson felt and the sofa with chairs arranged in front of it, one of them upholstered in the same crimson as the pool table. Her gaze travels further into the room, to the French doors and the terrace outside. She seems a touch surprised by the opulent surroundings.

I set the wicked angel on her feet behind the red armchair and, with my hands on her hips, urge her to lean back against it.

A semitransparent white curtain shields the floor-to-ceiling windows that I'm sure she can see from her position. But then I move between her body and the wall, blocking her view. My erection is tenting my kilt, and the lass gazes at it while licking her lips.

Stepping closer, I cage her to the chair's back with my hands on either side of her body, then I kiss her again—with more passion than I'd intended. This woman will drive me mad for certain. I settle my hands on her hips, tugging her into my body, compelling her to arch into me. She clamps her hands on the chair behind her, those bonnie tits rising and falling with her every labored breath. I nibble at her lower lip, and she sags against me while I skate my lips along her jaw.

"Want ye naked," I breathe into her ear. "Need to bury myself inside yer sweet little body."

Plunging my tongue inside her mouth, I devour her with demanding strokes while I struggle to unbutton my shirt but fumble. She pushes my hands away to take over the task, deftly freeing the buttons while we keep kissing. The second she unhooks the last button, I shrug out of the shirt.

Then I lunge both hands under her shirt, whisking it up her skin. Gooseflesh crops up on her arms. But whether from desire or a chill, I donnae have the brainpower right now to deduce the answer. I peel my lips away for only a second to tug the shirt over her head. I want all of her body. So I unzip her jeans and strip them off her along with the lass's knickers, without even hesitating in my ravishing of her mouth, not until I duck my head, meaning to latch onto her nipple.

But I stop, my attention riveted to the twenty-dollar bills sheltered between her breasts, inside her bra. She keeps money in there? Maybe that's what she'd been doing earlier, in the bar, when I watched her adjusting something inside her shirt. I cannae help smiling a little, because I have never before known a woman who kept twenty-dollar bills in her lingerie. I hook one finger inside her bra to pull it out just enough that I can peer down into the space between her breasts.

I raise my head, lifting one brow at her.

She shrugs. "Don't like to carry a purse in crowded places."

My cheeks feel tight, and I think I might be smiling more than a moment ago. She is the strangest, most adorable lass I've ever met. I pluck the folded-up bills out of her bra and toss them onto the table beside the chair, then move my arms behind her to unhook her bra. The last piece of her clothing flutters to the floor, near my feet.

I take one step back and allow myself a moment to admire her nude body, from her delicate throat down to the nipples that jut out from her full breasts, and across her flat belly with its perfect navel, then lower to the hairs on her mound and the sensual curve of her hips and thighs. I run my tongue over my lips. She is more than bonnie. She's the most beautiful creature I have ever seen.

Her gaze lands on my chest, and though her attention wanders down to my groin, she can't see anything with my kilt still covering my hips and thighs.

I unfasten the leather belt that prevents my kilt from falling off. With a swift tug, I shed the plaid. It settles into a heap on the rug.

The lass pulls in a shaky breath while she roves her gaze over the part of myself I've unveiled for her. She seems to like what she sees, considering that she bites her bottom lip and her eyes drift half-closed. She's fixated on my cock. It sways before me, curving up toward my belly, and the head glistens with moisture. I'm in this state because of her, because I need to quench my lust inside that beautiful body.

I stretch a hand out as if to touch her, but I stop an inch from her chest. My fingers curl into my palm. The need to touch her intensifies every second until it's too strong to deny. I place the tip of my middle finger on her breastbone and flick my tongue out to moisten my lips. Using only that one finger, I trace a line down her breastbone, onto her belly.

Her breaths shorten into wee gasps.

My gaze snaps to hers, and suddenly I can't catch my breath. I plunge my finger into her navel, swirling it slightly, then move it downward until I graze her mound.

The lass clings to the chair and bucks her hips toward my finger.

I groan, the ravenous sound vibrating in my chest. This isn't me. I don't behave this way with women I want to shag. Taking the time to explore her body... That's not me either, but I cannae stop myself. I sweep her up in my arms and stride back to the hall, through the doorway into the bedroom. I hug her to me with one arm while, with my other hand, I toss the covers off the large bed. When I lay her down on the mattress, on her back, I make sure her head rests on one of the plush pillows.

She brushes her palms over the smooth white sheets.

Does she like this room? I don't care, but I can't help glancing around at the decor, though I hadn't bothered to notice it before. Semitransparent curtains veil the windows, and a tall mirror reveals a reflection of her body sprawled across the length of the mattress. She can see me in the mirror too, I'm sure. As she regards her own reflection, she gets an odd look on her face, like she's thinking hard. Then she stretches both arms above her head, caressing the wooden headboard in the way she might stroke a lover. She arches her back just enough to elevate those bonnie breasts, with the nipples pointing toward the ceiling. Bending one knee, she spreads her thighs.

Fuck, I want her.

I suck in a breath, gazing at her with my eyes almost closed, drinking in the vision of this woman nude and aroused and ready for me.

She writhes on the sheets, making her breasts jiggle.

I rip open the top drawer of the nightstand. Snatching up a foil packet, I slam the drawer shut and get the condom on faster than I ever have before, faster than I knew I could. My pulse throbs in my veins, and something like excitement tingles over my skin.

She wriggles her erse, laying her hands at her sides on the silken sheets.

I scrape my tongue across my bottom teeth while I imagine all the things I want to do to her tonight.

The lass aims a smile at me that's so seductive it takes my breath away. "Come and get me."

I give in to the beast within and growl again while I rake my gaze over her entire body. "Yer the finest work of art I ever laid eyes on. A masterpiece of sensual beauty."

She catches her lip between her teeth while her breasts heave.

I climb onto the bed on my hands and knees, positioning my body over hers with our faces aligned.

She splays her palms over my chest. Her skin is almost as soft as the sheets.

Arms bent, I devour her mouth with all the hunger of a lion consuming his prey, rasping my tongue over hers and reveling in the sensations. I lick at the roof of her mouth, loving the soft noises she makes and the way she writhes against me. With every swipe of my tongue, the need to shag her intensifies, but I want more than a quick poke. The memory of our time in the taxi rushes through me, and I marvel at the way I'd kissed her for the entire ride back to my hotel, because I have never done anything like that. But tonight, with her, I want to let go and allow myself to luxuriate in the pleasure of this woman's body while I do things to her I've never done before.

The lass closes her hand around my cock.

I choke back a groan with my mouth still fastened to hers, but I hesitate for only half a second. Then I'm consuming her again, desperate to explore every inch of her body, starting with her mouth. Never have I kissed a woman this way, with our tongues colliding and our teeth gnashing. I can't stop myself. I wrap my hand around hers, where she's grasping my cock, then I take hold of her hips to tug her closer.

She glides her hand up and down my length.

Braced with one arm, I peel her hand away from my *slat*.

The lass makes a disappointed noise.

I lower my body onto the bed, lying on my side, and stretch one arm above her head. Her body nestles against mine, warm and pliant, and my cock brushes against her hip. I rest my free hand on her belly, easing my palm down inch by inch, taking my time so I can memorize every contour of her body until I reach the hairs between her thighs. She clenches her fingers in the sheets while I toy with those hairs, making her squirm and gasp. The second she spreads her legs for me, I push my fingers between her slick folds.

The heat of her body and the scent of her cream intoxicate me.

I glide my fingers up and down her flesh, caressing those glistening lips while I settle the heel of my hand over her clit. Underneath the surrounding flesh, it feels as rigid as my cock, and I know she's ready for me. But first, I need to give her pleasure. I marvel at the irresistible beauty of her body and the way the golden glow of the bedside lamp burnishes her skin. With my fingers, I torment her swollen flesh while I scrape the heel of my hand over her hard nub. She clenches my biceps, her nails pinching my skin, but I donnae care about the pain. All I see is her, and all I know is her body, while I pet her folds with measured strokes, increasing the pace gradually until I'm grinding my finger into her *brillean*.

"Ah!" she exclaims, bucking her hips while her entire face crimps from the release that's building inside her. "Please, oh God, please."

I thrust one finger inside her, then another. Her channel tightens around my fingers, and her body tenses, ready for the climax I mean to give her. Right now.

With the heel of my hand, I keep kneading her clit in quick, rough circles while I sink my fingers inside her and pull out, over and over, scraping her cleft with every movement. I bury my fingers inside her down to the last knuckle, kinking them so I can caress her on the inside, her velvety flesh giving under the pressure of my touch.

She cries out, thrashing under my hand.

The woman gives herself over to pleasure with abandon, and it's the most beautiful thing I've ever witnessed.

I latch my mouth onto hers, forging my tongue deep, every thrust synchronized with the motions of my fingers. The orgasm seems to detonate inside her like a bomb going off, robbing her of breath just as I tear my lips from hers. She clings to me, her mouth wide and her nails scratching my skin as she claws at me like she needs my body to anchor her. I watch her face, my features tight from the need pulsing within me, and I shift my fingers to rub her clit mercilessly until her body has devoured every last drop of pleasure.

Then I brush stray hairs from her face. "Ye come like a volcano, so wild and explosive. It's…maddening."

Her brows wrinkle in the most endearing way.

I withdraw my hand, wiping my fingers on the sheets, and smile at her apparent confusion. "I meant it's maddening how much it arouses me, seeing you come this way."

"Oh." Her chest is rising and falling with every labored breath, and pink dapples her chest and cheeks. But she seems unable to speak again, not just yet.

I skim my tongue over her bottom lip. "We're not done yet."

Chapter Three

No, I am not done with this woman. I haven't sunk my cock deep inside her body yet. I've already spent more time giving her pleasure than I ever have with another woman, but I can't stop until I've felt her come all over my *slat*. Lying on my side, I let myself appreciate her body one more time, admiring every curve and swell and dip until I'm sure I've memorized every inch of her skin.

I rest my hand on her collarbone, fanning my fingers over her throat.

Her eyes are half-closed, and her lips curl up a wee bit as if she loves my touch.

Christ, I love touching her. She's more responsive than any woman I've bedded before.

I smooth my hand down the center of her chest, over one breast and then the other, rolling her nipples between my thumbs. Dragging my hand down to her belly, I swirl my palm around her navel. She takes short, gasping breaths while her belly rises and falls in time with her inhalations. With my gaze, I track the path of my hand as I move it over her skin, so focused on the task that I compress my lips. My hand ventures lower, but when it dips to within millimeters of her mound, I sweep it over to cup her hip while massaging the hollow with my thumb.

Her lids flutter closed.

Sighing, I skate my hand down her thigh and over her knee to skim it along the side of her calf and past her slender ankle. Afflicted with a need to touch her everywhere, even in places where I've never touched another woman, I dance my fingers over the top of her foot and around to the sole, making the lass squirm. Already I've learned she wriggles like that when she fancies what I'm doing to her, so I rub her sole with deliberate strokes while I imagine what it might be like to spend an entire night with this woman, running my hands over her skin and pushing her toward one climax after another.

No, I will not stay the night. It's against my rules.

I shift my hand to her other foot, relishing her responses when I knead the sole with leisurely motions.

She exhales a breathy moan, every muscle in her body slackening.

But I cannae stop myself. I glide my hand up the inside of her leg until I reach her inner thigh. Then I graze my longest finger across the outer folds of her cleft, hauling in a long breath and letting it out on a groan that embodies all my carnal desires for this woman. "Yer scent drives me mad, it's like whisky and honey and musk." I comb my fingertips through those curly, silken hairs. "The scent of lust."

She opens her eyes, though they seem unfocused.

I hover my head over the flesh below those hairs while I coast my hand down her thigh, then slide it back up slowly.

The lass fists her hands in the sheets.

What is her name? I want to know, but I will never ask. That's another of my rules.

I curl my hand around her thigh and press my lips to her belly. Even her skin tastes like every decadent flavor ever invented. I kiss a damp trail up to her breasts, pausing there to nuzzle my face between them.

She flattens her palms on my back.

I dart my tongue out to moisten the peak of one nipple.

"Yes," she murmurs while her fingers sink into my flesh.

Taking one nipple into my mouth, I coil my tongue around the tip again and again, my cock jumping when she gasps and jerks as if the pleasure I'm giving her has hit her as powerfully as a lightning strike. I release her stiff peak, only to latch onto the other and repeat the process. She plows her hands into my hair while I give up her nipple so I can lie beside her again, my head near hers and my hand resting on her hip. I pull her snug against me, roll the lass onto her side, and tuck her head under my chin. Why am I snuggling with her? I never do that, but for reasons I can't comprehend, I want to feel as close to her as possible. I move my hand off her hip and down to her thigh, lifting her leg to expose her folds.

She stretches an arm over my torso as if to hold me close.

I hook her leg over mine, spreading my palm on her erse, and draw her toward me until my *slat* brushes her flesh. My pulse beats fast enough to pound in my ears, and I have trouble catching my breath, but I cannae think about what that means, not anymore. The need has grown too intense, obliterating everything else. I push inside her with one slow, smooth stroke, feeling her flesh stretch to conform to my cock until I'm seated deep within her body.

"All right?" I rumble in her ear.

She buries her face against my neck. "Yes. Don't stop."

"Willnae."

I grip her erse and begin to thrust in a controlled rhythm, struggling to keep the pace unhurried while I plunge inside her, only to retreat again, over and over until the lass is clinging to me and whimpering against my neck. I drive in and pull out, reveling in the sensations of her hot flesh around mine, the softness of her channel, the flexing of her thigh muscles, and so many other things that I can't focus on anymore. I blow out a breath with every thrust and suck in a breath every time I withdraw from her heat.

The lass locks her leg tighter around mine, pawing at my back as if wordlessly begging for more.

Bod an Donais, I need more, need all of her. I roll us both over so she lies flat on her back with my body above her, and I hold myself up with one straight arm. Then I whisk my free hand up and down her side, from her ribs down to her thigh, desperate to feel every inch of her even while I maintain the relentless rhythm of my thrusts. I bend my supporting arm to lower my head near hers, our foreheads touching. The mesmerizing color of her eyes draws me in and refuses to let me go, even while she rolls her hips up to meet my cock, opening her legs wider.

"Ah, lass," I groan. "Come for me now, come for me again."

She bolts her hands around my arms. "Faster, please, faster and harder."

Bracing myself on both elbows, I swing my hips back and slam into her with so much force that her body bows up and her mouth falls open on a strangled cry.

"More," she pleads.

I raise my body, using two straight arms to buttress me, and drive into her so many times so fast that my hips piston wildly and my cock pounds into her like the fevered rutting of a stag. Our bodies slap together with every punishing thrust, eliciting a wet sucking sound, and she fastens her legs around me, gripping my arms so fiercely it hurts, but I donnae care. I grunt with every lunge while sweat dribbles down my skin.

And she comes for me.

Every muscle in her body snaps taut, then the orgasm seizes her. She thrashes her head on the pillow while her inner muscles grip and release me repeatedly and the need to pour everything into her body becomes almost unbearable. Her frantic cries spur me to unleash a hoarse shout as I pummel her body twice more, punching into her so hard that I throw my head back and roar as the indescribable pleasure of coming inside her lush body seizes me.

Just as the first pulse of my release spills into her, she comes even harder.

With two more thrusts, I'm done, collapsing onto the bed next to her and rolling onto my side. Between gasping breaths, I say, "Thank ye for that."

She eyes me like she thinks I might kick her out the door now.

"Relax." I cradle her to my body and frisk my hand over her back. "It's a compliment. You are a passionate, spirited woman."

"Thank you." The lass snuggles into me with her face against my neck. "This was unexpected, but I'm glad you asked me to stay with you tonight."

"I'm glad too." I thread my fingers through her hair and kiss the top of her head. "A pleasant surprise. Most of my lovers aren't as enthusiastic as you."

She pulls her head back to look at me. "Are you saying you do this kind of thing a lot?"

"Aye." Why does it matter to women? I know it does, and so I squint at her, then curve my lips into a slight smile. "Well, not a lot. I indulge in the occasional fling, but it's not a long-time habit."

The lass is still watching me, though I cannae fathom why.

"No more talk," I say.

She doesn't object when I recline on the bed and pull her half onto my body with one of her arms over my chest and one of mine around her shoulders. I stretch out my free arm to shut off the light on my side of the bed, leaving only the lamp behind her for illumination. As I tug the sheet and blanket over us, I make sure to cover the lass up to her shoulders.

"Sleep," I whisper. "I've worn you out, haven't I?"

"Mm."

While I caress her arm with my fingertips and watch her slowly give in to sleep, I wonder what the bloody hell I'm doing. Staying the night? I never do that. Sleeping with her seems like a ruddy awful idea, one that's sure to backfire in the morning when she realizes I can't—won't—give her what she will eventually decide she needs.

I can't be her boyfriend or husband or even her lover. Not for more than tonight.

Her breathing grows shallower, barely a whisper against my skin. I can't resist sniffing her hair and running my fingers through the silky locks. She is bonnie and the best lover I've ever had, but that doesn't change anything. Still, with her warm body tucked against mine, I find myself relaxing and drifting away into sleep.

Sometime later, I wake with an inexplicable need pulsing inside me. I need to experience the American lass one more time, so I rouse her and lose myself in the sensual pleasure of burying my cock inside her body, swallowing her cries with my mouth. We both fall asleep again, but I wake later with the same need urging me to ravish her one last time. But I resist it, refusing to succumb to this hunger for her ever again. I know I could get addicted to her so easily.

Hours later, I rouse and extricate myself from her body so I can go to the window and peek out between the curtains. The sun is just rising, though I can't see the orb itself. The glow of sunrise has begun, which means it's time for me to leave. I walk into the living room, or whatever they call this large room, and find a pad of notepaper in the drawer of a table, plus a pen, so I write the lass a note. Keeping it simple seems best. I scrawl a brief message: "Thank you for last night. Don't forget your money." Does that sound bloody stupid? I've never been good at coming up with romantic words to impress a lass. I'm a solicitor, not a poet. And I don't care about romantic gestures. The lass I shagged last night was only that—a lass I shagged.

As I'm heading back into the bedroom to put my note on the nightstand, I catch sight of the twenty-dollar bills the lass had concealed in her bra and which I removed and set on the table by the armchair. Her mobile is also on the table. I grab both items, but the banknotes are wrinkled now, so I iron them out as best I can. Then I take the note and the money into the bedroom and leave both where I hope she'll see them, using her mobile as a paperweight.

I allow myself one more look at the beautiful, sensual lass in the bed.

And then I leave.

Chapter Four

For two hours, I wander the streets of New Orleans with no idea where I'm going or why. Finally, my stomach grumbles, reminding me that I need food. But I don't see any restaurants nearby. Pubs, yes. Tattoo parlors, yes. No place to eat a good breakfast, though. I hired a car so I can drive myself wherever I need to go, but I decide it's easier to hail a taxi. That way, I can ask the driver to take me someplace where I can get a normal meal. I want the sort that will leave me satisfied, rather than somewhere posh that gives customers tiny slivers of food that wouldn't fill up an ant's stomach.

The driver seems to think I'm off my head. Maybe I shouldn't have havered on and on about my opinion of modern cuisine.

While I eat my breakfast in a cafe that overlooks the Mississippi River, my thoughts keep returning to the lass I seduced last night. She was the bonniest, sweetest, most passionate woman I'd ever met. A night with her had become the most invigorating hours of my life. Why had I felt the need to take her again in the dead of night? Lust drove me to it, that's all. I do not need to see her again.

The lass's face flares in my mind's eye. Blonde hair. Hazel eyes. That smile, that laugh, the look on her face when she comes.

Mhac na galla. I will stop thinking about her right now.

That mental command works for about fifteen minutes. I order another breakfast just like the one I've already eaten, strictly to prevent myself from running back to the hotel to catch the woman I shagged last night before she leaves. But I eat so fast that it's not much of a distraction. Then I check my watch to see what time it is back in Scotland. The six-hour time difference means it's afternoon over there, so I could ring my brother Lachlan. To do what? Haver to him about what a sodding ersehole I am? The other women I'd screwed without knowing their names had left right after we finished. But this lass… I used her body for hours, then crept out at dawn while she was still asleep.

No, I will not call Lachlan.

That leaves me to wander the streets of a strange city or…go back to the hotel. She's probably gone by now. It's still early, though, and I did wear her out last night. She might still be asleep. The thought sends an odd shiver through me, not as if I'm cold, but as if I feel excited by the prospect of seeing her again.

That is ridiculous.

Maybe it is, but I can't stop myself. I hail another taxi and go back to the Ritz-Carlton. The elevator ride up to my suite seems to take forever. I tap my toes on the floor in a rapid rhythm that makes the other people in the car glance at me with strange expressions, almost as if they expect me to leap on them like a wolf and tear them to shreds. The other passengers get off on lower floors, leaving me alone when the doors open on my floor. I rush to the suite, unlocking it with my keycard, and shove the door open. I keep my head down as I step inside and turn to shut the door.

I make it halfway down the hall before I notice *her*. My feet refuse to move anymore.

The bonnie blonde stands near the French doors that lead to the terrace, facing me. The sun shimmering on her hair lends her the look of an angel with a halo encircling her head.

Bloody hell. What is wrong with me? She's no angel, but I am a devil.

All I can do is stare at the lass blankly for several seconds. Then I force myself to straighten my spine and act like a mature man, striding down the hall to stop an arm's length from her. I employ all the willpower I possess to keep from gawping at her like an eejit or staring at her breasts. "You're still here."

"Duh." She folds her arms over those luscious tits. "Did you forget your wallet and had to slither back in here to get it?"

"No," I say slowly while I try to figure out what sort of mood she's in. Anger would be appropriate. Throwing things at me would be too. But she doesn't do any of that. "I thought you'd be asleep."

"Sorry to disappoint."

"I'm not disappointed. I—" Shifting my weight from one foot to the other and back again does not ease my, well, unease at all. I scratch my neck instead while my face decides to cinch up into a pinched expression. "I am sorry for, ah…"

"Skulking out in the dead of night like a slimy worm?"

I sigh and give the lass a tight smile. "It wasn't the dead of night. I left at dawn."

"Are you expecting applause for waiting until sunrise?" She taps the toe of her shoe on the floor. "You could've, gee, maybe woken me up to say goodbye. And by the way, who leaves a thank-you note after sex? It's bizarre."

Early this morning, it had seemed like the gentlemanly thing to do, but I see her point. It was a strange impulse, but I've never been good at deducing what women will like or dislike. With my shoulders bunched, I avert my gaze to the wood floor. "I'm afraid that's what I do. Find a partner for the evening and satisfy our mutual needs with an hour or so of uncomplicated sex."

"Uncomplicated?" She narrows her gaze on me, which makes my skin itch. "Wait a minute. An hour? You stayed until dawn."

"Ah, yes." *Bod an Donais*, why must she be so clever? I have to admit I like that about her, but not right now. I wince and shove my hands into the pockets of my trousers. "I hadn't intended to stay, but… Donnae know."

Dead brilliant answer, MacTaggart.

"Hmm." The lass stalks over to the nearest chair, the same one I'd penned her to last night when I stripped her naked. She drops onto the cushioned crimson seat with her hands on the arms and drums her fingers. "With those other women, the ones you bang for an hour, do you say goodbye before you scurry off?"

"Yes." I trudge over to the seat opposite hers, a striped armchair with wood trim that isn't the sort of furniture I would buy, and I settle onto it. Perched on the chair's edge, I wedge my elbows on my thighs and study the rug at my feet. "I indulge in the occasional fling with a stranger. I'm not interested in relationships anymore, but I have…needs."

"Uh-*huh*." She swings one leg up to cross it over the other, which I can see because I roll my eyes up to glance at her. "You're a big old horndog, I get it. You prey on women you think are desperate and lonely."

"No." I utter the word in a harsh tone, but the anger is directed at myself, not her. I turn my head to the side so I can't see her even out of the corner of my eye. "I choose professional women."

A thump makes me look at her.

She has dropped her raised leg onto the floor. "You thought I was a hooker?"

For a moment, I have no clue what she's on about, then it hits me. I chuckle. Did the lass honestly think I mistook her for a prostitute? No one could make that mistake with her.

She huffs. "You think that's funny? Listen up, buddy, I am not for sale."

"You misunderstand." I lean back in the chair, smiling at her. "I meant women who have successful careers, the kind who have no time for relationships and want what I want. A casual encounter with no strings and no future."

She glances down at her shirt. "If you like professional women, why'd you pick me last night? A geek in a ComicCon T-shirt."

"You aren't a geek." But I have no ruddy idea what ComicCon is.

"I am a proud geek, a computer programmer who loves fantasy and science fiction movies. I don't have a high-powered career. I love to dress up in sexy costumes for Halloween or just to go to the Renaissance fair." She clasps her hands on her lap, seeming a wee bit embarrassed by her confession. "The point is, I'm no professional in search of a quick fling."

I give her an appraising look. "Do you often follow strangers to their hotel rooms?"

"No, of course not." She slouches in her chair. "I've never had a one-night stand before. Certainly never had sex with an anonymous stranger. I like to have fun, be wild and crazy, but even I've got my limits."

The lass has never done that before? I assumed she must have since she agreed to go with me minutes after we met. For a minute or two, maybe longer, I sit here observing her without blinking. I seduced a woman who has never done this sort of thing before. Not sure how I feel about that. But I do have an idea of how to make it up to her.

I exhale a gusty breath, slap my hands on my thighs, and push my body up off the armchair. Then I march over to her chair, offering her my hand. "Up."

She frowns. "I'm not a dog, you know. I don't heel on command."

"I'm aware of that." I grasp her right hand. "Please stand."

"Why?"

"Are you always this suspicious?"

She raises her eyebrows. "Only of men who won't tell me their names."

The lass won't get up, so I kneel before her with my gaze at her level and trained on her eyes. Then I hold out my palm again in the appropriate position for a handshake. "Rory MacTaggart."

"Emery Granger." She slips her palm into mine, hers feeling surprisingly cool, and we shake hands almost tentatively. When I curl my fingers around her hand, she clears her throat. "Nice to meet you."

"Nice to meet you too, Emery. You have a lovely name."

"Thanks." With her hand still enveloped by mine, she stares into my eyes for a moment before she speaks again. "Why were you wearing a kilt last night?"

I lift my shoulders in a half shrug, tipping my head to the side. "I like wearing kilts. They're quite comfortable, and they represent my heritage. Of which I am very proud."

Does she like my grey trousers and grey dress shirt? Not that I care. It doesn't matter if she approves of my clothing. I like hers, but then, she would look sexy in anything—though she looks best naked.

Emery bites the inside of her lip while her gaze wanders over my chest. "You look good in a kilt. But I like this businessman kind of stuff too."

I lift her hand, touching my lips to her knuckles. "I know I said it would be one night but… May I see you again?"

She straightens in her chair, seeming uncomfortable again.

Maybe she doesn't want to see me anymore. I did tell her it would be one night only, yet here I am all but begging her to let me bask in her presence a wee bit longer. I must be off my head. Nothing else explains my need to be with her even when we aren't having a poke.

Emery eyes the suite's door like she's calculating the best trajectory for fleeing.

I still hold her hand close to my lips, my breaths ghosting over her skin. "Do you have plans for today?"

"Not yet." She squints at me briefly, then relaxes. "Okay then. Come sightseeing with me."

"Sightseeing?"

"Don't you have that in Scotland?" With one finger, she tickles my lips. "Sightseeing is when you go to various locations to stare at a bunch of old junk or to admire the scenery, or maybe to make fun of goofy little niche museums. It's corny and cheesy and all that jazz. Geeks like me live for it."

She truly is the most enchanting woman I have ever met. I've never done any of the things she just described, so she might be disappointed by my reaction to her favorite activities. Still, at least I will get to spend more time with her.

Not because I want to date her. No, I'm done with that rubbish. This is companionship, nothing more.

I release her hand, placing both of mine on her knees. "All right. Let's go sightseeing."

"Awesome." She moves to get up, and I stand too, stepping back to give the lass more room. She aims a playful smile at me. "Hope you're ready to party hearty."

That sounds like the precise opposite of anything I would enjoy, but I will give it a go. This is my holiday, after all, even if I had intended to spend the whole time working. Now I have a reason to step outside my comfort zone for a day.

My attention returns to her shirt, and my lips struggle not to smile, though I only half succeed in not doing that. "One question first."

"Shoot."

I wave a finger at her shirt. "What is ComicCon?"

Chapter Five

*E*mery settles onto the sofa cross-legged, in the corner, relaxing into the cushions while angled toward me. She seems vaguely amused, but she's been like that ever since I asked her what the words on her shirt mean. At least she's not angry anymore. Maybe she had been hurt, not angry. That's worse, I suppose. But I can't worry about that. If she decides she doesn't like the everyday version of me, as opposed to the way I behaved last night, then she can walk out the door.

I suspect her amusement stems from the way I'm sitting. I sit straight, of course, positioned at the opposite end of the sofa from her and facing forward with the soles of my loafers planted on the rug. How else is a man meant to sit? Younger lads these days seem to think slouching is appropriate. Not me. I never slouch or slump or "hang loose."

Maybe I had been looser last night, but that is not what I'm like the rest of the time. I wouldn't blame the lass for being confused, but instead, she seems entertained by my behavior. Other women have never reacted that way.

I'm holding a plate of praline pancakes in one hand, while with my other hand I brandish a fork. I can't seem to keep the plate solidly placed while also holding a knife, so I'm calculating the best method for eating this meal without getting syrup on my trousers.

Meanwhile, at the other end of the sofa, Emery wolfs down her pancakes without worrying about making a sticky mess of herself. Never have I seen a woman eat with the sort of enthusiasm she displays. I don't think she gives a toss if she gets herself covered in maple syrup and butter and pancake crumbs. I observe her progress, fascinated by her method of hacking up her short stack into bite-size pieces, drowning the lot in syrup, and stuffing multiple chunks into her mouth at once. The whipped cream on top smears on her lips, but she swipes it away with long, sensuous glides of her tongue.

Bod an Donais. Is she trying to drive me insane? Not sure how long I can stop myself from dragging her down onto the cushions and fucking her. No, I won't do that. We will have sex again when and if I decide we should, and only in the manner that I decide is appropriate.

Aye, women call me uptight. Everyone does, in fact. My brothers and sisters especially.

Syrup dribbles down Emery's chin.

"Why do you eat this way?" I ask, unable to keep the humor out of my voice.

"Because I'm starving," she replies while chewing. The lass swallows her mouthful of food and wipes away the syrup on her chin with a cloth napkin. "Never got around to eating dinner last night. My flight was delayed, and after checking in at my motel and taking a cab to Pat O'Brien's, I barely had time to taste my first Hurricane before a certain foreigner seduced me."

I wince. Aye, that presumptuous foreigner would be me. I didn't ask if she'd eaten yet before I whisked her away to my hotel, and I failed to offer her any food after we, ah, enjoyed each other in my suite. But something else she said confuses me. "What is a Hurricane?"

"The signature drink at Pat O'Brien's. It was invented there. Didn't anybody tell you?"

"I wasn't interested in the bar's history." I fidget at my end of the sofa, and the plate of pancakes I haven't touched yet wobbles as if it might fall off my lap. I steady it with one hand. "I walked into the main bar at Pat O'Brien's ten minutes before I approached you. I was looking for company, not a strange red cocktail."

"The Hurricane is yummy. You missed out."

Emery wolfs down another mouthful of pancakes and syrup, then swigs from her glass of whole milk. Maybe I like that she drinks whole milk when most women worry about the fat content of everything they consume. She doesn't seem to care about that rubbish at all. I shouldn't be surprised by her passion for food since she showed me her passion for sex last night.

"By company," she says, "you mean you were on the hunt for a professional woman to screw."

"Uh, yes." I fidget again, though I have no idea why, and my plate almost tumbles off my lap. I catch it before the pancakes can spill onto the sofa cushion. "I saw no one who interested me. Then, as I was stepping out into the carriageway, I caught sight of a bonnie lass in the piano bar."

"What happened to her? Did she turn you down?"

The cheeky lass is teasing me, and I suddenly realize I like that. Since I seem to have forgotten how to smile lately—except for carnal expressions—I'm stunned when I feel my lips twitching upward at the corners, though only for a second. "Once I saw you, I lost interest in every other woman."

"Mm, I get it." Spearing a bite of pancake, she points her fork at me. "You've got a fetish for geeks wearing ComicCon T-shirts and worn jeans, and who haven't showered or brushed their hair."

"I have a fetish for beautiful women with stunning smiles and even more stunning eyes." I survey her from head to toe, remembering what every inch of her looks and feels like naked. "And a breathtaking body I couldnae wait to plunder."

"Plunder? You sound like a pirate."

Does she think what I said is barmy? Or that I sound like a numpty? Whether she thinks I'm crazy or stupid doesn't matter. I'm spending time with her strictly to expand my horizons—and get a few more good shags.

"Seriously, why pick me?" she asks. "You could've hooked up with any one of the hot little numbers strutting their stuff in that bar. I'm confused about why you'd pick me, the girl who'd just stumbled off an airliner. I hadn't even shaved my stubbly legs."

I shrug one shoulder. "Your legs seemed fine to me when I was fondling you from head to toe."

Oh, aye, the memory of running my hands over that body will stay with me for the rest of my life. Not because I like her. Because it was the best sex I've ever enjoyed. Her body truly is a masterpiece of sensual beauty. She must've thought I was lying, saying anything to seduce her, when I told her that last night. I might have many flaws, but lying isn't one of them.

I start to eat the plate of pancakes that I still have balanced on my thigh. With precise movements, I slice the stack into pieces that are exactly square and of equal size, then I stack them on one side of the plate and pour a small pool of syrup onto the other side of the plate. I proceed to consume my meal one bite at a time, dipping each piece into the syrup without dripping any of it. After each dip, I tap my fork on the plate to make sure no excess syrup dribbles off and slide the tines between my lips, withdrawing them cleanly. No mess. That's the way I eat.

Emery watches me the entire time, once again seeming highly entertained. She pulls out her mobile and aims it at me.

"Are you taking my picture?" I ask.

"Uh-huh. Gotta document this. Never seen anybody eat the way you do." She peeks over the screen at me. "Do you mind?"

"Do what you want."

The electronic click of the shutter indicates she's taken her snapshot of me eating. She lowers her mobile. "You're very photogenic."

I grunt. She is strange, for sure.

Since Emery has finished her breakfast, she settles in to watch me, like I'm a ruddy reality show on television. *World's most uptight man, tune in tonight at eight to see him iron his bath towel.* I don't iron bath towels, though. Emery probably thinks I do.

After I've consumed my fourth bite of food, she says, "You're fanatical about not getting even one molecule of food on your spiffy clothes, aren't you?"

"Messes are unpleasant. Though not to you, clearly."

"Are you implying I'm a slob?"

"Not at all. I admire your enthusiasm."

"Thank you." She scuttles across the sofa on her erse like a sexy crab until her knees nudge my leg. "I admire your efficiency, the way you eat with surgical precision. It's so cute." Though I open my mouth, she speaks before I can. "But you're kind of missing the point of eating pancakes."

"Am I?" Sliding another mouthful between my lips, I regard her with interest.

"Definitely. If you don't spill any syrup on yourself, how can I lick it off?"

I freeze with the fork poised near my lips, a pancake square pierced by its tines, and stare at her without blinking. "What?"

"Let me show you."

She plucks the fork from my fingers and dunks the pancake square into the syrup. Without bothering to tap the bite on the plate to remove the excess, she raises it to my mouth and skims the drenched bite of food across my lips to glaze them with sticky syrup. A drop rolls off the tines onto my chin. She holds the fork out to the side and leans toward me.

I cannae move. Cannae breathe either. Why I should get so aroused by syrup, I have no idea. But it's not the syrup, is it? Emery does this to me.

She thrusts her tongue out to skate it over my lips, then drags it down to lap up the syrup on my chin.

And I stare at her, eyes wide. Aye, this is definitely the way to eat pancakes.

She licks away the last molecule of syrup. Leaning back, she raises the loaded fork to my mouth. "Eat up, Rory. You'll need lots of carbs to keep up with me today."

All I can manage to do is keep staring at her while my breathing grows heavier.

Emery waggles the fork. "Don't you want another bite of soft, succulent flesh drenched with liquid?"

Mhac na galla. Why does she have to speak those words in a seductive tone? I'll never be able to look at pancakes again without imagining her naked with syrup drizzled over her skin. I'd love to lick it off her body, and the possibilities for whipped cream are endless. I cannae stop myself. I lunge my head forward, intending to claim her mouth, but I regain just enough of my senses to stop short of doing that. I open my mouth and enclose the entire pancake square plus all the fork tines, sealing my lips around them.

She pulls the fork away.

I devour the food like I haven't eaten in days, maybe months. But I haven't sampled the sweetness I most want to taste again, the kind only she can give me. I swallow my half-chewed bite of pancake and toss my plate onto the coffee table. It smacks down, making the pancake squares jiggle. I sling an arm around her waist, stunning a gasp from her, and silence her startled exhalation with my mouth. The stickiness that clings to my lips transfers onto her skin, and I can taste it when I lick at the seam of her mouth. She surrenders with a soft moan, sagging into me while I plunder her mouth—aye, like a pirate. She responds to every lash of my tongue with equally rough swipes of her own, even while her hands rise to bracket my face and her breasts mound against my chest.

Whisking my hands down to her erse, I wrench her closer.

She swings a leg out, and I know what she means to do. While I grope her body, I boost her onto my lap so she's straddling me. She crushes her body to mine and moans again, perhaps because my hardening cock is wedged between her thighs. I can feel the heat of her arousal even through our clothes while I massage her erse, plunging my fingers between her cheeks with every inward thrust.

Emery rocks her hips up so that my fingers dive down to graze her cleft.

What am I doing? Ravishing her in the living room? On the sofa? In front of the French doors and several windows? I cannae do this, not now. So I grasp her upper arms and push her away.

Breathing hard, and now half off my lap, she gapes at me. "Why'd you stop?"

I hook a finger under her chin. "Didnae want to."

"Then why? It was just getting good."

"Aye, it was." I rest my hands on her hips. "Losing control is not my strong suit."

"On the contrary, you excel at shedding your inhibitions."

I rub a hand over my jaw while I gaze into the far corner of the room. "I don't normally behave like a randy virgin." One corner of my mouth twists downward. "Until last night. Twice I've lost control with you, and twice I...didnae want to stop."

"Why did you stop? If you liked it."

"Told ye. Cannae abide a loss of control." I grasp her waist and hoist the lass off my lap, setting her down beside me. No, I can't understand my behavior with Emery. And it…unsettles me. Time to change the subject. I glance at her ComicCon T-shirt. "We should get you to your hotel. You must want a change of clothes."

"Yeah, I would."

With one finger, I trace the outline of the logo on her shirt. Earlier, after I'd ordered our breakfast, Emery had attempted to explain ComicCon to me. Being a bloody foolish erse, I first tried to define it myself based on the evidence before me.

"Is it a gathering of comedians?" I'd asked.

"Not that kind of comic." She had wandered to the pool table, running her fingers over the felt surface in an almost erotic manner. "It started out as a convention for fans of comic books, but these days it includes various kinds of popular culture not directly related to comics. Sci-fi and fantasy are popular topics. And there's a cool contest for masquerade costumes."

I couldn't stop my lip from curling. "Costumes? I cannae fathom why grown men and women want to dress up in silly outfits."

She smiled. "Everybody could use a bit of silly in their life."

I'm fair certain I pulled a face, a not entirely polite one, then I'd straightened my spine. "Do you wear costumes?"

"On Halloween and at ComicCon, yes." Emery sighed as if she were recalling her past escapades that involved costumes. "At the office party, my co-workers gave me a rinky-dink certificate declaring my costume the sexiest and skimpiest of all."

"Sexy and skimpy?" My voice came out huskier, probably because I was envisioning her in an outfit that barely covers her sensitive regions.

"Absolutely. Halloween is my favorite holiday because dressing up is so much fun." She stroked her fingers over the crimson felt of the pool table. "If you're super nice to me, I might show you photos of my costumes."

I swallowed hard because my cock wanted to see those photos. "You place a high value on fun, don't you?"

"Sure do." She had grabbed the eight ball then, rolling it between her palms while she leaned a hip against the table. "I'm getting the impression you don't."

"It's a waste of time."

Christ, did I sound like a sodding ersehole? Of course I did. But I honestly don't see the appeal of doing ridiculous things to entertain myself. Law journals provide all the enjoyment I need.

Which might be part of my problem.

Emery touched the eight ball to her cheek, nuzzling it. "What's your favorite thing to do? Favorite in the whole wide world?"

"Work."

Her jaw fell open. "You've got to be kidding."

"No." Desperate to spare her the depressing knowledge of what I'm really like, I had let my mouth slide into a suggestive smirk. "Fucking is a close second."

"Only second?" She set the eight ball on the table. "Seems to me that ought to be first on your list. I mean, you were so into it last night."

"Yes, but work is my passion."

And there I went again, saying things that serve to convince her I'm a boring, lifeless ersehole. So what if she does think that?

"That is so sad," she had told me as she flicked her finger to set the eight ball rolling across the felt. "Why are you in New Orleans? Business?"

"I'm visiting an American friend who's in the same line of work."

"Which is?"

No, I did not want to tell her. It was ridiculous, but I couldn't make myself say it. Instead, I coughed and glanced out the windows at the view of Bourbon Street below. When I finally convinced my eyes to look at her again, I avoided answering her question by asking one of my own. "Why are *you* in New Orleans? For fun?"

"Naturally." She sashayed up to me, so close the lass had to bend her head back to see my face. "I got enough work at work. This is a vacation. According to everyone but you, 'vacation' is defined as traveling with no useful purpose, solely to have a good time."

"I see." I tapped a fingertip on her lips. "How long are you here?"

"Leaving on the red-eye tomorrow night."

"Then I have two days with you." I touched my lips to hers but kept the kiss chaste. "Two days to plumb the depths of the mystery that is Emery Granger."

"Plumb away," she said, her tone sultry.

I leaned in as if to kiss her but stopped millimeters from her lips. "I look forward to it."

My thoughts return to the present, and I rise from the sofa to offer her my hand. "To your hotel."

"Um, it's more of a hostel than a hotel." She accepts my help in getting up. "Nowhere near as swanky as this pad."

I shrug. "Money isn't important."

"Says the guy who probably has his own private Fort Knox."

I compress my lips and hiss a breath out through my nostrils. "I need a change of clothes before we leave."

Should I tell her the truth about me? No, it doesn't matter. I'll spend two days with her in an attempt to teach myself how to relax. Then we will say goodbye. Simple. Clean. No entanglements.

"Yeah," she says, "you're not really dressed for a freewheeling day of sightseeing. Of course, a billionaire can get away with wearing anything, I guess."

"I'm not a billionaire." As I walk toward the bedroom door, I find myself blurting out the truth. "Only a millionaire several times over."

Before she can say anything else, I duck into the bedroom. And I don't look back. She probably wears a stunned expression. Whatever she thinks of me now, I'm sure spending two days with me will convince her to jump on the red-eye tomorrow night, and never think of me again.

I emerge from the bedroom several minutes later wearing clothing that seems more appropriate for a day of so-called fun—dark-blue jeans that sport sharp creases thanks to a professional pressing, and a golden-colored T-shirt. My sister Fiona gave me this outfit because she insisted I should try to have a good time in New Orleans, and she wanted me to look like I know how to do that. How do jeans alert everyone that I'm the good-time sort? I have no idea.

Emery gazes at my body while alternately chewing her lip and licking it.

I cock my head at her. "Are you ready?"

She nods.

Clasping her hand, strictly so we don't get separated, I guide her out of the suite. Aye, we're in danger of losing track of each other in the lift. As we stroll into the car, which is empty, I bend my head to whisper in her ear. "I'm yours for the weekend. What will you do with me?"

She smiles. "Show you how to loosen up and have fun."

"An impossible task. I dislike what most people consider to be fun."

"Lucky for you, I like a challenge."

Chapter Six

*P*erhaps I should have considered the ramifications more thoroughly before I agreed to do whatever Emery wants today. I don't understand her, but I feel oddly better when I'm with her. What barmy thing will she say next? I feel almost excited at the prospect of hearing whatever she might spout. I've never met anyone who surprises me as often as she does.

But I had no idea what would be involved in having "fun" with her.

The only other times I'd engaged in one-night stands, I hadn't stayed for more than an hour. Why couldn't I walk away from Emery? It makes no sense. But I've given myself these two days to explore the mystery of her, so maybe by tomorrow night I'll better understand my reactions to the lass.

The "fun" starts at Emery's hostel. I've heard the term before, of course, but I never knew what precisely that meant until today. I would've thought a clever lass like Emery would think to warn me what I'm walking into, but she does seem to relish every opportunity to shock me. That might explain the fact that she gave me no warning whatsoever.

The Quisby turns out to be an unusual hostel that occupies a historic building with the original Audubon Hotel sign still posted on its front. I appreciate the history and architecture, until we go inside. I seem to have developed a permanent wrinkle over my nose, one that I feel pinching my forehead, but it only appears once Emery leads me into the room she shares with three other women, a room equipped with two sets of bunk beds.

"Stevie and Ronnie are super nice," she tells me. "You'll like them."

My jaw goes slack. "You share a room with men?"

Emery shakes her head, clearly struggling not to laugh. "Chill out. This is a girls-only dorm. Besides, I'm not into orgies."

Thank heaven for that.

I do the only thing I can when she retreats into the bathroom to change her clothes, leaving me alone in this bizarre place. I resort to pacing the length of the room. By the time she returns a few minutes later, I'm examining the room from my stationary position near the door, with my hands linked behind my back. When I see her new outfit, I can't resist skimming my gaze over her entire body. I stand up a bit straighter, suddenly wanting to look… I don't know. Masculine? No, that sounds ridiculous.

She raises her arms and twirls for me. "Like my duds?"

"Aye." My voice sounds deeper now, almost lustful. Well, I cannae help it, considering the way she's dressed. I stride toward her, spanning the distance in two steps. "I like it very much."

And aye, that's no lie. Emery wears denim shorts that expose nearly all of her luscious legs and a neon-pink T-shirt that has short sleeves and a neckline so low that I can't stop my gaze from drifting down to admire a tantalizing glimpse of those bonnie tits. On the front of her shirt, images of colorful flowers stretch across her bosom and snake up on either side of her plunging neckline. I love the way she's drawn her hair up into a ponytail, and I even like the puffy pink thing she has used to secure her hair.

I glide the back of one finger up her arm, from her wrist to near her shoulder, where the sleeve of her T-shirt ends. "I liked the ComicCon shirt, but this one suits you better. It's full of color and life, like you."

Though I still don't know why I keep saying idiotic things like that, I've decided not to think about it today. Or tomorrow. Am I capable of forgetting to be uptight for two entire days? I'm about to find out.

I hook a finger inside the neckline of her shirt and peer down into the space between her breasts. "No cash?"

She holds up a small pink item that I think is called a clutch. "Got a purse today."

"Ah." I trace her neckline with the tip of my finger. "Stay with me tonight. You'll have more room and privacy."

"I don't know," she says, sounding far too uncertain for my liking.

Had I expected her to leap up and down while waving her arms in the air and shouting wordless cries of joy? Well, perhaps I did hope for that. A wee bit.

"Please. I have no expectations, for sex or anything else." I clear my throat. "I would very much like to have another night with you."

"I'll consider it."

Linking my hands behind my back again, I nod crisply. "Good."

Five minutes later, we climb inside my hired car, which is a luxury model. I can't decide if my wealth makes her uncomfortable, or if it's strictly me who makes her feel that way. I focus on driving as I navigate the car down the streets of New Orleans, which Emery informed me earlier is called NOLA for short. We've rounded one corner when Emery finally answers the question I asked her back in the hostel.

"Yes," she says, "I'd love to stay with you tonight."

My lips peel back from my teeth as if I might smile, but I resist the impulse, my mouth returning to a neutral expression. I hope it looks neutral, at least. Aye, it does. With my composure reasserted, I speak in a matter-of-fact tone. "I'm sure you'll be more comfortable at the Ritz-Carlton."

I had wanted to grin. The uptight solicitor wanted to smile like a dafty at the bonnie lass who has captivated him. My family would never believe it. I still remember what Aidan told me when he and Lachlan said goodbye to me as I was heading off for my working holiday.

"Donnae be an ogre," he said. "You'll scare the Americans. And try to dislodge that caber from your erse."

Why my brother insists I have a caber up my erse, I can't explain. Aidan is much younger than I am, and he thinks he should turn everything into an excuse for a great joke. The caber humor escapes me, though.

Today I am trying to be less of a caber-stuffed ogre by letting Emery pick the destinations for our sightseeing tour. While we tour the sights, she periodically brings out her mobile to take a picture—of me. The voodoo museum in the French Quarter forces me to exercise all my restraint, which seems contradictory to Emery's stated mission of loosening me up. But how does she expect me to react? Darkened rooms harboring strange altars, candles in glass holders that bear the names of voodoo deities… I am not equipped for this. Fortunately, Emery takes pity on me and suggests we head for a more mainstream museum, the Historic New Orleans Collection.

The museum consists of several historic buildings, and as we wander through them, I begin to enjoy myself. Every time I look at Emery—while we survey the displays of period clothing and weapons, or examine the artwork on display—she smiles sweetly. I find myself growing more relaxed and even becoming somewhat enthusiastic when we discuss the period furnishings. They remind me of my home, but I don't mention that to Emery.

After that, we visit the National World War II Museum. I share stories about my grandfather's aerial exploits during the war, but Emery seems to be tired of history. Outside the war museum, she stops me with a hand on my arm.

I gaze down at her, lifting my brows.

"We've done the history thing," she says. "Are you up for something a bit more audacious?"

"This would be your attempt to make me have fun."

"Yep." She slips her arm around mine, clasping my bicep. "Think you can handle it?"

"I can." I duck my head to meet her gaze. "If you're expecting me to become more like you, I'm afraid you'll be disappointed."

"Like me?" She pokes me with her elbow. "What am I like?"

"You are open and free, unafraid of what anyone thinks of you. I admire that, but I will never be like you."

"Do you want to be?"

I raise my head, my lips working though I can't formulate a response. So I reassert my neutral expression. "I'm comfortable the way I am."

Emery insists we should have lunch at SoBou, a Cajun restaurant in the French Quarter. It doesn't sound like my sort of place, but since I made her endure the war museum, I agree to the restaurant she chose. The lass gently pushes me to try gumbo with her. Once again, I give in. It's not the worst thing I've ever eaten, but the next dish she suggests forces me to put my foot down.

When the lass offers me a bite of her oyster taco, I jerk my head back and curl my lip. "No thank you."

She waves the taco near my mouth. "Come on, Rory, live a little. One bite won't kill you."

"Oysters can be appealing, but not in a…taco." I bar my arms over my chest. "Again, no thank you."

"This is a vacation day. Take a risk." She touches the taco to my lips. "One teeny bite."

I roll my eyes heavenward, sigh, and lower my arms. "All right."

Why can't I say no to this woman?

Leaning forward, I take a wee bite of the taco and chew carefully. I've tasted worse foods. Swallowing, I sink back in my chair. "Happy?"

"Yes. Wasn't awful, was it?"

"Not entirely." I almost smile again. "You do realize oysters are thought to be an aphrodisiac."

"Guess you'll find out later if that's true." She eyes me with curiosity. "How old are you?"

"Thirty-nine. I'll be forty in a month or so."

She gives me an assessing glance. "You don't look forty, but you act ninety."

"Thank you," I say crisply. Aidan has told me the same thing, but I don't glower at Emery the way I do when my brother speaks those words.

"Don't worry," she says, "your stuffiness is cute, and kind of a turn-on."

"I feel the same way about your silliness."

When we've finished our meal, Emery springs to her feet. "Buckle up, we're off to our next stop."

I get up and stretch. "What now?"

"I want to drive a Lamborghini at over a hundred miles an hour." She seizes my hand. "Come on, there's a place where you can do that."

My eyes must be bulging, and I'm dead certain my face has gone slack. She must be off her head this time.

"Relax," she tells me. "You can sit and watch while I take all the risks. Or, you could be my copilot. How brave are you, Mr. MacTaggart?"

"Not that brave."

Chapter Seven

I walk out of the bedroom into the living room, where Emery is reclining on the sofa with her feet propped on the coffee table. Her lips are curved into a soft smile of deep satisfaction, as if the food we consumed earlier fulfilled her every need. Her dietary needs, that is. I know the lass harbors deep, carnal hunger too, and I mean to tap into that later.

She had complained earlier when we ordered room service and I requested Cobb salad. Eating healthy is, I assume, a symptom of being an uptight erse. Emery naturally chose a large ribeye steak, but I refrained from commenting on her food choice.

Now, my salad lies half-eaten on the table.

Emery's plate is empty, though not only because she eats like someone who has just returned from a deep-space mission during which she ate only freeze-dried foods. Her plate is empty also because I had eaten some of her steak. I still can't believe I stole food from her plate, though I had asked permission first. Does that still qualify as stealing? Emery must think I am the most boring, stuffy person on the planet.

Not that I care. She can think what she likes.

For dessert, we had shared a massive piece of cheesecake, though I asked for two forks to go with it. She wanted to feed me, but I declined her offer. Emery had seemed mildly disappointed, but that's not my problem. I do not share forks, not even with bonnie, sexy lasses who beg me to "loosen up and live dangerously."

Emery pushed my tolerance to its limits today. The voodoo museum had been only the opening salvo in her battle to mold me into the sort of man she wants. When she had announced she wanted to drive a Lamborghini at over a hundred miles an hour, I assumed she was exaggerating in hopes of making me uncomfortable. She seems to enjoy doing that, and she usually calls me "cute" or "adorable" when I balk at her suggestions. I agreed to accompany her to a place called the Xtreme Xperience only because I believed it must be an arcade and she would "drive" that sports car virtually. Aye, I'm a complete sodding eejit. How was I to know there actually is a racetrack where people go to drive at outrageous speeds for fun?

Emery received a thirty-minute training session. Thirty minutes. Shouldn't a person need weeks or months of training before they rocket around a racetrack faster than an actual rocket flies into space? I sat in the stands, watching in mute horror as Emery drove a high-end sports car round and round the track, the engine screaming and the vehicle racing by so fast that I could barely see it. Maybe I'm exaggerating, but only just. I have never seen anyone drive that fast except in movies or televised car races. Christ, the woman is off her head.

By the time Emery trotted up to me in the stands, I felt sick, and I was swallowing against the bile that had crept up my throat.

She patted my shoulder. "You weren't even in the car, and you look like you're about to throw up."

"You were driving very fast," I said, my voice shaky. I had bloody well earned the right to sound like that after what I just witnessed. "I was sure you'd crash into the wall and die in a hellish explosion."

"You are so sweet to worry about me."

I scowled. "I'd worry about anyone as reckless as you."

"It's adorably sweet, Rory."

"Stop calling me adorable and cute and sweet." Though I tried to maintain my scowl, I failed, probably looking exasperated instead. "I'm a man, not a kitten."

Now, as I halt at the doorway to the living room where Emery waits, she opens her mouth on a big, loud yawn.

"Long day," I say, leaning against the doorjamb. "Time for bed."

The lass stretches her entire body, both arms above her head and all her toes extended. "Mm, yes, bedtime sounds good."

When she stretches her body like that, I can't stop myself from drinking in the length and breadth of Emery, from her bare arms and enticing cleavage to the exposed expanse of her legs and her sock-covered feet. My tongue darts out to wet my lips as I imagine licking her from head to toe. When I aim my focus at her face again, I struggle to maintain a neutral expression. "No sex tonight. You're exhausted, and so am I."

After the horrific trip to the racetrack.

"We can perk each other up," she says, waggling her delicate little toes. She lifts one foot to point her big toe at me. "Unless you're afraid you'll lose control again."

"I won't." Not sure I can reasonably declare that, but I don't need to tell her everything. I crook a finger at her. "Come, lass. Time for sleep."

She doesn't move.

I crook my finger a second time.

Emery rises and stretches again, boosting up onto her toes, then slaps her heels back down on the floor while her mouth gapes on another yawn. "We spent the day together, and now we're spending the night together with no sex. Sounds an awful lot like dating, wouldn't you say?"

"I don't date anymore."

With her hands on her hips, she tips her head to the side. "What do you call this?"

I scratch my cheek. "A casual fling, I suppose."

She strolls across the room to me and lays her hand on my shoulder. "Nothing about today was casual."

I spear her with a sharp look. "For me, it was."

Her mouth falls open again as the lass yawns loudly for a third time, and then a fourth.

Bollocks. I sweep her up in my arms and carry her to the bed, setting the lass on her feet beside it. "Get ready for bed. For sleep."

"Aye-aye, sir." She salutes me.

I can't help it. My lips tick upward a hair.

Then I march around the foot of the bed, yank the drapes closed, and dig my wallet out of my trouser pocket, tossing it onto the nightstand. I sit down on the bed's edge and begin to untie my shoelaces. I'm carefully removing my shoes when Emery takes hold of her shirt's hem and slides it up and over her head.

I bolt up off the bed. "What are you doing?"

"I sleep naked."

My *slat* loves the idea, but I throw my hands up. "Ye cannae."

No, I will go insane if she strips.

Wearing only her bra and shorts, she shakes her head. "Honestly, Rory, how can you be such a prude after last night? We were both naked. All night. In this bed."

I shift my weight from one foot to the other, grasping the back of my neck. My gaze flicks down to her lacy pink bra, and I'm fair certain my nostrils flare. I veer my attention to the pillow on my side of the bed. "Please, wear something to bed."

"Like what?" She flaps her arms. "Forgot to pack a nightie."

"You were planning to sleep in the nude in your communal hotel room?" I might be gaping at her. Can anyone blame me? The thought of Emery lying naked in a bunk bed in that place... Well, my cock wants me to keep imagining that, but my brain commands me to stop.

Rationality always wins.

Most of the time.

With a frustrated growl, she flings her hands up. "My roommates didn't care. Why should you? For pity's sake, we've had our hands all over each other's naked bodies."

I compress my lips and focus on the wall behind her. Am I being too...stuffy? No one will know what I've done with this woman. When I go home, the secret will go with me. Besides, it's not as if I'll be taking her in front of the living room windows. The bedroom curtains are closed. We could both sleep naked.

But I can't quite make myself tell her that.

I tear off my T-shirt and chuck it at her. "Wear this."

Emery catches the shirt. "Okay, but I have to take off everything else. Not sleeping in my bra, no matter how uncomfortable it makes you."

"Fine." I turn my back to her. "Undress quickly."

"I prefer sleeping naked, though. Hard to believe you're the same guy who tore my clothes off right there in the living room last night."

"That was different."

"Because you wanted to get in my pants then."

"I—" Yes, that's exactly right. I make a noise that feels like part growl, part hissing sigh. "Change yer bloody clothes, would ye?"

Soft noises indicate she's undressing.

Her bra drops onto my shoulder.

My entire body flinches. It's a bloody stupid reaction, I know. But it's her *bra*. Draped over my shoulder. Her pink lace bra. The woman has no shame. I take the garment between my thumb and forefinger, cautiously pluck it off my shoulder, and toss it onto the floor.

Maybe I like that Emery has no shame, but I can't live like that.

"Fit for viewing now, Mr. Fussy Pants."

I spin around to face her. My gaze swerves down to the hem of my shirt, which now covers her body, sort of. It hangs halfway down her thighs.

She braces one foot on the bed and rolls her sock down, casts it aside, and repeats the process with the other foot.

My eyes insist on watching her every movement.

Emery crawls under the covers and stretches out on her side with her head on the pillow.

I remove everything except my boxers, then climb onto the bed and move around until I'm situated on my side, facing her, with a gap of a foot between us. Should I move away from her a wee bit more?

She tucks her hands under her cheek on the pillow.

The lass looks even sweeter and more innocent lying beside me that way. I settle a fingertip on her upper arm, trailing it back and forth along her skin. "You mentioned you're a computer programmer. What is it you do?"

"Programming, duh. It's technical and very, very boring."

"I'd like to know. Do you create software?"

"I work for Travellis Games, a company that makes software for everything from the latest Kor the Space Viking game to online poker and digital slot machines." Her expression turns almost melancholy. "I don't really create anything, though. I fix what other people create. Debug code, rejigger scripts, that kind of thing. It's mind-numbing at times and always tedious."

"Why do it if you hate the work?"

"In college, I loved writing code. But the jobs I got after graduation were all programming, not actual creative coding." She withdraws one hand from under her cheek to pick at the seam of her pillowcase. "Being trapped in a cubicle forty hours or more every week, fixing someone else's creation, it gets to be a real drag after a while."

"You could find another career."

"Not that easy for us non-millionaires. Getting the training for something else takes time and money I don't have." She bites her upper lip when I draw an invisible line up to her shoulder. "My last job paid well enough, but I spent most of my income paying off my student loans. When the bosses ordered everyone to work longer hours, having fun became a rarity in my life."

I pull my hand away from her arm, closing it over her fingers to stop her from picking at her pillowcase. "You said your last job paid well, past tense. What about your current job?"

"Don't have one. Got laid off—downsized, as they say." She snuggles deeper into the pillow, and her chin grazes my knuckles. "I'd worked there longer than most of my coworkers, but I was the first to go."

"I'm sorry, Emery." I stroke her chin with my finger. "You deserve better."

"Why?"

I have no answer for her. "Why? Because—You do, that's all."

"What do you do for a living?"

I roll onto my back as if I mean to inspect the bed's canopy. "Nothing interesting."

She taps my nose until I look at her. "If you won't tell me your occupation, at least tell me how many times you've had one-night stands."

"Not often," I say in a measured tone.

"How often?"

"Four times. Including you."

"Only four? I got the impression you do it a lot."

"Why would you think that?"

She shrugs one shoulder. "You were so skilled at seduction, I figured you take strangers to bed all the time."

"No." I pinch the bridge of my nose with my thumb and forefinger. "My brother Aidan has convinced my entire family I travel the world seducing hapless women. No one should ever believe Aidan, though. He thinks it's humorous."

Why did I mention my brother? She doesn't need to know about my family.

Emery pokes me with her knee. "But you were looking for a professional woman to whisk away to your suite last night."

Will she never stop saying that? I punch my pillow, though I have no idea why. "I meant to have a whisky, enjoy the music at the bar, and find a companion for the night. I'd given up on the latter. None of the women I met interested me. Until I saw you."

"Why did you come back this morning?"

Emery and I gaze at each other while she waits for me to answer and I try to come up with a response. Since I can't, I cough and swerve my attention to the window. "I have no idea why I couldn't walk away from you."

She falls silent for a moment, then says, "I'd like to hear more about your family."

Mhac na galla. I punch my pillow again. Link my hands over my belly. Shift in place. Smack my hands down on the sheets.

"If you'd rather not talk about it," she says, "that's okay."

What's the point in refusing to tell her? I already mentioned Aidan.

I rub my forehead. "It's all right. I have two brothers, Aidan and Lachlan, as well as three sisters. They are Fiona, Catriona, and Jamie. Lachlan is the oldest, and Jamie is the youngest. I'm second, after Lachlan."

"What about your parents?"

"Alive and well. Most of my family lives in and around the village of Ballachulish in the Highlands, where we were born and raised." I move only my eyes to glance at her. "What about your family?"

"My parents moved to Australia ten years ago, for my dad's work. My sister, Hadley, got married four years ago and moved to Germany. She has beautiful twin girls."

"You must not see your family often."

"Haven't seen any of them since Hadley's wedding."

I brush the back of my hand over her cheek. "I can't imagine never seeing my family. Must be difficult."

"I get by. But yeah, I miss them a lot. Since losing my job, I feel more alone than ever. I know they didn't want to leave me, but sometimes I feel like an abandoned child. God, I have no idea why I'm telling you this."

She feels alone, like me, though for different reasons. That might explain why I lace my fingers with hers and study our joined hands. "Maybe you sense we have something in common. For quite a while, I've felt…lonely. You've provided a welcome distraction, if an unusual one."

"Is that a compliment or an insult?"

"A compliment. You are unusual in the very best way." I lift an arm, patting the bed between us. Once she snuggles up to me with her head on my chest, I slide an arm around her. "You're also beautiful, brave, sensual, ridiculous at times, and you have a wonderfully strange sense of humor."

Am I glad she's here? If I hadn't come back this morning, I would never have been given the chance to spend a day with her. She seems so different from me, and yet we have meaningful things in common. Loneliness, for one. And a love of family.

But I cannot become involved with her.

"Sleep," I say.

"Like I can do it on command."

"Try." I feel a powerful need to soothe her, so I sift my fingers through her hair in a steady rhythm.

"Admit it, you had a teeny bit of fun today."

"Perhaps a little." I skim my free hand up and down her arm, then bury my face in her hair. "Rest, Emery."

She seems to be having trouble relaxing, and I can think of only one other thing that might help.

I begin to sing softly. "*O chì, chì mi na mòr-bheanna, o chì, chì mi na coireachan, chì mi na sgoran fo cheò.*"

"What is that?" she murmurs. "Doesn't sound like English."

"It's Gaelic. A song my mother taught me, called 'The Mist Covered Mountains.' It's about how bonnie Scotland is."

"Sing to me some more, please. You have a wonderful voice."

I hug her tighter and sing for her while I wonder why my voice seems full of a strange yearning. For too long, I've wondered why I can't find peace—or love. But I don't want the latter, not anymore, and the former hovers out of my reach.

Until tonight. With Emery. The feel of her body, tucked against mine while she drifts off to sleep, affects me more than I care to admit, even to myself. Maybe I can keep her in my life, as long as I set the parameters. And as long as she adheres to my rules.

Aye, I want her. But can I do the unthinkable just to keep her in my bed?

Chapter Eight

In the morning, I wake at dawn just as I did the day before. When I'm at home, I always get up by six to start my day with a light breakfast before heading into my home office. Maybe I don't have an office here in New Orleans, but I decide I should use the suite's living area as a makeshift space for doing all the dull things a lawyer does. I'd meant this as a working holiday, anyway. Emery convinced me to try having "fun," but I still need to do something meaningful.

Aye, work is meaningful to me, more so than the sorts of activities Emery values above everything else.

But I have a wee bit of trouble getting out of bed this morning. I lie here, on my side, watching her sleep. She's facing me, and her lips are curved into a soft, sweet smile that makes me curious about what dreams she enjoys while she's slumbering. All right, I don't get up precisely at dawn, though I am awake then. It might be slightly after sunrise. After pulling on my clothes, I grab a terry-cloth robe from the bathroom and drape it over the foot of the bed for Emery.

Then I drag myself out of the bedroom and abandon the lovely lass who shared my bed for the past two nights.

Should it be this hard to stop gazing at a sleeping woman?

The answer hardly matters because I have made a decision. Several decisions, in fact. After ordering my light breakfast from room service and eating it alone on the sofa, I settle into a high-backed, upholstered chair positioned near the French doors that open onto the terrace. I don't open the doors, though. I don't plan to look out through them either, except for the occasional break from staring at my computer. As I set my laptop on my thigh and get started drafting legal documents for my personal use, I experience a twinge of guilt that I'm not slaving away for my clients. But this is a holiday, of sorts. Foregoing client work for something that will iron out the kinks in my life hardly seems like malpractice.

Aye, the documents I'm crafting will make my life simpler. My plan seems perfectly rational to me. Emery is a clever lass, so I'm sure she will appreciate what I've done.

At eight thirty, Emery ambles out of the bedroom into the living area.

Since my chair is angled partly away from the French doors, I see her out of the corner of my eye the moment she crosses the threshold. She's wearing the robe I left out for her.

I prefer the way she looked in my shirt last night, but that's not appropriate for the daytime. Not sure a robe is either, especially the way she looks while sashaying toward me with that body concealed only by terry cloth.

My clothing is casual but professional, which I have no doubt will amuse Emery. My charcoal slacks and pale-green dress shirt won't make her swoon, but that hardly matters. I pretend my attention is focused on my computer so she won't know that I might've been…watching for her to come out of the bedroom. Brows lowered, mouth tight, I study the screen with my reading glasses perched on my nose. I almost hadn't worn them, because they might make me look stuffy, but I can't read the computer screen without them.

Bloody hell. Now I care if she likes my glasses.

While I study the document on-screen, Emery crouches in front of me and lays her hands on my knees.

I glance up at her without lifting my head. "Good morning. Sleep well?"

"Yes, very." She squeezes between my knees, but my computer blocks her from getting too close. "Why are you doing boring things on your computer? You should join me for a bath instead."

"How do you know what I'm doing is boring?"

"Because you look tense. If it was interesting—or heaven forbid, fun—you'd look more relaxed." She places one finger at the corner of my mouth and pushes it up. "Might even smile."

"I'm not on holiday, Emery. This is a work-related trip."

"Come on, it's Sunday. Spend another day with me before I have to go home."

Should I share my idea with her? I'd planned to wait until later. But as I gaze at her, I find I want to tell her. I need to finish this document first, though.

I tip my head down to peer up at her over the tops of my glasses. "As much as I would enj—appreciate the company, I have to finish this contract."

She sinks back on her heels. "Contract? What kind of business are you in?"

"Later, I will explain. You have my word."

"Ugh. It's always later with you." She picks up my computer and sets it on the floor. I can't move, both curious and stunned while the lass wriggles between my thighs to loop her arms around my neck. "Be spontaneous, just this once. For me. I'll beg if you want."

My lips twitch against my will, but I repress the urge to wrap my arms around her. With my hands on my thighs, I shake my head. "Later is the best I can offer."

"What are we going to do later? At least tell me that."

The impulse I'd repressed seizes me again, stronger this time, and I lash my arms around her waist, then stand up while hoisting her with me. She lands on her bare feet. I ease her away from my body.

"Have a bath," I say. "I'll be finished soon."

"And then you'll join me?"

"I will come to you in the bathroom."

So what if I'm avoiding her question? I can't let my libido run my life anymore. Since it's a recent problem that started the night before last, I should have no trouble quashing the impulse.

Emery undoes the belt on her robe and lets the terry cloth fall open, exposing her naked body.

Aye, I could quash the impulse until she did *that*.

My focus snaps to her breasts. *Control the lust, don't let it control you.* I inhale a deep breath, and my body relaxes as I exhale it slowly. My gaze wanders down to the hairs between her thighs, though I hadn't meant to look there. I clear my throat. "Have your bath, Emery."

"I'll do that, Rory."

My voice sounded rougher when I told her to have a bath. My throat must be dry.

Her robe flutters around her as she spins on her heels and sashays into the bedroom.

I watch her hips swaying and that erse shimmying until she moves out of sight.

For the next five minutes, I force myself to focus on finishing the documents I need to create so I can get what I want without risking anything. Aye, that sounds like a one-sided deal, but I will offer Emery a hefty inducement. I shouldn't want to do this. It's ridiculous, but I can't back out now. Never in my life have I given up because a case proved challenging. Emery isn't my opponent in court, but I must treat her as if she were. It makes sense—to me.

Once I've polished my documents, I head into the bedroom to find Emery. As I approach the closed bathroom door, I hear odd noises coming from inside. It sounds as if she's breathing hard and grunting while water splashes around her.

I rap on the door.

"Yes?" she says, sounding out of breath.

"May I come in?"

She hesitates. "Yeah, come on in."

I swing the door inward and step into the bathroom, halting beside the tub. And all the blood in my body floods down into my groin. Emery lies in the jacuzzi, amid a swirling current of bubbles, with her arms draped on the tub's rim and her legs stretched out.

The lass is naked.

Of course she is, ye eejit. She's taking a bath.

Last night, I might've acted like a bampot when Emery tried to undress in front of me. This morning, however, I feel no such panic. Not a lunatic after all. I sweep my gaze over her body and feel my lips trying to tighten into a smile, but I prevent it from becoming anything more than a slight curving of my lips. Can't have her thinking I want her so much that she can renegotiate the terms I intend to offer her.

I run a fingertip along the tub's rim, imagining it's her skin I'm touching. "Enjoying the amenities?"

"Absolutely." She raises one knee, moving it about so the water splashes high enough to lap at my finger. "What's the point of staying in a luxury hotel if you don't avail yourself of its pleasures?"

I tilt my head to the side, unable to stop my gaze from flicking down to the hairs between her thighs, visible every time her knee moves to the right. *Bod an Donais*, I want her right now. But I never enter into a negotiation from a position of weakness. So I stare at the opposite wall instead, though my eyes insist on stealing glimpses of her nude body.

"Out of the tub, please," I say gruffly. "I need to speak with you."

"We can talk here." She braces her ankle on the tub's rim, poking my leg with her dainty toes. "Hop on in."

"No thank you." I lean my leg against the tub and fold my arms over my chest. "I will wait for you in the dining room."

She feigns a pout. "You're no fun."

"Yes, I stipulate that fact."

Emery squints at me for a moment as if she can't quite figure me out. Good. I don't want her to understand me. The agreement I mean to present to her does not require the lass to like or understand me.

She lifts her leg, stretching her toes as she tries to reach my arm, without success. Instead, she wiggles her toes in the air near my hip. "I'd rather have a conversation in this tub. I think better naked."

I choke on a panicked laugh that I barely manage to squelch. "I rather doubt it. Even if it's true, I will not think properly while naked in a tub with you."

She smiles in her sweet, sexy way. "You're that hot for me. Wow, I'm super flattered."

An impulse I can't deny spurs me to snare her foot with my hand and trace circles on the ball with my thumb. "As tempting as you are, I need to discuss a serious matter with you." I slide my thumb down the side of her foot. "We'll talk in the dining room."

With another fake pout, she drops her arms, and they splash down in the water. "If you insist."

"I do." Releasing her foot, I move to the doorway. "And put on some clothing, please."

As I exit the bathroom, I do not glance back. No, I will not give her any more reasons to believe she has power over me simply because I hunger for her body. My rules will make certain of that.

I get everything set up in the dining room while I wait for Emery.

When she enters the room, I'm seated at one end of the rectangular wooden table. Though a gold chandelier hangs above the table's center, most of the light comes from the two windows. A white pot in the middle of the table holds purple flowers, but I didn't put that there. It was already here when I checked into my suite the other day.

Emery wears dark-blue jeans that cling to her body and a yellow peasant blouse. Even the loose-fitting shirt can't disguise her lovely body, not from me. I've explored every inch of it and know the contours by heart.

I place a neat stack of papers on the tabletop while my portable laser printer spits out more sheets. Seconds later, the printer has completed its task and ceases its whirring. I add the newly printed sheets to my stack.

Emery watches me the entire time.

"Have a seat," I say, waving toward the chair at the opposite end of the table.

She seems confused for a moment, but then she pulls the chair out and drops her erse onto it, propping her feet on the table. Her elbows rest on the chair's arms, and she links her hands over her belly.

I twist my lips into a tight pucker. Why must she always behave in such a haphazard fashion? *Feet off the table,* I want to say, but that would not be professional.

"What's up?" she asks.

I tap my fingers on the table while I avoid looking at her. Though I shouldn't ask, I find I can't make my mouth obey my wishes. "What were you doing in the bathroom when I knocked? I heard noises."

"Oh, that." She grins. "Since you wouldn't join me, I decided to have a good time all by myself. I was seconds away from my happy ending when you interrupted."

I gawp at her. "You were touching yourself?"

"Bingo. You must've suspected as much, or you wouldn't have asked what I was doing."

I square my shoulders, re-stack my papers that don't need to be stacked again, and struggle to reassert my calm demeanor. "I simply can't understand why you would do that in the daytime."

Why the bloody hell did I say that?

Emery clamps her teeth over her lips while her body shakes faintly with what I take for restrained laughter. "It's okay, Rory. I like your hang-ups. Makes me want to nibble them away one by one with my teeth, my tongue, my lips, my—"

"Enough. I've deduced your meaning."

"Is this what you wanted to talk about?" she asks. "Whether I masturbate in the tub, in the daytime, while you're standing outside the door. Bet you were listening at the keyhole."

"There is no keyhole on the bathroom door."

"Don't be so literal. I'm cool with you being a lech."

"I am not—Never mind." I snatch up a pen and twirl it round and round my middle finger.

"Out of curiosity, what do you do for a living?"

"I'm a solicitor."

"That like a pimp?"

I slap the pen down on the table. "No, it's like a lawyer."

"Chill out, I was kidding. I watch BBC America, I know what a solicitor is." She relaxes into her chair. "And you are a very solicitous solicitor."

I grunt, then pick up the papers I'd printed out and rap their edges on the table to ensure their perfectly aligned tops are...even more perfectly aligned. *Off your head for sure, MacTaggart.*

While I ignore my inner voice, I set the stack down again. "I have an offer for you."

"What kind of offer?"

"One I hope you'll consider." I shut my laptop's lid with a soft click and fiddle with the papers a bit more. "You seem as if you'd be amenable to this sort of—"

"Spit it out, Rory."

I reposition my hands on my lap and lean back against my chair. "I want us to marry."

Chapter Nine

Emery stares at me as if I've grown five red, lumpy heads and a pair of devil horns. She says nothing, seems not to blink, and the only movement she makes is when her jaw goes slack. I've shocked the lass, and though I expected this response, I hadn't anticipated the strength of her reaction. A free-spirited woman like Emery should jump at the chance. Shouldn't she?

But I haven't explained the details to her. That's why she can't speak or blink. Once I lay out the parameters, she will understand and appreciate the elegance of my solution. The problem is my unquenchable lust for her. My rules will clear up that issue.

Aye, they will.

"Perhaps I should explain," I tell her.

"Yeah, I think you really should."

Head bowed, I flatten a palm on the tabletop, curling my fingers and then spreading them. That is not a nervous reaction. It's…something else. I study my reflection on the polished surface of the table since I cannot look at her. "I've been divorced three times, and I have no desire to marry again."

"So naturally, you propose to me."

My fingers tense into a claw-like position. "I said I have no desire to marry, but circumstances require that I do."

"This isn't the Middle Ages. People aren't required to get hitched."

"You don't understand." I slump forward, elbows on the table, my hands flat on the slim stack of papers. "In the past two years, both my brothers have married. First Lachlan, then Aidan. This has resulted in my family insisting what I need to set me right is another wife."

"Set you right?" She bends forward, crossing her arms on the tabletop. "You mean because you're so uptight and pent-up and determined to make yourself miserable when you could be having a rollicking good time?"

Memories of the other night explode in my mind. Emery naked. The scent of her desire. The look on her face when she came.

I stab my tongue into the inside of my cheek. "Yes."

"You've decided they're right, and that marrying a stranger is the solution."

Mhac na galla. I scratch my head. "This will not be a love match. It will be a business arrangement."

"Better explain in more detail, before I run for the phone and call nine-one-one to report a man is kidnapping me for sex slavery."

I roll my eyes, and with a huff, throw my body against the chair's back. "No slavery of any sort. You are intelligent enough to consider my offer and decide whether to accept it."

"Gee, thanks. But you haven't explained your offer yet."

No, I haven't. *What a bloody stupid erse you are.*

I steeple my fingers under my chin, elbows balanced on the chair's arms. "I need a wife, to appease my family. As I said, they've grown rather insistent that marriage is the cure for what they believe ails me, to the point they've begun to contrive seemingly accidental meetings with eligible young women every time I go out in public. They convinced my housekeeper to bring her divorced daughter to work with her in hopes I'd find her appealing."

"You didn't."

I rest my forehead on my steepled fingers. "She's bonnie, but I'm not interested. Besides, she was a wee bit frightened of me."

"Frightened? Of you?"

"I realize I have no such effect on you, but some people find me intimidating." I glare at the papers on the table. "The salient fact is this. I tried marrying for love three times, and three times I was…disappointed."

Despite the overpowering urge to glance at her, I refuse to do it.

But I swear I can feel her watching me.

"This time," I continue, "I will marry for pragmatic purposes. If I go home with a new wife on my arm, my family will have no choice but to stop blethering about my personal life. You and I would remain married for one year, then you will leave, and I will tell my family our marriage is over. There will be a legally required one-year separation after that, but you will receive generous compensation as soon as you move out."

"How generous?"

"Five hundred thousand American dollars."

She draws her head back as her arms tumble off the table onto her lap. "You're paying me half a million bucks to be your wife for a year."

"Precisely. I have more conditions, however." I reach for the papers but then grab my pen instead, twirling it between my fingers. "You will live with me, and we will have sexual relations on a regular basis."

Slack-jawed, she stares at me.

I raise a placating hand. "Of course, you're free to say no if I want sex and you don't. But I will require it at least twice a week. Sex with strangers has been less than fulfilling, and even the risks involved couldn't provide enough stimulation for me. A monogamous arrangement seems the most prudent alternative."

There. That sounded reasonable and even appropriate.

Emery grips her chair's arms. "We were strangers the other night, which means you're saying sex with me was less than fulfilling."

"That's not—I meant the others, not you."

"Mm-hm." She glances at the windows, then at me. "This is sounding an awful lot like I'll be your live-in prostitute."

"Donnae be ridiculous." I clench my jaw. "You will be my wife, with all the benefits of such a relationship."

"Like what?"

"Free access to my financial accounts and the freedom to do whatever you wish." I rise, gather my papers, and stalk down the table's length to where she slumps in her chair. Poised on the table's corner, one leg bent, I set the papers facedown on my thigh. I decide she might need more of an inducement, so I speak in a rougher tone, the sort she seemed to like on the night we met. "You told me you've spent years working hard to pay off your student loans, and that you had little opportunity for the fun you value so highly. It sounds to me as if you've been stifled by responsibility. For a woman like you, that must've been torture."

She watches me without any discernible expression. "Not torture. I got sick and tired of working forty hours a week—often fifty, sixty, or more—to make my employer rich while I lived in a teeny apartment and never took a single vacation day."

I nod because I understand being shackled to a job, though I've done that by choice. She hasn't.

"What I offer," I say, slanting toward her, "is liberation from those responsibilities. With my wealth, you can do anything you want. Consider it an extended holiday, or start your own programming firm if that's what you like."

"Oh no, I've had it with that stuff."

"Discover what you do want. Even after we separate, you'll have a significant amount of money and no need to rush to find employment." I settle a hand on the back of her chair, our faces inches apart and her golden gaze glued to mine. "I'm offering to fund your search, so you can take all the time you need to find your passion."

Though she continues to gaze at me without expression, I see her pupils have dilated and her breaths are coming faster. I'm seducing her into a marriage of convenience. Maybe I feel the slight tug of guilt, but it's not as if I'm kidnapping her. She has a choice.

I drag a fingertip down her jaw to the corner of her mouth. "Who else can offer you this sort of freedom?"

"How do I know you'll stick to the bargain?" she asks. "What's to stop you from using me and throwing me away when you get tired of my silliness?"

"This." I proffer the papers to her. "A contract."

"A—huh?" She blinks rapidly, her focus flitting between the papers and my face several times before she settles on staring into my eyes. "I don't understand."

"These papers include two documents—a prenuptial agreement, and a marriage contract. Combined, they detail our arrangement." I set the papers on her lap. "Read them. Carefully."

"Should I have a lawyer look at this?"

"For the prenuptial agreement, yes. As for the marriage contract, a lawyer would tell you it's unlikely to be enforceable."

"How is the contract different from the prenup?"

"You'll see when you read it."

She looks down at the papers on her lap. "If the contract's not enforceable, what's the point?"

"The contract is a promise between us." I snap my spine straight, though my erse remains lodged on the table's edge. "Essentially, these documents obligate you to remain my wife for one year and to perform your marital duties at least twice each week. You will have access to my financial accounts, as I've said, but you are free to open your own accounts should you wish to do so. You further agree to attend social functions and to maintain the pretense we are in love."

A frantic laugh spurts out of her, accompanied by a light spray of spittle that barely misses me. "Are you serious? I have to pretend we're madly in love. You better hire an actress because I don't think I can be that convincing."

"I believe you can." I slant my body forward and cup her cheek with one hand, while with the other I palm her breast through her clothing.

Her mouth opens on a silent "oh." She pushes up on the chair's arms, lifting her erse off the seat.

Cannae stop my lips from curling into a smug smile, though it's only a slight one. "You won't have to fake your reactions to me."

"That's lust, not love."

"No one will notice the difference." I flick my thumb over her stiffening nipple, rewarded by her wee gasp. "If you need a bit of encouragement to fulfill your social duties, I can provide it."

"I'm still not sure." She waves a finger in a circle in front of my face. "As far as I can tell, you've got at least three people living inside that pretty little head of yours. Not sure I can handle psychological bigamy."

"There's no one else in my head. Only me."

"I don't mean actual split personalities. You have these distinct facets to your personality, and they come and go like flipping a switch."

I frown. "If you think I'm insane—"

"No, that's not what I mean either." She searches my gaze but seems not to find what she hoped to see there. "You're very complicated, Rory."

"I've been told as much before. By my family."

She freezes, her eyes widening. "What about my family? What am I supposed to tell them?"

"The same thing we tell mine."

"A lie, you mean." She squirms. "Would you please remove your hand?"

I peel my palm away from her breast, then settle one hand on my thigh and the other on the table. Something in her expression makes me think she might be seriously considering my offer. My pulse accelerates, and a strange sort of excitement races over my skin.

She clenches the marriage contract in her hand. "I need to think about this."

"Take all the time you need." Though I want to know her answer now, I must give her a chance to adjust to the idea. I stand up. "I can wait in the other room."

"No." She shoves her chair backward and springs to her feet. "I need to think while I'm away from you, away from your crazy-hot sexiness and charming little idiosyncrasies. I'll change my airline ticket and fly home as soon as I can—today."

Disappointment floods through me so heavily that my head falls forward and my shoulders cave in.

"I promise I will think about your proposal," she says. Since I'm blocking her path to the door, unintentionally, she lays a hand on my chest and pushes. "Please move. You're in my way."

I wrap my hand around hers, afflicted with a sudden need to convince her my plan will work. While I keep her hand caged in mine, I back her up to the table, forcing the lass to brace her erse against the edge. I ease my knee forward to push her thighs apart. She grips the table in one hand.

And I press her other hand to my chest. "What can I do to convince you?"

"I-I don't know. You're suggesting I marry you for sex and money." She leans backward, though she can't escape me that way. "The money I get. But the sex… We only did it the one time. Maybe it'll stink from now on."

I can't help chuckling. "It won't. And for the record, we fucked more than once."

"Twice in a single night. I'm counting that as one time."

"You came three times."

She wrestles her hand free of mine. "What did you do, make a spreadsheet to keep track of our sexual encounters? Bet you like spreadsheets. You're so…meticulous."

With my mouth a breath away from hers, I smirk and murmur, "You make 'spreadsheet' sound filthy."

And aye, now I'm fantasizing about making spreadsheets of every last thing I want to do to her body. While I'm shagging her, I'll recite my list of erotic options, whispering it into her ear. I'll spread her thighs and calculate the odds I can make her come four times in a night. With the right pivot table, I can do anything.

My lips tease her while I speak. "Stay until the red-eye tonight. I'll show you how meticulous I can be."

She flings her arms around my neck and latches her legs around my hips. The heels of her shoes dig into my erse. "Why wait? Show me now."

"Can't."

"Excuse me?" She pulls her head back. "Why not?"

I'd hoped not to need to explain this to her, but if I intend to marry her, she must understand. Still, I suspect I'm wearing a pained look. "It's daytime."

"Huh?" She jerks her head back even more, narrowing her gaze on me. "Oh Rory, you have got to be joking."

"No joke." I disentangle myself from the lass and shuffle backward a few steps. My arms hang stiffly at my sides, and my fingers twitch. "It's daytime. Sex is a nighttime activity."

"Uh-huh." She pushes away from the table. The contracts I'd given her lie strewn across the floor, as if they fell out of her hand when I backed her into the table. "Listen, I better go home right away. Your hang-ups are cute and all, but I need to seriously consider whether this is a good idea for either one of us."

She collects the papers in a haphazard bundle and hurries past me toward the doorway.

"Emery."

She half turns to glance at me.

"If the answer is no, tell me now and be done with it."

"I'm not saying no. I'm saying give me a little time and space." She hugs the sheaf of papers to her chest. "When do you go home?"

"Wednesday."

"You'll have my answer by then."

I stare at the papers she holds, feeling my fingers twitch again. "Where do you live?"

"Oh. Sorry." A nervous laugh bubbles out of her. "Forgot to tell you, didn't I? Colorado Springs."

"I'll wait until Wednesday." I motion toward the papers. "Those must be out of order."

"Yeah, I'll sort them out later." She tilts her head, her lips ticking upward a touch. "You really, really want to come over here and straighten these papers yourself, don't you?"

"*Mhac na galla*," I hiss. "I'm not that uptight."

"Glad to hear it." She taps the pages against her chest. "One more question. Why me? Out of all the women in the world, why pick one who drives you crazy?"

"I loved my previous wives. You're nothing like any of them, nothing like the sort of woman I've been attracted to in the past." I shove a hand into my trouser pocket, then yank it out. "There's no danger involved. I can't love you."

"Better call the airline and change my reservation. I'm leaving as soon as possible."

I watch her scurrying out of the room with those papers clutched in her arms. What will I do if she says no? I'll go on with my life, just as it was before I walked into that piano bar and seduced a sexy American. If she rejects my offer, I won't be fashed.

No, it won't bother me at all.

Chapter Ten

Monday, I tried to focus on learning about the American legal system, but every time my mate, Alan Fitz, tried to tell me something, I wouldn't hear it. He would wave a hand in my face or speak my name sharply—and once, he whistled with such piercing intensity that my ears rang for several seconds afterward. I couldn't blame Alan, though. I kept falling into an Emery trance.

I need to know her answer, and the suspense is driving me mad.

That explains why, on Tuesday, I fly to Colorado Springs. I have no ruddy idea where exactly she lives, but I do know she works at Travellis Games. A quick search on my mobile garners me the company's address. I hired a car at the airport to spare myself the agony of a taxi ride. Though I also hired a driver, a pane of glass separates us provided I keep the window rolled up. Privacy is paramount in my world, but drivers always want to interrogate me.

I park in the large lot outside the building. It wraps around the entire structure, which has multiple floors and seems to house various kinds of businesses. I know which floor Travellis Games occupies, thanks to my online search, so I won't need to ask for assistance. I dislike doing that almost as much as I dislike taxicabs. A lift ferries me to the correct floor, where I disembark and stride down the hall to the glass double doors marked with the Travellis logo.

Then I hesitate. If Emery says no, I will have come all the way to Colorado for nothing. But, for no sensible reason at all, I need to see her again and hear her answer, even it's a rejection. At least it will be over then, and I can go home. Traveling is not something I enjoy.

I push through the doors, pausing briefly at the front desk to inquire where I might find Emery Granger, then I'm off again. This entire floor seems to be a cubicle farm with each stall identified by a number rather than a person's name. I pass one cubicle after another as I make my way to where Emery works—or worked. She said she was being made redundant, but I hope she's here today. Otherwise, I'll need to find another way to contact her. I forgot to ask for her mobile number.

At last, I reach the collection of cubicles where I should find Emery. I know I'm in the right place when I spot the back of her blonde head. I would recognize that hair and that erse anywhere. I stride across the room toward her, navigating the maze of vacant cubicles, with my head held high and my shoulders square. Emery thinks my posture is amusing. She told me so on Saturday. But as I march toward her, she's not laughing. The lass looks stunned. Will she like my clothes? I dressed the way I usually do, wearing a charcoal suit, but I'd opted to go without a tie and leave the top button of my white dress shirt open. Maybe I had hoped Emery would think I'm less uptight this way.

No, that's not the reason. I felt like being more casual.

Even stunned, Emery is the bonniest woman in the world.

I reach her seconds after I first spotted her. Two other employees loiter nearby. The man sits in a chair that looks like it could double as a torture device but that I'm sure employers think qualifies as an ergonomic office chair. The woman, who has blue-streaked hair, stands in the cubicle behind his, with her arms resting on top of the flimsy wall.

"There you are," I say to Emery, with all my focus trained on her and her alone.

"Here I am," she concurs.

The man glances between me and Emery with an irritable look on his face. "Who's this guy? You know him?"

"I do," Emery says. She lays a hand on my bicep and squeezes it. "This is Rory MacTaggart. My fiancé."

What did she just say? Fiancé? I'm fair certain I'm staring blankly at her, and I can't swear that my chin hasn't dropped to my chest. She wants to marry me? Why?

Because ye asked her to, ye bloody bod ceann.

"Fiancé?" the woman with blue streaks in her hair says, then she breaks into a wide grin. "Congrats, Em. Why didn't you tell us you were seeing somebody? You sly puppy."

"Um, it just happened. We met in New Orleans."

"Love at first sight? That's so romantic."

The bloke who seems to dislike me twists his face into another irritable expression. "I asked you out four times, and you turned me down cold. You meet this guy a few days ago and decide to marry him?"

"Yes." Emery hooks her arm around mine, snuggling up to me. "You know how spontaneous I am. When I met Rory, we clicked, and I ran with it."

She ran with it? Emery is leaning her body into mine, a moment ago she squeezed my bicep, and now she says I'm her fiancé. If I'm still asleep, this is one barmy dream. Somehow, though, I manage to remain calm and unaffected—on the outside.

The bloke who clearly lusts for Emery shakes his head, but a slight smile tugs at his lips. He rises and offers me his hand. "Congratulations, man. Em's an amazing girl."

I shake his hand, strictly to be polite. "I'm well aware of how fortunate I am."

Emery's friends swarm her, tearing the lass away from me so they can suffocate her in a group hug, havering nonsense I can't understand because they're crying and speaking quickly. They act as if I'm spiriting her away to my underground bunker where I'll lock us in until every other human on the planet has died in the nuclear holocaust I initiated.

The blue-streaked woman releases Emery, spins around, and flings herself at me.

I have no choice. I catch the daft woman and give her a light hug. I don't enjoy hugging anyone, but especially not a stranger.

"Take good care of her," the woman says.

"I will." Is that a lie? Cannae say for sure.

The bloke who dislikes me finally lets go of Emery.

She sidles up to me, and we both say goodbye to her friends, then make our way out of the cubicle farm with her arm snugly curled around mine. Once we've exited the building onto the sidewalk, I halt us. Grasping her shoulders, I turn her so she faces me. If my expression is grim, I can't help that.

"Did you mean it?" I ask. "You called me your fiancé. Are you accepting my proposal?"

"It's more of a proposition than a proposal." She splays a hand on my chest, fingering my lapel. "But yes, I'm accepting your offer."

My lips twitch faintly. It's the best sort of smile I can offer.

"I have two conditions, though," she says.

"Name it. Whatever you want, it's yours."

"First, I need total honesty. No secrets, no lies. This is nonnegotiable, and I'll do the same for you."

I stare at the space beyond her shoulder while I weigh my options. She won't marry me unless I promise total honesty, but there are things I cannot tell her. My convenient wife doesn't need to know everything. Is not sharing every detail of my life a sort of lying? Donnae know. But I need Emery to marry me, so I have no choice.

Before I answer, I require full disclosure from her. "The other condition?"

"Sex and money are great, and of course I love the freedom you're offering." She pats my chest. "But I need to be useful."

"I don't understand."

"Being your trophy wife isn't enough for me." She rolls her shoulders back, lifting her chin. "While I search for my true calling in life, I need something to keep me busy. I need a mission, and I've picked one."

I have the sinking feeling I don't want to hear the rest. "What is it?"

"You."

Blinking slowly, I stare at her. "What?"

"Think of me as your private therapist." She smiles brightly while bouncing on her toes. "I'm going to help you remember how to enjoy life, Rory."

Mhac na galla. I groan. "You want to change me. Do you think my previous wives haven't already tried it?"

"I don't want to change you. Only you can do that. I want to help you."

"There's a difference?"

"Absolutely. I'm not dragging you kicking and screaming into the fun zone. I'm illuminating the path for you." She inches closer, tipping her head back to meet my gaze. "You've gotten a taste of what I'm like. You understand I'm no wallflower, and I won't be the trophy wife you trot out at parties and put away in a closet the rest of the time. Are you sure you want me?"

Aye, I want her—for sex. As for her mission to save me… I study Emery for a long moment. She can try to make me enjoy "fun" things. But she will fail. I grasp her upper arms. "I'm certain. And I accept your conditions."

"Good." Emery wrestles with her purse, which is slung over her shoulder, and pulls out the contract I'd given her. She holds it up. "Signed and delivered."

She signed it. The lass intends to marry me and follow my rules.

A strange sensation rushes through me, enlivening every part of my body. Is this happiness? No, I'm extremely relieved she said yes.

I drag her into me and lash my arms around her while I crush my lips to hers. She opens for me without hesitation while I invade her mouth, both of us thrusting our tongues, and she teases the roof of my mouth. She always tastes better than any food or drink, better than any other woman I've kissed, better than anything in the world.

Stepping back, I snatch the contract from her fingers. I glance at it, then fold the papers in half and tuck them into the inside pocket of my jacket. I'll sign them later.

Why am I delaying? It's ridiculous.

"Are you going to sign it?" she asks.

"Later. We marry today and leave for Scotland in the morning."

"Today?" She shakes her head. "Don't know how it is in Scotland, but here we've got licenses and blood tests and whatnot."

"Not in Colorado. Didn't you know that? You've lived in this state for how long?"

"Six years. But I've never been married. Engaged once, but never married. I didn't have a reason to learn about the marriage laws."

"I researched the process last night."

"Of course you did." She hesitates, her lips puckering slightly. "How did you find me here?"

"You mentioned Travellis Games and Colorado Springs. I didn't expect to find you at work, but I hoped your colleagues might point me in the right direction."

"Impatient, huh?"

"Today is Tuesday. I leave tomorrow." I fiddle with my shirt collar. "I needed your answer."

"You've got it."

I check the time on my mobile. "We should hurry if we're going to do this today."

"What's the rush? Don't you want to have a wedding in front of your family?"

"No." That's the last thing I want. This isn't a long-term relationship, and I don't want my family watching while I enter into a legally acceptable farce. I don't know why, but I slip a hand under my jacket only to realize I have no idea what I was reaching for, so I withdraw my hand. "Are you sure you've read the entire contract and understand it fully?"

"Yep." She rises onto her toes and pecks a kiss on my lips. "I'm a smart girl. I know what I'm getting into."

She claims to be sure. Time will tell. Once she sees what I'm really like, she might abandon the fortune I'm offering her and run back to America.

I guide Emery to the limousine parked along the curb.

Aye, I'd hired a limousine. Might as well travel in comfort. I'm not trying to impress Emery.

I swing the door open and wait for her to climb inside.

She gets in, sliding across the seat while I drop onto the cushioned leather beside her.

By this afternoon, I will be married to Emery Granger. What happens after that… Heaven only knows.

Chapter Eleven

Somehow, I had forgotten how much rubbish goes into getting married, even if the ceremony takes place in a magistrate's office. Luckily, Emery already has a passport, so I don't need to "steamroll the American legal system," as she called it, to get one for her on short notice. I also don't need to stay in this country until that happens. Going home is all I want right now. Well, that and Emery's body. But before I can shag her again, I must go through the rubbish. That means buying wedding rings. She doesn't have an engagement ring, but that seems superfluous, and she doesn't act as if she cares.

Am I a blind eejit? Does she want a diamond ring?

No, she wouldn't be marrying me if she wanted all the bells and whistles of a genuine marriage. The contract and prenuptial agreement spell out the parameters.

Though I make certain everything is arranged quickly and properly, Emery doesn't seem to mind the rush. She told me I'm "polite but ruthless" in my determination to get this done, but she also said it's "sexy as hell." Am I ruthless? Only when necessary, but I don't think I've treated her that way. I reserve my ruthless side for defending my clients from lawsuits or whatever bollocks they're going through. Emery hasn't really seen that side of me.

When I suggest we go to a high-end jeweler for rings, Emery points out that we can't get bespoke wedding bands on such short notice. To meet my "adorably uptight, self-imposed deadline" for leaving the country, I give in and take her to a store that can deliver rings immediately. Emery called my deadline that. I don't see what's adorable or uptight about finishing this as soon as possible. It's efficient. My fiancée also calls me "adorably snooty" because I would've preferred more expensive rings.

She is a strange woman.

"Uptight *and* kind of a snob," Emery teases while we study the options inside the glass case at a jewelry store.

"I like quality and originality."

"Originality, hm? Is that why you wore a kilt Friday night?"

"No." I wave to the clerk. A laddie who looks like he's barely out of his teens approaches us, and I indicate a pair of simple gold bands. Emery will think they're expensive, but to me, they are average. While the clerk retrieves and boxes the rings, I angle toward her with a hip braced on the jewelry case. "I told you why I wore a kilt."

"You fed me a mouthful of BS, and being a polite lady, I let you get away with it." She moves closer, and I realize I've subconsciously rested a hand on her hip. "Seeing as I'm about to uproot my entire life for you, I think the least you owe me is the truth about your choice of clothing that night. Why a kilt?"

No, my fiancée won't give up until I tell her. So I exhale a long sigh. "Aidan."

"Your brother?"

I nod, my mouth crimped, while I recall my conversation with my younger brother. "Aidan dared me to wear a kilt in public, in a location where no one else would be wearing one and no one would expect to see a man dressed that way." I scratch my jaw, and my lips keep twitching as if they want me to smile, but I don't. "Aidan thought it would be funny."

"Because you're...you."

"Aye. The dare turned into a wager."

"You won. What do you get?"

"A favor from Aidan. Whatever I want, whenever I want."

"Wow, that's quite a wager. What are you going to make him do?"

"Haven't decided yet."

Emery insists on taking a picture of us in the jewelry store, and I acquiesce with a roll of my eyes. Women are so barmy about this sort of thing. It's not as if we're in love. It's an arrangement, nothing more. Once I've paid for the rings, we go to her apartment so she can pack.

Emery has just finished packing one suitcase when I announce, "Time to go."

How many bags does the woman need? One seems plenty to me.

"But—" She flaps her arms in a gesture I can't interpret. "All my stuff. I can't live out of one suitcase for the next year."

"You can buy new things."

"What's the big rush?"

I shove my hands into my trouser pockets and hunch my shoulders. "I want to go home."

What a bloody stupid confession. But it's true. I miss my home, meaning more than just the place where I live. I'm referring to my family too, and the Highlands.

She flies at me and throws her arms around me. "You miss your family, I get it. We can rush, and maybe I can get my friends to pack up the rest of my stuff and somehow get it shipped to me."

I gaze at her with bemusement. Aye, I'm sure I look this way often when I'm with Emery. The lass confuses me so often that it shouldn't surprise me anymore, but it does.

She kisses my cheek and releases me, backing up a few steps as if to give me space. I must admit she is a very thoughtful lass.

I survey her wee, one-room apartment. Cannae believe she lives in such a cramped space. Emery seems like the sort who needs plenty of room and plenty of soft pillows and quilts. I will make certain all her possessions get to Scotland as quickly as possible to ensure she'll feel at home there. "I'll hire someone to take care of your belongings."

The lass flies at me again and plants another kiss on my cheek. "Thank you, Rory. You're a real sweetie-pie."

"Donnae say that in front of my family, or Aidan will be calling me 'sweetie-pie' for the rest of eternity."

"I will try to restrain myself, but no promises. I'm impulsive, you know, which you really ought to like since it's the impetus for me marrying you."

She makes a valid point, but I need a moment before I can admit to the truth. "I can live with your outlandish enthusiasm."

"Thanks a bunch, sweetie-pie."

I grumble and pick up her solitary suitcase.

Emery watches me in silence while biting her lip.

The lass seems to want to say something, but it fashes her for some reason.

At last, she pulls in a deep breath and tells me, "There's something you should know before we tie the knot, in case it changes your mind."

"Nothing will change my mind."

"You haven't heard my confession yet."

I set down the suitcase. "Tell me, then."

"Remember how I said I hate secrets and lies?" Her gaze flits around the room, everywhere except to me. "That's because my ex took naked pictures of me and posted them online without my knowledge or consent. I mean, I consented to him taking pictures of me. But I had no idea he'd post them on social media. He swore they were just for him to look at. After I broke up with him, he got revenge-y."

"Revenge-y?"

"It's called revenge porn." She looks almost sick, though she keeps talking. "I'll spare you the details. The gist is I got the photos taken down from his social media accounts, but there's always a chance the images had been propagated elsewhere. Our contract talks about moral obligations, and I don't want you to be humiliated if nudie pictures of me turn up somehow, somewhere."

A flash of movement makes me glance down at her belly, where she's wringing her hands. She honestly worries I won't want her anymore if I see those pictures.

"I won't be humiliated," I tell her, doing my best to sound soothing. Not my strong suit. I squeeze her shoulder, then wrap my hand around both of hers. "And I haven't changed my mind."

Now she chews on her lip and pinches her face.

I duck my head to look into her eyes. "I don't treat women that way, no matter what they do to me. Do you believe me?"

She nods once.

Peeling her hands apart, I release one but keep hold of the other, threading our fingers. "All of that is in the past."

I lead Emery out of her depressingly small apartment. Earlier, I'd spoken to her landlord to take care of terminating her lease. The man had gawped at us both when Emery informed him that she was marrying me and moving to Scotland, but eventually, he'd offered us both his congratulations and wishes for good luck.

Aye, I'll need luck on my side. My family will be...surprised by the news. I haven't told anyone I'm bringing a wife home with me.

Just a few hours later, we stand before a magistrate who solemnizes our marriage. That's the official term for it. I wear the same suit as earlier, but Emery has changed into a knee-length, cream-colored sundress with a modest neckline. Even sedate clothing can't diminish her sex appeal. Though she wears shoes with heels that add another three inches to her height, I still sort of tower over her, though not on purpose. I avoid looking at Emery during the solemnization ceremony, even when we slip the rings onto each other's fingers. My new wife must, of course, take a picture of us with her mobile, while we're still in the magistrate's office. The second the deed is done, I rush us back to the limo. We head for the Garden of the Gods resort for our wedding night, and in the morning, we will fly to Scotland.

Perhaps I shouldn't have arranged for our wedding night to take place at a posh resort, since I don't want Emery to think I'm being romantic, but I felt compelled to give her something nice in exchange for the arrangement I've convinced her to sign onto with me.

What have I done?

Exactly what I need to do. I ensured my family will stop harassing me and stop shoving poor lasses at me at random moments. But aye, I've also ensured that I will have free access to Emery's body for one year. By then, I'll have her out of my system. She will leave, and I will go back to my life—alone. I feel slightly nauseous, but that has nothing to do with Emery. It's only… I have no sodding clue what it is, but I do not feel nauseous because I know I'll have her for only one year.

I look at my wife, and she smiles at me. My wife. I've done the thing I swore that I would never do again. I've shackled my life to a woman's.

Bloody hell.

Once we've checked in at the resort and the bellboy who brought our luggage has left, I clap the door shut behind us. "I need to ring my family in private."

"Ring them?" Emery asks.

I articulate each syllable with painstaking care as I explain, "Call them on the telephone. To explain what—what I've done."

"You make it sound so romantic."

"This is not romance, it's a business arrangement."

"Yeah-yeah, I know." She flings a hand in the direction of the balcony and its sliding glass door. "Go, make your call in private. I won't listen at the keyhole like a certain someone did when I was having a good time in the jacuzzi."

My entire body stiffens, and my features warp into an expression that likely conveys my exasperation. Why must she keep mentioning that incident? I did not listen at the keyhole.

She skims her hands up my lapels. "You are so easy to tease. And so much fun to tease too."

I lift my gaze to the ceiling, then march out onto the balcony and jerk the glass door open and shut. Dropping into one of the chairs positioned around a circular table, I turn my back on my wife. A glass door isn't enough of a barrier. A concrete retaining wall wouldn't be enough to keep my wife from harassing me with her inappropriate humor and outlandish behavior.

Now that I'm settled in on the balcony, I dial Lachlan's number.

"Do you have any idea what time it is?" he grumbles. "It's the middle of the bloody night, Rory."

"This is my revenge for when you called me at an ungodly hour because you'd cocked it up with Erica."

"All right, I suppose I deserve that. What do you need?"

Suddenly, I feel itchy all over, but scratching doesn't alleviate the problem. "I have some, ah, news that might be of interest to the family."

"What is it?"

"I got married."

Silence follows. The only sound is my pulse thumping in my ears and a faint hissing on the line.

"Are you there, Lachlan?"

He clears his throat, and I hear a shuffling sound as if he's moving around. "Aye, Rory, I'm here. But I cannae believe what I thought you just said. You're...married?"

"Yes."

"But how—I mean, when did you meet the lass? Aren't you the man who swore he'd never, never, never take a wife again?"

I scratch my arm, but that bloody itch still won't go away. "Aye, I said that. But I changed my mind. Her name is Emery, and I'm bringing her home tomorrow. Please alert the family."

"Aye, I'll do that. But..." His tone is rife with confusion when speaks again. "When did you meet this woman?"

"Friday night."

"Friday night?" Lachlan shouts. "Erica, wake up. Rory's having a stroke or a psychotic break. We need to ring Jack."

"I do not need a therapist, Lachlan, so donnae be ringing our cousin."

"But you married a woman you met *Friday night.*" He still sounds more shocked and confused than I've ever heard him sound before. "You must be off your head."

Perhaps I am, but I hadn't anticipated how my brother would react to the news of my marriage.

"Are ye sure ye didn't hallucinate it?" Lachlan asks. "Maybe someone slipped you drugs and—"

"Just tell the bloody family," I growl. "We'll be there tomorrow."

I hang up on Lachlan. Once he recovers from the shock, he'll do as I asked. Now, I need to pray that the entire MacTaggart clan doesn't turn up at the Inverness airport—with Jack carrying a straitjacket.

Time to return to my wife.

I heave my body out of the chair, tucking the mobile in my pocket, and slide the glass door open so I can stride inside. When I catch sight of Emery, I lift one brow in a silent question. She's talking to someone on her mobile.

"Mom, Dad, please," she says, "try to be cool about this, okay? I know you haven't met Rory but—"

I commandeer her phone. "Mr. and Mrs. Granger, this is Rory MacTaggart."

Even I'm surprised by how calm and almost pleasant I sound, considering that my face feels as if it's tightening up like papier-mâché that's drying on my skin.

My wife gawps at me.

"Please accept my apologies," I say to her parents, "for sweeping your daughter off her feet with a whirlwind courtship and marriage. I need to go home tomorrow, and I couldn't bear to leave without her. However, I should've spoken to you first, so this wouldn't have been such a shock. I hope you can forgive me."

"You'd better treat our baby right," Emery's mother says. "We're not afraid to use physical force if you hurt her."

"That's right," a male voice says, and I assume it's Emery's father. "We don't want our girl to end up alone in a foreign country, abandoned by the man who seduced her into marrying him faster than I can get my car detailed."

Emery pushes up off the sofa, staring at me so intently that I feel as if she's trying to read my thoughts.

"You have my word," I inform her parents. "I will do everything in my power to ensure Emery is happy. She will not be alone in a foreign country. She has me—and my family. But you should visit as soon as possible. I'm certain you'll feel more comfortable with the situation once we've met."

"We live in Australia," Mrs. Granger says. "And we're not rich like you. We can't just hop on a plane. And what about her sister? Hadley will be worried too. They're very close."

"Never mind the expense," I assure the Grangers. "I'll send my jet for you. And of course, I will have Emery's sister and her family flown in as well. Let us know when you can take a holiday, and I'll arrange everything."

My gaze veers to Emery. Is it my imagination, or does she seem aroused? No, that's barmy.

She tears the mobile from my hand. "We'll be in touch to talk travel details. It's our wedding night, so forgive the rude goodbye but—goodbye."

Emery tosses her mobile onto the coffee table.

I can't help smiling a wee bit. My wife rudely hung up on her parents. And she thinks I'm gruff.

"Thank you," she says, "for handling my parents like that. Once they calm down, they'll be stoked about getting a free trip to Scotland."

"I look forward to meeting them."

"One more thing." She jabs a finger toward my chest. "Don't ever butt into my life again. I don't like being bossed around, even if it turns me on big time the way you take charge and get things done."

With deliberate slowness, I retrieve my mobile from my pocket. "Should I order dinner?"

"Later." She seizes the lapels of my suit jacket and hauls me closer. "Take me into the bedroom and fuck me."

"Whatever my wife desires."

Chapter Twelve

My fourth marriage is off to a brilliant start. I'm slumped at the foot of the bed, naked, with my feet flat on the floor and my elbows on my thighs. My hands hang slack between my legs. And another part of me lies slack too, though it should be proudly waving. But no, my cock decided now would be the right time to turn as limp as a wet noodle. That explains why I'm glaring down at my hands and not speaking to my wife, much less looking at her.

This has never happened to me before. Why tonight? I crave Emery like mad, but as soon as we walked into the bedroom, I'd started to feel off. Maybe a wee bit anxious. No, not anxious. Tired. Aye, that's right. I'm exhausted from the whirlwind that has blown around me since the night I met Emery.

She lies nude on the bed, studying the ring on her left hand.

I can see her doing that out of the corner of my eye.

"You okay?" she asks.

Mhac na galla. How can she not know the answer? I flash her a dark look that I hope conveys the fact I am the opposite of okay.

She sits up. "This is completely normal. It happens to everybody."

"Not to me." I drop my face into my upraised palms. "What have I done?"

I met a woman Friday, had a poke with her five minutes later, and married her on Tuesday. That's what I've done. Suddenly, I don't feel as comfortable with this arrangement as I had fifteen minutes ago.

Our wedding night had begun very well. We kissed and groped and undressed each other, then we kissed more and kept on doing that while we made our way to the bed. Even as I pulled the covers back, we kept our mouths fused, and I lifted her up to set her on the mattress. Gazing down at her body, I felt my cock hardening and my lust growing with every passing second.

Then she smiled.

Aye, I've seen her do that before. But this time, she smiled as if she genuinely wants me to be her husband, as if she hopes for more than the arrangement we agreed to, despite what I told her. She gazed at me with…affection. And I swallowed so hard my throat hurt. Standing there frozen, I stared at the woman I'd married this afternoon. A stranger. A sweet, passionate lass who, for reasons I will never understand, bound her life to mine.

She lay on the bed, seeming more and more puzzled by my lack of action.

Naturally, I stumbled backward instead of pouncing on the lass the way a husband is expected to do on the wedding night. Worse, my *slat* had dropped like a stone in a pond.

"What have I done?" I repeat, my voice hardly a whisper, my face still in my hands.

Emery crawls across the bed to kneel behind me, settling her soft hands on my shoulders.

I jerk my head up and go stiff—though not in the way I want to be stiff.

"Take it easy, baby," she says, twining her arms loosely around my neck, her hands draped over my collarbone. She touches her lips to my ear. "I know you don't have a physical problem, which means this is emotional. We can work through it together."

"Cannae."

She nuzzles my cheek. "You're awfully morose for a man who got what he wanted today."

I drum one knuckle on my thigh.

"What is it you're afraid you've done?" she asks.

"Doesnae matter."

She skates her hands down my chest, swirling her palms over my skin. "The night isn't a bust yet. We had a weird, stressful day. That's bound to make you anxious." She coils her tongue around my earlobe. "Let me help you relax."

"Ye can try, but it willnae work."

"Don't be such a pessimist." Emery presses her lips to the pulse point on my throat, while her hands travel lower and lower, caressing and exploring. "I have skills too, ya know."

I pull in a ragged breath. Her touch is arousing me, for sure, but I don't know if it's enough to overcome whatever the hell is wrong with me tonight.

She drags her mouth down my throat, tasting my skin with light licks.

My drumming knuckle stops moving. I've stopped breathing too, and my *slat* is wide awake.

"Mmmmm," she moans as she curls one hand around the base of my cock. "I love the flavor of your skin."

Her hand glides along my length, and she sinks her teeth into my shoulder.

A breath explodes out of me.

With her chin on my shoulder, she slides her hand down my cock. "I can feel your enthusiasm growing."

Aye, my *slat* is getting hard. Fast. But if she keeps this up, I'll come before I've even touched her. So I pry her fingers away from my cock. "You first."

"Me first what?"

I rotate my head to see her face. "Lie down and you'll find out."

My wife stretches her lithe body across the silken sheets.

Bod an Donais, Emery is perfect. I crouch at her feet with my hands on her ankles and my focus on the hairs between her thighs. "Yer so beautiful, ye make my *bagais* ache, *cho cinnteach is a tha bod's an each*. I want my face in your *camas*, my mouth on your *brillean*."

I spread my hands on her thighs.

She sucks in a breath and blows it out, her hard nipples bouncing with her breasts.

"*Leannan*," I murmur, "I wanted ye in the tub the other day when ye tickled me with your wee bonnie toes. I wanted to give ye the happy ending ye needed, but I held back." I push my hands under her thighs and lift them until her knees bend slightly. "Ahmno holding back tonight."

Because I want her so badly I cannae restrain my lust.

I shift my hands to her inner thighs, easing them apart, then I settle my body between her legs while keeping my hands on her thighs. Stroking my tongue across my lower lip, slowly, I picture all the things I want to do to her tonight. When I brush my lips over the hairs of her mound, she curls her fingers into the sheets. Using only the index fingers of each hand, I part her outer folds to expose her clitoris and her rosy inner folds.

Her cheeks have turned pink, but it's the scent of her that proves she wants me as intensely as I want her.

I skim my fingers up and down her folds while she bites down on her lip and breaths bluster out of her nostrils. Eyes half-closed, I pucker my lips and blow a stream of cool air across her rigid nub.

"Please," she moans.

I flick my tongue over her clit lightly, teasing her flesh while I keep the pace measured and steady. She throws her hands above her head, clenching the pillow tightly. I whisk my fingers over her folds, grazing her opening and swirling my tongue around her nub while her breaths shorten.

"Oh, God," she moans between staccato breaths. "Please don't stop, please."

Chuckling, I puff soft breaths over her slick flesh.

Emery closes her eyes.

"Stop," I snarl. "Donnae close your eyes."

Her lids fly open, but she seems dazed. "What?"

"Donnae close your eyes." I compress my lips, but then force myself to relax. She won't understand why I need her to look at me, and I will not explain. "Please."

"Okayfinewhatever," she says in a breathless rush.

The tension in my body melts away. At least she didn't demand to know why I ordered her to keep her eyes open.

"Just don't stop, Rory," she says. "For heaven's sake, don't stop."

"Donnae say my name either."

The lass gapes at me, still breathing hard. "What, like, ever?"

"Not while we're being intimate."

She hoists her head up and sharpens her gaze on me. "What should I call you? How about 'asshole'?"

"Anything but my name."

Emery frowns for a split second, then collapses back onto the mattress and whimpers, though it doesn't sound like lust spurs that noise. "Why did you have to tell me these crazy rules right in the middle of things, when I was about to—to—"

Tears shimmer in her eyes but don't escape her lids.

"Donnae cry," I say, trying to sound comforting, though I've never been good at that. "I'm sorry for shouting."

"I'll get mad at you later. Finish what you started before I rip my hair out."

She's angry, but wants to have sex with me. I'll never understand women. But I lower my mouth again and lap at her clit.

Emery comes so quickly that I cannae believe it. Her back flattens into the mattress, her hands grip the pillow, and her teeth are clamped together while desperate cries erupt from her. I keep licking until the last wave of her climax fades away. Then I raise my head, giving up the taste of her flesh.

While she recovers, I quickly roll on a condom.

My wife goes limp, her gaze unfocused and her lips parted. "Oh, God. That was… You are…"

I crawl up her body to crouch on my hands and knees above her. "Have I exhausted you?"

"In a good way."

She seals her hand around my sheathed cock and sweeps it up to the base. "When did you put this on?"

"While you were coming down from the clouds. You had your eyes closed."

She winces. "Oops. Sorry, I meant to keep my eyes open."

"Donnae worry." I rest my head next to hers, our cheeks touching. "You looked at me when I was pleasuring you and when you came. That's what I needed."

Emery folds her arm around my neck while methodically pumping my erection. "We're not done yet, are we?"

With my cheek lingering on hers, I grasp her wrist to halt her hand. "We are nowhere near done."

"Good, because I can't get enough of you."

For a moment, I hold perfectly still. She can't get enough? No woman has ever said that to me. I draw my head back and study her expression. "I want you more than I should. We have a business arrangement, not a traditional marriage. Sex for us should be a mutual satisfaction of needs and nothing more."

"Stop making this so complicated." Despite my hand on her wrist, she manages to rub her fingers over my *slat*. "I'm your wife. Kiss me."

I lunge my head to within millimeters of her mouth.

She parts her lips, silently begging me to do what she asked.

And I plant a kiss on her shoulder.

"You rat," she says, slapping my arm.

I chuckle. "Rat is better than 'asshole.' "

"You might earn the asshole designation soon enough."

Aye, that I might. But I won't think about it now. Instead, I nip her chin. "Patience, my sweet wife."

"I want to be fucked, not appeased."

"Of course." I raise onto one straight arm. "I promised to deliver anything my wife desires."

Plunging my free hand under her erse, I elevate her hip until she lies twisted at the waist with her shoulders on the bed. Then I coast my hand over her hip and down the side of her thigh while I feather my lips over the back of her knee, encouraging her to bend it with light pressure from my hand.

"Not quite sure what you're doing," she says, "but I'm game for anything."

"One of your most endearing qualities."

I shift one leg to push it between both of hers so that her bent knee is hooked around my hip. Maybe I saw this in a book, and maybe I bought that book the other day when I was waiting for Emery to accept or reject my proposition. This is not me trying to impress her again. No, I have never done that. I wanted to make sure she would enjoy our wedding night, that's all.

She watches my every move as I lodge one knee firmly on the mattress, with her body between my legs. My erection brushes against her folds.

Emery shudders and reaches for me.

I capture her wrists with one hand, pin them above her head, and brace my other hand alongside her shoulder. "Ye want to be fucked, aye?"

"Oh yes, please."

Whatever my wife desires. I drive into her with a single strong thrust, then pause there, buried inside her hot, lush body to the hilt. My eyes want to roll back in my head because of how wonderful this feels, but I don't do that. It would be ridiculous.

My wife makes a strange noise, apparently annoyed that I've stopped moving.

I let my lips slide into a slow grin, imbued with the heat of all my wicked intentions for her body.

She surrenders to me, relaxing into my hold on her wrists as if she'll wait hours for me to start shagging her again. I roll my hips in a circle, my cock penetrating her deeply, and somehow maintain enough control to keep the pace unhurried despite how good she feels around me and how badly I want to feel her come all over my cock. Bound by my hands, she can't clutch me the way she seems to love doing, so she clutches me with the leg she has locked around me instead. She rocks her hips in time with my movements, her expression so blissful that I almost wish I could pull out my mobile and snap a picture of her, the way she looks right now while I'm rotating my hips to experience every inch of her perfect body.

She nestles her face against my neck.

With a groan, I impale her body with powerful, vigorous strokes. My pace accelerates as I thrust hard every time, pounding into her until we both bounce on the mattress. With her face mashed against my neck, I can't see if she keeps her eyes open. Donnae care. With her, all I want to do is let go and drown in the pleasure of her body while I pump my hips, scraping her *brillean.*

Emery goes rigid a second before her body convulses, and her inner muscles pulsate around me. I come too, my cock spilling everything inside her while she thrashes under me and her orgasm rolls on and on, and I keep thrusting, slower every time, until at last we're both spent.

I disentangle our bodies to lie beside her.

My wife is struggling to catch her breath.

"Shh," I whisper. "Breathe slow and easy."

I rub her belly, hoping to calm her while she recovers from an orgasm that clearly left her dazed, though in a good way. I hope.

"Wow, I love your ingenuity," she says once her breathing has returned to normal. "That position was amazing."

"I'm not ingenious." I cease rubbing her belly and spread my hand over her skin. "That position appears in numerous books about sex."

Emery shoots me a sidelong look. "You read sex manuals?"

My cheeks start to feel warm, but I am not blushing. That would be unmanly. "I, ah…bought a few of them over the years."

For my ex-wives. I tried to make them happy in the bedroom, since I seemed to be incapable of making them happy in any other way. I failed in the bedroom too. But not with Emery. She loves what I give her, and that's why I'd bought yet another sex book.

My wife wriggles to lie on her side facing me. "Nothing wrong with looking for ways to spice up your love life. I've read sex books too, even the Kama Sutra."

I lift my gaze to hers. "I wasn't brave enough to read that one."

"It's not as lewd as most people think." She places a sweet kiss on my lips. "We could look at it together sometime. If you want."

"Perhaps," I say cautiously, not at all sure I could handle that.

"No rush." She dances her fingers along my upper arm. "Are we done for the night?"

"Aren't you tired?"

"Nope."

I drape a hand over her hip. "Should we go again?"

"Oh yes, baby. Yes indeed."

Maybe tomorrow, I'll wonder why she's called me "baby" twice tonight. But right now, I need to shag my wife again.

Chapter Thirteen

I rise earlier than usual in the morning, though that has nothing to do with the fact I'm taking Emery home with me today. I cannot be nervous about introducing her to my family because I do not get nervous. But I also don't like being away from home. Although I wake up at three fifty-two, I sneak out of bed so I won't disturb Emery.

She looks so bonnie and sweet when she's sleeping.

After going through my morning ritual, I check my emails on my computer, then check the weather between here and Scotland. Maybe that is a bloody stupid thing to do, and I'm sure Emery would call me uptight for doing that, but it eases the tension inside me and makes me feel as if I have a small measure of control over my life.

It's five a.m. now, and I can't convince myself to wait any longer. Emery can have a nice long nap on the jet, but I need to get out of Colorado. So I wander over to the bed, where she lies on her side, facing away from me, and I sit down behind her. The sheet has slid down to her waist, exposing her naked torso to me, though her arm hides her breasts. A curtain of hair has fallen over her face. I gently slip my fingers under it to lift those hairs away from her cheek and sweep them behind her ear.

How should I wake her? We don't have time for sex, not with the schedule I've arranged for our departure. Since I can't rouse her the way I prefer, instead I slide my hand over her hip and onto her belly. Then I lean in to touch my lips to her throat and drop light kisses on her skin. She always tastes good enough to devour.

Emery moans faintly, stirring just enough to brush her hair against my cheek.

I keep kissing her neck while I inhale the sweet scent of her.

She opens her eyes halfway and wriggles her hips, which makes my long-sleeved shirt brush her skin.

Her lids fly open. "You're dressed."

I trail the backs of my fingers across her belly. "I don't generally board an airplane in the nude."

"Maybe I will."

She laughs, probably because I look stunned. My wife says the most outlandish things, and I can't be certain she won't do what she said. The woman has no shame.

Emery slaps the back of her hand on my chest. "That was a joke. I'm not an exhibitionist." She fingers a button on my shirt. "Unless you want me to exhibit myself for you."

"Not at the moment." I straighten, then smack her erse. "Time to get dressed. We leave for the airport in thirty minutes."

"Thirty—" She springs into a sitting position. "I need a shower and breakfast and—What time is it?"

"Five o'clock. You can freshen up in flight." I rise and flap my hand. "Up, Emery."

Mumbling under her breath, probably cursing at me, she clambers out of bed and reaches for the robe that's draped over the foot. As she pulls it on, she gives me a mulish look. "Just so you know, bossiness at five a.m. does not turn me on. Why the stampede to get outta Dodge?"

"I want to take you home, and I'm not known for dawdling."

She rubs her forehead. "Jeez, Rory, it's still dark out. I need a shower to wake me up and food to keep me from passing out from hunger."

I fist my hands, then stretch my fingers taut. "I will feed you on the jet, which has a full bathroom. A bed too. Please, may we get on the plane quickly?"

"You're super anxious to get home, hey?"

"Aye."

"Why is that?"

Bloody hell. Why cannae the woman just do what I say? I drop onto the foot of the bed, slumping forward, and rest my elbows on my knees. "I've been gone for ten days, the longest period I've ever been away."

Her expression softens, and she sits down beside me. "This seems like more than missing home. What else is bothering you?"

I frown at the floor. "My family is anxious to see you. I convinced them not to meet us at the airport, but they insist on coming to the house tomorrow."

Aye, Lachlan had texted me at midnight to let me know.

"They want to check out the trophy wife," Emery says.

"You are not a trophy."

She hesitates briefly, though I can't decipher her expression. "I can deal with meeting your family. And I promise not to embarrass you if that's what you're worried about. Your family will meet a well-behaved American."

"Not worried about you." I roll my shoulders back. "You can handle yourself. My family... They don't understand what I've done."

"Do you regret marrying me? This wasn't exactly a well-thought-out decision. You were lusting after me, and you got this crazy marriage idea in your head. I'd understand if you have buyer's remorse."

"I haven't bought you."

"You kinda did. Half a million dollars after a year, remember?"

Mhac na galla. I grind my teeth, because I don't like hearing her remind me of our arrangement. "I haven't bought you. All of my ex-wives received generous settlements when we divorced."

But I am paying for Emery, in a way. She isn't marrying me for love. I've offered her a large sum to put up with me for one year.

"My family can be overly protective," I tell her, "particularly my brother Lachlan. He almost frightened away the woman Aidan married. He terrified my first two wives, and the third kept her distance from him."

A smile tugs at her lips but doesn't quite form. "Are you afraid your big brother will have me fleeing in terror? Your concern is adorable but unnecessary. I'm not that easy to get rid of, baby."

"Why do you keep calling me that?"

"What?"

"Baby."

"Don't know. Didn't realize I was doing it." She bumps her shoulder into mine. "Guess it means I like you. Which is a good thing since we'll be living together."

She likes me? That's the last thing I want.

I launch my body off the bed. "You'll change your mind about that soon enough."

Before she can tell me anything else I don't want to hear, I stalk out of the bedroom and into the living area, where she can't see me and I can't see or hear her.

Ten minutes later, Emery walks into the living area.

I'm seated on the sofa with my computer on my lap, typing away as if I'm working, though I'm only pretending. I clap the laptop shut. "Ready?"

"Yep." She watches me get up off the sofa while holding the laptop in one hand. "We don't know each other very well, so I need to ask you something. Are you a pervert who's into BDSM—bondage, sadism, that kind of thing?"

"No."

"It's not a ridiculous thing to ask. You told me I'd change my mind about liking you, and I couldn't help wondering if that means you've got a tawdry secret at home. Maybe you'll lock me in your sex dungeon."

I roll my eyes. "I may live in a castle, but I don't have a dungeon."

"So, you're not into the twisted shit."

"I am not." Do I seem like the bondage sort? I ponder that question while I stow the laptop in its carrying bag. "Time to leave."

Grabbing her suitcase, I wheel it toward the door where my bag waits. Then I swing the door open for her. She's still watching me, but with a dubious expression now.

"You live in a castle?" she asks.

"I do."

With a hand on her back, I urge her to walk out the door.

For the entire journey to the airport, and while we walk out onto the tarmac, I keep thinking about her BDSM question. Maybe my rules and my rigidity have convinced her that I must need an extreme sort of release. But I do not have a sex dungeon.

As we approach the jet, Emery stumbles to a halt.

I touch a finger to her chin. "Your mouth is hanging open, lass. Insects might fly in there if you're not careful."

She closes her mouth, but her lips stretch into a teasing smile as she points toward the jet. "This is yours?"

I shrug one shoulder. "I share it with Lachlan. After he married Erica, he wanted a private means of getting wherever he might need to be." I'm smirking, for certain, but I think I might almost be smiling. "I think he wanted a flying bedroom so he could ravish his wife up in the clouds."

"I'm sure you have no such plans." Emery sidles up to me, looping an arm around my waist. "Did you guys go halfsies on the plane?"

"It's a jet, but I'm not sure what you're asking."

"Did you each pay half the cost."

"Ah, no. Lachlan insisted on buying the jet himself. I do pay for the fuel, and I tried to convince him to let me pay a portion of the cost. He wouldn't agree. This was the first of two jets he bought."

"Two jets?" She rests her chin on my arm, her face angled up toward mine. "How rich is your brother?"

"I'm not certain, but I'd wager it's at least ten times more than I have."

"Ten times? I suppose your brother Aidan has twenty times more."

"Aidan is not wealthy," I explain, "though he has rebuilt his construction business into quite a success. He nearly lost the company after he was injured in a rock-climbing accident, but he's worked like the devil to bring it back to life."

Before my wife can ask more questions, I usher her up the stairs and into the jet. Well-cushioned seats line both sides of the cabin, their ivory-colored leather pristine. A group of seats face each other with a table between them, and a sofa occupies a space along the right-hand side. Beyond that, boxes fill an empty area. More compartments lie at the rear.

"Through there are the bedroom, bathroom, and galley," I say, gesturing toward the back of the jet.

"What are those boxes?" Emery asks.

"Your belongings."

Her gaze flies to the boxes and then back to my face. "You said you'd hire people to pack up my stuff and get it to me. I assumed that meant shipping it. How did you get anybody to do it this fast?"

"I paid them a great deal of money." I curl my hands around her upper arms. "I'm spiriting you away to a new country and a home you've never seen. You'll feel more at ease if you have your belongings."

"Thank you. That's unbelievably considerate."

"Don't thank me. I've asked a lot of you, and this was the least I could do in return."

Her mouth opens wide as she yawns.

I pick her up, cradling her body in my arms. "My wife needs a lie-down."

She rests her head on my chest as I carry her toward the bedroom, her lips curling into a sweet smile of contentment.

Even if she genuinely likes me now, I will disabuse her of that fondness. I won't mean to do it, but I will. The last thing I want is for my wife to develop stronger feelings for me, so maybe I will need to make certain she doesn't care for me.

Aye, I'm a bastard.

Chapter Fourteen

mery sleeps on the jet, and though I rouse her so we can climb into my car at the Inverness airport, she falls asleep again within minutes after we start our journey to my home. The lass wakes up just as we're driving through Ballachulish, the village where I was born and raised. My parents and some of my siblings live there now, but I'd moved to a more private location a few years ago.

When we'd first gotten into my car, a Mercedes S-Class, Emery had teased me about the luxury vehicle. She seems to think it's amusing to remind me of my wealth. Everyone knows I have money, but it never bothered me until I met Emery. I don't want her to feel uncomfortable with my lifestyle.

We've just crossed the Ballachulish Bridge over Loch Leven when my wife speaks.

The village is disappearing in the rearview mirror as she sits up, leaning forward slightly to squint at the scenery. "What was that lake?"

"Loch Leven."

"Where are we going?"

"Home."

"Gee, you're so helpful with the details." She falls back against her seat. "We passed the village. I thought you lived in Ballachulish."

"I said I was born and raised there. I live an hour from Ballachulish, near a village called Loch Fairbairn."

"This house of yours, is it out in the boonies or close to town?"

I wince and fidget in my seat. "I suppose that depends on your definition of boonies."

"Rory, honestly." She twists around in her seat to look at me. "Why are you avoiding my question? Will I be living in the middle of nowhere or not?"

"You will. In a way." I can't help wincing again. "I don't think of my home as remote, but you may have a different perspective."

"Are you afraid I'll be horrified when I see where you're taking me and flee as fast as I can?"

"Some women would."

I focus on the road so I won't see Emery, but I swear I can feel her studying me. Soon, we're crossing over another bridge with lochs on either side.

"What's that?" Emery asks, pointing out the window. "Is it still Loch Leven?"

"No, that is Loch Linnhe." I exhale a frustrated sigh. "Are ye planning to question me for the entire trip? Why donnae ye go back to sleep?"

"What's got you so grumpy? Worried about seeing your family?"

"If I promise to point out every notable place we pass by, will you cease talking?"

"Absolutely not." She slants toward me until her breasts graze my arm. "If you wanted a wife who doesn't speak unless spoken to, you shouldn't have picked me. You knew damn well what I was like when you practically begged me to marry you. I talked plenty over the weekend in New Orleans."

"Incessantly, yes."

"Watch it, buster. I'm this close"—she holds one hand in front of my face with her thumb and forefinger almost touching—"to forfeiting that half a million bucks by refusing to do you for at least two weeks."

I shrug as if I don't give a toss. "I survived without sex for thirteen months before I met you."

"Thirteen months?" She slouches into her seat. "It was six months for me. How many women have you slept with, total?"

"In my life? Twelve, including you." If she's going to interrogate me, I'm owed the same chance. "What about you? How many men?"

"Five. You mentioned before that you've had four one-nighters."

"Three."

"Four including me."

I throw her an irritated glance. "I've spent more than one night with you."

"So, three one-nighters, me, three wives... That's seven. You've had five other lovers."

Why is she havering on and on about this?

"Um, those other five women—"

"Christ, Emery. What the devil is it you want to know?"

"Not sure."

Like hell she isn't sure. I huff and steer the car off the left side of the road, alongside a field lined with trees. Mountains hem in the valleys and the dark, glassy lochs, but I cannae focus on the scenery. My wife wants to know every minute detail of my sex life, and she willnae be satisfied until I tell her.

I grimace and massage my forehead with my thumb and forefinger. "You want my full history? I fucked a girl in high school, but she preferred my brother Aidan, not that he'd have her. Even Aidan was never that callous. I fucked three more girls in college before I met my first wife. After she left me, I fucked one woman, but she threw me over. Satisfied?"

Emery gazes at me with a deceptively calm expression, though the slight puckering of her lips tells me I have upset her. "Listen, if you're trying to make me feel like an idiot for asking, forget it. I'm not that easy to cow. Like I told you, I've had five lovers in my life. One I almost married, another who humiliated me, and two who just didn't give a damn. Oh, wait." She waves a hand in my direction. "Make that three who didn't give a damn."

Ye bloody cacan, MacTaggart. I've hurt her, and that…bothers me. Moaning, I slump forward to rest my head on the steering wheel between my hands. My entire body sags as I mumble curses at myself.

"Didn't catch that," she says. "Take your face out of the steering wheel if you want me to understand."

I hoist my head up, though it seems to have mutated into a granite boulder.

"I don't regret marrying you," I say without looking at her, "but I suspect you'll regret marrying me soon enough. If you don't already."

Silence echoes between us as a sliver of sunlight peeks out through the clouds.

"When was the last time you slept?" she asks.

"Last night."

"For how long?"

I hesitate. "Two hours."

"No wonder you're so testy." She combs her fingers through my hair, caressing my cheek with her thumb. "Let me drive for a while."

"You have no idea where you're going." I glance at her out of the corner of my eye. "And you'd need to drive on the left side."

"If you can handle right-side driving, I can manage the wrong way."

"Driving on the left isn't wrong in the UK."

"But it's unnatural." She tickles my cheek with her soft fingertips. "Why do you think they call it driving on the *right* side?"

I grumble something that isn't quite a word, then tell her, "I'm fine to drive."

"At least take a nap." She nods toward the dashboard. "The car's got GPS. Punch in the address, and I'll drive for a spell."

Let her drive? The woman who wanted to race a Lamborghini at one hundred miles per hour? But I could use a rest. I grip the steering wheel with both hands. "All right."

She claps once. "Yay, my first driving experience in Scotland."

"You will wake me in twenty minutes. I need your word."

"Fine, I'll wake you up."

"In twenty minutes."

"Yes, Mr. Bossy."

We climb out of the car and switch sides. Emery needs to move the seat forward, since her body is shorter than mine. After a brief instructional session that involves me behaving like a ruddy eejit, telling her which pedal is the accelerator and that she should avoid running into trees or lochs, I relinquish control.

Emery pulls out onto the road, on the left side.

So far so good.

Though I don't expect to fall asleep, I do.

Emery wakes me precisely twenty minutes later.

We're parked along the edge of the road, on the left side. We switch places and resume our journey while Emery peers out at the view without speaking. Should I report this miracle to the nearest priest? Maybe I don't dislike her frequent need to chat to me as much as I'd let her believe. I might sort of…miss hearing her voice. That's ridiculous, though. She's sitting right next to me, so I can't miss anything about her. Still, I develop a strange need to fill the silence by announcing landmarks and towns along our route, sometimes offering bits of information, but sometimes just reciting the names.

I am not a tour guide, after all. Havering is not in my nature.

The further we travel, the more we retreat into the countryside, which must seem to Emery like the back of beyond. She lived in the city of Colorado Springs, not in a remote home in the Scottish Highlands. We pass a house now and then, but there are no more villages to delight her. Everything delights her, though. Even the trees make her smile.

As I execute our last turn, onto a narrow dirt track, I announce, "Almost there."

"Where?" She bends forward, squinting out the windscreen.

"Home. This is the drive."

"You're saying this is your driveway, and we're almost to your house."

"If you insist on repeating everything I say, yes."

She leans forward more to stare up at the treetops. "I'm excited."

"We'll be there shortly."

Emery swerves her head left and right, up and down, craning her neck to take in the surroundings while a sweetly excited expression lights up her face. "You said there was a village, Loch Fairbairn."

"Can't see it from here. The village is past the mountain, Beann Dealgach, behind my home. Our home."

"Beann Dealgach?" She struggles to pronounce the name. "Is that Gaelic? I can't keep up."

I settle a hand on her thigh. "Easy, lass, we'll be there soon. And yes, many of the names in the Highlands are Scots Gaelic or Anglicized versions of the Gaelic."

She taps her foot on the floorboard, hands pressed to her thighs, her gaze riveted to the driveway ahead of us. I maneuver the Mercedes around potholes for a few minutes longer while my wife gnaws on the inside of her lower lip. Cannae believe how excited she is to see my home. I hope she won't be disappointed.

The dirt drive transitions into gravel that ticks on the undercarriage. Then we break out of the trees, and the house comes into view.

My wife gapes at the building.

Aye, it's a ruddy castle. So what? This is my home, not a museum. It has all the typical features of a medieval fortress, from its boxy contours to the wall that surrounds it and the large wooden gates that offer entry. The four-story structure, built from grey stones, features twin turrets. A flag flies above the highest turret, waving in the breeze.

Emery's attention is riveted to the blue flag emblazoned with a white X. "Is that the flag of Scotland?"

"Yes."

"How much land do you have?"

"One hundred acres."

She moves her head this way and that, almost like a bird, as she takes in more of the compound. A covered walkway joins the tower to the shorter structure behind and to the side of it. An old wooden fence extends from the covered walkway, past the smaller building, and around the backside of the compound. That's where we're going. The gates stand open, waiting for our arrival.

Honestly, I never close the gates. I'm not a medieval warlord.

And I do not have a sex dungeon.

I park the car behind the main section of the castle.

Emery's eyes have grown so large I keep thinking they'll spring out of their sockets.

My home isn't that shocking. Is it?

On the opposite side of the drive lies another walled space, but this one holds a garden and isn't one-fifth as large as the wall that surrounds the castle compound. Emery can see into the garden from here, so I imagine she's admiring the naturalistic way my gardener, Tavish, has cultivated the flowers and bushes, not to mention the large pots that hold more blooms. He chose a variety of plants and colors, turning the once dying garden into a spectacular oasis. The wooden arbor holds more flowers that have wound their vines through the latticework.

Since Emery seems incapable of moving or speaking, I get out and stride around to her side, swinging her door open.

My wife yelps and jerks upright, bumping her head into the windscreen.

I offer my hand to her.

She places her palm in mine, letting me help her out of the car, and she stumbles on the gravel because she's too busy gawping at my home to notice where she's walking. Emery shakes off my hand, spinning in circles as she gawps a bit more. "Holy shit. This is amazing. I assumed you were pulling my leg when you said you live in a castle, but this…" She throws her head back and whoops. "I love Scotland!"

A smile tries to tug at my lips, but I can't quite let it take hold. Aye, my wife is adorably thrilled to see my castle. It makes me want to shag her right here on the hood of the Mercedes.

"The garden," she says, swinging an arm in that direction. "It's so…free-wheeling. Did you design it?"

"I gave Tavish, the groundskeeper, a few instructions. Then I told him to do what he wanted and have at it."

"The garden is gorgeous. This whole place is stunning."

"It's home," I say as I shut the car door. "Come inside. You'll have plenty of time to explore the grounds later. Let's get you settled."

Although I march toward the main door, she lags behind me because the lass can't stop staring wide-eyed and slack-jawed at my home. Our home. She will be living here for one year. We reach the wooden door to the vestibule, which juts out from the rest of the building, and I reach for the knob.

The door bursts open. My housekeeper rushes out to drag me into an overly firm hug, her grey hair tickling my chin.

I pat her back. "Hello, Mrs. Darroch."

She releases me, grabbing my face with both hands, and aims her blue eyes at me. "Rory, ye naughty *chuilein*. Sneaking off to America to bring home a bride and not telling anyone until the deed was done."

Mrs. Darroch always makes me feel like a bairn, especially when she calls me her laddie in Gaelic. I duck my head, shoulders slumped. "Well, I…"

She looks as if she's been baking, since her apron has streaks of flour on it.

I seize my bride's hand, hauling her into my side. With my arm latched around her, I clear my throat. "This is my wife, Emery Granger."

"MacTaggart," Emery corrects. "I may be unconventional in many ways, but I have a traditional streak. My mother raised me to believe a woman should take her husband's name."

I stare at her, not blinking, surprised that she wants to take my name when we'll be married for only one year. But I shake off my shock and nod toward the other woman in my life. "Emery, this is Mrs. Evelyn Darroch, my housekeeper."

Emery holds out her hand to Mrs. Darroch. "Pleasure to meet you."

Mrs. Darroch clasps my wife's hand, the lines around her eyes deepening as she beams at Emery.

Why is everyone so bloody thrilled that I've brought home a wife? They don't even know her. I don't know her.

"Lovely to meet ye, dearie," Mrs. Darroch says. She wrests Emery away from me and into a hug as fierce as the one she'd given me. When she lets go, she takes hold of Emery's upper arms, apparently so she can size up my wife "My, ye are a bonnie wee thing."

"Emery is intelligent," I say. Do I sound defensive? "And very…adventurous. She was a computer programmer, but she's taking time to find a new vocation."

"No need for excuses, *mo luran*," Mrs. Darroch says. She winks and adds, "Ye must love her, or ye wouldnae have made sure to tell me how clever and adventurous she is."

Love? She assumes that because we're married. No one will ever know the truth about our relationship.

I hug Emery to my side again and kiss her cheek. Then I smile at her, strictly to convince Mrs. Darroch I genuinely care for my wife despite the fact our marriage is a farce.

Emery gazes up at me with a soft smile on her lips.

Mrs. Darroch snares my wife's hand. "I'll show you around your new home, Mrs. MacTaggart."

"Call me Emery."

"What a charming name." Mrs. Darroch tugs Emery's hand, luring her away from me. "Come, lassie. Cannae have ye getting lost your first night here."

I grab Emery's other hand, forcing the lass to stop. "Mrs. Darroch, I will show my wife the house. You should be home in bed."

"Tosh," she says, as she relinquishes my wife's hand. "It's early evening, and my home is behind the garden, not in Devonshire. Thought I should stay to be a neutral party, considering."

I halt on the threshold. "Considering what?"

She gives me a look that implies I'm a complete dafty. "Ye've forgotten, haven't ye? Jamie's here."

"Jamie—" Bloody hell. I mutter an oath and turn to Emery. "My sister Jamie has been living with me for over a year."

"It's no big deal, Rory. I want to meet your family. Might as well get started today and test the waters with one sibling, since I'll be meeting the whole gang tomorrow."

"Are you sure? Jamie can be…energetic."

"Oh, you mean like me." She tickles the soft underside of my chin. "If I can handle being me, I can handle your energetic sister."

"I imagine you can."

Mrs. Darroch retreats into the house, waving for us to follow. "Ye'll be wanting to see your new home. It's called Dùndubhan."

"What's that mean?" Emery asks while I lead her inside.

I answer her question. "It means fortress of the black water. Either that or fortress of the fishhook."

"Fishhook?" she says with a laugh. "Not very imposing."

Trying not to frown, I end up harrumphing instead. "You're in the vestibule of the not-imposing castle."

We trail Mrs. Darroch past the spiral staircase and out of the vestibule, entering the ground-floor hallway.

Someone shrieks.

Emery whirls to the right, straight into the path of my sister Jamie, who's barreling down the hallway. Her long, light-brown hair flies wild around her face. Jamie grins and shrieks again as she descends on my wife.

My sister flings her arms around Emery. "You must be her. Rory's wife, the one he met in America and couldn't wait to marry so he went on and did it and never told us until yesterday but—Oh! You must be exhausted from the trip, but how romantic and—"

"Jamie!" I shout.

Unfazed, my sister releases Emery only to snatch up my wife's hands and beam at her.

Aye, my sister and my wife will get on well. They're both barmy.

"Don't be a humbug," Jamie says to me. "I want to meet your wife."

I grind my teeth, and terse introductions are all I can manage. "This is Emery. And this is my youngest sister, Jamie."

Emery grins. "I kinda figured that one out, but thanks for the super-friendly intro."

What was wrong with what I said? I bar my arms over my chest, but none of the women surrounding me seem even the slightest bit intimidated.

"Ignore him," Jamie says. "I'm friendly enough for both of us. And I'm sooooo happy to meet you, Emery."

"Likewise, Jamie."

My sister grabs my wife by the arm. "Let me give you the tour. This house is really a castle, do ye know? Built in the Middle Ages."

"I knew it was a castle, yeah, but Rory hasn't been forthcoming with the details."

No details? I told her its name, and she thought it was funny.

Jamie drags Emery down the hall. "We'll start the tour here."

"Stop," I all but bellow, my voice echoing in the hall. "I will show my wife our home. If you please, Jamie."

"No need to shout at me. Ahmno deaf, Rory."

"Why don't you go to bed?"

Jamie snorts. "Ahmno five years old. It's only seven o'clock."

I glower at her, or try to, but I find I can't pull off the expression with enough sternness to convince anyone.

"All right," Jamie says, her hands raised in surrender. "But I want to talk to my new sister over dinner."

"Fine," I hiss. "Stay down here. The top floor is for myself and my wife alone."

Jamie salutes, clicking her heels together. "Aye-aye, admiral. I willnae step a toe on the third floor, so you and Emery can make all the noise ye want when you're shagging."

I flash her a frown, then tow my wife down the hall.

Jamie and Mrs. Darroch chuckle as they retreat into the vestibule.

"This is the ground floor," I announce. "The house has four levels."

"Cool."

Though I feel as if I might snarl again at any moment, I won't disappoint Emery by refusing to give her a tour of our home. "We have a landline, and every room has a telephone. You can dial out, but you can also ring the kitchen, my office, or the master suite."

Perhaps I march a bit too swiftly as I guide her through the castle, pointing out the rooms on each level, but I can't get rid of the tension inside me. Still, I show her the ground-floor bathroom with its claw-foot tub and a separate shower, then I point out the laundry room, dining room, cloakroom, and exercise room. The dining room opens into the guest wing which, I explain to her, houses bedrooms, bathrooms, the kitchen, and a sitting room. I don't take her down that hallway, though. She glances out every window we walk past, but I'm sure she notices this is not a brightly lit structure. It was meant to be a fortress, not a mansion.

When we head upstairs and reach the next level, I say, "This is the first floor."

"Downstairs isn't the first floor?"

"That's the ground floor," I say, rather proud of myself for not snarling. "This is the first floor."

"But it's upstairs."

"You will adjust to the oddities of castle living."

We march through the great hall. Then we come to the closed door that I'm sure will pique my wife's curiosity.

"At our right is the library, my office," I say. "Inside that is the old study I've converted into a file room."

"Your law office is in your castle?"

"I work from home quite a lot, but I do have an office in Loch Fairbairn. I go there for client meetings."

She comments on the fact that my office door is closed, and I don't offer to show her that room. Every man needs a sanctuary from his wife.

We climb the stairs to the second floor.

"Is there an elevator?" Emery asks.

"No. This is a castle, not a shopping mall."

"Just asking, sheesh."

On the second floor, I show her the long gallery and the tower bedroom. She trails behind me a few paces, probably because she can't stop gawping. Emery has to jog to keep up with me, and I know I should slow down. But I can't. Something inside me pushes me to get this over with as quickly as possible. When we ascend to the third and final floor, Emery once again seems confused by the numbering of the levels in this building. We're on the fourth level, but it's the third floor. What's so bloody hard to understand about that?

I halt in the long hallway. "Our bedrooms are up here, along with a shower room, bathroom, and dressing room. There's also a third bedroom accessed through yours, with stairs leading down to it."

"Um..." She rubs her eyes and her temples. "The last bedroom is actually on the second floor, but its door is up here?"

"No, it's between floors."

"I'm never going to get any of this, am I?" She takes a deep breath, exhaling it slowly. Then she squints at me. "What do you mean the third bedroom is accessed through mine? You mean *our* bedroom, right?"

"You'll sleep in that room." I point toward the door at the right end of the hall. "I sleep in the master suite, there."

I hook a thumb toward the left end of the hall.

She nails me with a hard look. "Separate bedrooms? That wasn't part of the deal."

"We hadn't discussed sleeping arrangements." I stride toward the door at the left end of the hallway while Emery trails after me. I open the door just enough to let her glimpse what's inside. "The dressing room. My bedroom is accessed through it. When the boxes of your belongings arrive tomorrow, you can store any of them that you don't need in here. We share a bathroom, there."

I gesture toward another doorway.

My wife regards me for a moment, one hip cocked with a hand balanced on it. "What happens when we have sex?"

"I don't understand the question."

"We screw, and then what? Do you scamper back to your master bedroom, leaving me alone in my hole in the wall?"

"Your room is not a hole in the wall."

"Well, this explains why you ordered Jamie never to come up here." She narrows her gaze on me. "Wouldn't want your sister to find out you don't sleep with your wife. A quick roll in the hay, and you're off to your private suite for the night."

"You make it sound unseemly."

"What about Mrs. Darroch? Does she know?"

Head down, I scratch my brow with one fingertip. "She does. Mrs. Darroch cares for the whole house, and I had her prepare your room for you. I told her we'll sleep in separate rooms because you snore."

"I snore? Thanks a bunch, Rory."

"Everyone knows I don't snore."

"Guess that was a fly snoring in the car while I was driving."

I assume my best deadpan expression. "It must've been."

She gazes at me with an almost rapt expression, her eyes turning softer, her lips slightly parted.

"What's wrong with you?" I demand.

"Huh?" She shakes her head, blinking swiftly. "What do you mean? Nothing's wrong."

I scrutinize her. "You looked…dazed."

A half-suppressed laugh snorts out of her. "Dazed? Guess you only know how to sweet-talk a girl when you want to get lucky."

I glance up at the ceiling, accepting that I will never understand my wife, then I gesture toward the stairwell. "Jamie's waiting for us to have dinner with her. We should go."

Emery trots to keep up with me as I rush downstairs.

Chapter Fifteen

For an hour, I listen to three women blethering. Jamie and Emery get on well, and that means they never stop talking. Do I want my sister to become friends with my wife? I'll only be married to her for one year, which means Jamie will be disappointed when Emery goes back to America. She might even try to…help us. Then she'll get the entire MacTaggart clan behind her to meddle and "fix" my relationship with my "wife."

I might be panicking prematurely. No, I'm not panicking at all. I have legitimate concerns that my sister might get overly attached to my wife, the woman I mean to shag regularly but not sleep with or develop feelings for, no matter what anyone else thinks.

When Mrs. Darroch brings us our meal, she joins in the blethering too. Fortunately, my housekeeper has enough sense not to tell any stories about me or to mention my ex-wives. Una had lived here at Dùndubhan with me, so Mrs. Darroch knew her. They never got on, though. Emery seems to enchant everyone who meets her, even my overprotective house-keeper who thinks she's my second mother. And aye, my actual mother loves my housekeeper and vice versa.

Emery listens intently when Mrs. Darroch tells her all about the meal we ate. Few Americans are familiar with Scottish food, so it usually needs a wee bit of explaining. We have Lorne sausage as well as tatties and neeps. Emery laughs at those two words, but she's not denigrating our traditional foods. She thinks tatties and neeps are "such super-cute names" for the dishes. It's potatoes and turnips. I don't see why that's entertaining, no matter what we call them.

Emery yawns throughout dinner. The lass is exhausted, because I dragged her out of bed at dawn to satisfy my selfish need to get home quickly. She can sleep as late as she likes tomorrow morning.

My wife gets almost giddy when she sees our dessert—blueberry tray cake. Emery rubs her palms together and licks her lips, her eyes alight. She gets excited about everything. I can't remember the last time I felt as happy as she seems to be all the time. Maybe I've never felt that way.

Except, perhaps, that day in New Orleans when she convinced me to go sightseeing.

After her second piece of cake, Emery suggests we all drink hot cocoa. Jamie loves the idea, of course.

"That's for bairns," I say. "Grown men donnae drink cocoa."

"Sure they do," my wife tells me. "As long as they don't have big old sticks up their fine asses."

I can tell by the way her eyes sparkle that she's teasing me.

"Try it, Rory," Jamie says. "Cocoa will soothe your jet lag and help you sleep better."

"Donnae have jet lag. It's a mental state, not a physical condition, and I do not let it affect me."

Jamie and Emery seem dubious, though they stop harassing me.

But I must disappoint the lasses by not drinking cocoa.

Emery takes another sip of her chocolate drink and yawns again, slumping into the chair she occupies, her eyes half-closed.

Jamie relaxes at one end of the adjacent sofa with her legs tucked under her, while she hugs a pillow to her belly.

As for me, I sit upright in a high-backed chair angled to face halfway toward the windows and sip whisky while I gaze out one of the three tall windows that overlook the castle compound. The flaming ribbons of sunset unfurl across the sky with streamers of clouds scudding along in their wake.

Earlier, when Emery had seen me pouring myself a dram of whisky, she'd asked me why the word was misspelled on the bottle.

"Not misspelled," I told her. "In Scotland, whisky is spelled without the E."

"Because all you stubborn Scots just have to come up with your own way to spell words." Her eyes had sparkled again when she said that. My wife seems to relish teasing me.

Now, my wife asks, "What kind of Scotch is that you're drinking?"

"It's whisky. Single malt Scotch whisky."

"What brand?"

"Ben Nevis," I say. "It's made in Fort William, which is near Ballachulish."

"Do all MacTaggarts drink Ben Nevis?"

"No. My brother Lachlan prefers Talisker, and my brother Aidan will drink anything."

Peripherally, I can see Emery watching me. "What about your sisters? Do they like whisky too?"

Jamie pretends to gag. "Och, no, we hate that rot. Men have no taste buds. They'll drink anything. But I like Irn Bru."

"That's not a real drink," I say with genuine disdain. "It's orange soda."

"I'd like to try it sometime," Emery says, and Jamie nods her approval.

I grunt in disgust. "Donnae think I'll kiss ye after ye drink it."

Yet another yawn grips Emery.

"You two are so sweet," Jamie says, for no reason that I can see.

I cast her a sideways glance. "My wife would say I'm grumpy."

"She'd be right. I meant overall, the way you are together." Jamie absently rubs circles on the pillow she holds over her belly. "When will you have bairns?"

Coughing and sputtering, I just manage to keep from spilling my whisky.

"Bairns?" Emery asks.

Jamie gives her an impish smile. "Babies."

"Mind your own business," I snap.

Jamie tosses her pillow aside and hops off the sofa. "I'm for bed. You can go upstairs to your king-and-queen's bedroom and make all the noise you like. I can't hear a blessed thing down here."

I'm fair certain I make an exasperated face.

Jamie skips out of the room while humming "Scotland the Brave."

Once the sitting-room door clicks shut, Emery wanders over to the windows. She takes a seat on the wide sill of the middle window, the one closest to my chair. Her feet are bare, and her toenails are painted pink.

"Do you want kids?" she asks.

I don't sputter this time, mostly because I've just lifted the glass to my lips but haven't taken a sip yet. While I assess my wife over the glass's rim, I tap a finger on it. "Why do you ask?"

"Curiosity." She bends one leg and wraps both arms around her raised knee. "You're on your fourth marriage. Did you want kids with your ex-wives?"

While I swirl my whisky, I peer into the glass to avoid looking at her. "Doesn't matter."

"I'd like to know, please."

But you don't need to know.

Instead of saying that, I slouch into my chair and stretch out my legs, crossing my ankles. Maybe I'm feigning relaxation. And maybe I stare into my drink, not sipping it, simply to avoid Emery's gaze. "I tried with my first wife, Isobel, but it never happened. Lilias, my second wife, wanted to wait until she felt more settled in her position as a schoolteacher. She divorced me nineteen months later. Left me for someone else, and they had a baby. Una never wanted children, but she didn't tell me that until after we were married."

"That was rotten."

I shut my eyes and sigh. "I should've asked before marrying her. Turned out Una didn't want a bairn with me, but she was happy to have one with her next... partner."

Why am I telling her about that? Maybe she'll give up on this line of questioning. Aye, because Emery isn't stubborn at all.

"You haven't answered my question," she says. "Do you want children?"

I crack one eye open. "Leave it alone, Emery."

She watches me for a few seconds, then her mouth gapes open on a noisy yawn.

I toss back the last of my whisky, surge to my feet, and reach Emery in one stride. With a hand on the window frame, I slant in close enough I can feel her breaths tickling my lips. "Time for bed."

She slides off the windowsill. Hoisting herself onto her tiptoes, she leans in and tilts her head back to meet my gaze.

My breaths quicken. My pulse quickens too because I recognize that lustful look in her eyes. When she splays her hands on my chest, I feel my *slat* awakening.

"Yes, please," she says. "Let's go to bed."

"To sleep, Emery." My voice grows rough. "You need rest, to recover from the jet lag."

"So do you." She glides her hands up to my shirt collar, pressing her supple body into me, and I feel her nipples hardening as they rake over my chest. "Might as well lie down together."

"I doubt either one of us would sleep that way." I lower my head, intending to nuzzle her neck, but catch myself. "We will lie down. You in your room, and I in mine."

Her hands sweep up and over my shoulders, where she links them at my nape. "Your perfect grammar makes me so hot."

"Behave, Emery." My command probably lacks vigor since I'm experiencing a powerful need to rip her clothes off and have her on the coffee table.

"You like it when I misbehave." She twirls her fingers at my nape, and I suck in a sharp breath. "Never asked me what kind of whisky I like."

"Try Ben Nevis. I think you'd like it."

"I'd love to taste it." She feathers her lips over mine, licking at the seam of my mouth. "Think I'll sample it now."

She spreads her delicate fingers over my scalp and clasps the back of my head with both hands as she fuses her mouth to mine. I shouldn't let her do this, but my body overrules my brain. I part my lips in a silent invitation for her to take whatever she wants, and she dives her agile tongue deep, exploring with leisurely strokes, teasing the roof of my mouth and coiling that tongue around mine until I cannae stop myself from responding with hungry thrusts. I grip her waist and tug her body into mine while plunging deeper, tasting more of her.

She must taste the whisky on my tongue—its rich, smoky flavor, imbued with hints of nut and chocolate and with an undercurrent of fruit.

"Mmm," she moans into my mouth. Then she peels her lips away from mine with a slowness that leaves me fighting for breath. The lass massages my nape as her lips curve into a lazy smile. "Delicious."

I stare down at her as the need to claim her body pulses inside me.

She dances her fingers over my cheek.

The siren has entranced me, again, and I blink rapidly until the spell fades. "To bed, Emery. You in your room—"

"And you in yours. Yeah, I heard you the first time." Her hands fall away from my shoulders, and she rocks back on her heels. "I'm not crazy about this separate-bedrooms thing."

"Once you've lived with me for a while, you'll be glad of the privacy."

She studies me the way she often does, as if she's trying to unravel a mystery. I'm not mysterious. I told her exactly what I can give, and she agreed to the arrangement.

"You are my husband for the next year," she says. "I'd rather share a bed with you, but if separate bedrooms makes you feel safer, I'll go along with it. For the time being."

"Thank you."

"You're welcome."

I pivot on my heels and head for the door. "Upstairs, to bed."

She jogs after me as I rush down the hallway and through the door to the dining room, out into the main hall, and up the winding stairs to the top floor. At Emery's bedroom door, I halt. My shoulders are stiff, and my chin is elevated. Why am I assuming my solicitor stance? I use it in court, not with my wife.

"Sleep well," I say, then I turn to leave.

Emery settles a hand on my arm to stop me. "No good-night kiss?"

"You had your kiss downstairs. Good night, Emery."

I hurry down the hall to my bedroom at the opposite end of the hall, as far from Emery as I can get, unless I move into the guest wing on the ground floor. The door clicks shut behind me.

While I undress for bed, I begin to seriously consider moving downstairs. Emery will not give up. She insists on trying to reshape our arrangement into a genuine marriage, but she signed the contract and the prenup. She knew what I could offer and what I can never give her. Yet she insists on testing me.

I stay awake half the night, tormented by thoughts of the beautiful, sexy, bizarre woman I've brought into my home, into my life. No one has ever crawled under my skin the way she does. No more playful kisses from my wife. I don't need intimacy from her. Only sex.

Sometime after two o'clock, I start to drift off. Then I remember what will happen in a matter of hours, and I lose any chance I might've had to sleep.

Tomorrow, my family will descend on Dùndubhan.

Chapter Sixteen

Why my family insists on turning this into a big do, instead of a simple meet-and-greet, I have no bloody idea. MacTaggarts love a party, though, and they especially love meddling. At least they won't drag any hapless lasses to this gathering in the hopes I'll fall madly in love with one of them and get married, so my mother can have the bairns she keeps pestering me to give her. Lachlan and Aidan have taken care of that, so she has no reason to harass me.

I find Emery in the vestibule, apparently hiding under the spiral staircase. She stares at the door to the outside, not blinking, her expression tight. I've never seen her this anxious. Emery takes everything in stride—but not today. I hover just outside the vestibule doorway, in the hall, and watch her nervous movements as she smooths her pale-blue shirt and touches each button in turn as if double-checking that she fastened them all correctly. Then she glances down at her blue jeans and makes a face I can't describe, but it seems like she's on the verge of panic.

Over her clothes? I don't spend that much time worrying about what I wear. My tan, long-sleeved shirt goes with my khaki trousers, and I shined up my leather boots. But I didn't fixate on my clothing the way she seems to be doing. It's my family out there, not the Spanish Inquisition.

I do love the blouse she's wearing. The neckline dips low enough to reveal her cleavage without being unseemly. She looks as bonnie as ever, so I can't understand her discomfort about her clothes.

Just as I step into the vestibule, Emery whirls around as if she means to flee back into the house. But she collides with me instead.

Yelping, she flails backward.

I catch her around the waist and hold her snugly against me.

She pulls in a deep breath, but instead of calming her, it seems to make her more miserable.

"Are you all right?" I ask.

"Yeah, sure." She unleashes a pitiful moan. "No, I'm not. Jeez, I was never this nervous for job interviews. I'm a disaster. Why do you have to look so good and smell so good? It's not fair."

"Emery." I drop my hands to her erse, which looks fantastic in those jeans. "You are beautiful, but my family doesn't care about superficial things. They want to know who you are, and you have no reason to be fashed about that. Jamie worships you after one evening in your presence."

"Your sister worships you too. You're her hero." Emery glances toward the hall doorway. "Where is Jamie?"

"She went out to keep the family from storming our castle."

Her face blanches, and her mouth drops open. "They're mad? Oh God, I—"

I seal my mouth over hers, strictly to short-circuit her panic. Though perhaps I let my lips linger there for a bit longer than necessary. "No one is angry. Relax, Emery. I've never seen you frantic before."

"You've known me for less than a week." Our lips scrape against each other when we speak. "To be fair, I've never been this frantic before. Never had to meet the in-laws, seeing as I called off my last engagement. And considering your opinion of me, I'm not sure what your family will think. Jamie might be an aberration."

I give her erse a gentle squeeze. "What do you think my opinion of you is?"

"I'm crazy and annoying."

She believes that? The daft lass.

I nibble on her upper lip and flick my tongue against hers. "You're wrong."

"Then what do you think…" Her voice trails off as I push two fingers between her thighs to rub her through her jeans. She clamps her hands over my biceps.

And I caress her while my breaths mingle with hers. "We can discuss that later."

I lift Emery onto her toes and devour my wife with a rough, demanding kiss while I massage her folds, though the fabric prevents me from feeling her slick heat.

A moan vibrates in her throat.

I set my wife down and peel my hands away, then pat her shoulders. "You're ready."

"I'm—huh?"

"You're not nervous anymore," I declare, and I don't even try to erase the self-satisfaction from my voice or my expression.

"Terrific," she says, sounding irritated. Straightening her blouse, she staggers backward a step. "I get to meet your family while I'm on the verge of orgasm."

"At least no one will doubt we married for love." I tap a finger on her nose. "You look like the adoring bride."

Not that I want her to honestly adore me. She only needs to convey that effect.

She jabs a finger into my chest. "Don't ever do that to me again."

I arch one brow.

Smoothing her shirt, she rolls her shoulders back. "Unless, you know, I ask you to do it."

"Of course. Only when you beg me for it."

A fist bangs on the outer door.

Emery jumps.

I stiffen, my gaze nailed to the door.

"Rory!" Aidan shouts. "Are ye coming out to see us? Or should we let ourselves inside?"

I stomp to the door, rip it open, and confront my brother. "Aidan, what the bloody hell are you doing? We'll come out when we're ready."

"When you're ready," Aidan repeats with a sly smile. "Would that be before or after you have a quick poke in the vestibule?"

He enunciated "vestibule" with great care—because I've chastised him in the past for referring to this room as the entryway. He thinks I'm "rigid" about using the proper terms for the various parts of this building.

I make a sound that's somewhere between a growl and a huff. "I don't have a poke anywhere."

Emery raises her hand. "What's a poke?"

Aidan's lips spread into a mischievous grin. "It's a word for sex."

My wife steps up beside me, though my arm blocks her from getting too close to Aidan. I had set my hand on the doorjamb for that very purpose.

Emery tells him, "We weren't doing that."

"What a shame," Aidan says, still grinning. He thumps his fist into my shoulder. "I see why ye married her so fast. She's bonnie and braw."

"I'm what now?" Emery asks.

"Braw means fine, and bonnie means beautiful."

"Thank you for the compliment, then. I'm Emery, by the way, since my husband won't introduce us."

She ducks under my arm to squeeze in front of me and offers her hand to Aidan. He shakes it, his smile deepening when I squint and flatten my lips. Why do I care if Aidan smiles at Emery? I don't. But his self-satisfied expression annoys me.

Aidan turns sideways, motioning for us to go outside. "Everyone's waiting."

Naturally, a horde of MacTaggarts—men, women, and two bairns—observe us from the other side of the courtyard, near the garden. I grasp Emery's shoulders, anchoring her in place.

Aidan waggles his eyebrows. "Willnae let her out of the house, eh? From what Jamie said, Emery's not the sort to let you lock her indoors."

My wife glances at me over her shoulder. "I'm also not the sort to do whatever my husband says."

"Aye, Jamie said that too," Aidan informs us. "A strong-willed, feisty American. Just the sort of woman Rory needs, whether he knows it or not."

My wife hops up to give my brother a quick hug. "What a nice thing to say. Thank you, Aidan."

She drops back down, sideways to me.

I roll my eyes. "You can stop thanking my brother for being an erse."

"He means ass," Aidan explains.

"Rory, your brother is not an ass," Emery says. "Now, let's go greet the rest of your family."

Might as well get this disaster over with.

I shouldn't be surprised that my family has turned this into a spectacle, but I find that I am surprised. Or maybe I'm annoyed. Both, probably. Instead of a casual get-together, this has become a courtly spectacle in which my wife and I receive our guests like a medieval laird and his lady. We stand in front of the arbor while every MacTaggart in the entire Highlands files past us to offer their congratulations.

Emery looks even bonnier surrounded by fragrant vine roses and lush rhododendron bushes.

All right, maybe it's not *every* MacTaggart in creation. But it feels that way. My palm is sore by the time I shake hands with the ninth family member. They all express their joy and relief that I finally settled down with the right woman. What makes them think Emery is the right one, I have no idea. They're a crackbrained lot. Emery is nothing like my ex-wives, and I suppose that's why they assume this marriage will work.

Aye, it will. For one year. According to my rules.

Naturally, my wife hugs every person she meets.

Lachlan slaps me on the arm. "Did ye kidnap her, Rory?"

Erica, my brother's bonnie American wife, holds their toddler son in her arms while she shakes her head at her husband. "Give the poor girl a break. She's not used to the MacTaggart tradition of incessant, well-meaning harassment."

Though I ignore Lachlan's comment, he still seems thoroughly entertained. Why? I haven't done or said anything. But maybe I seem…harried. Can anyone blame me?

Aidan breezes past Lachlan, towing the lovely Calli in his wake. That would be *his* American wife, the lass he pursued relentlessly last year. Aidan claims her hand while she cradles their baby daughter in a contraption that looks like some type of sling. It hangs over her body at a diagonal.

"Out of the way, Lachie," Aidan says briskly. "Donnae get to hog the new girl."

Lachlan scowls at Aidan's use of the diminutive Lachie. Aye, my older brother hates that nickname. I should start calling him that too, since he sees fit to harass me with abduction comments.

I might be almost smiling, but the expression fails to take hold.

Gavin Douglas approaches too, offering his congratulations. He is Calli's brother, but now the *cacan* is making my sister unhappy with his "long-distance relationship" bollocks. Emery seems to bond with him, though, in the way two strangers might do when they've both come to a new country. Emery lives here, with me, but Gavin is only around when he visits Jamie. And he's leaving again this afternoon.

No, I don't like the way he's treating my sister.

Emery gets anxious again when I introduce her to my parents, though I doubt anyone else notices. Niall and Sorcha MacTaggart treat her like a true daughter-in-law, as if she'll be in the family for good. I can't tell them this will last one year only, and I married Emery primarily to appease them. Acid churns in my gut, rising higher with every minute that we chat to my parents.

I'm deceiving them. The whole family, in fact. And I'm forcing Emery to share in my deceit.

My mother latches her arms around my wife. "Welcome to the family, Emery. We couldn't be more pleased to meet anyone."

I snort out a half-stifled laugh. "Don't let Lachlan or Aidan hear you say that. They think their wives are the bonniest, most charming women in all the world."

"They are. All our American daughters are equally bonnie and sweet and welcome. But Emery is a wonderful surprise."

"Aye," my father says, remaining stoic about it. A family trait, I suppose. "We were afraid those other ones had put Rory off marriage for good."

"Niall," my mother chastises, "we agreed not to mention the others in front of Emery."

He makes a dismissive noise. "Sorcha, ye cannae treat him like a bairn. Rory's a grown man who can abide hearing his ex-wives mentioned."

I tense up, my expression blank and my eyes trained on my wife. No, I can't abide hearing anyone mention my ex-wives. It fashes me, though I wish it didn't. And I wonder what Emery feels right now, hearing about the three women who left me. She must think there's something wrong with me, which there is.

My three sisters push past our parents, determined to corral my wife. Emery met Jamie yesterday, but my youngest sister still greets her with a hug. Fiona, my oldest sister, offers my wife a friendly introduction and states her agreement with Aidan's idea that she's perfect for me, then Fiona hugs Emery too.

Emery is perfect, but only as a tool to satisfy my family. She is not my soul mate. That's rot, anyway.

Jamie and Fiona wander away while Catriona stays to talk to my wife.

Lachlan shouts to me, "Get over here, Rory! It's time for a brotherly blether."

Men don't gossip. I want to shout that to Lachlan, but instead, I trudge over there so I can tell him in person. When I glance back at Emery, my sister Catriona is engaged in conversation with her. Do I want to know what Cat is telling Emery? It might be women's rubbish about how to handle a man. Not sure that's what lasses blether about, but it seems as likely as anything.

Lachlan and Aidan pull me into a conversation about all the absurd things their wives have done, and they joke about what married life is like with an American woman. At first, I listen but don't contribute much to the conversation other than the occasional grunt. Gradually, though, I start to relax and insert my own sarcastic comments, and soon I'm laughing right along with them.

This is what I used to be like, when I was a strapping lad who hadn't married the wrong woman, three times. I used to date. And dance. And laugh. Though I'd never been as outgoing as Aidan, I had my moments. How did I end up here? Thrice divorced. Engaged in a marriage of convenience. Too closed off to tell my wife what I think of her or let her share my bed.

I glance toward Emery.

My wife has just thrown her arms around Catriona. My sister pats her on the back and walks away, heading toward Jamie and Fiona.

Aye, Emery loves everyone. My family loves her too.

I let my brothers pull me back into the jokes and laughter. I might be letting myself think, for a little while, that my wife might genuinely care for me. I shouldn't want that. I don't want it. But letting myself entertain the idea...

I get a strange sensation in my chest.

Every few minutes, I glance at Emery. Calli and Erica are talking to her now.

Lachlan slaps a hand on my shoulder. "Don't worry. Wives need to blether, and I'm sure they're discussing how Emery can tame the Ogre of Loch Fairbairn, but it's only talk."

Aidan chuckles. "No, I think Emery is serious about giving Rory a mental makeover."

"Mental makeover?" I say with a slight growl. "Donnae need that."

"Aye, ye do." Aidan leans in to whisper, "Let her shag ye until that caber falls out of your erse."

I see Calli and Erica walking away from Emery, so at least their blethering hasn't gone on for hours.

A few minutes later, my mother marches up to me, seizes my arm, and tows me back to my wife with my father hurrying to catch up to us. She waves a hand, encouraging me to stand beside Emery, just as my father reaches us.

Sorcha MacTaggart claims both of her daughter-in-law's hands, sandwiching them between her palms. "Rory told us you haven't seen your family in a long time. I hope ye donnae mind, but I asked for your parents' number, and Rory gave it to me. I had a good chat with your mother last night."

Emery is probably wondering how I got her parents' number. I can explain that later. Or not. Will she be angry when she finds out?

Emery smiles at my mother. "That's great. I imagine you and my mom commiserated over being left out of the loop on this marriage thing. I really have to apologize—"

"Hush, lass." Ma squeezes her hands. "I'm happy to see Rory awake to the world again. He's been hiding in his castle keep for too long, like the ghost of a medieval laird."

Emery's smile broadens. "That's a perfect description, Mrs. MacTaggart."

"Och." She waves a dismissive hand. "Call me Sorcha."

My mother gazes at my wife as if Emery is the answer to her prayers.

Ma frees my wife's hands. "Penny and I had a wonderful idea. Since you and Rory eloped, neither family had the chance to witness your marriage."

Penny? I suppose that must be Emery's mother, though I'd never asked what her first name was.

I secure an arm around my wife's waist. "Mother, what are you on about?"

She gives a decisive nod. "We're having a wedding for you. A proper, traditional ceremony."

I groan out a sigh. "If it'll make you happy, we can plan it for a few months out."

"No." Sorcha MacTaggart anchors her hands on her hips. "It'll be on Saturday in two weeks."

Chapter Seventeen

"*Bod an Donais*," I hiss. "Ye cannae order us to—"

"Rory Niall MacTaggart, don't you curse at me," my mother says in the stern tone I know well. "You decided to sweep the lass off her feet and bulldoze her through a marriage ceremony in a magistrate's office, in another country. This wedding is for Emery as much as for me and Penny and our families."

I moan, like the pathetic numpty I am. How did I not anticipate this? "Mother..."

Ma arches one brow, quite like the way I often do. "Lachlan and Aidan gave us weddings."

My shoulders slump. "I gave ye three ceremonies. How many do ye need?"

"One for every marriage. Lachlan didnae complain about another wedding."

"He's only had two."

Emery whispers to me out of the corner of her mouth, "Let her have this."

Bloody hell. But she's right, and I know it. I shut my eyes and hang my head for a moment, then pull myself up to face the inevitable. "You can have your wedding. In three weeks."

"It's your wedding, Rory," my mother says. "And you will pay for it, won't you."

Though the statement is phrased as a question, I know she means it as a command. Her tone confirms it.

I grimace a wee bit. "I will pay."

Aye, in every way imaginable.

"Then you can have three weeks," Ma says. She winks at Emery.

Does my wife need to look so happy about the prospect? It will be a ridiculous spectacle, even more so than this garden party nonsense.

Ma grasps my face and plants a firm kiss on my cheek. "Good lad."

I aim a resigned look at my wife.

She winces, her lips tight.

My mother kisses my wife's cheek. "This is for you, Emery. We willnae do anything you don't want."

No one cares what I want. That's a husband's lot, isn't it? To let the women in my life cram a sodding wedding down my throat and expect me to enjoy it.

My parents leave us, though only so they can tell everyone about the "fairy-tale wedding" that will happen in three weeks. Da glances back at me and shrugs, as if he's silently telling me there's nothing a man can do in a situation like this.

Emery smiles and bumps my shoulder. "I like your parents."

I grunt. "You want a posh wedding."

"No, but this will make our mothers feel better. Don't you want your mom to be happy?"

I grunt again. "Arguing with women about weddings is a futile endeavor."

"Did you have big weddings the first three times?"

"Not extravaganzas. Tasteful ceremonies."

"I'm sure our mothers won't go hog wild with this one."

She doesn't know my mother. It had taken an enormous amount of nego-tiation to stop my brothers' weddings from becoming outlandish events.

"I should speak to Lachlan and Aidan," I say. "Maybe their wives can help us keep this bloody wedding under control."

Emery kisses my cheek. "You do that."

As I leave to go seek my brothers' advice, I glance back at Emery. She's standing under the arbor, alone, looking a touch melancholy. Does she want an outrageous wedding? Or is she uncomfortable being alone amid a gathering of MacTaggarts? She can't want me to stay with her, to keep her company.

When I find my brothers, they commiserate with me about the wedding rubbish. But they also find ways to lighten my mood, as only Lachlan and Aidan know how to do. Soon, I'm laughing at a stupid joke Aidan told me.

Something makes me look around for my wife. She's still hiding under the arbor. Alone. Her shoulders hunched. My smile fades into a slight frown as Emery's gaze meets mine. I shouldn't have left her, should I? She doesn't know my family.

But Lachlan says something, drawing my attention away from my wife.

She'll find someone to talk to. Emery is outgoing and sweet, and unlike me, she attracts people to her instead of chasing them away.

After a few more minutes, Aidan leaves to…do whatever he does. Lachlan keeps talking, so I don't see where Aidan goes, but I know he loves to blether almost as much as the women do. Lachlan eventually excuses himself to go find his wife, since he can't seem to stay away from Erica for more than ten minutes at a time.

I search the garden for Emery—and see her talking to Aidan. He glances around with his infamous impish look on his face, the one that always means he's about to say something sarcastic and inappropriate.

Emery smiles and smacks his chest with the back of her hand. Then she says something to him.

And I march over there to find out what the bloody hell my brother is doing with my wife. I know he's being friendly, not trying it on with Emery, but I still experience an overpowering need to pry my brother away from my wife.

"We all agree," Aidan says as I draw nearer to the pair of them. "Rory's gone doolally for ye."

He's the one who's off his head, if he believes that.

I arrive just as Emery hugs Aidan and says, "You guys have all been so sweet. I feel like part of the family."

"Ye are family," Aidan assures her right before he wraps his arms around my wife. "You're our sister."

"Aidan, unhand my wife, if you please." My hard tone, the one I use often in the courtroom, has no effect on my brother.

But Emery pulls away from him.

Aidan bunches his shoulders, hands spread wide. "What? She hugged me, Rory. Would've been rude to shove her away."

I cross the distance to Emery, slinging an arm around her waist to haul her into me. "Maybe I should wrap myself around your wife, Aidan."

He grins at Emery. "Doolally, see?"

That's complete rubbish, but I see no point in telling him that.

Aidan claps me on the shoulder and ambles off in the direction of Lachlan.

I rub my forehead. "Must you fling yourself at everyone you meet?"

"I was expressing gratitude. Aidan said I'm part of the family, which was very sweet of him."

"The pair of you were having an intimate discussion, by the look of it."

She tries to wriggle in my embrace, apparently wanting to turn toward me. "Aidan wanted to know why women like you."

"I see. What did you—"

My gaze swerves past her shoulder as someone enters the garden. All the blood in my veins hardens into ice. I stop blinking. Stop breathing. My entire body goes stone-still.

That fucking ersehole.

I push past Emery and stalk toward the intruder, halting a few feet from the opening in the garden wall.

The rangy man standing at the entrance is no stranger to me. I know him on sight—from his brown hair salted with grey to the crow's feet around his eyes, and the sagging skin under them, not to mention the sallow coloring of his skin. Being a chain smoker for years will do that to a person. As usual, he wears rumpled khakis and a polo shirt with his hair unkempt.

"What do you want?" I ask in a flat voice. "You weren't invited, and you are not welcome here."

"I'm a journalist, MacTaggart," he says. "Your new bride is big news in the village. Everyone wants to know if your taste in women has improved, or if you'll be a victim of another failed marriage."

The *bod ceann*'s smug look implies he relishes the idea that I might lose another wife.

"You are a journalist as much as I'm a sheep farmer," I say. "At least sheep shit washes off your clothes. The stench of being a *bod ceann* can't be cleansed."

When I risk a backward glance, I discover the rest of the MacTaggart clan has gathered behind me. Aidan and Lachlan stand at either side of me, though they keep back a few paces.

"Graham Oliver," Lachlan says, his tone making it clear he disdains the man as much as I do. "Rory told ye to leave, so go on. Before I skelp your sorry hide raw."

My brother cracks his knuckles.

Unfazed, Graham juts his chin and stuffs his thumbs into his waistband. "Is it my fault ye donnae have security? I've got journalistic privilege, at any rate." He switches his attention to someone behind me, his eyes bright with interest. "Mrs. MacTaggart, what a pleasure to meet ye."

I glance back at Emery, who seems confused. If this bastard drags her into his muckraking, I will beat him bloody.

Emery gives me a small, encouraging smile.

"Need your wife's permission to speak?" Graham says. "Ye married her so fast, she must've put a hex on ye. Led around by the short hairs, MacTaggart?"

I shake my fist at him. "*Falbh dàirich fhein*, ye bawbag."

Lachlan steps up beside me, laying a hand on my shoulder. "He's not worth the sore knuckles, Rory. Donnae let this wee shit ruin a family celebration."

Graham sniggers. "Ahmno staying, Lachlan. Stopped in to give my congratulations to your brother. Let's hope the fourth time is the charm, and this one can stand ye for more than eight months. Isobel must've had an iron constitution to stay all those years, but the others—"

"Shut up," I snarl.

The self-described "journalist" saunters out of the garden, swinging his hands at his sides and whistling a jaunty tune. Graham climbs into a black sedan scarred by scratches and dents. Once his vehicle rolls down the drive, Lachlan thumps me on the shoulder and heads back toward the crowd, waving for them to disperse. The family fans out around the garden again, and I return to my wife.

"Who was that?" Emery asks.

"Graham Oliver."

"Am I supposed to know the name?"

"Only locals know him. Graham fancies himself a publishing magnate, but his newspaper is nothing more than a muckraking scandal sheet on the verge of collapse." My lips twist into a nasty smirk. "Graham is as rotten as the smut he peddles."

"Don't hold back, honey." She winks. "Tell me what you really think of him."

"He's a right scunner." When I note her confusion, I explain, "It means he's a bloody nuisance. His newspaper is the *Loch Fairbairn World News*, but everyone calls it The Bletherer."

"Kinda seemed like he has a grudge against you."

I grasp the back of my neck. "He does. I represented his wife in their divorce last year. Negotiated a generous, and well-deserved, settlement for her. Graham's financial fortunes have taken a tumble since then, mostly because he's a boozing gambler."

She nudges me with her elbow. "You've been speaking a lot of Gaelic today, haven't you? Care to enlighten your American wife? Your mother said you cursed at her."

"*Bod an Donais* means the devil's penis, and it's a curse I picked up from Aidan." I might be smirking again, but not because I'm disgusted. "Aidan's a bad influence, but I've developed my own favorite insults. *Falbh dàirich fhein* means go fuck yourself, and a *bod ceann* is a dickhead."

"What about bawbag?"

"It's a reference to a man's... ah..." I gesture vaguely downward. "You know."

Emery tries to stifle a laugh, though it makes her mouth twitch. "Are you pointing to your balls?"

"Aye." Why on earth couldn't I say that? I'm a man, not a wee laddie.

"You can say dickhead, but not balls. You're the cutest." She bounces up on her toes to kiss me. "Let's go mingle with your family and forget that bawbag was ever here."

Chapter Eighteen

It feels like days elapse while we "mingle" with my family, but I suppose it's been a few hours. I do not like long get-togethers. They leave me jeeked. I need to rest, but I don't want to do it. The arrival of Graham Oliver hadn't helped matters, and my mind keeps replaying that moment no matter how hard I try to avoid thinking about it. Graham must want something, or he believes he can hurt me somehow by talking rubbish about my wife.

I will never let Graham drag Emery through the muck.

Perhaps I haven't given her the sort of marriage a woman like her deserves, but I've done the best I can. Loving my wife is out of the question, whether I want it to be or not. Besides, I'm incapable of it.

After the confrontation with Graham, I find myself becoming the stoic and grumpy ogre everyone thinks I am. Maybe I don't growl at anyone, but I realize I'm retreating into myself again and ignoring my wife, giving her the occasional cursory glance while I herd my family out of the garden and to their vehicles. I try to encourage them to leave, politely, but I doubt I pull that off. Since my relatives each flash Emery a sympathetic smile, I suspect I have failed.

When we return to the house, Mrs. Darroch insists on making lunch for us. Emery tries to engage me in conversation, but I manage only the occasional grunt or obligatory "aye." This day so far has been a right fankle. I like order and reason, not a tangled mess of confusion.

After lunch, Emery decides to go upstairs to her bedroom while I retreat into my office with the door closed.

I sit at my desk and stare down at the file folders I've set on the surface, but I don't do anything. I stare. At the folders. What am I meant to do? Work, obviously. My clients need my help. I had told them I'm still on holiday until tomorrow, though, so I can't decide what work I should do. At least here, in my private sanctum, I can find a bit of peace and quiet. After the garden party nonsense, solitude appeals to me.

But I get bored with that after five minutes.

Organizing my calendar and my files keeps me occupied—for another ten minutes. Then I decide to call my mate at the Home Office to check on the progress of my wife's visa. Stephen Beckham answers on the second ring.

"It's Rory MacTaggart," I say.

"Good afternoon to you too, Rory," he says with a hint of sarcasm. Everyone knows I waste little time on pleasantries, but like my family, Stephen enjoys teasing me about that. "How's the weather in bonnie old Balla-whatever?"

"Ballachulish. But you know I don't live there anymore."

"Of course. You live in a castle in the dark and forbidding woods, like a character in a Grimm Brothers tale." A clicking noise alerts me to the fact he's extending and retracting the tip of his ballpoint pen while he talks, a habit he's had for years. "What can I do for you, Rory?"

"Can you check on the status of my wife's visa?"

"You want me to expedite it in any way possible."

Aye, he knows I prefer to get things done quickly. "Yes. Can you speed it up at all?"

"For you, of course. I'll do whatever I can. You did save me from a legal nightmare, and I will owe you for the rest of my life."

"You're being melodramatic. It wasn't that bad."

"No, it was worse. I'm grateful, so stop being humble and let me repay the favor."

"All right. Thank you, Stephen."

"Cheers, Rory."

Just as I hang up the phone, someone knocks twice on my office door.

"Come," I say.

The door swings open, and Emery waltzes into my sanctum.

She scans her gaze over the entire room as if she's cataloging every element. The office has dark wood paneling on the walls and shelves packed with books that take up three of the four walls from floor to ceiling. Many of the books are about the law, but I also have history texts. She smiles slightly when she sees the trio of tall windows that admit sunlight into the room and the upholstered bench positioned beneath them.

I'm hunched over my desk, which features wood the same dark shade as the walls. My leather executive chair suddenly feels too formal, at least when Emery is in the room. She likes "fun" things, so I doubt she appreciates the style of my office.

She glances at the computer that occupies one corner of the desk.

I try to focus on the papers spread out across the desktop, resting my arms on the surface, but I feel lines creasing my forehead. I'm dreading whatever my wife wants to say to me. She seems determined to pry me open and rummage about in there.

Emery approaches the two smaller chairs positioned across from me, which sit at a respectable distance from my desk. She glances down at the rug that covers most of the floor, her brows rising briefly.

Then she grabs one of the chairs and drags it across the rug toward my desk.

I peer at her over the tops of my reading glasses. "What are you doing?"

She drops into the chair and folds her hands on her lap as she props her sock-clad feet on the desk, crossing her ankles. "Oh yes, my darling husband, I'm so pleased to see you too."

Her breezy tone and bright smile are pure sarcasm. I know this, but I can't stop staring at her socks. Why is she using my desk as a footrest?

I nudge her sole with one finger. "Your feet are on my desk."

"Yep."

"What do you want, Emery?" I aim a pointed glance at my papers and then spout pure bollocks. "I have work to catch up."

"I have questions."

My wife will not give up. I know this. Slumping back into my chair, I exhale a defeated sigh. "Go on, then."

"First of all, have you seen my phone? I can't find it. Had to do a video chat with my family on my laptop."

Mhac na galla. I'd hoped she wouldn't notice that, and I could return her mobile to her room before she needed the device. Eyes downcast, I open a desk drawer and produce her mobile. I set it on the desk, pushing it toward her feet. "I went into your room while you were asleep and borrowed your mobile. Only so I could switch it to local service."

"You sneaked into my bedroom while I was sleeping to steal my phone?"

"To switch it to local service," I say again, enunciating each syllable with knife-like precision. "It was a favor."

"One I didn't ask for. Is that how your mom got my mom's number? You snooped on my phone?"

I rearrange the papers on my desk, not having a clue why I'm doing that. "Yes. My mother asked me for the number, so she could surprise you."

"Did she ask you to steal my phone?"

"No, I—" Why won't she drop the subject? I shove a hand inside the back of my shirt collar because I swear ants are nesting there. "I didn't know another way to get the information."

"Rory, honestly." She pitches her head back and makes a frustrated noise. But she sounds calm when looks at me again. "Let's forget that for the moment. I have more important questions."

More questions? *Bod an Donais.* I brace my elbows on the desktop and rest my cheek in one hand.

"Erica asked if I'd applied for my spouse visa yet," she asks while wiggling the toes of one foot in the air. "Told her I had no idea what that is. She and Calli explained it's an immigration thing, and I'd better take care of the formalities ASAP. Am I going to be deported for not doing that right away?"

"No." Her toes are distracting me, the way they move in such a haphazard fashion. I pluck up a pen and twirl it around my fingers, rapping it on the desktop with every third revolution. "I'm handling it. Started the process before we left America."

"You—" She gapes at me. "Let me get this straight. Without telling me, without consulting me at all, you took it upon yourself to secretly apply for a visa for me. Meanwhile, you skulked into my room in the dead of night—"

"Not the dead of night. It was daylight, but you were asleep." I shift uncomfortably in my chair. Every conversation with my wife makes me feel like I've got an itchy rash all over my body. "I planned to tell you about the mobile service change, but I didn't have the chance yet. Then you flounced in here asking your bloody questions."

"Flounced in?" She laughs and shakes her head. "You are so weird. Lucky for you, I like your weirdness. It's kind of hot."

Without my permission, one side of my mouth quirks. "Am I meant to thank you for the compliment?"

"No, you're meant to apologize for your stealth mission to get me a visa."

I toss the pen across my desk, and it rolls into the computer keyboard. "I was trying to spare you the stress."

"Should've told me what you were doing."

"You were exhausted from jet lag and worried about meeting my family." I flatten my hand on the desktop, but her feet snare my attention again. I'd loved massaging her soles on the first night in New Orleans, loved the way she responded to my touch. "As I said, I was trying to spare you the added stress of dealing with immigration issues. I should've consulted you, I'm sorry."

She says nothing for a moment, just seeming to consider me. Then she announces, "Okay, I forgive you. What you did was thoughtful and efficient. Thank you."

I jerk my head back. "You—thank me?"

"I do."

This must be shock I'm feeling. She thanks me? I lean over my desk again. "But I invaded your privacy."

"If you're talking about the phone incident, don't worry about it."

"You should still be angry."

She stretches out a leg to tap my nose with her big toe. "Lighten up, Ror. I'm over it. You get a onetime free pass on keeping secrets."

I push my glasses down to study her over their rims. "Ror?"

"Yeah, I'm trying out a nickname for you."

"I don't require a nickname. And 'Ror' is bloody ridiculous. I'm not a lion." I catch her big toe to stop her from waving it in my face. "My name is Rory. Say it with me. Ror-ee."

She wiggles her toe in my grip. "I knew you had a sense of humor, baby."

"Must you call me 'baby'? I am not a bairn."

"Don't worry. I'll find a good nickname for you." She smiles. "But it might include the word baby."

"As long as it's not 'Ror.' "

"No, that wasn't working for me either."

"Glad to hear it." I release her toe, skating my middle finger down the sole of her foot, rewarded by her subtle intake of breath. "Any other questions?"

"Not really a question. More of a request." My wife sets her feet on the floor, sits up straight, and rests both hands on her thighs. "Do you remember what I said about needing total honesty?"

I link my hands on the desktop. "You need to understand two things. I can't discuss my clients or their private legal matters."

"Of course. I get that."

"There are also parts of my past I don't care to discuss at all."

"Rory, you can tell me about—"

"No."

I can see her nails digging into her thighs, but she pries them loose. "Total honesty. It's nonnegotiable."

Though I have no idea why, I finger my wedding ring.

"This is the deal," she says. "I won't pester you to tell me about your past. I will ask questions, though, and the longer we live together and you don't tell me, the more it'll make things uncomfortable between us. I can't help that. We need to be friends, Rory."

"Asking questions sounds like pestering."

"Not the way I do it." Emery rises and perches her sexy erse on the edge of my desk. "I'm your therapist, remember? While I search for my true bliss, my mission is to help you relearn how to have fun."

"I assumed it would be sex therapy."

"Sex is a part of it, but you need way more than that."

"I shouldn't be your life's purpose."

The lass spreads a hand over the smooth, dark wood of the desk and leans toward me. "You aren't my life's purpose. You're my current mission. I've set my sights on making sure you come out of your office prison for more than sleeping and eating, and that you remember how to enjoy life. I plan on helping you lift that weight you carry around. I'm beginning to suspect it's an ex-wife-shaped burden."

"You mean to save me." I'm slightly dismayed by how resigned I sound.

"I'm not trying to save you, unless you want me to. I told you before, I love a challenge and I love an adventure. You are both."

"I see." While I mull my options, I survey the room to avoid meeting my wife's gaze. "May I ask a personal question?"

"Ask me anything you like." She holds up one finger. "Be warned, though. It goes both ways."

"Fine." I relax into my chair, one ankle lodged on the opposite knee. "You mentioned a fiancé. Why did you call off the wedding?»

"I didn't call off the wedding. I ended the engagement." Straightening, she dances her fingers over the computer keyboard near her hip. "Luke and I were together for three years before he proposed, and I took six days to give him an answer. Two weeks after I said yes, I realized if we'd really loved each other, we would've tied the knot a long time ago. So, I broke up with Luke. He wasn't devastated."

"He let you go without a fight?"

"Yep." She bends one knee, tucking her foot under the other leg. "I told him I couldn't marry him, and he shrugged. Literally. He shrugged and walked away. Moved his stuff out of our apartment the same day. Six months later, he's living with a woman who owns a pot shop."

"Ceramics?" I have no idea if she realizes I'm teasing her. But I suspect she does. Emery is a clever woman.

"Marijuana," she says. "It's legal in Colorado."

I rise from my chair and angle over the desk toward her. "You haven't said if you were upset when you ended your engagement."

"I wasn't. Relieved would be the best description."

"Why would you stay so long with a man who cared so little about you?"

"Luke and I had been friends since college," she says. "Four years ago, I started dating somebody I thought was a nice guy. We got along, and Sebastian was game for any silly thing I wanted to do. Gradually, he became more and more withdrawn, even lost interest in sex. He blamed work stress. About eight months into our relationship, I ran into one of his coworkers. He told me Sebastian had been fired six weeks earlier, for watching internet porn at work."

Though I want to touch her, to comfort her, I don't do it. That would be inappropriate, considering our arrangement.

She scratches her arm. "When I confronted him, Sebastian admitted he'd been lying to me about a lot of things, not just being fired. Instead of looking for a new job, he'd spent eighteen hours a day watching porn on two dozen different websites. He didn't want to sleep with me because reality couldn't compare to his fantasy women. He liked jerking off while watching them more than he cared about me. I begged him to get help."

"What did he say?" I ask gently.

"Flat-out no." She wraps her arms around herself. "I had no choice. I broke up with him."

I walk around the desk to sit on its edge facing her and settle a hand on her knee. "This is where revenge porn comes into the story."

She nods, though she won't look at me. "Six months earlier, Sebastian talked me into posing for nude photos. He swore they'd be for his eyes only, and I was kind of flattered he'd ask. What an idiot, huh?"

"No, Emery, you are not an idiot."

"I trusted him, and he turned out to be a damn liar." She swipes at the tears gathering in her eyes. "He posted the photos on social media. I told you before, I got them taken down. For all I know, some other sleazebag might've copied them."

She's locked her hands around her upper arms.

I tug them free and slide closer to clasp her hands on her lap. "How does this relate to your engagement?"

"When the shit exploded in my face, Luke was there to support me." She takes three slow breaths. "My family was far away, and I was ashamed to tell them what happened. Luke convinced me I needed to. He sat beside me, holding my hand, when I called my parents. He helped me figure out how to get the photos taken down. I was so grateful to him, I guess I mistook gratitude for love. Three months after the photo fiasco, I moved in with Luke."

"You stayed with him for three years."

"Because it was easy." She inhales another deep breath. "I swore I'd never let Sebastian's actions affect my future, but I guess they did. I got into this rut with my life. Boring, dead-end job. Boring, dead-end boyfriend. Standing still was easier and safer than uprooting my whole life. Computer programming wasn't my life's passion, and neither was Luke. Both looked good on paper, but all of it stifled me more than I realized until I got laid off and had to reexamine my choices."

"That's why you married me."

"Kind of." She lifts her face to gaze at me. "You are not boring, that's for sure."

I absently draw circles on the desk with my finger. "What's the full name of the scunner who shamed you?"

"Sebastian Zegers. Why do you ask?"

I grab a pen and jot down the name. "I want to make certain he can't hurt you again."

"Are you planning to exact vengeance on my behalf? That's adorable."

"Not vengeance." I click the pen to retract its tip. "I'd like to hire an investigator in America to check on this Sebastian man. Find out what he's been doing and determine whether he kept those photographs. If so, I will ensure they are destroyed. Permanently."

"Um, thanks. That's an amazing thing to do for your trophy wife."

I smack the pen down on the desktop. "Never call yourself a trophy again. You are my wife, full stop."

"And you are a truly awesome husband."

Though I grimace, I don't speak. Awesome? I've treated her like my chattel.

"My turn," she says. "What did Graham mean about your first wife having an iron constitution?"

Bloody hell. I cough and grimace again. "I'm not sure. Isobel wanted things I couldn't give her, left me because I was boring and—"

I flinch as I realize how much I've said. Too much.

"Is that why you keep telling me I'll get tired of you?" Emery asks.

All I can do is glare into the darkest corner of the room. "I met Isobel near the end of my traineeship, the final step in becoming a solicitor. I was twenty-five, she was twenty-three. We married six months later, and only after that did she start to complain about my work. She thought being a solicitor was dull and unglamorous, kept telling me I should at least become a corporate lawyer where I'd make more money. Isobel despised the fact I often worked pro bono for those who couldn't afford a solicitor's fees. When she walked out, she told me I would never find a woman who would tolerate the long hours I put into my work, the late-night calls from panicked clients, and what she called the 'pittance income' I earned."

"How long were you married to her?"

"Five years."

Neither of us speaks for a moment. She probably can't figure out what to say. Why had I told her about Isobel? She asked, and I...answered, without thinking.

"Thank you for telling me all of that," Emery says. "It couldn't have been easy to talk about."

"You are the first person I've told the whole truth."

"May I ask one more itty-bitty question? Not about your exes."

"Go on."

"What's the real reason you got irritated when I hugged Aidan?"

I slither off the desk and retreat behind it, dropping onto the chair. "It's ridiculous."

"I love ridiculous. You know that."

Ducking my head, I scratch my scalp. "You hugged everyone, even Gavin Douglas. You hugged Aidan twice. But you haven't hugged me today."

"Sure I have."

I shake my head slowly, feeling like a bloody eejit for confessing to her.

"I haven't?" When I shake my head again, she slides off the desk. "I can remedy that right this minute."

Before I realize her intent, she circles behind the desk and sits down on my lap. When she winds her arms around my neck, I stiffen. Then she rests her cheek on my shoulder.

"What are you doing?" I ask.

"I upgraded your hug to a cuddle."

"Hmm." I link my hands over the small of her back, having no idea why I do it. "Ye willnae do this with Aidan."

"Only you."

We sit here for several minutes, and Emery snuggles closer to me, her warm body molded to mine. Have I ever been given a cuddle before? No, never. It's oddly relaxing. But I can't let her crawl under my skin, the way she seems determined to do. I need to reassert the parameters.

At last, I clear my throat and try to sit up straighter, but her body hinders me.

"Something wrong?" she asks, without lifting her head from my shoulder.

"It's about the wedding." I clear my throat again. "We shouldn't have sex until after the ceremony."

Her head pops up, and she sets her hands on my chest. "You've got to be kidding."

"No."

"We're already married. Everyone assumes we're getting it on twenty-four seven."

"Out of respect for our mothers, we shouldn't have sex until after the wedding."

Laughter splutters out between her closed lips and through her nostrils, resulting in odd piglike noises. "Respect for our mothers? That's the lamest excuse in the history of lameness. You're trying to use our moms as a wedge to keep some distance between you and me. I get that you're feeling weird about confiding in me but—"

"Ahmno feeling weird." I sound petulant, don't I? *Mhac na galla.* "We should take a break to become accustomed to… well… until we're accustomed to living together."

She traces a finger along the seam of my lips. "You are full of it, Mr. MacTaggart, but I'll make a deal with you. Or rather, a little bet."

"What are the stakes?"

"If I win, you agree to participate in one activity of my choosing. No bitching, no growling, no eye-rolling. Agreed?"

"All right." I tighten my arms around her. "And if I win?"

"The same. I'll participate in one activity of your choosing."

I glide my hand down to her hip, probing the hollow with my fingertips. "What is the wager?"

"No sex, like you suggested." She sweeps a hand up my neck, toying with my earlobe. "I bet you we'll both be naked in my bed inside of four days."

"I can wait until the wedding day."

"Oh, sure." Her voice has grown huskier while she fingers my earlobe with her thumb. "There's no way you'll make it three weeks without at least one good fuck. You're way too passionate to go cold turkey."

I massage her hip with more vigor, pressing in deeply. Her wager excites me, and I cannae stop my lips from opening, ready to possess her mouth.

"Do we have a bet?" she asks.

"We do."

Her mouth hovers millimeters from my lips. "Three weeks, Rory."

I stand, picking her up with me, and spank her erse. "I have work. You'll need to entertain yourself."

"Oh, I'm really good at that." She tips her head back to expose her slender throat. "Maybe I'll entertain myself in my bedroom for a while."

With that, she flounces out of the room.

And aye, her tone made it clear she means to masturbate.

I want to run upstairs and fuck her like mad, but I need to prove to her I have the willpower to win our wager. The terms she suggested fit within my rules. Three weeks without sex. If Emery were any other woman, I'd feel confident in my ability to win.

But with my wicked little angel…

I might end up participating in a silly spectacle instead of proving my inner fortitude.

Chapter Nineteen

Emery stays upstairs, as far as I know, for the rest of the afternoon. Jamie has decided to stay with Aidan and Calli for a while to give me and my new wife "some alone time to settle in," which she said with a wink and a sly smile. My sister assumes I will shag my wife several times a day. I need to do that, but I won't forfeit our wager. When I've survived three weeks without ravishing her body, she will understand she can't use sex to get what she wants from me.

The woman thinks she can save me and "help" me. Emery will be disappointed. I'm beyond salvation.

My wife and I say goodbye to my sister, then we go our separate ways.

I grab a piece from the kitchen, eating it at the island, then return to my office and shut the door. For seven years, I've haunted this castle like a ghost searching for the doorway to heaven. I haven't found it. Why had I married Una? The lass had lived here with me for eight months before she walked out. No one can abide being married to me. So why had I seduced Emery into becoming my fourth wife? To appease my family, that's what I'd convinced myself was the reason. They kept throwing lasses in front of me, hoping one day I'd find another wife.

I did, but not for love. Not forever either. One year only.

What have I become? A bastard who uses a lovely, sweet woman. Emery will leave me, but whether she stays for the year or walks out sooner, she will never be mine.

Sinking into my desk chair, I yank out a drawer and retrieve a bottle of Ben Nevis and a glass. I never used to keep whisky in my desk, but lately, I've needed to have it on hand. For reasons I can't fathom, I pull out our marriage contract and the prenuptial agreement. As I lay the stack of papers on the desktop, I extricate the contract and lay it on top. Then I pour whisky into the glass, filling it up.

While I stare at the marriage contract, I drink. And drink. And drink.

Before long, I get drowsy. The blessed oblivion of whisky beckons me, and I lean back in my chair to rest my head against it. The world spirals away from me, drawing me into the sanctuary of sleep.

Something warm and soft touches my cheek, but I only half-rouse.

"Wakey-wakey," Emery says, and I feel her hand cradling my face. "Rory, wake up."

My lids flutter open, and I come to full wakefulness with a start. "Emery?"

"You got another blonde, American wife stashed in a closet?" She straightens from her half-crouch and pats my shoulder. "Get up. You are not sleeping in your office."

I push her hand away. "I'm fine here. Have work to—"

"Nope." She seizes my hands and leans back, compelling me to rise. "I decree you shall not spend the night in your office when you have a perfectly good bed upstairs."

Grumbling, I struggle to my feet. My mouth splits open on a wide yawn.

"Come on," Emery says, supporting me with an arm around mine as she encourages me to move toward the doorway. When I stagger a wee bit, she glances up at me. "How many glasses of whisky did you have?"

"One." Filled to the brim, but still only one glass.

She clucks her tongue. "Alcohol and jet lag aren't a good combo."

"Ahmno jet-lagged."

"Says the man who was found unconscious at his desk." As we exit the office, she straps her other arm around my torso. "It's beddy-bye time for Rory baby."

I grunt but keep walking, shuffling now instead of staggering. I did not get drunk, but I'm too jeeked to argue with my wife about it. She guides me through the great hall and up the stairs, passing the second floor.

At the third-floor landing, I halt before she can drag me through the doorway into the hall. Then I point toward a door at our left. "There."

"Where's that go?" She cranes her neck to see around me.

"My room. It has a private entry and exit. Lairds needed a way to escape their wives."

Emery stares at me, her lips tight, and I know she wants to complain about our sleeping arrangements. But she doesn't do it. The lass has tact, at least, even if she enjoys being outlandish.

She rotates us both toward the closed door and tries to turn the knob. "Locked? Is the main door to your room locked too? It wasn't the other day when you showed me around."

"It's locked now."

"Rory, Rory, Rory," she says on a long exhalation. "This extreme need for privacy from your own wife is going to change. Are you afraid I'll sneak in and steal your underwear?"

I excavate a set of keys from my pocket and select the right one. As I insert it into the door lock, I mumble, "This is how I live."

"No, honey, this is how you hide from life."

I stand frozen with the key in the lock, my fingers holding it there, and my gaze veers to my wife. For a moment, I can't move. My eyes start to burn because I'm not even blinking. She thinks I'm hiding from life. Perhaps I am, but I'm too old to change now. Too old, and too damaged.

Unlocking the door, I ease it inward just enough to accommodate my body. "Good night, Emery."

I shuffle into the bedroom, keeping the door mostly shut so my wife won't see inside the room. It's a bloody stupid impulse, but I can't help it. Privacy matters to me, and now that I've taken another wife, my options for solitude have dwindled to one. Emery invaded my office sanctum earlier. My bedroom is my last bastion.

"Good night, Rory." Emery hops up to kiss my cheek. "Sleep late for once. You need the rest."

Uttering a noncommittal noise, I shut the door.

The next morning, I rise at five o'clock as usual. Emery will be disappointed that I haven't heeded her advice and slept late. I don't do that. Not ever. Not even the slight hangover I'm experiencing can make me sleep past five. Today, I do have legitimate work to handle. That gives me an excuse to avoid my wife. I hide—ah, remain in my office until lunch, at which point I ring Mrs. Darroch on the house phone and ask her to bring me lunch.

Occasionally, I get up from my desk to stretch and look out the windows. Once, I see Emery walking into the garden. She seems to have decided to explore the castle compound, and I'm glad for that. At least it will distract the lass from her barmy mission to improve my life. Later, I observe Emery inspecting the garage, which used to be a carriage house back when this castle was a fortress. Now, I keep a Range Rover in the garage, though I park my Mercedes in the drive.

What does Emery think of my wealth? She'd been stunned when I told her I'm a multimillionaire, and now she lives in my castle and sees all the things I've bought. The Mercedes alone costs more than a computer programmer could hope to earn in a year. I don't want her to feel uncomfortable, but I can't change the fact I have money.

Maybe I'm the one who's uncomfortable. Cannae figure why.

I spend the rest of the afternoon working. The sun sinks below the horizon, and I keep poring over documents that I've already examined twice before. Anything to avoid my wife. I've become a bloody coward.

Someone knocks twice and pushes the door open.

My wife traipses across the room with her head held high, as if she is the lady of the castle. Her confidence and the way her hips sway make my cock twitch. Though I've lifted my gaze, I keep my head bowed as I observe her approach. "What are you doing?"

"You ask me that a lot." As she comes up alongside my chair, Emery drops into a deep curtsy and speaks with mock graveness. "Your presence is requested in the dining hall, my laird."

My cock jerks again, though I doubt she can see that. I slap my pen on the desktop and battle to restrain a smile. "I eat in here. Mrs. Darroch will bring—"

"Not tonight." Emery grasps the top of my chair and forces it to rotate toward her. "I'm tired of eating alone. We're having dinner together, in the dining room, like normal people."

With my head at the height of her tits, I can't resist admiring them. "I take my meals here."

She bends from the waist to level our gazes. "You take your dinners with me from here on. No arguments. Listen to your therapist, Rory baby."

"You called me that last night, but I assumed it was sarcastic."

"It was—then." She brackets my face with her hands. "I've decided this nickname's a keeper. Rory baby."

"As I've told you before, I don't need a nickname."

"Yes, you do." She straightens and holds her hands flat, palms up, bouncing them in the air. "Get up. To the dining hall with you."

Grudgingly, I heave myself out of the chair and skim my gaze over her body while the blood in my brain swiftly pours down into my groin. "Why are ye barefoot?"

"I don't wear shoes at home, inside the house."

"You have no socks."

"How observant. I like being as naked as possible at all times."

Though I give her a look that implies I think she's barmy, I give in because I know my wife will not relent. I do need to eat, anyway. So I let her lead me downstairs to the dining room and take a seat at the head of the table where Emery has laid out my meal. She settles her bonnie erse onto the adjacent seat where she's laid out her dinner. A bottle of red wine sits stationed between our plates, uncorked, waiting for one of us to decant it.

I pick up the bottle, pouring wine into her glass first, then mine. I set down the bottle. "I see you found the wine cellar."

"Yep. Hope you don't mind me stealing a bottle."

"It's not stealing. This is your home."

We both take sips from our glasses, though Emery swirls the wine and inhales a deep draft of its scent before she drinks.

"Mrs. D went home," Emery says, "to her cottage in the garden."

I assume she means Mrs. Darroch. My wife needs to give everyone a nickname, apparently.

"We've got full privacy, if you'd rather eat your meal off my naked body."

My fork tumbles from my grasp, clattering onto the plate. "*Bod an Donais.*"

"It's not the devil's penis I want to suck."

"You're a wicked angel, for sure."

She cants her head, studying me. "Which part of *bod an Donais* means penis?"

"*Bod.* Your pronunciation of Gaelic is impressive. You are impressive, Emery."

To stop myself from saying anything else she might misinterpret as being romantic, I start to eat my meal, applying my usual precision and care to the task. My wife still seems to find that amusing. Emery dives into her food with an enthusiasm that both disturbs me and makes me want to do what she suggested and eat my meal off her naked body. I marvel at the way she devours her T-bone steak and garlic mashed potatoes.

Most women won't even eat steak. Not in my presence, at least.

Christ, I need to fuck her. But I won't forfeit the bet.

Emery notices me watching her eat, and she swallows a mouthful of steak. "What? Do I have food on my face?"

"No." I sit back in my chair, still observing her with fascination. "Your enthusiasm for eating continues to amaze me. Isobel ate like a bird, and Lilias was a vegan. Una latched onto whatever diet was most popular at the time."

She sips her wine. "I've never dieted, unless you count not being able to eat hardly anything when I had the stomach flu. Never understood the appeal of depriving yourself in the hopes other people will like you better if you're thinner."

I raise my glass near my mouth while I roam my gaze over every luscious curve of her body. "You don't need to be thinner."

"Most guys I've dated would disagree. One jerk told me he didn't mind being with a chubby girl, and another one asked if I'd had a baby recently." She shoves a bite of steak into her mouth, speaking while chewing. "Men these days expect every woman to have a stick figure. With big boobs, of course."

Frowning, I set down my glass. "Those men are eejits. You're perfect. I love your body, love running my hands over every curve and swell."

"I've never thought I was fat. But thank you for that…compliment."

"You're welcome." My voice has grown rougher with a hunger that has nothing to do with food.

Emery sets down her glass and stretches one leg under the table, though I can still see it. Her bare foot nestles between my thighs. My breaths turn into blustering gasps while she slithers lower in her chair, determined to burrow her foot deeper between my thighs. My body tenses, and my cock swells.

"What are ye doing?" I ask.

"There you go again." She strokes my hardening erection with her toes. "Asking questions that have obvious answers. If you insist I explain…" She rubs the length of her foot along the length of my cock. "I'm trying to get you so hot you'll throw me down on this table and fuck me mindless."

I clap my hands on the chair's arms, gripping them hard. "This is your plan to win the wager."

"Partly." She pets me with her wee toes. "I want you all the time."

I want her all the time too. But I cuff my hand around her ankle and exert just enough pressure to force the lass to bend her knee and retract her foot from my *slat*. "May I finish my dinner without you…tempting me?"

"I may be shameless when it comes to winning our bet, but I promise." She moves her foot to the floor and sits up in her chair. "I won't tease you, but I can't guarantee you won't feel tempted. I can't be held responsible for your lustful tendencies."

"My lustful tendencies?" A smirk tightens my cheeks. "You are the most passionate woman I've ever known. Full of lust and vigor, unafraid of your desires."

"You're full of compliments tonight."

"Well-deserved ones."

If I'd meant to appease her with compliments, I succeeded. But I hadn't planned it. The words flowed out of me unbidden, though I meant every word. Emery lets me dine in peace, of a sort, while she asks questions about the castle grounds. The peace only lasts until we've finished our meal.

Emery thrusts her empty plate away. "Last night, when I found you sleeping at your desk, you had a document out. It looked like our marriage contract."

I feel my face contorting into a pained expression.

She turns her chair toward me. "Why were you looking at—"

"Preparing to file it in the proper folder."

"Filing. Sure." She swings one leg over the arm of her chair. "Do I look that gullible?"

I pick at the upholstery on my chair. "Donnae know why I brought out the contract."

She regards me in silence, probably trying to decide whether she believes me. I told her the truth. I have no ruddy idea why I was staring at the contract. The longer she stays silent, the more I fidget in my chair. But the way she has one leg draped over her chair's arm exposes her groin, shielded by her trousers, and I find myself snaking a hand down to adjust my erection, as if that will help.

Emery pushes her chair back and stands, one hip buttressed by the table. "You know, we could have sex—right here, right now—and you wouldn't lose the bet."

My brows inch upward. She must have an alternate definition of sex.

My wife slopes her sensual body over the table, leaning toward me, supported by one palm splayed on the smooth surface. "We're not naked in my bedroom."

I whisk my tongue back and forth along my bottom lip. Once. Twice. Three times. Imagining I'm licking up her cream. "You may be right about the bet. But we are not having sex until after the wedding."

Even if it kills me. I have an overpowering need to prove to my wife that I can survive three weeks without shagging her.

"Aw, Rory baby," she purrs, crawling across the table, "you look like you need a cuddle."

How am I meant to resist that? I let my body go slack, resigned to a cuddle. No sex, though.

Emery crawls onto my lap, straddling me. I lay my palms on the small of her back as she ropes her arms around my neck. My fingers are trembling. Because I want her, that's all. She molds her body to mine with her lips a hair's breadth away. "Better?"

"Depends on your definition of 'better.' "

She closes her eyes, pulling in a deep breath, and her lips curve into a contented smile. "You smell so good. I love being close to you."

I press my hands into her back because I love being close to her too.

Emery opens her eyes. With a breathy moan, she seals her mouth over mine and plunges her tongue inside. I clench my fingers in her shirt, crushing her to me while I surrender to her kiss and respond by curling my tongue around hers until she goes limp against me. Her breasts are mounded against my chest, and the heat of her arousal penetrates both our clothes, the scent of it wafting in the air. The chair creaks beneath us from every small movement while I spread my hands on her back, desperate to clasp her as close to me as possible.

But I shouldn't be kissing her like this. She'll get the wrong idea. It's not an expression of raw lust. This is something else, something I won't even try to figure out. She tears her lips away from mine and gazes into my eyes like she wants to plumb the depths of my soul. Her expression reveals a tenderness that makes my chest ache. Though she adjusts her position on my lap, rubbing her body against my cock, my erection has already flagged. Why? Because I'm tired, that's all. It has nothing to do with whatever I thought I might have felt a moment ago.

I yawn, though I try to stifle it.

"You need sleep," Emery says. "It's bedtime."

"Not yet."

I crush her body to mine, forging the kiss into one of possession and almost dominance, driven by my need to scour away any tender feelings she might have stirred in me. I can't allow myself to feel anything except lust. If I care for her, and she leaves me, I don't know if I'll survive that. I abandon myself to the kiss, to my carnal need for her, and use my lips and tongue to brand her as mine, even while I glide my tongue around hers with delicate strokes. She surrenders to me willingly, her body sagging against me. With a guttural groan, I give up her lips and drag my mouth down her throat, licking and nibbling at the hollow. I close my hand around her breast. Her head falls onto my shoulder, and her mouth grazes my skin.

"Oh," she murmurs. "Oh, Rory."

We both freeze. I'd told her days ago never to speak my name while we were being intimate, but...

"I'm sorry," she hastens to say, hiding her face from me. "I forgot the rule—"

"Say it again."

My wife stays motionless in my arms, though she lifts her gaze to mine, surprise evident in her eyes.

"Please," I say, my voice hushed but rife with emotions I refuse to examine, and I lash her tighter against my body with both arms. "Please say it again."

"Rory." She almost whispers my name, like a hushed prayer.

I bury my face against her neck and fist my hands in her shirt, then loosen them again, repeating the motion over and over while I brush delicate kisses over her skin. I shouldn't want her to say my name, not in a moment like this, but every time she speaks the word, warmth tingles over my skin.

Emery peels herself away from my body and places her hands on my shoulders. "You said I shouldn't speak your name when we're getting sexy together."

"Changed my mind."

"But why?"

My first impulse is to growl at her. But I promised her honesty, and for once, I want to speak the truth. With one fingertip, I chart the lines of the tendons in her hand. "When you say my name, I...like it."

She looks up at me through her lashes. "Does this mean the prohibition on me speaking your name during intimate moments is lifted?"

"Aye."

"Hallelujah." She plants a firm kiss on my lips. "It's super hard to make sure I don't accidentally say your name in the throes of passion."

I turn her hand over to trace the lines on her palm with my finger. "You were right, though. It is time for bed. In our separate rooms."

Her posture wilts, her expression too.

These are the rules, though. I push my chair back, set my wife on her feet, and stand up. "Good night, Emery."

I kiss her cheek and leave the dining room.

But all night, I toss and turn while remembering *that* moment, when our lips met and something changed. It doesn't matter what I might feel. I can't let her into my soul because, if I do, the disaster that's sure to follow will destroy us both.

Chapter Twenty

No, I did not sleep well. But I get up at my usual time anyway and start my daily routine while forbidding myself to think about my wife. Aye, that works—for two hours. That's how long it takes me to shower, dress, eat breakfast, and abscond to my office before *she* wakes so I can bury my nose in work. But at the close of the second hour, I realize I forgot to wear socks. This won't do. My lack of socks makes it seem like I'm so frazzled by my wife's kiss last night that I forgot how to dress myself. I return to the bedroom to put on socks, then walk out onto the landing.

I glimpse Emery at the bottom of the stairwell, just exiting the vestibule.

How am I meant to avoid thinking about her when she turns up everywhere I go? Well, it is her home too. I can't lock her in my dungeon since, as I've told everyone repeatedly, I do not have such a room.

Shortly after I return to my office, Mrs. Darroch barges into the room. "Emery asked me to tell you she'll be outdoors all morning exploring the grounds. The lass thinks you need a break from her, but that's tosh. What you need, dearie, is to be with your wife, not avoid her."

"Ahmno avoiding her. I have work to do."

"Be nice to her, Rory. She's a lovely lass." Mrs. Darroch turns to leave, but glances back at me. "The last one didn't suit you, *mo luran*, but Emery is good for you. Donnae cock it up."

She marches out the door, shutting it behind her.

Mrs. Darroch assumes I want my wife to love me, or that I love Emery, and she knows nothing about our arrangement. Perhaps I am cocking it up, but not the way Mrs. Darroch thinks. I cannot let Emery think she means something to me, and I absolutely cannot let myself slide down that slippery slope.

It's easy to be fond of Emery. She's…endearing. Therein lies the slippery slope. I won't fall down it. Never.

Mrs. Darroch won't call me *mo luran*—"my darling boy"—anymore if she learns why I married Emery.

Several times during the day, I gravitate to the windows in my office to gaze out at the grounds and the forest beyond the castle compound. I see Emery returning from a walk, coming up the trail that leads out to the river. She shouldn't walk out there alone. She shouldn't need to be alone at all. Emery is the sort who wants to be with people, not like me, the Ogre of Loch Fairbairn who prefers to hide in a castle that has become my personal prison.

Emery heads into the house.

I stand here for a few minutes, debating whether to find her and…say something. Cheer her up. But I have no bloody idea how to make her feel better, and I don't want to confuse things between us even more than I've already done. Still, I know her belongings arrived late yesterday, and she might need help unpacking. I can at least carry any heavy items for her. That isn't romantic. It's polite.

First, I ring Mrs. Darroch on the landline to make sure where Emery is. "Do you know where my wife might be?"

"Said she was going to her bedroom."

"Thank you."

Now that I've rationalized my need to see my wife, and confirmed her location, I make my way up to the third floor and Emery's bedroom. The door is open. I step onto the threshold, taking in the sight of the ten boxes she has arrayed on the floor around her. Emery is kneeling on the floor. But she must've heard my footsteps because she'd been looking at the doorway when I appeared.

"This is a nice surprise," she says. "What's up, honey?"

"Mrs. Darroch said you were in here. Thought I'd help you unpack."

"I'd like that." She pats the floor beside her. "Have a seat and dig in."

Approaching Emery, I squat beside her and flip open the flaps of a cardboard box. One by one, I extract items of her clothing. Cardigans. Blouses. Skirts. Jeans. Her clothing got rumpled by the trip to Scotland, but it doesn't matter what she wears. Emery always looks beautiful, even in nothing but a terry-cloth robe. I sit back on my haunches and contemplate each item before carefully folding it and placing it in a stack of similar items. That way blouses don't wind up in a pile with jeans. It makes sense to me. Emery probably thinks it's more evidence that I'm uptight.

Peripherally, I watch her sort books and knickknacks, keeping some and dumping others back in the box once she's emptied it.

I pick up a crumpled blouse and fold it, settling it onto the appropriate stack. Then I notice *it*. The bizarre object looks like nothing I've seen before. Maybe I have an inkling of what it might be, based on its shape. Though I feel like I shouldn't touch the object, I need to remove it from the box. So I lay the item on my palm.

I clear my throat with deliberate emphasis.

Emery tosses a speckled, polished rock back into a box and glances my way.

Aye, I'm still staring down at the item poised on my palm. The long, cylindrical item with a rounded tip and a battery compartment on the opposite end. I tip my head from side to side while I mull the pink object. "What is this?"

"My vibrator."

I snatch my hand away, and the device plummets to the floor.

"Don't break it," she says, grabbing the vibrator. "Haven't you ever seen one before?"

"No." Maybe I'd seen one in a magazine once, but that model had a far more complicated design. And I won't admit to Emery I looked at a magazine that has ads for that sort of device.

She waves the vibrator in my face.

My eyes track the object's movements.

"It won't bite," she says. Then she drapes an arm around my neck. "Can't promise I won't, though."

"Yes, I'm aware of that." I touch my shoulder where she'd bitten me on our wedding night. "You are a she-wolf."

"Salvaged our wedding night, didn't I?"

"You did."

She tosses the vibrator onto the bed.

I wish she would put it in a box where I can't see it.

"Got a question," she says. "Can you recommend a local doctor? I have a prescription that'll need refilling soon."

I drop the scarf I'd been folding. "Prescription? Are you ill?"

"No, I'm on the pill."

"What pill?"

"Birth control, Rory."

I tug at the collar of my shirt. "I see. I'll arrange an appoint—"

"Uh-uh. I can do it myself."

Annoyance flashes through me, but I square my shoulders and shake it off. "I will give you the number for my GP, Dr. Buchanan. He's in Loch Fairbairn."

Emery kisses my cheek. "Thanks. You're the sweetest."

I roll my eyes.

She turns to another box, bringing out a small photo album that has a plain grey cover. Her lips tick up at the corners as she flips through the pages.

"Catch," she says, hurling the photo album at me, and I catch it in one hand. "Think of that as your menu for excitement."

Menu? Cautiously, I thumb through the four-by-six-inch pages. Each holds a photo of Emery in a different costume. Greek goddess. Wonder Woman, I think. And this one looks like Princess Leia from one of those *Star Wars* films, the scantily clad version of her. I know about those movies only because Jamie made me watch all fifty of them. Well, it might've been slightly less than fifty. I'm not a science fiction addict.

One picture intrigues me, and I pause to inspect it.

"Like that one?" Emery asks, leaning over to peek at it. "That's my ancient Egyptian dancer costume."

"Are you naked?" I ask, humiliated by how excited I sound. I've seen my wife's nude body before. But this photograph...

"Not naked. I'm wearing a flesh-colored bodysuit." She swirls a fingertip over the image. "For you, I'd nix the bodysuit. You'd get me wearing nothing but a skinny belt and a long black wig."

In the picture, a braided wig drapes down to shield her breasts, while the end of each braid seems to be weighted with beads. She also wears a white headband and sandals.

"You wore this in public?" I ask, gawping at her.

"Uh-huh. It was an office Halloween party held at a nightclub, organized by me and my work buddies. The two you met, Pam and Sabri."

"Men saw you dressed this way?"

"You betcha." She trails her finger up my thigh. "For you, I'll even put on a belly-dance show."

I absently pet the photo album with one finger. "You know how to belly dance?"

"Sure do, baby." She shuts the album and closes my fingers around it. "Look at the pictures. Take your time. Let me know which costume you like the best, and I'll make your fantasy come true."

I study the album for a moment, then tuck it in my pocket.

We resume sorting through her boxes. My eyes decide to keep glancing at the pink vibrator, but we unpack the remainder of her belongings without any additional surprises. Emery stays in her room to organize the closet or some such bollocks, while I rush downstairs to my office and peruse the photo album.

That costume. The bodysuit. The dark Egyptian eyeliner that makes her eyes look even more entrancing.

But my wife isn't done shocking me. I get another surprise when I walk into our shared bathroom that night. Emery has decorated the space with womanly rubbish. A pink towel. A furry pink bath rug. Packages of…maxi pads with wings, the package tells me, along with pink disposable razors.

Bod an Donais.

This is my punishment for telling Emery it's her house too.

Of course, I sneaked into her room after she went downstairs and left a surprise of my own for her. When she opens the drawer on the nightstand, she'll find a box of condoms with a note on them: "For later." Aye, I need to shag my wife—but not until I've won our wager.

Though Emery had declared we would dine together every evening, she doesn't hunt me down to enforce that law, not tonight, or the one after that. Mrs. Darroch reminds me that Emery will be eating in the dining room, but I have a feeling my wife encouraged her to do that. On the third day, I'm sitting in my office shortly after lunch, intending to focus on work but thinking about my wife instead. I fling open a drawer and pull out Emery's photo album, flipping to the ancient Egyptian costume.

Then I dump the album back into the drawer and slam it shut.

If I keep looking at the blasted thing, I'll voluntarily forfeit our wager.

The door swings open, and my wife sashays onto the threshold, wearing only minuscule denim shorts. They look like the same ones she wore the day after our first night together in New Orleans. She leans against the doorjamb with one foot braced on it and her arms loosely at her sides. The powder-blue halter top she wears shows off a lot of skin, and the lush waves of her hair kiss her shoulders.

I try to act as if I've been browsing the files laid out on my desk. Then I look up at her. "No shoes again, I see."

"Told you, I don't wear them in the house." She aims a pointed glance at the leather loafers on my feet, which I'm sure she can see under the desk. "How can you be comfortable in those shoes? I mean, aren't you itching to kick them off?"

"I dress for work."

"You work at home. Locked up in this office. Nobody will see if you ditch the loafers."

I recline in my chair, holding a pen between my thumb and forefinger with its tip planted on the desktop. "Did you pop in to chastise me for my choice of wardrobe?"

"No, I'm here to tempt you."

"Are you." I tap the pen on the desktop while my mind flashes back to the photo album. "You mentioned you're shameless when it comes to winning our wager, but I don't have time to play with you. I have work."

"You always have work." She slides her foot higher up the doorjamb, bending her knee more deeply, and strokes her hand along her exposed thigh. "Do you dream about files and cases and clients? Or do you dream about me?"

I stop tapping my pen. My gaze is nailed to her thigh, and her palm resting on it.

With one hand positioned at the hem of her shorts, she trails the fingertips of the other hand along the neckline of her shirt, skimming it down the inner slope of one breast. "That's a nice, big desk. Have you ever fantasized about stripping me naked, laying me over that smooth wood, and having your way with me right here in your office?"

Of course I have. Repeatedly.

I grit my teeth, clenching my hand around the pen tightly enough to make my fingers ache. My attention gravitates to her breasts where her fingers tease her own flesh.

Emery pushes away from the jamb, padding toward me with her hips swaying. "You have. I can tell from the way you're devouring me with your gaze."

My hand pops open, and the pen drops to the floor. I grip my thighs, my breaths shortening as my *slat* thickens inside my trousers, straining the fabric and my self-control.

She perches her erse on the desk right in front of me. "Would you like me to sit on your lap the way I did the other night? This time, I'll take your cock in my hand and stroke you while I whisper your name."

"Bloody hell." I grind the words out between my teeth.

Emery falls to her knees between my legs, her body cradled by my thighs. "You can have me anytime you want, anywhere you want, any way you want."

I shut my eyes, swallow hard, and struggle to control my erratic breathing. Only then can I look at her. "Not in the daytime, and not outside the bedroom."

"Okay, baby, whatever you want." She uncoils her body inch by inch, granting me a close-up view of her cleavage and her naked legs. With my face too close to her groin, she tousles my hair. "If you change your mind, let me know."

My wicked angel skates her fingers down my cheek, over my chin, across my lips.

I stop breathing, my attention fixated on the fly of her shorts. Christ, I want to tear the zipper open with my teeth.

Emery walks away, her hips undulating. Outside the doorway, with her hand on the knob, she pauses. "Oh, I forgot to tell you—because I haven't seen you since yesterday morning. Got a doctor's appointment tomorrow. I'm having lunch with Erica and Calli after."

I rip a Post-it note from a dispenser, but I can't remember what I meant to write on it. "Tomorrow. Fine."

"Have a good afternoon."

I mumble, producing no words.

My wife shuts the door behind her.

Chapter Twenty-One

espite the way Emery tormented me yesterday with that body, I enjoyed a better night's sleep. Maybe the finger of whisky I drank before bed helped. I've never been a solitary drinker, and I do not get intoxicated—not until I met Emery. Lately, I find myself sneaking a wee dram in my office or the sitting room, whenever my wife isn't around. It relaxes me.

If I shagged my wife, that would relax me even more. But I need to win our bet, for reasons I don't understand. I probably want to win because it will prove to Emery that I can live without her body. It's not as if I can't sleep or breathe or do anything unless I've fucked her. She has no such power over me.

Once, when I'm coming back from the kitchen after having a piece, as I'm walking down the first-floor hallway toward my office, movement outside the windows catches my attention. I approach the glass, leaning forward slightly to see what's out there. It's my wife. She's on the front lawn, spinning round and round with her arms outstretched. After a moment, she halts and drops her arms to her sides, then tips her head back as if she's communing with the sky.

What on earth? Spinning? Why would she do that?

Emery trots back into the house.

And I give up trying to understand her.

My wife refrains from harassing me all morning. I know she's going into the village for her doctor's appointment and to have lunch with Erica and Calli. The fact that I walk over to the windows in my office at precisely the time when I know Emery will be leaving is a coincidence. The occasional break from staring at legal documents keeps my mind fresh. I'd done that before I ever met her. The fact that I stand at the window until she has climbed into the Mercedes and the car is rolling down the drive, then I return to my desk, means nothing.

Aidan rings me after lunch.

"What do you want?" I say instead of hello.

"The ogre is alive and well," my cheeky brother says. "So, sweetie-pie, have ye heard what our wives are calling themselves?"

I stifle a groan because my wife must have told his wife about that ridiculous pet name. "I have no idea what you're on about."

"Calli told me all about it when she got home from her lunch with the other lasses." Aidan pauses, most likely because he's about to tell me something I won't like. "They've started a group. Emery named it the American Wives Club. Clever, eh?"

"A group? To do what?"

He chuckles. "They're women. What do you think they want to do? Meddle in everyone's lives, of course. Erica and Calli started the ball rolling months ago with you. Now your wife is taking the lead. Best get used to it, sweetie-pie."

Oh, bloody sodding hell. Emery honestly is trying to drive me barking mad.

"I have work," I tell Aidan, then I hang up without saying goodbye.

The American Wives Club? Those crackbrained women.

Seventeen minutes later—which I know because my computer has a clock in the corner of its screen, not because I'm counting the minutes—I start to wonder what has become of my wife. If Calli arrived home a little while ago, then Emery should arrive any second. I fight the impulse for as long as I can, which is a dismayingly short time. Finally, I can't stand the suspense anymore. I march to the office door, intent on...going into the hall so I can stare out different windows to watch for my wife to come back.

That realization stops me for a moment. Then I shake off the ridiculous notion and swing the door open, stepping out into the hall.

I stop dead when I see Emery walking this way.

She trots up to me. "Hi, honey. I'm home."

Pursing my lips, I glance around and scratch my arm, which I'm fair certain makes me look like a numpty who's been desperately hunting for his wife.

"Everything okay?" she asks, peeking around my shoulder. "Were you getting your rocks off in there?"

"What?" I gape at her like a ruddy cartoon character, jerking my head back. "Why would you ask such a thing?"

"Because you look guilty."

Not guilt. Not desperation either. Donnae know what this is, but I don't like it. Shuffling my feet without moving an inch, I glance toward the hall windows. "I, ah, wanted to...watch out the windows for you."

What a dead stupid confession.

"Waiting for me to come home?" Her lips curl into a soft smile. "Aw, that's so—"

"Do not say sweet or cute."

"Endearing. How's that?"

"Acceptable, I suppose." Turning sideways to the door, I gesture toward the nearest chair inside the office. "Come in."

Emery follows me inside and drops onto the chair I'd indicated. Her chair. That's how I've come to think of it, since she often throws her body into that seat when she invades my sanctum.

I set my erse on the desk's edge in front of her, my hands loosely linked over my lap. "Your visa has been approved."

"Wow, that was fast."

"I have a friend at the Home Office. He had your application expedited." My lips twitch into a near smile, but not because of Emery. It's a reflex or…some such rot. "Stephen Beckham is an old friend from university, and he was extremely grateful for my help in sorting his father's estate after the old man passed away. His father had been senile and married an exotic dancer, then tried to amend his will."

"Makes me look like a sane choice, huh?" Emery rocks back in her chair, the front legs lifting off the floor a touch. "Thought you couldn't talk about your clients."

"The details appeared in newspapers. It was quite the scandal at the time."

"Were you mentioned in the stories?"

I lift one shoulder. "A few times, but no one cared about the solicitor. Thanks to his venture capital business, the old man had been a celebrity of sorts even before Graham Oliver defamed him."

"Graham? You mean the *bod ceann*?"

"Very good. Maybe I'll teach you naughty Gaelic later."

"Sounds like fun." She eyes me with curiosity. "What did Graham do to your friend?"

"He published a story about Stephen's father. Though there was a kernel of truth to it, Graham perverted the facts into a sordid tale worthy of a Roman emperor. A London tabloid latched onto the story."

Emery nudges my leg with her foot, which is covered by what my wife calls a sneaker. "Never told me you're a famous solicitor."

I close a hand over the desk's edge. "I am not famous. No one would remember my name, it was years ago. The case did…elevate my financial standing, however."

She sits forward, both hands on the chair's arms. "Are you saying you made a lot of money off this Stephen guy's case? Is that how you got so rich?"

"In part." I fiddle with the cuff of my sleeve. "Stephen was very grateful, as I said, and generous with more than his money. He recommended me to a few others in need of legal assistance, people who could afford to pay a high price for it and were more than willing to do so. Lachlan advised me on how to invest and grow my earnings."

"At least that's one mystery solved." She leans back, crossing her shapely legs. "Damn, your first wife must really hate herself for dumping you. If she'd stuck around a little longer, she could've had the rich husband she wanted."

I reach behind me to retrieve a sheet of paper, then offer it to her. "Information concerning our bank accounts. You can access them online with my sign-in credentials, but you'll need to visit the bank with me to become a signatory. We can take care of that whenever it's convenient for you."

"No rush." She takes the paper. "Thanks. The way you're so on top of things makes me want you on top of me."

"After the wedding, Emery."

"Whatever you say, Rory baby."

I extricate a set of keys from my pocket and toss them to her. "For the house doors, interior and exterior. We rarely lock the doors, no need to. You also have your own keys for the vehicles and the carriage house where they're kept, so you won't need to borrow mine again."

"Cool." She tucks the keys into her hip pocket. Then my wife stands and stretches, extending her arms above her head far enough that her shirt rides up, attracting my attention to her belly. "I hope you won't be a grump about the wedding when my family's here."

"I am not a grump."

"You are, but I think it's cute." She eases her body between my legs, resting her hands on my thighs. "You could at least try to think of our wedding as a cause for celebration. Do it for me."

Without thinking about it, I settle my hands on her hips. "I'll try. For you."

"Aw, you're such a sweetheart."

"Emery," I all but moan.

She raises her hands, palms out. "Sorry, sorry. Can't help it, though. You are adorable, not a demon at all."

"Who says I'm a demon?"

"It was discussed over lunch." She gets that familiar teasing look on her face. "Erica said you must be a demon holding me hostage in your dungeon to do naughty rituals with me, and that's why I hadn't left the house since coming to Scotland. Then Calli wondered if you might have a forked penis. After that, we got distracted when Erica started grilling me about what it's like sleeping with an uptight solicitor."

"Forked penis?" I contemplate that statement for a moment but decide I'll never understand women. What else did they discuss? My hands tense on her hips. "Did you tell Erica and Calli about—about our arrangement?"

"I wouldn't do that. It's private."

Relief slackens my fingers, and I tug her closer. "How did you answer Erica's question?"

"About our sex life?" Emery wriggles even closer, the proximity of her body stirring my cock. "I told her you are a demon, but only in the bedroom. We have mind-blowing, earth-shattering, screaming-hot sex and you do me so hard all night long I can't walk or speak for two days after."

"What?"

"Chill, Rory." She presses her body into mine, moving her hand up my thigh and across my hip to cup my erection. "I didn't tell the girls anything private. But I did tell them you're awesome in the sack."

My mouth slides into a smirk, and I let my hands drift up to her waist. "I'm awesome, am I?"

"Absolutely."

Maybe I shouldn't care if Emery thinks I'm awesome at sex, but I can't help liking the fact that she does.

"I spoke to Aidan earlier," I say. "He called me 'sweetie-pie.' Twice."

Emery winces, and her lips peel back from her teeth. "Whoops. Erica said Lachlan told her you can be a grump sometimes. I told her maybe, but you're also a real sweetie-pie." She bites her lip. "Calli must've told Aidan what I said."

"Heaven save us from blethering wives. I warned you if Aidan heard your silly names for me, he'd be calling me 'sweetie-pie' for the rest of eternity."

"I'll make it up to you, promise." She slithers down my body until her face hovers in front of my swollen cock. "If you'll let me."

My chest swells as I suck in a deep breath.

With her hands on my thighs, she grasps my zipper with her teeth.

The breath explodes out of me.

Emery pulls the zipper down millimeter by millimeter with her gaze locked on mine.

I grasp the back of her head, halting her progress. "No, Emery."

"Why not? Because it's daytime?"

"Because… Just donnae." If I let her do this, I'll lose control. That's one thing I cannot ever do again with her. Keeping my wits in order is the only safe choice.

She hoists her body up, using her hands on my thighs as leverage. "Okay, your loss."

I rise and slap her erse. "Off with you. I have work."

As Emery heads for the door, she waves her fingers at me. "That excuse won't work forever, you know."

No, it won't. But I will never relinquish control to my wife. If I let her unravel me, I'll never get the strings tied together again.

Control. That's what I need. Isn't it?

Chapter Twenty-Two

For the remainder of the day, I struggle not to think about the moment when Emery knelt before me, ready to take my cock into her mouth. Control—of my work, my life, and my passions—has been the impetus for everything I've done for longer than I can remember. Then I'd seduced an American and convinced her to marry me for money. Was I in control of the situation then? Donnae know anymore.

Perhaps I've been unraveling since that first night in New Orleans.

And I've fought it with every iota of self-control I have left.

Though I know Emery wants me to dine with her every evening, I've resisted that too. Tonight is no different. I steal some food from the kitchen, while Mrs. Darroch is elsewhere in the castle, and eat at my desk.

Have you ever fantasized about stripping me naked, laying me over that smooth wood, and having your way with me right here in your office?

Ever since Emery spoke those words the other day, I've hungered to do just that. Sex on my desk? No, that wouldn't be proper. A bed is the only place I will ever shag my wife. But the memory of her sultry voice, the way she'd looked at me when suggested it... I yank open a desk drawer and snatch up the bottle of Ben Nevis, removing the cap. Just as I'm about to pour the whisky down my throat straight from the bottle, I freeze. Even the best single malt can't compare to the intoxicating pleasure of taking my wife's body.

I return the bottle to the drawer and kick it shut. Then I race upstairs.

There in the hallway, I strip off my clothes, letting them fall where they may, not giving a toss about the mess I'm making. When I reach the door to Emery's bedroom, I hesitate. Better wait until my breathing normalizes and my pulse slows down. I'm not excited because I'm about to shag my wife. I'm out of breath from running up the stairs from my office.

Once I've calmed myself, I knock on the door twice.

I should wait for her to open the door, but I find myself grasping the knob, twisting it, and pushing the door inward.

Emery stands beside the bed wearing only a satin dressing gown that stops halfway down her thighs. It's pink, naturally. The bed covers have been thrown back. Her mouth hangs open, surprise lighting up her face as her mouth tightens into a sexy smile.

She glances at my cock that's waving in front of my body.

I shut the door on my way to her, halting near the foot of the bed. "You win."

"Just like that? I mean, you could wait a couple more hours and it'll be day five. You'll have won the bet."

"Donnae care about winning." The sight of her naked legs transfixes me, and my cock jerks. Donnae care that my face has cinched up with a need I cannae deny anymore. "I need to fuck ye, *m'eudail*. Now."

"Oh God, I want you too, baby. So much."

I move closer, my hands rising of their own volition to rub her upper arms. "The wager was we'd be naked in your room in four days. Cannae wait another day to feel the heat of your soft, slick body around my cock."

She sags into me, angling her head up as if she's begging me to possess her mouth.

I skim my hands up to her shoulders and down along the neckline of her dressing gown until my fingertips tease her breasts. With one hand, I free the belt around her waist, and the gown falls open, revealing her flat belly and the tits I've needed to devour more than food. I push the satin off her shoulders, letting it flutter to the floor.

"*M'eudail*," I whisper while I drag my fingers over her breasts, down to her belly, "you are the most beautiful thing I've ever laid eyes on. Or laid my hands on."

She spreads her palms on my chest. "I want to touch you the way you've touched me, the other times we were together. I want to feel every inch of you."

"This is what you want for the bet?"

"No. This is extra, and you can say no."

Grasping her upper arms, I pull her body into mine. "Have your way with me, *m'eala-fhiadhaich*. Donnae let me fetter your wings."

"My wings?" She hops up on her toes, twining her arms around my neck. "What was that you called me? It sounded lovely."

"*M'eala-fhiadhaich*. It means my wild swan." And I called her my darling a moment ago, but I won't think about why. I massage her flesh with my fingers, keeping my touch gentle. "You are a free and untamed lass, and as elegant and beautiful as any swan."

She moves back half a step, roving her gaze over me from head to toe. The golden light from the bedside lamp lends her skin a heavenly glow, as if she is a genuine angel—the sort with a wicked streak. She lays her palms on my belly and glides them up, her skin grazing all the fine hairs, awakening every nerve until I feel like I'm electrified from the inside out. My lids slide almost shut, and I gaze at her through the barest of slits, relishing the lustful yet soft expression on her face. She explores me as if she means to memorize every contour of my body, her hands traveling up my chest, across my shoulders, down my arms until she reaches my hips. Then she lays her wee palms on my erse, seeming surprised that she can't span my cheeks with her hands. Her body is flush with mine as she runs her palms up my back.

The scent of her desire fills the air, and I cannae resist inhaling deeply to savor it.

I exhale a jagged breath, and my voice comes out rough. "Ye plan on killing me, then, lass?"

"You won't die from lust."

"Maybe not." I shudder with a sharp intake of breath. "But I might *caith* before you're done."

As my cock throbs against her belly, her confusion melts into understanding. "Do you mean ejac—"

"Yes," I hiss. If she speaks the word ejaculate, I will *caith* right this second.

"I can help with that."

She drops to her knees at my feet, her face positioned before my *slat*. As she regards my cock, the bead of moisture poised on its head seems to capture her attention, and she licks her lips. Then my wife leans in, opening her mouth.

I stop her with two fingers on her lips. "Don't. Please."

All I want is for her to take me into her mouth, but I'm not ready for that. Maybe I never will be. Coming here tonight, all but begging her to let me fuck her… That's the biggest loss of control I've ever experienced. While Emery gazes up my body at me, the look on her face suggests she realizes I've made all the concessions I can tonight.

She rises and lays her hands on my chest again.

I sweep her into my arms and settle her onto the mattress. Then I climb onto the bed, hovering over her with my knees on either side of her thighs. With her beautiful body stretched out beneath me, I ease one knee between her legs, urging her to part them. She complies without a second's hesitation, spreading her thighs for me as she raises both arms over her head with her hands just above the pillow. I skate my palms up her belly, molding my fingers around each breast while I push my thumbs under them, rubbing in slow and delicate circles.

Her body arches into my touch, the delicate curve of her spine lifting those breasts.

I sweep my thumbs up to toy with her taut nipples, and her neck arches this time, forcing her head deeper into the pillow. I'm breathing harder now, and my pulse pounds in my ears. Though I know it's ridiculous, I don't care because this feels too good to stop. I smother her nipple with my mouth, saturating her skin until it glistens. The areola pebbles and darkens to a dusky shade of pink.

The breath catches in her throat.

With my gaze glued to her, I slide my tongue around her stiff peak, coiling it round and round her flesh with deliberate slowness, needing to arouse her as deeply as she always arouses me. Emery clenches her hands around the rails of the headboard, her back arching even more, and a whisper of a moan escapes her lips. My need to devour her grows too intense to hold back anymore. I lick and suckle and rasp my tongue over her nipples while I flick my thumbs over the tips, again and again, my breaths almost as hectic as hers while she writhes beneath me. My erection grazes her belly when she bucks her hips.

Her eyelids flutter half-closed.

Then her lids spring open, wide and unblinking.

I can't think about why she looks that way, not when I've got her on the verge of orgasm, so I keep tormenting her flesh until that stunned expression fades and her eyes gradually slide almost closed.

Then they pop open again. She grips the headboard tighter and lets out a frustrated whimper.

I lift my head, stilling my thumbs. "What's wrong?"

"I—" Her eyes shimmer with nascent tears, and her lips tremble a touch. "I'm trying not to close my eyes, but I don't think I can stop it. I'm sorry, I know I promised, I'm sorry."

Christ, what a bastard I am. Bracing my body with one arm, I lay a hand on her cheek. "I'm the one who should apologize. Please forgive me, *m'eudail*. I never meant to cause you pain."

She takes a few breaths, seeming to calm her anxiety. "It's okay. You didn't do it on purpose."

I smooth my hand over her hair. "Forget what I said. Close your eyes if you need to."

"Are you sure?"

"Aye. That rule is rescinded."

She gazes at me with an expression I can't describe, something like wonder and sadness intertwined, but the look vanishes before I can even try to understand it, her playfulness returning. "Kiss me, Rory."

I stretch my lips into a closed-mouth smile, feeling a bit mischievous. "I will."

Then I kiss her nose and crawl backward down her body until my face hovers over her hips.

She raises her head. "You didn't kiss me."

"Ahm about to. Feel free to close yer eyes and scream mah name." With two fingers, I separate her folds and revel in the scent of her lust. "Mah lass loves pink. So do I, when it's the rosy color of yer succulent, slippery skin."

I glide my tongue straight down the center of her cleft, dipping it inside her opening only to snatch it away.

"Don't stop," she pleads. "Kiss me the way you did on our wedding night."

One side of my mouth kicks up as I place a soft kiss on her clit. "Mah woman needs to come, and ahmno letting ye down."

She lashes her hands around the headboard rails again, her chest heaving with every breath and dappled with rosy pink.

I draw her clit into my mouth but keep my gaze riveted to hers even while I maintain a measured pace of lapping and suckling, groaning softly because the flavor of her makes me starved for more, for all of her, wrapped around me while I take her body. My cheeks cave in as I suckle her flesh vigorously, and my lips pucker around her nub while I rasp my tongue over it. She writhes like a wild thing, her hips bucking every time I pull on her flesh, only to bounce down onto the mattress when I release the pressure—though only for a heartbeat.

She thrashes her head and whimpers, but it's not anguish this time. She loves what I'm doing to her.

I wedge a hand between her thighs, questing with my fingertips until I find her entrance.

"Rory," she gasps.

That simple word, spilling from her lips, ignites a bonfire inside me. I dive a single finger inside her and whisk it back out, only to punch in again and retreat. Then I add a second finger, pushing both inside her slick channel and pulling them out in a leisurely thrusting motion.

"P-please," she begs between harsh breaths. "Please, oh God, make me come."

My brows inch upward, and my lips tighten as I smile with her clit still caught in my mouth. Even while my cock pulses, its need for her as intense as mine, I don't let up for even half a second, determined to suckle her flesh until she comes for me. I crook my fingers inside her, stretching them toward a spot I've read can push a woman over the edge, and I stroke it while I nip at her clit and chafe my thumb along the center of her cleft.

Her back flattens into the mattress as she hoists her hips. She clings to the rails, her mouth falling open.

And she comes for me, screaming my name.

The climax rips through her in pulsating waves that grip my fingers, but I keep rubbing that spot inside her. Sharp cries erupt from her while she flails and shouts and screams my name again. When her release finally wanes, she goes limp beneath me, her gaze unfocused, struggling to regain her breath.

I've never seen anything as beautiful as Emery when she comes. To have her eyes on me the entire time... It affected me in ways I don't want to examine right now.

Rising onto my hands and knees, I crawl forward until my face is above hers. "Ye didnae close yer eyes."

"Couldn't. You were—" She gulps in a breath. "Didn't want to stop looking at you."

I fan a hand over her belly. "I love the way yer always wet and ready for me."

She lifts her trembling arms to clasp my nape. "You make me hot and wet without even touching me, just the look in your eyes does me in."

I nuzzle her throat. "You make me hard as granite with only a smile."

"Really." She frees one hand to wrap it around my cock. "Oh. You weren't exaggerating."

"Complete honesty, that's what you wanted."

She moves her hand up to the base of my erection, then slides it down my length. "Honesty can be so hot."

I throw an arm out, fumbling for the drawer on the nightstand. When I locate the metal latch, I yank the drawer open. My breaths huff out of me while I grab for a condom packet, and it slips from my grasp. With a spluttered curse in Gaelic, I snag the packet and slam the drawer shut.

"Let me help," Emery says, reaching for the foil packet.

I close my fist around it and growl, "I'll die from lust if ye lay even one of yer wee, dainty fingers on me."

"Told you before, no one dies from lust."

"With you, a man could." I tear the packet open with my teeth and spit out the fragment. "Ye turn me into a bampot, with yer smiles and the way ye move that body."

"What's a bampot?"

"Me."

I rise to my knees, rolling the condom over myself with more calmness than seems possible. Only Emery turns me into a lunatic, so desperate to have her that I cannae think. When I fall to my hands and knees again, she frisks her palms over my chest, the light caress making me suck in a breath.

"Oh, Rory baby," she drawls, her voice turning husky, "I want you, all of you. On top of me, inside me, any way you want me."

"Emery, *mo leannan*, I want ye every minute of every day."

I let out a long, deep groan that embodies all my hunger for her in a way I could never express with words. Then I lunge my hips to plow my length deep into her hot, silky flesh. I pause there, my arms shaking from the effort of holding still, but I need to revel in this feeling for a moment longer.

Emery shackles her hands around my biceps.

A need I can't deny compels to me speak. "Say that again."

"What?"

"Call me—" My lips quiver. "Call me Rory baby again. Keep saying it. Please."

She squeezes my arms. "Rory baby."

I pull out and plunge deep inside her, taking it slow and easy, withdrawing and thrusting over and over, every stroke stealing my breath away as her heat surrounds my cock. Her body hugs my length while I drive in and out, trying so hard to keep the pace measured that sweat beads on my skin and dribbles down my temples.

She moans my name, gasps my name, shouts my name, every cry of "Rory baby" intensifying the sweet tension that's building inside me. Her body tenses, and I know she'll come again any second. With an anguished groan, I bend to cover her mouth with mine, swallowing her cry as her climax strikes and she clings to me through every undulating spasm. That's when it happens. The last thread of my control snaps, and I give in to the unbridled pleasure of making love to my wife, pumping my hips so forcefully that her breasts bounce every time I pound her body into the mattress. Fire sears down my spine, electrifying every nerve in my body and shooting down my cock, triggering a storm of spasms. I throw my head back and roar, unleashing everything inside her with two more powerful thrusts.

I collapse on top of Emery, my head landing on the pillow beside hers, my face buried in her hair.

She cradles me in her arms, seeming not to care that my weight is on top of her and my *slat* is still nestled inside her body.

A sigh of pure contentment rushes out of me. "My Emery, you are irreplaceable."

I roll off her body. Maybe she didn't notice what I just said. Hadn't meant to say it, but the words tumbled out of me. It means nothing.

Emery flips onto her side and burrows against me, and I curl an arm around her. She pushes herself up with one elbow. "Why did you not want me to close my eyes?"

Though I keep my arm around her, I scrub my face with my free hand. "Does it matter? I rescinded the rule."

"I think it does matter, Rory. To you, for sure. And what matters to you affects me."

But it shouldn't. I've let this happen, this closeness between us, and now I've inadvertently drawn her into my mental prison. Now I have to tell her the truth.

I cover my eyes with one hand. "My third wife, Una. Whenever we were…intimate, and I would, ah…" I feel every muscle in my face cinching up tight. "When I gave her oral sex, she would keep her eyes shut the entire time. I assumed it was a sign she enjoyed it. Only when she left me did she confess the truth."

Emery watches me with a neutral expression.

I need a moment to convince myself to go on. "I had noticed she rarely achieved orgasm during intercourse, but she always came when I used my mouth on her." I squirm but keep my arm around Emery, though I stare up at the ceiling. "On the day she walked out, Una told me she'd made a terrible mistake marrying me. She couldn't be with me or any man because she's gay."

No, I will not look at Emery now. Couldn't stand to see pity on her face.

"I asked her how long she'd known," I say, "about her preference for women. She said she'd always known, for as long as she could remember. I couldn't understand how that could be, since we'd had sex many times. Una told me she could only have an orgasm during oral sex, and only if she closed her eyes and imagined I was a woman."

Emery shifts a little in my hold, but she doesn't speak.

I strap an arm over my face to shield myself from seeing her expression. "During intercourse, she would pretend to like it when she really wanted it to be over as quickly as possible. Our eight months together were, according to Una, the most painful of her life. She cried while telling me all of this, apologized repeatedly for lying to me."

Neither of us speaks for so long that I start to feel nauseous.

"Um…" Emery trails off without speaking a single actual word.

"Go on. You have a question, ask it."

"You don't have to tell me any more than you already have." She lays her hand over mine where it's draped over my arm. "I can't help wondering. Why did Una marry you in the first place?"

With half my face concealed behind my arm, I answer in a flat voice. "She believed her family would despise her for being gay. That turned out to be wrong, but she believed it for many years."

Her silence speaks loudly.

I lower my arm. "Say it. Whatever it is, go on and say it."

She wiggles around until she's on her knees, sitting back on her heels with her hands on her thighs. "Una caused you a lot of pain, the kind that sticks around for years. Deceiving you like that was mean and selfish."

"Una's not a bad person. She worried about what others thought of her, and I believe she cared for me in a certain way, but her fears were of her own making. Those are the hardest to overcome. I have no ill will toward Una. She did the best she could."

"Fine, maybe Una's not evil." Emery studies her hands, twirling her fingers with jerky motions. "But don't tell me Isobel wasn't selfish and mean, bitching about your job and how much money you made. You're my husband now, and I won't pretend I'm okay with the harm they did to you, whether it was intentional or not."

I stare at her, confused by the stern tone of her voice. She shouldn't feel...whatever she feels right now. I keep my tone guarded when I speak. "That sounds rather possessive."

"I stand up for the people I—" She stops, staying silent for a moment, then starts again. "As a rule, I assume everybody's doing their best and doesn't mean to hurt anybody else. But I stand up for my family. We are married, whatever the reason for it, which makes you family."

"That's...generous of you. I have a family of my own, though, so it's not necessary."

"I know you have a family, and they're amazing. But you haven't told them the whole story about your exes, have you?"

"No."

"Then it's up to me to say 'oh hell no' to what they did to you." She squints at me. "Am I the only one who knows?"

"Yes." I raise a hand when she opens her mouth to speak again, silently asking for her patience. "I'd rather not discuss this any further at the moment."

"Okay. Thank you for telling me, even though it couldn't have been easy for you."

I rub my eyes with the heels of my hands and force a faint smile. "You won the bet. What do you want for it?"

She taps her chin as if she's weighing her options. "Hmm, what do I want from Rory baby?"

A smile tries to take hold, but I can't quite let it. Not after the conversation we just had.

Emery swings a leg over me to sit astride my thighs. "I want to see the ocean."

My brows shoot up. "That's all?"

"I've never seen the ocean, but no. That's not all."

"You have never seen the ocean?"

"I lived in landlocked states. Born and raised in Idaho, moved to Colorado after college. Plenty of lakes, but no seashore."

I clasp my hands behind my head. "What else do you want, then? This was supposed to be one activity of your choice, not a Christmas list."

She rakes her nails down my belly, to within inches of my groin. "It will be one activity, Mr. Persnickety. I want to see the ocean as part of a broader tour of the Highlands. And I want you to be my tour guide."

I make a face. "I have work."

"One day." She braces her hands on my shoulders, those tits dangling in front of my eyes. "That's all I'm asking. A day trip."

"Jamie would be a better guide."

My wife nips my nose. "No dice. You agreed to our wager, and this is the one thing I want." She sits up and slaps my chest. "Don't be a grouch. Show me your homeland, Rory."

I regard her in silence as the minutes tick by on the bedside clock.

She wriggles her erse, making me grimace. And my cock rouses.

I surge up and flip us both over, making her squeak, and Emery lands flat on her back with me poised above her, my knees penning her legs. I strap her hands to the pillow with my palms and lower my head, meaning to kiss her senseless, but I pause a hair's breadth from her lips.

"Again?" she asks. "I'm up for anything, you know that. On our first night together, I loved the way you woke me up in the middle of the night to make love to me one more time."

Everything inside me goes cold, as if someone has doused me with ice water. Make love. Why did she have to say that? A few minutes ago, I'd thought those same words, but lust had driven out any comprehension of what it meant.

It means nothing. It's a phrase people say, not a declaration of…anything.

"What's wrong?" she asks.

I leap up to kneel over her, step off the bed, and walk out of the room.

The door clicks shut behind me.

And I stumble down the hall into my bedroom, sagging against it as the latch snaps closed behind me. I do not love my wife. Thinking the phrase "making love" doesn't mean I have deeper feelings for Emery. She shouldn't want that, and if she does, she'll come to regret it.

But as I spend another restless night alone, those two words echo in my mind.

Chapter Twenty-Three

The sunrise gives me a measure of clarity, and I no longer feel like I've committed a crime by thinking of sex with my wife as making love. It's a common expression. Why did I panic when I heard her speak those words? It's ridiculous. But I do enjoy shagging my wife, and I don't even mind that I've agreed to take Emery on a tour of the Highlands. If she wants to see the ocean, I will show it to her. After everything I've put her through, with our light-speed marriage and hauling her off to Scotland, where she spends most of her days alone, I owe her whatever barmy activities she wants to undertake.

And I feel an inexplicable need to show her an activity I enjoy. She won't participate in it, but I want her to see me in action. For once, I don't analyze the impulse. I go with it.

That means I sneak into her bedroom while she's still asleep and leave a note on her nightstand. I keep it brief and simple: "Meet me on the green."

I change into the appropriate attire and head for the green, aka the lawn behind the castle compound, just outside the walls. The garden doorway opens onto the green, and I shut it behind me. Then I gather the necessary equipment for my display. I'm not showing off. Emery wants to know more about me, and this activity is something I used to enjoy.

While I wait for my wife to arrive, I warm up with stretches and lunges. Then I lay out the only item I need, settling it onto the grass lengthwise in front of me.

The second I hear the garden door creak, I know Emery is about to emerge onto the green.

I take up my position at the foot of the wooden pole, facing away from the castle walls.

The garden door bursts open with a thud. Aye, it always requires a bit of force.

A quick, furtive glance over my shoulder assures me Emery has stepped onto the lawn.

Only a few clouds dot the blue sky, as if the heavens approve of my plan and have given me perfect weather for it. I stand at the center of the green, wearing only a kilt and tall leather boots. The sun warms my back, but I'm hoping that in a few minutes it will be more than sunshine making my wife feel hot.

Aye, it's time for the caber toss.

I crouch to grasp the wooden pole with both hands, heave it up, and walk my hands down its length until it rises above my head. I now hold the pole, a tree trunk with its branches shaved off, straight up in front of me. I risk a quick glance and see Emery sidling up to the wall, her fascinated gaze riveted to me. But I don't want her to stare at my back while I do this. Keeping the caber between my hands, I move around until I'm facing the opposite direction, facing Emery. Since I don't want her to think I'm doing this strictly for her benefit, I scan the green as if I'm just enjoying the bonnie day. When I finally look at my wife, I let my chest puff out.

Which is barmy. But I don't care right now.

"There you are," I say. "At last."

"What are you doing?"

I smack the pole. "Practicing my caber toss."

"You're seriously planning to chuck that thing?"

"I am."

Her tongue darts out to slide across her bottom lip.

Aye, this will arouse her for sure. I shift my hands down the pole to squat at its base, then heft its end up with both hands beneath it. The muscles in my arms and back tauten with the effort.

The caber wobbles a wee bit.

Emery watches me, seemingly entranced.

With a harsh yell, I thrust my hands up and out, hurling the caber end over end. I estimate my throw landed fifty feet away.

"Holy shit!" Emery shouts.

And I smirk. "I'll take that as a compliment."

My wife sweeps her lustful gaze over me, her fingers touching her throat delicately. She glances at the caber. "Is it safe to practice flinging trees by yourself?"

I roll one shoulder in a careless shrug. "Safe enough. I used to practice with Lachlan, but I gave up the sport three years ago."

"Why?"

I give her another casual shrug, though her question triggers a pang of unease.

"When did you start up again?" she asks.

"Last week."

She lodges her hands in the pockets of her lavender shorts. "After we got married."

I nod, though I lower my gaze to the grass. Why does she care when I stopped or restarted my caber tossing?

"Would ye like to watch me go again?" I ask, my voice colored by lust, thanks to the hungry look on her face.

"Love to."

I raise the caber again and launch the pole end over end.

Emery pulls out her mobile and takes a picture. Then she leaps away from the wall, clapping and whooping. "Go, Rory baby!"

I quirk a brow at her, unable to stop my lips from ticking up slightly. "Ye like to watch."

She bites her lip.

I stride toward her, halting an arm's length away.

"Wow," she says, "you're like Hercules."

That's the sort of flattery I can handle. Though I've gotten used to being called "sweet" and "cute," those aren't masculine compliments.

She studies me, her focus squarely on my eyes. "You invited me here. You wanted me to see you flinging trees."

I hook a thumb inside the waistband of my kilt.

Emery cocks her head, leaning into the wall. "Are you showing off for me?"

"Why would I?"

"You tell me." She braces one foot on the wall and bends her knee. "Therapy is a journey of self-discovery, after all."

In a single stride, I erase the distance between us. Her bent leg brushes my kilt. I slip a hand around the curve of her naked thigh, curling it around the underside. "Do I need to prove my masculine prowess to you?"

She settles a hand on my belly, tracing her fingertips over my skin. "I'm fully aware of your virility and stamina."

I drag my hand up the underside of her thigh, sneaking it inside her shorts and knickers to palm her buttock. As I slant my body into hers, she lets her head fall back against the stone wall, exposing the curve of her throat to me. I lay my other hand on the rock alongside her and rest my chin on her shoulder while I knead her erse.

She latches her leg around mine, pulling my erection into her belly.

With my lips, I trace a path up her throat. "Have ye ever fucked up against a castle wall?"

"Oh yeah, dozens of times."

I tug her hips into me. "Liar."

"Let's go for it."

My body goes as rigid as the stone behind her, and I suddenly realize what the bloody hell I'm doing. Suggesting we have sex outdoors, in the daytime, where anyone might see us. I glance around, slowly waking from the spell my wicked angel has cast over me yet again.

No, it's not her fault. I'm the bastard who can't deal with my own feelings and desires.

"*Mhac na galla*," I hiss, and shove my body away from her. "We cannae."

She frowns at me, but the expression is swiftly overtaken by a confused look. "What the hell is *mhac na galla*?"

"It means son of a bitch." I lay a hand on my forehead. "We cannot do this."

"Come on." Pure frustration rings in her voice. "Getting me worked up and yanking the rug out from under me again? After the way you sprinted out of my bedroom last night? Not cool, Rory. Not cool at all."

"I believe you're mixing several metaphors."

"Screw metaphors." She raps her wee fist on my chest. "Show a little respect, or at least common courtesy. I'm your wife, not your concubine."

I knife a hand through my hair. "I didn't—You're right. I'm sorry, you deserve better, but you knew what I am when you agreed to our arrangement. You said you understood the terms."

"Thanks so much for reminding me."

Her sharp tone cuts into me more than I would've expected. I lurch backward, gesturing toward the garden door. "I'm sure you have other things to do. Twirling about on the lawn, perhaps."

"You saw me yesterday?"

"I did."

"That was spinning and skipping, not 'twirling about.' " She flaps a hand in the direction of my discarded caber. "Not any weirder than hurling giant sticks."

"The caber toss is a feat of strength and control. What purpose does spinning serve?"

"It's fun. And I was soaking up the sunshine." She takes a deep breath and throws her arms wide, just as she'd done yesterday on the lawn. "Why don't you come out and join me this time? Instead of peeping on me from the first-floor hallway."

"How did you know where I was?"

"Simple deduction. You were in your office, like always, and it's on the first floor. The office windows don't face the front lawn. To see me, you would've had to walk out into the hall."

I almost want to smile, though I shouldn't be surprised she figured that out. "My clever wife."

"Would you come for a walk with me?"

"Can't. I'll be spending the day at my office in Loch Fairbairn." I turn away and start to roll the caber toward the pile at the edge of the green.

Emery starts for the garden door, then hesitates on the threshold, glancing back at me. "Will I see you for dinner?"

I push the caber into the pile with the others. "Don't wait for me."

My wife slams the garden door behind her.

The door is difficult to maneuver, but I don't think she slammed it for that reason alone.

I go inside to change clothes, and as I steer the Mercedes down the drive, I stare into the rearview mirror. The shape of Emery watching from the ground-floor windows recedes from view.

Emery releases a long string of wordless cries, her voice growing hoarse as the intensity of her climax gradually subsides and the final spasm clench-es my cock. Her knees are hooked over my shoulders while I have my palms firmly on the mattress on either side of her body, hunched over while frozen with my cock still buried deeper inside her than ever before. I'd never tried this position before, but I like the way it feels, as if I've melded with her in a new and more meaningful way.

And it's turned me into an eejit who havers about how much I love fuck-ing my wife. *Bod an Donais.*

Perspiration trickles down our bodies, and droplets tumble from my skin to land on her belly. The scent of sex permeates the air. The scent of her.

When Emery had rung me at my office in the village this afternoon, she wanted to know when I would be home for dinner. I told her, repeatedly, not to wait up for me. Despite arriving after ten o'clock, I found my wife still awake—and naked in bed. I discovered that fact when I sort of sneaked into her bedroom to check on whether she had indeed waited for me.

Not that I wanted her to do that. But I had a feeling the bloody-minded woman would wait.

I didn't give her a chance to chastise me for abandoning her yet again. I meant to seduce her, plain and simple, but something strange happened to me during the act. I started to feel a twinge of anxiety about whether she might be annoyed with me and for how long she'll put up with my behavior before she moves to a flat in the village. Will she do that? I shouldn't care, but I think the idea makes me...uneasy. To avoid thinking about that, I fucked her hard and deep, as if I were trying to shed all my neuroses inside her body.

She doesn't like us having separate bedrooms. I know that, but I can't change my nature overnight. Or ever.

I crawl out from under her legs and kneel at her feet. Emery's knees remain bent, her glistening flesh still exposed. I want to shove my face between her thighs and make her come again, but I shouldn't stay any longer.

My gaze shifts to the door.

"It's okay," my wife says. "You can leave."

I swing my legs over the bed's edge, hesitate for only a second, then lean over to kiss her forehead. "Good night, Emery."

She forces a half-hearted smile. "Good night, Rory."

And I slide off the bed, shuffling toward the door.

On the threshold, I pause. "I ran into Graham in the village today. He's developed an odd fascination with you, asked how you were adjusting to your new home. Cannae understand what he wants, but be cautious if you see him. Anything you say might be printed in his grimy paper."

"I won't tell him about our arrangement or the contract."

"Graham has a way of wheedling things out of people."

With two fingers, she draws a cross over her heart. "I'm wheedle-proof, promise."

I believe her. But I'm not worried about what she might accidentally tell Graham. I'm concerned about what lengths he'll go to in his quest to punish me for doing my job too well. Maybe I won't share a bed with my wife, but I still want to protect her.

Back in my bedroom, I lie awake for an hour while I try to sort the mess I've made of my life—and Emery's. Though I have no solutions, I do come up with stopgap measures. And at breakfast the next morning, I explain them to my wife.

I march into the kitchen and announce, "I'm having a gate installed at the end of the drive. No car will approach the house without permission again. The entrance doors are to remain locked at all times. I'll give you a remote for opening the gate once it's installed."

Then I leave the house.

My way of explaining might not be appreciated, but I don't do well with soft-pedaling things. My clients usually appreciate my directness. I don't know if my wife feels that way, but I didn't stay to listen to her complaints. I'm an erse. I know that, and I don't need more reminders of my countless flaws.

For the next two days, I avoid my wife during the day and shag her relentlessly every night. Then I hurry back to my room to hide from the woman I convinced to marry me. And every night, she seems more forlorn when I walk out the door. I get a pang in my chest, but I think that might be gas. The alternative is nothing I dare consider.

But I can't stop all my ridiculous impulses. Since I refuse to sleep in the same bed with her, I let myself indulge in another kind of intimacy. Every day, I hunt down my wife and kiss her. At first, I simply peck a kiss on her lips and hurry away. But soon, I'm teasing her with playful kisses and long, lingering ones that turn into extended sessions, with our lips and tongues speaking all the words neither of us wants to say. Or maybe I'm the only one who can't speak the truth. No, I won't think about that. Not now. I want to relish these days with her and the sexy smiles she gives me every time I stride up to her and surprise her with a kiss.

I even kiss her outdoors, under the larch trees, while birds serenade us.

Emery takes to driving out to visit members of my family, because she says she needs to "find a new life's purpose." I assume she's given up on reforming me, and I can't decide how I feel about that. She drives out to the homes of Erica and Lachlan, then Aidan and Calli, though she doesn't share the details of those visits with me.

Why should she? I haven't treated her like my wife. Maybe I could be a bit more accommodating without risking that she might fall in love with me.

All day, every day, I work. Except when I'm kissing my wife.

One afternoon, we've just separated our lips after a sensual kiss that's left me halfway to an erection when I feel the need to say something moronic.

I coil a lock of her hair around my finger, studying the strands to avoid looking at my wife. "You haven't come to my office lately."

"Thought you'd rather be alone."

"It seems…quiet without your visits."

She stares at me, clearly stunned by my foolish statement.

"I'll see you at dinner, then?" I ask.

"Yes, at dinner."

I release her hair and nod crisply. "Good."

Then I rush back to my office.

We meet in the dining room that evening to share a meal and casual conversation. Afterward, I shag my wife in her bedroom and walk out the door, kissing her goodbye on the way out.

Though she tries to hide it, I sense the sadness in her wan smile.

And I get that pain in my chest again.

The next morning, my wife bursts into my office and slams the door shut.

I flinch, my head jerking up. "Emery?"

Shadows darken the skin under her eyes, and I imagine I have a similar look. Emery sprawls in the chair across the desk from me with one leg draped over the arm and her foot swinging. "We need to talk about the separate-bedrooms thing."

I drop my pen, sitting back in my chair. "We've already discussed it."

"No, you issued your decree, and I went along with it." She sets a hand on the knee of her dangling leg. "Separate bedrooms isn't in the contract. Did you make your ex-wives sleep alone?"

I compress my lips into a sharp line.

"Well?" she demands. "Did you?"

"No."

"Mm-*hm*." She raps her knuckles on her knee. "Did you order them not to say your name during sex?"

I finger the top button of my shirt, though I have no idea why.

"I'll take that as a no," she says. "What about your one-night stands? Did you tell them not to speak your name or close their eyes?"

Tugging at my collar, I scratch my throat. Are insects nesting in my clothes?

"Another no," my wife declares. She scrapes her nails on her jeans, almost as if she's sharpening them. "Why do you invent rules for living with me? I'm trying to understand this, Rory, but you've got to help me out. Why am I the special one who gets banished to the other end of a very long hallway?"

I absently rearrange the papers on my desk. "You're not banished."

"Sure as hell feels like it. Either I'm your wife or I'm your mistress. Make up your mind."

Though I jolt forward, I keep my head down and pretend I need to stack the papers on my desk, then I insert them into a file folder where they don't belong. "This is our arrangement. You agreed to it."

"I never agreed to these cockamamie rules. I know you have issues with trusting women, but I'd like to know what I've done to give you the impression you can't trust me. I've been supportive and understanding, right? Haven't I accommodated all your hang-ups?"

"You've done all of that," I admit, though I can't look at her.

"Do you trust me?"

I snatch up my pen, hovering it over a page that has…some sort of words on it. Since I can't decipher them, I set my pen down again. "I can't sleep with you. It's that simple."

"No, it's this simple." She shoves out of the chair. "Sometimes I'm not sure if you like me, or if you tolerate me because you require the use of my body at least twice a week."

The acid in her tone spurs me to meet her gaze. "I have never said I require the use of your body."

"It's in the contract." She slaps her palms down on the desktop, the sound reverberating through the room. "You require sexual congress at least twice a week. Since you can't bring yourself to spend the night with me, that means you need my body and nothing else."

"Emery."

"Shut up and listen, Rory." She spears me with a razor-sharp glare like nothing I've ever seen from her. "I tried to be cool with you screwing me and running off to your room, to hide behind a locked door. I tried to be patient and not question your hang-ups, to wait until you were ready to talk. And you have, a few times, and I appreciate that."

My eyes widen, though only a fraction.

"But it's not enough," she says. "You're making me feel like your in-house whore."

"You are not a whore."

"Aren't I? You're paying me half a million dollars to fuck you for a year."

"You signed the contract." My voice has hardened as I'm sure my expression has too, and I twist my mouth downward. "If you're waiting for me to fall in love with you, it will never happen."

A cold spike pierces my chest, but she needs to understand, to stop waiting for me to become a different man.

"I'm not trying to make you love me," she says. "A few days ago on the green, after your impressive demonstration of caber tossing, I asked you to show me a little common decency. You stayed with me on our wedding night, for heaven's sake. You fell asleep with me the night we met and only left at dawn. Is it really such a hardship for you to let me into your bedroom?"

"If you leave me now, you'll walk away with nothing. Not one pound of my money."

Her glare softens into something much worse—pain. "I know what you're doing. This is how you keep your distance. You want me to think you're a cold bastard, so I won't like you anymore, but I'm on to you. If you were really a bastard, you wouldn't act like one."

"Your bum's oot the windae."

"I am not talking nonsense." She must see the surprise on my face, because she straightens and lifts her chin. "Erica told me what that saying means. You're the one who spouts nonsense on a regular basis."

Says the woman who likes to "spin" on the lawn.

"What I said about bastards," she explains, "means they are bastards, all the time, it's no act. You have to put on a show to convince me you're a jerk, but I see what you're doing, and I don't buy it."

I crook my fingers on the desktop like claws. "Separate bedrooms. That's my final word on the matter."

"Your summary judgment, you mean. I don't want your money, I never did. If you think that's why I married you, then you are the most clueless, blindest man on earth."

She whirls toward the door.

I catch up to her at the threshold, snaring her arm. "Don't love me, Emery. I will only hurt you. Willnae mean to, but…"

My voice trails off, and I let my hand fall away from her arm.

"You are hurting me," she says, "every night when you walk out the door. You'd better think about what you really want, Rory. If we keep going this way, I'll have to do whatever is necessary to protect myself."

She walks away from me without glancing back.

I sink into my chair again, shutting my eyes, and pray she heeds my warning. Loving me is the worst mistake any woman can make.

Chapter Twenty-Four

I'm chasing another wife away. That seems to be what I'm best at, because no matter how hard I try to make women happy, they end up frustrated and miserable. Though I will never love Emery, I don't like knowing I've ruined her cheerful disposition and brought her nothing but pain. How did I expect this arrangement would go? That she'd be grateful to have a husband who ignores her? A *bod ceann* who creeps into her bedroom at night, then runs away?

I never wanted to become this man. But here I am, destroying another marriage.

After a few more minutes of brooding while slumped in my office chair, I consider getting drunk. That bottle of Ben Nevis is still inside the desk drawer. But no, that won't solve a bloody thing. I get up and shuffle over to the windows. The sun has come out again, as if even Scotland can't bear to see Emery languishing under cloudy skies. She belongs in the sun.

A figure emerges from the vestibule doorway.

Emery exits the house and heads straight for the garden, disappearing through the entrance into the walled space.

I can't see her anymore, though I crane my neck hoping to catch a glimpse, just to know she isn't crying or…something. Should I go out there and apologize? We might not have a normal marriage, but that's no excuse for me to treat her with disrespect. My mother would have my hide if she knew what I've done to my wife. Yes, that's the reason I hurry downstairs and outside to the garden. My upbringing pushes me to do it.

When I find my wife, she's lying on the grass under the arbor with her eyes closed, seeming more relaxed than I've ever felt. A ghost of a smile tugs at her lips. She's so bonnie, lying there under the rose vines while the sunlight that filters through the foliage casts a subdued glow on her skin. She starts to hum softly, a tune I know well.

On our second night in New Orleans, when she hadn't been able to sleep, I'd soothed her the only way I could think of. Will that work again? I need to try, if only to show her I'm not a heartless bastard.

And so I sing, "Alas, my love, you do me wrong—"

Her eyes fly open, those beautiful eyes aimed straight at me.

I keep singing until I've finished the song, though she's stopped humming. Then I ask, "What are you doing?"

"Don't you get tired of asking me that? It should be fairly obvious, anyway. I'm lying in the grass."

"I can see that." I drop into a crouch. "If you were trying to get away from me, I can go."

"Hiding isn't my thing. I wanted some fresh air, that's all."

For a moment, I just look at her, uncertain of how she'll react to my next question. "May I join you?"

"You want to lie in the grass?"

"I want to lie beside you, wherever that might be."

My wife shimmies sideways to make room for me and pats the grass.

And I stretch out beside her, our shoulders brushing. We glance at each other at the same instant, and something in her tender gaze brings on that pain in my chest again, the one that's not entirely unpleasant. I gaze up at the mesh of roses and leaves above our heads and slip my hand into hers. The warmth of her palm pressed to mine feels good, and I can't resist threading our fingers.

I don't lie in the grass. It's a frivolous thing to do. But Emery needs kindness from me, and I can't make myself remind her of the rules. Not right now. She has a light inside her that I'd seen that night in the piano bar, a warm and sweet glow that burns within her every moment of every day. At least, it did until she married me. I don't want to be the one who extinguishes that light.

She seems to be admiring the rose-covered lattice above us.

"That's a sad song," I murmur, "the one you were humming. Greensleeves."

"Guess it is."

"The song and the look on your face earlier, they mean you weren't angry. You were hurt. It's worse, isn't it? Worse than if you'd shouted at me."

"I hate being angry. I hate being miserable too."

With my thumb, I knead the back of her hand. "I've never done well with upset women. No idea how to respond to it."

"Congratulations. You're a typical man in at least one way."

"I have behaved like a bastard." I raise our hands to my face, laying her palm on my cheek. "I trust you, *m'eudail*, and I will make this up to you."

"Why did you have to point out I'd get nothing if I left you today?"

"It was—I don't know." I turn my face into her hand. "That will never happen again."

Does she believe me? Perhaps she shouldn't. I might hurt her again before I realize what I've done.

I move her hand to my chest, resting it over my heart, and settle my hand on top of hers.

"Listen," she says, "what you said really hurt me. I can't pretend it didn't, but I also realize this might be partly my fault."

"It isn't. I'm to blame."

"Let's call it ninety-ten, with you being ninety percent in the wrong." She hesitates as if she's considering how to proceed. "I never told you the real reason I married you. It's—"

My mobile rings. I dig it out of my hip pocket and sit up, relinquishing her hand while I answer the call with a gruff hello.

"It's Mike Jeffries, Mr. MacTaggart."

Emery sits up too, squinting into the sunlight beyond the arbor.

"Hate to bother you," Jeffries says, "but the search has taken longer than expected. This guy doesn't have much of a digital footprint anymore, which means I needed to bring in some of my associates to look for him the old-fashioned way. I think we've almost got him. But this means more expenses because he's now in Alaska, apparently hiding out in Anchorage. I'll need to fly there. Are you okay with that?"

"Yes, whatever you need. I'll pay any added expense. Let me know as soon as you find him."

Without another word, I end the call. Donnae give a shit about the money. I want to know what my wife had been about to tell me before my mobile rang.

"Everything okay?" Emery asks.

"The investigator thinks he's found Sebastian Zegers. He needs to fly to Alaska. Your former love seems to be hiding in Anchorage."

"Alaska? Sebastian hates the cold."

"He's been in and out of psychiatric facilities for years, Emery. You don't know him anymore." I pull her into my arms, pressing my cheek to hers. "I want to fix this for you."

"I'm okay, even if you don't find Sebastian."

"But you worry the photos are still out there." I clasp her a wee bit tighter. "What he did has affected you more than you believe. I think it's why sleeping in separate bedrooms makes you feel like a concubine. I should've realized sooner."

But naturally, I only realized that a moment ago. I'm an eejit.

I brush my nose against hers. "I have a call with a client, but I will see you for dinner. Won't I?"

"You will." She kisses me. "Don't work too hard."

We stroll back into the house hand in hand, kissing each other goodbye in the vestibule.

As I turn to leave, I find myself hesitating, needing to say something. "For the record, I don't pay you to fuck me. I'm paying you not to leave."

I take two steps toward the stairs, but stop when she calls out to me. "Rory."

My shoulders tense up as I glance back at her.

"I was trying to tell you earlier," she says, "before your investigator called. I didn't marry you for money or sex."

"You did it for the adventure and excitement."

"Partly."

Gazing into her eyes, I suddenly understand. "You were lonely."

She draws back a little, as if I've surprised her.

I haven't been a good husband, but I have listened to everything she told me.

"Yes," she says, "but that's not the main reason."

"Why, then?"

"Because you have potential."

I give a slight shake of my head. "Potential for what?"

"To break free of your past and become the best version of yourself. That's what I'm trying to do, to reclaim who I used to be, and that's what you want to do too."

I grunt. "You may be disappointed with my potential."

"Stop telling me you suck." She takes a single step closer, never breaking eye contact. "I see you, Rory. Not just the parts you show everyone, but the pieces you try to hide. I see *you*."

She sees me? I can't decide what that means, but a strange tingle sweeps over my skin. I nail my gaze to hers, struggling to see something in them that will explain why she insists on believing in me no matter how often I hurt her. "Perhaps what you see is what you want, not what I am."

I turn away and begin my slog up the stairs to my office.

But she calls out to me from the stairwell. "That's crap."

Though I hesitate for a second, and my pulse speeds up, I force myself to start walking again.

For the rest of the day, I keep hearing her words in my mind. *I see you, Rory. Not just the parts you show everyone, but the pieces you try to hide. I see you.*

Emery and I have dinner together in the dining room, and something odd happens. I enjoy myself. We tease each other and tell jokes that make us both laugh, then I share stories about my family. She loves the one about teenage Lachlan showing his dokey to a silly lass, and Emery figures out "dokey" means penis without me telling her. Aye, she is clever. Though I have no idea why I'm doing any of this, I like seeing her smile with that light glowing inside her the way it should. I don't want to become the shadow that engulfs her. Perhaps I have been too rigid, refusing to eat with her and refusing to give her my time. I do need to work, but I can spare a few minutes now and then to make her happy.

We'll be living together for a year. Ensuring we get on reasonably well seems prudent.

After dinner, we go to our separate bedrooms.

I stare at my bed, the one that's large enough for three or four full-grown men. Not that I care to invite several lads to sleep with me. But suddenly, the bed—the entire room, in fact—seems empty. I strip off my clothes and change into the pajama bottoms I always sleep in, then I stand here staring at the bed again. The empty one. I have, quite literally, made my own bed and have to lie in it alone every night.

Well, Mrs. Darroch makes my bed every morning. But still—

Stop whingeing in yer head, ye damn eejit.

I picture Emery lying in this bed, her sensual body stretched out across its length. She's nude, of course, in my mental picture. Nude and aroused and—

Mhac na galla. I stalk out into the hallway, then freeze halfway between my room and Emery's. What am I doing? Going to my wife's bedroom so I can fuck her and walk away? Though I've been doing that for a while now, I don't want that tonight. I want—I need something else.

To make amends for the way I've treated her.

I march to her door and throw it open.

Emery yelps and spins toward the doorway, clutching an armload of clothes.

I stalk up to her, not unaware of the fact she's dressed in only her short satin dressing gown.

"What's up?" she asks, though her dilating pupils and the rising and falling of her chest belie her casual tone.

She wants me as much as I want her.

I lean over, lash my arms around her waist, and sling the lass around my shoulders with her bare feet hanging over my chest on one side and her head and arms dangling down the other side. Her midsection is crushed to the back of my neck and head while her tits brush against my ear. My arms strap her to my torso.

My wife's clothes tumble from her grasp, fluttering to the floor.

"Hey!" she says. "What's with the fireman hold?"

"I'm making it up to you."

That explains everything, doesn't it? I stride out of her bedroom and down the hall to the door of the master suite. I enter the room and kick the door shut behind us.

"Put me down," Emery says, "before I pass out from too much blood in my brain. I'm getting tired of staring at your pajamas. Is that silk? Sheesh, for a guy who doesn't care about money you sure like the luxury comforts, don't you?"

"And you never stop havering." I bend my knees to let her body slide off my shoulders and set her down on her feet. "Are you angry I made another decision for you without asking?"

"Not this time." She glances around the room at the four-poster bed with its golden-brown sheets and the windows along the opposite wall. "You want to have sex in here tonight? I'm surprised you let me into your bedroom."

"Our bedroom." I hook a finger inside the belt on her dressing gown and tug her closer. "You'll be sleeping here."

"Just for tonight."

"Forever." No, not forever. Until she leaves me at the end of one year. But I won't think about that tonight.

Her hands float up to my chest. "Are you sure about this?"

"Aye." My fingers fumble with the bow that secures her belt. "I want to fall asleep beside you and wake up with you in the morning. Every day."

She grins. "Sharing a bed. Now that's progress."

Bowing my head, I focus on freeing her belt. "Progress toward what?"

"You fulfilling your potential." She bats my hands away and liberates the belt, letting her dressing gown fall open. "Before you know it, you'll be doing me in the daytime and on every surface in this house. Maybe outside too."

I make a pained face. "Not certain I'll ever be like you."

"Don't be like me. Be yourself—the real Rory, the one who desperately wants to come out and play."

Maybe I do want that, but it's not in my nature. I sweep my hands under her dressing gown and push the satin fabric off her shoulders. The garment tumbles to the floor, lying in a lump at her feet. "No sex tonight. Sleep only."

She feigns a pout.

Trying not to smile has gotten more difficult every day, and I feel my lips twitching as if they want me to stop fighting it. I can't, not yet. "It's been a trying day. Sleep is what we both need."

"Have you browsed your menu of fantasies yet?" She skates her palms over my chest and down to the waistband of my pajama bottoms. "Pick a costume, and I'll make you forget about everything in the world except for me."

"Yes, I'm sure you would." I grasp her hands. "But you were upset earlier, and it's clear you haven't slept well."

"Didn't realize it was that obvious."

I cup her cheek. "It's my fault. I'm sorry."

"I know you are, and I forgive you."

"Get in bed, *mo leannan*."

The fact that I've started calling her my sweetheart in Gaelic means nothing. It's a reflex, that's all.

Emery crawls under the covers and rests her head on one of the two pillows on the bed.

I strip off my pajama bottoms and join my naked wife beneath the silk sheets, lying on my back with one hand under my head. When I raise the other arm as an invitation, Emery cuddles up to me, her head nestled in the crook of my shoulder. I curl my arm around her.

This feels…right.

"Why did you get naked?" she asks. "Since we're not having sex tonight."

"Hush." I stretch an arm out to turn off the lamp on the nightstand. "Time for sleep, Em, not talking."

A slight giggle escapes her lips. "You called me Em. The man who hates nicknames called me by my nickname."

I grumble.

She snuggles closer. "Maybe tomorrow you could take a break from work and do something fun with me."

I enfold her in my arms, my chin on the crown of her head. "Sleep, Emery."

"Promise you'll wake me up before you go downstairs in the morning, every day."

"If that will make you happy, I will."

"Thank you. Night, Rory."

I kiss the top of her head. "Good night."

Whatever happens tomorrow, or the day after that, at least I've made her happy for one night.

Chapter Twenty-Five

The next evening, after a long day of handling contracts and divorces and other legal grievances, I decide it's time to give my wife something other than sex and a shared bedroom. Every little thing I do for her makes me feel lighter somehow, but I'm sure that's only because the weight of guilt has hung around my neck since the day we said our vows in a magistrate's office. As much as I don't want an overblown wedding, I can tell Emery does want it. But I have other things to offer her too.

My wife had told me she planned to take a bath in the ground-floor tub before bed, so I hurry downstairs, taking the steps two at a time. I'm not excited to see Emery. It's simply the most expedient way to get to the ground floor. Taking things slow has never been my strong suit.

The door to the bathroom hangs open. Emery lies in the large, claw-foot tub with her arms on the rim and her fingers lazily swishing in the water. Her head rests against the tub, and her nude body is on full display, with the water lapping around her breasts and a thin layer of bubbles floating around her.

I barely notice the sunset outside the windows across the hall, too distracted by the vision of her. "Emery."

She peels her lids apart.

"A bubble bath?" I say, sounding baffled because I am. Aren't bubbles for children? But she looks delectable surrounded by translucent pockets of suds.

Emery dunks her arms into the water, then raises them above her head. Suds drizzle off her creamy skin while the water slides down her arms, leaving only a few bubbles on her flesh. She lays her arms on the tub's rim, bending one knee to raise it above the water level.

"Bubbles are fun," she says, and hoists her leg fully out of the water, lifting her foot high and wiggling her toes. "Why not join me? It's warm and slippery in here."

"I don't lie in tubs." But I can't resist watching the suds as they glide over her foot and dribble down her leg. "I have showers."

"Mm, we could do that together too."

I curl my fingers into my palms. "We can fuck later. I need to speak with you in my office first."

She pushes away from the tub's edge and stretches her arms out to me. "Give a girl a hand?"

While I have no doubt she can get herself out of there, I cross the room and take her hands, helping my wife stand up inside the tub. I drink in the sight of her nakedness, moistening my lips three times before I can tear my focus away from her body.

"Getting chilly," she says.

Though her nipples have hardened, I know it's not from a chill. Perhaps I haven't learned everything about her, but I'm well acquainted with my wife's insatiable nature.

I grab a towel from the rack nearby and wrap it around her torso. Sized for me, the terry cloth drapes down to Emery's knees. I tuck in one corner of the towel to secure it, sling my arms around her, and lift my wife out of the tub. Soapy water sloshes over the rim.

Although her feet are flat on the tile floor, I keep her bound in my arms.

"Thanks for the assist," she says. "One of these days, I will get you in a tub with me."

"Dry off and meet me in the office."

"Sure thing, Rory baby."

I give up her body and hurry out the door.

Ten minutes later, my wife sashays into the room while I'm focused on the papers on my desk. Peripherally, I notice when she sits down on the chair across from me, but I still have my arms on the desktop on either side of a neatly arranged spread of folders and papers. I have my reading glasses perched on my nose, and glare on the lenses makes it difficult to see my wife without raising my gaze to her. I'm too engrossed by the documents in front of me to look up. That might be an excuse. Her behavior in the ground-floor bathroom left me on the verge of an erection.

Emery props her bare feet on the desk in front of me and crosses her ankles.

I have no choice but to notice that since her feet are inches away. Glancing up from my papers, I flick my gaze to her naked feet and follow a path up her legs. Reclining in my chair grants me a measure of distance, though I still feel my mouth crimp at one corner.

The cheeky lass is wearing nothing but her short satin dressing gown.

"I said to get dressed," I remind her in the most patient tone I can muster. "A robe is not clothing."

"Sure it is." She wags her foot. "Besides, you said dry off, not get dressed."

I fasten a hand over her wiggling toes. Her foot feels cold, probably from walking barefoot across the wood floors.

When she shifts her erse, as if to find a better position, the halves of her robe fall away from her legs, revealing nothing but skin up to her hips. Only her crossed ankles prevent me from glimpsing the hairs between her thighs.

I rock forward, tip my head down, and peer at her over my glasses. "You are not a biddable wife, are you?"

"Uh, no." She hits me with a sarcastically cheerful smile. "But I give you great sex to make up for it."

"Aye." I release her toes. "I have something for you."

I hold out a sheet of paper.

She drops her feet to the floor and strains to accept the paper across the wide desk. As she peruses the document, which I had typed up with bullet points to separate each item of interest, she struggles to restrain a smile. She undoubtedly thinks my organizational skills are amusing.

"What is this?" she asks.

"A list of my holdings."

"Is that like stocks and bonds?"

"No, it's an inventory of properties I own. I thought you should be made aware of this information."

"I'm definitely aware," she says with a teasing smile and a sultry tone in her voice. She browses the document again. "This isn't a huge list for a rich guy. An apartment in Edinburgh, the castle here, and—" She squints at the sheet. "You own property on Skye? The island?"

"Yes. It's a house."

"Cool." Emery sets the paper on her lap. "How often do you go to Skye?"

"I've been there once, when I looked at the property."

"Once? If you never go there, why did you buy it?"

I shrug one shoulder. No, I don't care to explain my reasons to her. It would sound pathetic.

She eyes me in a way that makes my skin itch because it feels like she can see through my flesh, down to my soul. "Don't try to convince me you have no idea why you bought it. You don't want to tell me, that's all."

I arrange and rearrange the folders and papers on my desk while avoiding eye contact. "You'll see the property soon enough."

She jerks upright, her hands on her knees, and the document sails down to the floor. "I will? When?"

"During our sightseeing holiday."

"Thank you, Rory." She claps her hands, beaming at me. "Yay! I get to see the ocean and the famous Isle of Skye."

I'm fair certain I'm giving her a baffled look, which has become a bad habit since I married Emery. "It's not as exciting as you seem to think."

"Maybe to you." She sways in her chair, both arms extended above her head with her fingers fanned out. "This is awesome! Do you have any idea how long it's been since I took a vacation? Years. I mean, seriously, *years*. I should come over there and smack a big one on you."

My gaze has landed on her breasts, now exposed because her dressing gown has come undone and gapes open.

Emery glances down, noticing what's happened. She lowers her arms and starts to pull her robe closed, but then hesitates.

I can't stop gawping at her tits and the pearls of her nipples that I want to devour.

She lets go of the dressing gown, her lips parted and her gaze glossy.

A tortured groan resonates in my chest as I scrub my face with both hands. "Ever since you mentioned it, I cannae stop thinking of—*bod an Donais*—taking you on this desk."

She ties her robe closed. "Sorry. Didn't mean to flash you a full-frontal shot."

"Wasnae blaming ye. I was enjoying the view."

"Oh, I knew that. It was written all over your gorgeous face."

I spread my fingers on the desk, then curl them. Stretching them straight, I curl them again, repeating the action several times while I imagine I'm stroking her *brillean*. "Ahm burning for ye, Em."

The sun has almost set, so I won't be breaking my rule about not shagging her in the daytime.

I sag into my chair, though my arm remains on the desk. Powerless to resist the impulse, I gesture with one finger, inviting her to come to me. The only time she obeys me is when she knows I want to fuck her.

My wife ambles around the desk, sidling up to my chair. She rotates my chair toward her while I keep my arm on the desktop.

My face lies at the level of her breasts, and I can see her stiff nipples through the fabric of her dressing gown. I hook a finger inside the belt and untie it slowly, letting the strip of fabric fall away so that her robe hangs open. I glance at the hairs between her thighs and shut my eyes while I inhale a deep breath, hauling in a hint of her scent. My groin tightens, and my lids ease open.

I pat my thigh.

Emery climbs onto my lap with her knees straddling my hips and her slick folds poised over my thighs. "Do you need a special kind of cuddle?"

"Aye."

With a hand on each of my shoulders, she kneads my bunched muscles until they soften and I sigh. Her touch always soothes and arouses me, but with her, the contradiction makes sense. She glides her palms up my throat, tenderly feeling the pulse point as if she's measuring the acceleration of my heartbeats. My lips fall open because I need to kiss and taste her everywhere. She slants in, skimming her palms up to my cheeks, and rubs her lips over mine.

My cock throbs for her.

I rest my hands on her hips, then coast them up her sides, brushing them against her breasts. "Yer bonnie, soft, sweet…perfection."

She sways into me. "Kiss me. Touch me. Anything you want, please."

For a moment, I just sit here unmoving while my breaths grow uneven and harsh. With my hands positioned alongside her breasts, I lazily stroke my thumbs along the undersides, then let my hands wander down to her waist while I draw circles on her skin with my thumbs.

I let one hand roam down to cover her mound.

She rocks her hips into my touch, pressing those silky curls into my waiting palm. The heat of her arousal warms my skin, and her wetness dampens my fingers. A soft moan whispers out between her parted lips. When I tease her damp hairs with my fingers, she releases another moan, this one so low and throaty that it makes my cock throb again.

"*M'eudail*," I murmur, my voice strained by lust. I whisk my hands up to her shoulders, under the robe, and slip it off. The fabric flutters down to the floor.

And I'm gazing at my naked wife.

Sinking into my lap, with my erection trapped beneath her, she yanks my shirt out from inside my waistband.

I settle the weight of my palm over her mound, molding my fingers to the swollen lips of her sex.

Her fingers scrabble to unhook my shirt buttons, failing in the attempt. Then she grasps the shirt and tears it open. Buttons rain onto the rug.

My eyes bulge, but gradually narrow as I give her a wicked smile. "I love your enthusiasm."

"Too amped to be subtle."

She rakes her nails down my chest.

I shove my hand between her legs, diving into her slick heat.

"Yes, baby," she moans, rocking against my palm as she finds a slow and sensuous rhythm, shuddering when I caress her with my middle finger. "I want you so bad I can't think. Take me hard, do it fast, I need you inside me."

"Ah, *mo leannan*, yer so wet and hot." I rasp two fingers along her outer folds while I swirl my longest finger around her entrance. "Ahm starved for ye, Emery."

I plunge a finger inside her.

With a sharp cry, she latches onto my shoulders. As I pump my finger in and out, I scrape my other fingers along the insides of her folds and rub the heel of my hand on her mound, grazing her clit with every swipe. She moves her hips, rolling them in sync with the thrusts of my fingers. She's panting now, writhing while her tits splash against my chest. Then she raises onto her knees, placing her groin inches from my face, and rides my hand while clinging to my shoulders.

"Rory," she gasps. "Yes, oh God, yes."

She clutches my head, and I bury my face against her belly while showering her skin with wet kisses and circling my tongue around her navel, then plunging it inside at the same instant I push my finger into her opening. Her body tenses as her jaw goes slack, and I know she's on the edge.

"Oh shit," she whimpers. "Please, Rory, please, I need your cock inside me."

I snarl in Gaelic, not even sure what I'm saying.

She grinds her body into my hand, her wetness coating my palm and dribbling down my wrist. I'm breathing hard, so aroused that I'm almost gasping.

"Fuck," I growl, and yank my hand away.

Emery gapes down at me. "What…"

I launch out of the chair, dumping my wife on her feet.

She wobbles a touch, seeming dazed. "It's dark out, but we can go to the bedroom if you want."

"Ahmno worried about the location." Struggling to breathe, I palm my raging erection through my trousers. "Cannae wait a second longer."

I glance at the desk as two needs war within me—keeping to my rules, or fucking my wife on this desk until she screams. I've never had sex anywhere except in a bed. Never.

Rolling my shoulders back, I sweep one arm across the desktop and send everything on it except for the computer toppling to the floor. Papers spew across the rugs and wood flooring. Then I pick her up and spread her body across the desk.

She grins. "Rory baby, I love this new side of you."

I allow myself five seconds to absorb the sight of my wife's nude body laid across the wooden surface. The floor lamp spills golden light over her skin and shimmers in her hazel eyes. When she smooths her hands over my chest, I grasp her hips and drag my wife closer until her erse rests on the very edge of the desk. Her legs dangle there, and though she shivers faintly, I know it's not from the cool air in this room.

I unzip my trousers and shove them off my hips along with my boxers, not giving a toss that my ankles are trapped by my clothes. My cock springs free, bouncing as it curls up toward my belly, and Emery licks her lips as her gaze lands on the moisture beading on my crown. With all the focus I usually reserve for work, I brace myself with both hands on the desk on either side of her head, then position my cock between her thighs. The head nudges her entrance.

Any semblance of control I might've had left disintegrates.

I pull my hips back and plunge inside her, penetrating her body with one powerful thrust.

Emery gasps, clinching her hands around my biceps while I consume her, sinking my length deep inside her. She clasps her ankles behind my erse. "Oh Rory, don't stop."

"Say the other thing."

She hesitates, her brows knitting together. Then realization dawns. "Rory baby, my Rory baby."

I devour her mouth in a brutal kiss, my tongue lashing and my teeth scraping on her lips while she digs her fingers into my shoulders, scratching them down my back, and grips my erse.

"*Bod 'a chac*," I growl. "Ye feel so fucking good, *m'eudail*."

She thrashes her head, hips undulating, while her muscles pulsate around my shaft.

I jerk my hips back, then slam into her again. And again. And again. The feel of her silky heat around me drives out reason and rules. She cries out, bucking her hips and clawing at my erse like she can't get me deep enough inside her. My heart pounds in my chest, and the power of my need for her robs me of breath. Every punishing thrust pushes me deeper inside her body and binds us to each other in a way I can't understand, not now when we're both about to come any second. She flings her arms around me and mashes her face into my shoulder while her cries echo off the walls and mingle with my grunts and shouts.

The desk jounces and thumps.

I grip the desk's edge above her head and piston my hips in a wild rhythm. The room reverberates with the slapping of flesh on flesh while the pressure in my *slat* mounts until it's almost painful.

Emery's whole body convulses around me, from her arms and legs to the muscles deep inside her. "Oh God, Rory!"

"Emery, ahhhh!"

I punch into her once more, and my climax yanks my entire body taut as steel wires while I come so hard that my eyes roll back in my head.

She cradles me in her arms as I fall on top of her, both of us fighting for breath.

"*M'eudail*," I murmur in her ear, "I love—fucking you."

Had I almost said something else? No, I wouldn't do that. I don't love her.

She freezes for a moment, while my cock softens inside her.

Does she think I'd been about to say… No, she understands I can't give her that.

Emery skims her hands over my back. "This is another milestone. We had sex somewhere other than the bedroom. Next thing you know, we'll be ravishing each other in broad daylight in the garden."

I raise my head to smirk at her. "Donnae hold your breath for that one."

"No need to hold my breath." She squeezes her muscles around my cock, earning a wince and a slight gasp from me. "You take my breath away every time you touch me."

And now my *slat* is firming up again.

She smiles. "Again?"

"Mm." I run a hand down her side, over her hip, up to her thigh that's still latched around me. "In the bedroom this time. The desk is too hard to do everything I want to do with you."

I pull her up with me as I straighten, withdrawing from her body with a sigh. My gaze travels down her body, then to my own. I'm naked from the waist down, and my chest is also exposed thanks to Emery tearing my shirt open. Then I realize something. "Bollocks."

"What's the matter?"

"Forgot to use a condom."

"Relax. I'm on the pill, remember? We're covered."

My expression might have…lit up when she said that, though I don't smile. "We are, aren't we?"

"Mm-hm."

"Well then—" I scoop her up in my arms. "To the bedroom."

She points at my feet. "Might want to fix your pants first, or you'll dump us both on the floor."

"Ah. Yes. Can't have that."

I set her down and tug my trousers up, zipping them hastily. Then I carry my wife to our bedroom, where I shed all my clothes and my inhibitions, again. For tonight, I'll throw away the rules and make love to my wife until our bodies are slicked with sweat and she's too exhausted to move a muscle, so satisfied that she will never want to leave me. By the time we're done, I've kept the promise I made to myself. Emery lies limp and satiated beside me.

And we fall asleep entangled in each other's arms.

Chapter Twenty-Six

Something strange has happened to me this morning. Maybe waking up with my wife snuggled up to me has done it. Maybe her silliness is contagious. Whatever the cause, I develop a bizarre and irresistible desire to act like an eejit, if only to make Emery smile. She might think I'm off my head, but I'm hoping she will appreciate the effort.

I gently peel the covers back, trying not to wake her yet, and slide down the bed until I can rest my chin on her hip and my elbows at either side of her body. Then I move my fingers over her belly as if they're wee people cavorting on her skin.

She rouses little by little, her gaze sleepy as she struggles to understand what she sees. Emery blinks rapidly, then jerks her head up, her attention riveted to my fingers.

"What are you doing?" she asks.

I aim a sly smile at her. "Isn't that my line?"

"Usually." She tousles my hair. "What are your finger-people doing on my tummy?"

"Playing shinty." I make one finger-person run toward her belly button, then thrust my thumb out. "You have to imagine the caman he's swinging."

"The what?"

"Caman. The stick every player carries and uses to hit the ball."

She pushes up on one elbow. "What is shinty?"

"Something like lacrosse." I smile. "Only better."

Why does she look almost sick? I thought she wanted me to smile, but she doesn't seem happy about it. I order my finger-people to take a timeout while I study my wife. "Are you all right?"

"Fine, yeah." She drops back onto her pillow and waves a hand. "Go on. Don't let me interrupt your important shinty game."

"It's a match, not a game." I kiss her belly. "You'll learn the lingo when you watch the MacTaggarts play the Buchanans."

"You play shinty?"

"Aye."

"When will this game—sorry, match—happen?"

I shrug. "We play whenever both families can get twelve members to join in. For the MacTaggarts, that means our cousins need to be available. Lachlan may think he's the equivalent of ten men, but we need actual bodies on the field, not just his ego."

Her lips curve into a sweet wee smile.

And I end the timeout, letting my fingers play out their shinty match. A few minutes later, the MacTaggarts have won the match and defeated the Buchanans amid stage-whisper cheers, which I create. With my team victorious, I lay back on the bed with my head beside Emery's. Then I thread our fingers, holding her hand while we enjoy a comfortable silence. I'd never known silence could feel nice, but this time it does.

Emery bites the corner of her lip. "Do you think we'll be smote by a bolt of lightning?"

She does ask the strangest questions.

I feather my lips over her fingertips. "Why would that happen?"

"Because we're going to take vows and swear we love each other."

I give her a patient smile. "If everyone who married without love were smote down, hardly anyone would've survived the Middle Ages. Arranged marriages used to be the norm."

"Right, I forgot about that." She sits up and twists sideways to look at me. "So, there won't be any smiting. That's good news. But we still have things to discuss, about our wedding."

I exhale a long sigh. "Must we?"

"Yes."

She swings one leg over me to mount my lap. Though I enjoy the view of her breasts from below, I dread whatever she might say next.

Emery plants her hands on her hips. "My family will be here in two days. We haven't talked about where they'll stay."

"I've made hotel reservations."

"You made a decision without telling me. Again."

Distraction seems like my safest option. I trace the contours of her thighs with my hands, following them down to her knees, then retrace my path back to her hips. "You didn't mind when I decided to carry you into this room without asking."

"That was different." She starts to breathe more heavily as I run my hands up her inner thighs and tease the hairs at the apex with my fingertips. "Stop trying to distract me."

I smile with self-satisfaction, my mission accomplished.

She gives my chest a half-hearted slap. "That won't work, you sneaky, sneaky man. My family is not going to stay in a hotel. I haven't seen them in years. I want them to stay here."

My plan almost worked.

I try a different approach and glance around while pretending to be confused. "I doubt we'll all fit in this bed."

She pokes my chest with her index finger. "Figures when you suddenly decide to be playful, it's because you want to distract and confuse me in order to get your way."

"Am I succeeding?"

She captures my hands, prying them away from her inner thighs, and claps them down on my belly. "Keep your hands to yourself, Mr. MacTaggart. No matter how cute and sexy you are, I am not letting you bamboozle me into having my family stay in a hotel. I want them here with us, in this ginormous castle. This place has enough bedrooms to host an army."

"I hope you're not implying your family has come to destroy me in battle."

"Only if you tick them off." She snakes a hand down to stroke my stiffening *slat*. "If you agree to let them stay here, I'll make it worth your while."

"In what way?"

"Any way you want." She caresses my length with gentle sweeps of her hand. "Say yes, Rory baby. You have no choice but to bend to my will."

Surrendering to my wife used to sound like the worst sort of pain. But today, with Emery, I can't think of it that way anymore. At least for the moment.

My wife massages my cock with both of her soft hands until it's steel-hard and the head is moist. My body tenses, and I crimp my face—not from pain, but from the intense need to let her have her way with me. I have trouble catching my breath, and I can't stop my hips from rocking up into her strokes. My hands fist in the sheets, though I didn't do that on purpose.

She bends low over me, her breasts swinging in my face, and speaks in the huskiest, most erotic voice I've ever heard. "If you give me what I want, I'll give you what you want."

"Bargaining with your body?" I try to smirk, but the way she's touching me makes it impossible. "Isnae that—too much like—ah God, woman. Yer killing me."

She licks at the seam of my lips. "Say yes, and I'll use my mouth on you. Don't pretend it's not what you want."

I don't *want* it. I *need* it. Sucking in a breath, I let the words pour out of me. "Aye, yer family stays here."

"Thank you." She waddles backward until her face hovers above my erection. "I've wanted to taste you since the night we met."

Though I can barely breathe, a coldness rushes through me. "Emery…"

"Please don't tell me no again. You want me to do this, I can tell."

"I do, but—" I swallow hard. "No one has ever touched me this way. Considering how much I want you, ahmno sure I can keep still. Donnae want to hurt you."

"Relax, baby, you won't."

"Better restrain me, just in case."

She sets her hands at either side of my hips. "I am not tying you up. Stop worrying and tell me yes or no. Do you want this?"

Yes, I fucking want this. But I might lose control, like I did yesterday in my office. As I gaze at my wife—my sensual, adventurous, understanding wife—I remember last night and the way we'd shagged on my desk. Maybe losing control isn't a bad thing. And Emery wants to do this. For me.

"Do you want this?" she repeats.

"Aye."

She lowers her head to kiss and lick my inner thigh, working her way up to the base of my cock. Breaths gust out of my open mouth, making me feel lightheaded, and my gaze remains riveted to every swipe of her tongue. She flicks it out to lap at my sac, slowly moving her mouth onto my cock while lapping at my flesh as she works her way toward the crown.

My heels dig into the mattress. Every muscle in my body tightens.

She runs her tongue over the slit on the underside of my cock.

I shudder, spluttering out a ragged breath. "Please, Em, donnae go slow. Ahmno calm enough to take it."

"Whatever you need, honey."

She covers her teeth with her lips and engulfs my crown with her mouth, closing one hand around my sac. Fuck, she's going to give me a heart attack. My head rolls to the side as my lids shutter and my heart pounds. She drags her mouth up and down my length, kneading my thigh and moaning with pleasure as she tastes the beads of moisture gathered on the head of my cock. She keeps the pace measured, alternately cupping my *bagais* and skimming her hand along my thigh while I grunt and groan and lock my hands around the headboard rails, gripping them hard. She makes hungry little noises in the back of her throat that make my *slat* pulse. Then I roll my hips into the downward strokes of her mouth, half-mad from the need to come inside her mouth. But she won't want that. Will she? My balls tighten and retract into my body, and I know I won't last much longer.

My eyes spring open. With my gaze nailed to her, to my wife's mouth enclosing my cock and her fingers manipulating my flesh, my face twists with a mixture of pleasure and agony as I balance on the razor edge of climax.

She swipes at my flesh with her tongue, gliding her mouth up and down while maintaining a steady pace.

"Ah!" I shout as my release erupts in her mouth, powered by the swift jolts of electricity that grip my cock.

She keeps licking me, tenderly, until the orgasm dwindles and I stay her movements with a hand in her hair. She braces her chin on my thigh, smiling up at me.

"God, Em," I say, almost breathless, as I comb my fingers through her hair. "You are wonderful. I've never felt anything like that, it's almost as good as taking your body."

She levers up to sit back on her heels. "Why wouldn't you let me do that before?"

"Donnae know."

"Baloney. You know as well as I do, but I want to hear you say it." She stretches out on her side next to me, twirling her fingers on my chest and tickling the fine hairs on my skin. "This is part of your therapy. Tell me why."

I probably make an annoyed face as I pinch the bridge of my nose. "I was afraid of losing control. When we have sex, I can't help losing it a wee bit. But your mouth on me… I knew I could never withstand the onslaught."

"How did it feel to let go and give in?"

"Extremely satisfying." I aim a crooked smile at her. "You're a wicked little angel, *m'eudail*, and I love it."

"You're sinfully sexy yourself, Rory baby."

I fold an arm around her, letting my hand drift down to her erse.

"We should get up," she says. "It's after six."

"In a while." I shift my hand down to her belly, sneaking it lower, and dive my fingers between her thighs to find the taut bud of her clitoris. "Once I regain my strength, it's your turn."

She smiles in her playfully angelic way.

Maybe I should worry about why I want to lounge in bed with my wife, but I don't care. For a wee while longer, I want to enjoy making my wife come for me without thinking about anything else.

Chapter Twenty-Seven

"Come on, Rory," my wife says, "you can't stay holed up in your office twenty-four seven. Get your fine ass out of that chair and come outside with me. It's a beautiful day, and fresh air is good for you. So instead of drinking whisky in here, by yourself, try a little sunshine on the lawn with me."

"Why do you assume I drink whisky in my office?"

She gives me a look that implies we both know I do exactly that. Not every day, though. On occasion. Mostly after Emery has gotten annoyed with me.

My wife settles her bonnie erse onto my desk—right in front of me. She's not on the opposite side where the chairs are. No, she took it upon herself to commandeer my desk, though I still control the executive chair. "Give in, Rory baby. You know you want to come outside with me, so just say yes."

"I have work."

"Uh-uh-uh. That excuse is super old and not acceptable."

"The lawn hasn't been mowed yet."

"Yes, it has. Tavish mowed an hour ago."

What's the point in arguing? I might as well get some fresh air. "Fine. I will go outside."

"Yay!" She claps, though not loudly.

Then Emery seizes my hand, hauling me through the house and out onto the lawn, which has been neatly mown.

At the edge of the grass, I dig in my heels to halt us. "What are we meant to do out here?"

"Dance on the grass."

"I don't dance."

"Well then, spin with me."

"Spin?" I might've shouted that word. If she'd told me to strip naked and prance about like a bampot, I would've have reacted with less shock. I shake my head. "Emery—"

"Chill out, Rory." She releases my hand, spinning and skipping across the lush green grass, twirling even faster as she returns to me. My wife offers me her hand. "Give it a try. Please. For me."

My entire face "scrunches up," as Emery would say. And she has said it, several times lately. I "scrunch" when I'm "uptighting" myself again. Not sure if "scrunch" is a legitimate word, but "uptighting" absolutely is not.

She grasps both my hands, leaning back. "No skipping or prancing, I promise."

"But you expect me to spin."

"This one time. If you hate it, I'll never ask again."

I screw up my mouth this time, instead of scrunching it, though I'd rather be screwing my wife. Then I sigh with all the resignation of a condemned man. "What am I meant to do?"

"Hold my hands, lean back, and then we both turn in a circle together. Slow at first, but faster and faster with each circuit."

I plant my feet on the ground opposite hers and slant backward.

As one, we rotate in a circle. At first, I feel my face "scrunching" again because this is bloody ridiculous, but I discover the motion relaxes me more with every rotation. As our pace increases, I realize I sort of like this feeling of spinning round and round for no good reason. The faster we whirl, the more her hair flies around her face and the centrifugal force stretches our arms. I stop trying to see our surroundings, instead letting the world blur into the background while we keep spinning and a strange sensation of weightlessness overtakes me. Emery starts laughing, her smile so full of joy that I can't help myself. I laugh too. Soon, we're spinning so swiftly that all I can see is her eyes gazing back at me.

One of us trips—hard to say who—and we tumble to the ground. Emery lands on top of me. I wrap my arms around her. We both keep laughing for a moment, but then it fades away, and we just lie here gazing into each other's eyes.

I smile, really smile, for the first time in…I don't know how long. Since Lachlan's wedding, I think. No, it must've been Aidan's wedding. Aye, I'd been happy on those days, but it wasn't the kind of smile I'm giving my wife right now. She grins in response, looking more beautiful than ever because I've made her this happy.

Spinning made me happy, but only because I'm with her.

The clouds separate, admitting a golden ray of sunshine that lights up my sweet and wicked angel. And I laugh again.

Emery joins me, though she's still sprawled over me.

Is this joy? I don't think I've ever felt anything like it before.

She stops laughing, her expression turning softer, and she catches my face in her hands to kiss me.

I roll us over with my body covering hers, but even that can't interrupt our kiss.

Emery hooks her legs around mine, looping her arms around my neck.

Something happens then, as if a switch inside me has been flipped. I abruptly realize what I'm doing—lying on the lawn, in the daytime, kissing my wife with enough passion that we both know we'll be shagging right here on the grass in a minute or two at most. I pull away and spring to my knees, then sit back on my heels while straddling her feet.

She gazes at me with…adoration.

And I regard her without expression. What have I done? She'll think I can give her things I can't. I should never have let my loss of control last night and this morning affect her expectations. Shinty on her belly? Spinning on the lawn? I've lost my mind.

I cough. "That was interesting, but I have—things to do."

She lies there on the grass, studying me, but I can't decipher her expression.

Rising, I help her up. "I'll see you at dinner."

Then I rush back into the house.

My wife does not waltz into my office to tease me or call me Rory baby.

In the evening, I find Emery asleep on the sofa in the sitting room with an empty glass on her lap and an open bottle of Ben Nevis on the coffee table. Now I've driven her to drink. Christ, I should never have let things go this far, but I can't take back what I've done. I let her believe I might love her, though I've never spoken any such words. I rouse Emery to inform her dinner is ready and usher her into the dining room. Our idle conversation during the meal feels rather forced, but neither of us mentions the incident on the lawn.

Emery seems even more melancholy now, though she tries to hide it with tight smiles and breezy comments.

When we retire to the bedroom, we simply go to sleep. I hold her in my arms as we both drift off, and I wonder whether I have any idea what I'm doing. No, I don't. Not anymore. Emery tempts me to do things I never would've done on my own, or with anyone else. Why she has this power over me, I don't understand.

But it scares the fuck out of me.

Chapter Twenty-Eight

A countdown clock ticks in my head today, marking the hours and minutes until the invasion begins. I have one more day until Emery's family arrives. Meeting her parents and her sister doesn't fash me. Perhaps I do worry a wee bit about how they'll react to me since, as my wife claimed recently, I can be "a growly bear with the heart of a teddy." That's ridiculous, but I've given up trying to disabuse Emery of her silly notions. No one on earth would call me a teddy bear, though thanks to my wife, Aidan now calls me "sweetie-pie" every time I speak to him.

In the afternoon, Emery waltzes into my office the way only she can.

"To what do I owe this honor?" I ask.

"Your own neurosis." She braces her erse on the front edge of my desk. "We need to talk about yesterday."

I flip through a sheaf of papers, pretending not to care about anything. "Yesterday?"

"Come off it, Rory." She slaps her palm down on my papers. "You know exactly what I'm talking about. That moment when you actually had fun, out on the lawn. When you gave me a real smile for the first time in the history of us."

I remove my reading glasses and set them on the desk beside her hand. "I've smiled before. Many times."

"Uh-uh." She crosses her arms under those bonnie breasts. "You smirk. You almost smile. You kink your lips like you might be about to smile, but you don't go all the way. Not for me, at least. You grin and laugh with your family, but with me, you hold back like you think the universe will smack you down if you let on you like being around me."

"That's ridiculous."

"Ah, your favorite word." She taps the fingers of one hand on her arm. "Case in point, that day in the garden when you were happy until you looked at me. Then you frowned."

I huff. "I did not."

"You did." She leans in. "Are you accusing me of lying?"

"Of course not." I twirl my pen on the desktop. "If I frowned at you that day, I apologize. I had no idea I'd done that."

"Apology accepted." She settles her hands on her thighs. "About yesterday…"

I rub my chest, wincing slightly due to a pain that has no rational source. "What about it?"

"You had fun, admit it. Spinning made you smile."

"I suppose it did. And I had fun."

Though I've said what she wanted to hear, which happens to be true, she seems less than satisfied with my response. What does she want from me?

"Spinning may have been enjoyable," I say, twirling my pen faster, "but it wasn't as much fun as the night before." I catch the pen, halting its movement, and spread my hand over the desktop. "When I shagged you right here."

I pet the wood, gratified by the desire that warms her expression and makes her breathe harder. Distracting her with lust has become my only method of escaping uncomfortable conversations.

"I'm glad you had fun that night," Emery says, hopping off the desk. "Maybe tonight we can reenact that pivotal moment on a different surface. Maybe someday we'll even do it in the daytime."

She sways her hips as she exits my office, in a deliberate attempt to get me hard. It works, of course.

When she turns to pull the door closed, I utter a single word suffused with hunger. "Perhaps."

My wife shuts the door.

But I don't have a poke with her later. The wedding nonsense has begun early, and Emery is too busy chatting to her mother and her sister on her mobile. I pretend to sleep, an act she seems to believe, and wait for her to curl up beside me under the covers. I need to have her body tucked against me every night.

I can't sleep without her anymore.

I rise at six o'clock the next morning, and in accordance with Emery's wishes, I wake her so she knows I'm up. I'd promised to do that, and despite my numerous faults, I always keep my word. We eat breakfast together before I go into my office. This is my last chance for peace and quiet before the horde descends and the wedding insanity begins in earnest.

Though Emery insists on going to bed at the same as I do and rising at the same time too, I know it's not natural for her to sleep on such a rigid schedule. Every day, she yawns frequently, and I've caught her having a lie-down in the sitting room on multiple occasions. She does look like an angel when she sleeps. And when she's awake. Especially when she gives me one of her joyful smiles.

I haven't seen many of those lately—except for two days ago, on the front lawn.

After a few hours of solitude in my office, I start to feel…antsy. Maybe I should check on Emery. She must be feeling at least a wee twinge of anxiety over her family's imminent arrival and the upcoming wedding. My wife had worried about getting smote during the ceremony, after all.

She's not in the sitting room or our bedroom, so I go down to the ground floor in hopes of locating my wife there.

I find her in the kitchen.

Emery doesn't notice me hovering just outside the doorway. She's focused on the various food items arrayed on the island—three packages of ice cream plus jars of fudge and caramel sauce as well as a can of whipped cream.

"In the mood to indulge your cravings?" I ask.

Emery turns toward me, leaning back against the island, and sets her hands on the rim of the granite countertop. "I am jonesing for something decadent."

I pore my gaze over her body, my eyes narrowing at the sight of her denim shorts that seem barely to qualify as clothing. They expose every inch of her shapely legs, and the short-sleeved top she wears reveals the lush swells of her breasts. The neckline just covers her jutting nipples, and the edge of her lacy pink bra peeks out from under her shirt.

"Ah, Emery…" My voice has roughened, as it always does when I have her alone. I rub my jaw, suddenly realizing I forgot to shave this morning. Lusting for my wife all day every day erases every other thought. "Your erse looks divine in those shorts."

"I wore them for you."

"And I appreciate it." I saunter across the kitchen to her, and my attention flicks to the ingredients on the island. "Donnae need food to be decadent."

"You have an alternate suggestion?"

"For a more satisfying dessert." I frame her body with my arms, penning her to the island with my hands on the granite surface. "A feast of pleasure."

I trace the shell of her ear with my tongue, following it down to the lobe, and tug her flesh into my mouth. The full length of my body bears down on hers, and I almost groan as the warmth and suppleness of her flesh yields to mine, the temptation to have her right here, right now too irresistible to fight. My cock presses into her belly, a steel-hard line against her willing body.

"Sex in the kitchen?" she says, and pushes her hand between our bodies to palm me through my trousers. "And in the daytime, with Mrs. Darroch somewhere in the house. My goodness, Rory, you're tossing out all the rules."

"Hell with the rules." I roll my eyes up, though not because she's vexing me. The lass has started to fondle me with her delicate, but strong, fingers. I flatten a hand over the small of her back. "I'll be taking my wife whenever and wherever I please."

"So do it. Right here."

Heat ripples through me as my gaze lands on the neckline of her shirt. "Do ye let your bra show in public?"

"No, baby. Only for you."

I groan and crush my mouth to hers, loving the way her lips yield to mine even while she thrusts her tongue between my lips, and I cannae stop myself from ravaging her mouth while she devours me with a matching hunger. I'm starved for her, every moment of every day, and the only thing that will satisfy the need is her body clenching my *slat*. She wraps her free arm around my neck while I lap at the roof of her mouth and slide my hand down to her erse. She rasps her thumb over the slit of my cock, exposed above the waistband of my trousers.

My body jerks as an electric shock rips through me. I grunt into her mouth, and my fingers sink into her erse.

Our fused lips muffle her frustrated whimper.

With my mouth fastened to hers, I grasp her erse with both hands and hoist her onto the island. Her bottom rests on the granite, but her bare legs dangle at either side of my hips, the perfect frame for my body. She wriggles against me, lashing her tongue around mine like she cannae get enough, and she opens wider for me. No man could resist an invitation like that. I need to shag her so badly that I hardly notice it when my ears start to ring because I can't take in a full breath while I'm ravishing her mouth. I unbutton her blouse, keeping one hand on her erse to hold her still while I free each button. Spreading the halves of her top, I mold my hands to her breasts and stroke my thumbs over her nipples.

Emery fumbles with the buttons on my shirt. I've shoved a hand inside her bra to claim one breast long before she gets my shirt undone and lays her palms on my chest. She races her hands down my skin and straight to the button fly of my trousers.

I coax her down onto the island, flat on her back, then unbutton my trousers and let them slump down to my ankles, suddenly glad I'd gone without underwear today. I lay my body over hers. She moans, the sound rife with need. I kiss a path down her throat and chest, spurring her to arch into my mouth. When my lips find the lacy edge of her bra, I dive my tongue beneath the fabric to drag it down the inner seam until I graze her areola.

She hugs my head to her breast and slings both legs around my waist. "Bloody hell."

We both freeze. I did not speak those words.

Slowly, I rotate my head toward the doorway, though Emery still clutches my face to her tits. I clamp my lips into a hard line as I see who has interrupted us.

Emery glances at the doorway too—and yelps.

Lachlan stands there, his eyes large and his mouth agape. He swerves his head to the left and throws a hand up to block his view of us. "For Christ's sake, Rory. Put some trousers on."

I leap backward and yank my trousers up, hastily zipping them. The button hangs open, but I don't bother with that, not when my brother has just seen my wife half-naked on the granite island. Emery lies there with her shirt gaping and one breast mounded up to expose everything except the nipple. And Lachlan saw that. I swallow a growl and lift her into a sitting position, then struggle to button her shirt. My fingers can't manage the task.

Emery shoos my hands away. "Cool down, baby. I'll take care of my own clothes."

Lachlan chuckles. "Is he a sweetie-pie baby?"

I shoot him a dark look.

While my wife tucks her breast back into her bra and buttons her shirt, I stalk across the kitchen to glare at my brother, though I doubt my expression seems menacing enough to cow him. "Donnae be looking at my wife."

"I wouldn't have minded a good look at her." Lachlan lowers his hand, smirking at me. "Unfortunately, all I saw was you. Didn't need such an unobstructed view of your erse."

My face feels hot, which is ridiculous. "Then maybe ye shouldnae be walking into our home like it belongs to ye. Havenae ye heard of knocking?"

Lachlan gives a careless shrug. "Mrs. Darroch let me in. She said Emery was in the kitchen and you were in the office."

I squint at him. "What do you want with my wife?"

"Calm down, man." Lachlan raises his hands, palms out. "Emery told Erica I could pick up the book she's borrowing today. Didn't mean to storm your castle while you were under your good wife's skirts. Isn't this a Wednesday, one of those days when medieval husbands couldn't bed their ladies?"

My shoulders bunch so tightly it almost hurts. I'm not angry with Lachlan. I'm silently chastising myself for even thinking about shagging my wife in the kitchen in broad daylight. Of course someone walked in on us. That's my curse.

Emery hops off the counter, with her clothes now set right, and trots up to lay a hand on my upper arm. I throw her a sideways glance, and the tender look on her face melts away some of my anxiety. She slips her other hand into mine, though I can't seem to relax my fingers.

"Are you planning to pummel your brother?" she asks, her tone as sweet as her smile. "Go ahead, if it'll make you feel better. But honestly, Rory, I don't think it's the most logical response. Lachlan got a gander at your bare ass, not mine."

"He saw you—on the—with your—"

Now I can't piece together a complete sentence. What a ruddy eejit I am.

Emery squeezes my hand. "It was an accident. I'm not embarrassed, and you shouldn't be either. Tell Lachlan you forgive him and let it go."

The breath I hadn't realized I'd been holding floods out of me. My shoulders deflate, and my entire body follows suit while I fold my hand around hers. Only Emery knows how to melt the cold ball that's been lodged in my gut since the day she married me.

I grudgingly tell Lachlan, "Sorry. I may have…overreacted."

My brother's brows hike up, and he gives my wife an appreciative nod. "You are a miracle worker, Emery. Getting Rory to admit he was wrong is one of the signs of the apocalypse."

I huff. "Didn't say I was wrong."

"Haven't heard forgiveness yet." Lachlan is smirking again, hoping to get me up to high doh one more time. My brothers both enjoy prodding me until I bark at them. They think it's entertaining.

I growl, then mutter, "I forgive you. Just donnae do it again."

He raises one hand. "I solemnly swear never to breach Rory's castle again without permission."

I look at Emery. "Happy?"

"Yes." She boosts herself onto her tiptoes and kisses my cheek. "Thank you, Rory baby."

Her eyes flare wide at the instant she realizes what she said, but it's too late.

Lachlan bursts out laughing, the uproarious noise reverberating through the kitchen.

"Rory baby?" he says between guffaws. "Wait till I tell Aidan about that one. He'll love it more than 'sweetie-pie.' "

I feel my lips stretch into a tight line as I bore my gaze into Emery. "You promised never to speak that phrase in front of anyone but me."

"I'm sorry, I really am." She bites her lip, hunching her shoulders. "It slipped out."

Lachlan's laughter finally subsides, but he still seems inordinately amused and quite pleased with himself. He claps a hand on my shoulder. "It was bound to come out sooner or later. Can't keep something like this a secret in the MacTaggart family."

I warp my mouth into a half frown, half-smile. "Not when we enjoy tormenting each other so much."

"I won't tell Aidan." Lachlan winks. "Probably."

Emery eyes us both. "Can I trust you to behave yourselves without me? The book Erica wants is in the bedroom."

"Aye, you can trust me," Lachlan says. "Can't speak for Rory, though. He seems to need his wife to keep him in line."

I purse my lips.

Emery pats my cheek. "Try not to kill each other until I get back."

"No promises," I say with a slight smile. "Lachie might deserve a right skelping."

"Lachie?" my brother says with a chuckle. "Oh, I am for certain telling Aidan what your wife calls you."

Shaking her head, Emery jogs off down the hall, out of sight.

I take her advice and let go of my humiliation. Lachlan and I spend the next few minutes discussing when we should hold Highland games on the green again, and when we might trounce the Buchanans in another shinty match. I prefer playing shinty on my wife's belly, but I will not admit that to my brother.

Emery returns, holding a book in one hand. A bit of newspaper covers the book, so I can't tell what it is.

Lachlan accepts the package. "Best get home. We'll see you two on Saturday. Your big day, as Erica calls it."

The wedding. *Bod an Donais.*

Once I hear the door to the outside clap shut, I relax at last. Setting a hand on the island, I lean into it. "What book are you lending Erica?"

"My copy of the Kama Sutra."

"What if I wanted to read it?"

"Happy to demonstrate my favorite parts for you." She bounces on the balls of her feet and rubs her hands together. "What should we do now?"

I push away from the counter, pick her up, and deposit my wife on the island beside her collection of dessert ingredients. Grabbing the can of whipped cream, I touch its tip to her breast. "I have ideas. And we have time before we leave for Inverness to meet your family."

She smiles, locking her legs around me. "Show me, Rory baby. You always have the best ideas."

And I donnae care that it's daytime.

Chapter Twenty-Nine

My sanctum is in shambles. I stand on the tarmac at the Inverness airport with Emery at my side while we watch four adults and twin toddlers pour out of the jet I'd sent for them. My in-laws have arrived. Perhaps I've jumped the gun a bit in declaring my ordered life has been shattered, but I can tell these people will not respect my need for privacy or my rules. Not that I plan to tell them my rules. Those are for Emery. I wouldn't want her family to think I'm a rigid bastard.

I am like that, but they don't need to know.

The children and the women voice their joy at seeing each other with an outrageous amount of squealing and shrieking. I expect that from bairns. But grown women? The twin lassies fling their wee arms at me and my wife, but Emery's sister and her brother-in-law grab the bairns before they can latch onto us. Her parents wave and grin at us, then Mrs. Granger takes hold of one of the children.

Emery's sister, now free of her bairn, throws her arms wide and rushes at my wife, bounding like her children had done. She shrieks, "Emmy!"

My wife shrieks too, her arms spread wide. "Haddie!"

The women bolt for each other, colliding in a jumble of arms and a cacophony of overjoyed noises that make my eardrums ache.

This is insanity. My wife has turned into a raving bampot, all because she's seen her sister again for the first time in years. All right, maybe I can understand feeling very happy about that. But screaming? Leaping about? It's utter nonsense.

Emery drags her sister over to me. "Rory, meet Hadley. She's married to Cole Wilson, the hottie over there with my parents and the two kiddies."

"Pleasure to meet you," I say as I offer my hand to Hadley. "Welcome to Scotland."

"Thank you, Rory," my sister-in-law says. "Wow, you sure swept my sister off her feet, didn't you? It's okay, I forgive you for the whole whirlwind marriage thing. Now you get to make it up to her with a big bash."

Aye, the word bash makes this wedding rubbish sound so much more attractive. I might need a good whack on the head to survive this insanity.

Emery introduces me to her brother-in-law, who seems like a decent bloke. Ted Granger, Emery's father, shakes my hand vigorously and smiles. Not the reaction I was expecting given our brief phone conversation a few weeks ago. Penny Granger, my mother-in-law, hugs me and kisses my cheek while havering about how happy she is that Emery found "the right man."

I'm not the right one for Emery. She won't find a happy ending with me.

Hadley's daughters, Madison and Mackenzie, giggle shyly when I kneel to greet them.

"You two are the perfect couple," Ted Granger announces just as I rise from saying hello to the bairns. Then he slaps my back. "I ordered a full background check on you, but it came back clean. Welcome to the family."

When I glance at Emery, she shrugs and shakes her head. The slight uptick of her lips suggests she enjoys this mad spectacle. I feel like I need several fingers of Ben Nevis.

I guide Emery's parents and her brother-in-law, along with the bairns, toward the limousine I'd rented for the occasion. Can't have my in-laws crammed into the Mercedes. We wouldn't all fit, anyway.

Emery and her sister keep back a short distance, seemingly engaged in a secret conversation.

Once we arrive at Dùndubhan, my wife and I show her family to the quarters I've arranged for them in the guest wing. Aye, they will sleep in bedrooms on the ground floor while Emery and I will have the third floor to ourselves. And aye, that arrangement is no accident. I plotted this scenario early in the morning in my office. I know Emery will want privacy as much as I do so we can shag each other until we're too exhausted to do anything else except fall asleep. We will need to forgo sex in the kitchen, office, or anyplace where someone might stumble onto us in flagrante. It's a sacrifice I make for her.

I mention my disappointment to Emery that evening.

She pastes her body to mine while I'm in the middle of undressing. Since she's naked, her breasts scrape over my chest when she wriggles against me. "It's only for a little while, baby. Then you can have me anytime, anywhere, as often as you want."

Then she drags me onto the bed, shoving me down on my back, and unzips my trousers.

Aye, she knows how to placate me.

The next day, I drive the grown-up lasses into Loch Fairbairn so Emery, Hadley, and Penny can meet up with Erica and Calli for what my wife calls "a dress-hunting expedition." My mother and my three sisters join them too. I retreat into my office in the village, leaving my wife to deal with eight women who, I'm fair certain, all think they know what's best for Emery. The bairns stayed at home with Cole, as did Ted.

I gave my wife strict instructions for choosing a dress after she suggested she might buy something inexpensive. She doesn't want to make use of our joint bank account. So I told her, "Spend the bloody money, it's yours too."

She smiled and kissed me. "You really are a big old teddy bear."

I've given up trying to convince her I am not a teddy bear or a sweetie-pie.

For the next three hours, I try to focus on work. But my thoughts keep returning to Emery and the wedding. We will stand before our families and a minister, vowing to love and honor each other forever. I have no idea if Emery will mean those words. I will be forced to lie. Whatever I might feel for her, it can't be love since I'm no longer capable of that. And I won't stay with her until I die. I can't. Three torturous journeys down the matrimonial path have left me too scarred to be any good for Emery.

If one of us gets smote down on our wedding day, it will be me. I belong in Hell.

The front door opens, then bangs shut. A moment later, Emery sprints into my office. She's breathing hard, her cheeks pink from exertion.

I leap out of my chair, rushing to her. "What's wrong?"

She takes a few slow, deep breaths until she's calmed herself. "Graham. I bumped into him outside his office, and he said…things."

I grasp her shoulders. "What things?"

"He mentioned 'those pictures' and said you—Well, that's about it. How can he know about the photos Sebastian took? That must be what he meant."

Aye, she changed the subject deftly, but it's clear Graham must've said something about me. Emery doesn't want to tell me about it, though. "I don't know how Graham found out about the pictures, but I will contact my investigator to ask him."

"Okay."

I study her for a moment, then decide to just ask. "What did Graham say about me?"

She hunches her shoulders, turning her face away from me. "He said my past will be too much for you once you see it splashed across the newspapers for everyone to gawp at."

That bloody ersehole.

I resist the impulse to clench my fists and instead cradle her face in my hands. "Ignore the goddamn scunner. He wants to start trouble, that's all."

She nods, though she seems unconvinced.

Maybe I should've told her nothing will make me think any less of her, not even seeing her nude body displayed on the front page of *The Loch Fairbairn World News*. But I can't summon the words.

I hustle her out to the Mercedes.

For the rest of the week, we don't discuss Graham or that bastard who humiliated Emery. The wedding rubbish occupies all our time, and the days rush past in a blur until The Day arrives.

I'm about to swear I love my wife, in front of everyone I know.

I wait at the edge of the lawn, near the castle wall, and watch the guests file past me to take their seats in the chairs set up on the grass. Most of the guests are MacTaggarts—my immediate family as well as my cousins, uncles, and aunts. Emery's family sits in the first row with my parents and siblings. My wife and I had agreed not to have groomsmen or bridesmaids, just the two of us standing at the altar with the minister. No one minded.

Though I should make my way to the altar, I can't move from this spot. I'm about to vow I love Emery. My chest feels tight, as if a lead weight is settling onto my ribs little by little, compressing my lungs and making it hard to breathe. That pang has returned too, stronger and sharper than ever, no longer a vaguely pleasant sensation but more like a knife stabbing into me.

What have I done?

I'd spoken those words aloud on our first wedding night, when I'd suffered from a wee problem related to my cock. The anxiety I'd experienced then seems like a trifle compared to what I'm feeling now. Can't catch my breath. Can't move a muscle. My ears have started to ring, and a coldness sifts through my body, infiltrating every cell.

What have I done? Emery deserves better than this, better than me. I had no right to drag her into my life and treat her like my sex slave. I should march up to the altar and announce the wedding is off. But we're already married. It won't do any good unless I shout that I don't love my wife and never will, that she married me because I'm paying her to do it.

Except Emery swears she didn't marry me for the money. She sees my potential.

The pressure has mutated into an itch deep under my skin, in a part of myself I can never reach. I scratch my neck, my cheek, then push a hand inside my shirt to scratch my chest.

"Got fleas?" Lachlan says as he comes up beside me.

"No, I do not have bloody fleas."

"Ah, then it's wedding jitters. Erica told me this would happen, but I couldn't believe it. The Steely Solicitor never gets nervous."

"Why must everyone invent ridiculous nicknames for me?"

"To fash you, of course." Lachlan winks. "Relax, Rory. This is a happy day."

He heads into the crowd, taking a seat beside his wife.

The last thing I feel today is happy. That single question echoes in my mind. *What have I done?*

All the guests have arrived and been seated. Lachlan turns to wave for me to take my place.

I trudge up the silver-carpeted aisle, dressed in my kilt with a waist-length black jacket, a white shirt, and a black bow tie as well as black boots. Emery has no idea I've worn this outfit. I know she'll like it, though, and that's why I chose it. She loves me in a kilt.

Loves me. Acid roils in my gut, threatening to creep up into my throat.

At the altar, I turn to face the crowd.

Emery's mother and sister trot up the aisle to sit beside their husbands.

And my wife emerges from the house, walking slowly up the aisle toward me.

My heart stutters. She is an angel, a genuine vision of a heavenly creature who, for reasons beyond my comprehension, wants to pledge herself to me—again. Her lace-covered dress hugs her upper body, then flares out into a flowing skirt, while the neckline reveals a tasteful suggestion of her cleavage. Her blonde hair cascades over her shoulders in loose waves, with wee roses clinging to the locks. Instead of a full veil, she has a length of lacy material pinned to the back of her head with a silver clip.

I can't breathe again, my chest tightening as if a vise is gripping me harder and harder every second. My mouth goes dry. My pulse beats so fast I think I might pass out, but somehow, I stay conscious and upright.

She glances at the crowd, and I can tell she's noticed the three surprise guests I invited. Her friends from Colorado—Pam, Sabri, and Luke—smile and wave at her. Emery gives her mates a friendly smile, then beams at me.

That pain. In my chest. I swallow but can't dislodge the rock in my throat.

She's beautiful. Perfect. And I don't deserve her.

Our gazes connect, and I go stiff, unable to look away or even blink.

Her smile falters, and her lips quiver, but she doesn't seem to be sad, not this time. She seems overcome with emotion.

No, I don't deserve her, but I can't let her go either.

She manages a gentle smile, her lips no longer trembling, as she joins me at the altar and we face each other. I have nothing else to do except stare into her eyes and try to understand my reaction to seeing her in a wedding dress. As the minister begins to speak, delivering the usual words, Emery and I never break eye contact, not even when the minister asks us to recite our vows. Love, honor, cherish, till death.

Then it's time for those two words: "I do."

Emery gets choked up, her eyes shimmering with the start of tears, but she utters the syllables while gazing straight into my eyes.

I mumble "I do" while struggling not to cock it up, though I hesitate before speaking the words. Never in my life have I been like this, a mass of raw nerves and tangled emotions, too confused to understand what's happening. I've been married to Emery for weeks. Why should a second ceremony turn me into a bampot?

When we exchange rings, I glance away from her only long enough to get the gold band on her finger.

"You may kiss the bride," the minister says.

I take her face in my hands, slant forward, and touch my lips to hers.

Her body slackens as if she's let go of everything, as if nothing else matters except this moment when our lips meet. She sways into me and tips her head back, all but begging me to kiss her, *really* kiss her. I press my mouth to hers more firmly and dive my hands into her hair, the soft wee petals of the silk roses in her hair brushing against my fingers. Her lips relax too and open for me while she exhales a delicate breath that teases my skin.

I pull away, though my hands linger on her cheeks.

Clapping erupts. Then someone whistles, and the clapping escalates into cheers and whoops from dozens of voices, male and female, young and old.

Emery rotates her eyes to scan our audience, and I follow her gaze.

Aidan whistles with two fingers in his mouth, then grins and pumps his fists in the air.

I might find that amusing if I weren't still entangled in my own raw nerves.

Ted Granger whoops.

Why should he celebrate the fact I've married his daughter, again? The man barely knows me. I remove my hands from Emery's face, drawing her attention back to me. Since I'm positive I can't speak yet, I graze my thumb over her chin.

Then I claim her hand and guide her back down the aisle.

Chapter Thirty

Wedding receptions are meant to be... What? Fun, I suppose. It's a celebration of the couple's love for each other and their bright future together. But I don't feel like celebrating. How can I? Emery married me because I seduced her into believing our arrangement would benefit her, that she would have the freedom to do what she wants. Yet all she seems to want is to change me. I'm not the sort of man she needs. We both know that. I should give her the money and let her go, now, tonight.

But I can't give her up. I want Emery to be mine. I can't love her, or anyone, but I need to possess her. It's selfish and wrong, but I lost all my senses on that day when I dragged Emery into a magistrate's office in Colorado Springs. She has done everything I demanded of her, and I've given her nothing.

The reception takes place on the first floor—not the ground floor, as the American guests believe, until I explain the layout of this castle to them. The buffet is downstairs in the dining room, but the actual event takes place in the great hall on the first floor where Scots and Americans gather to dance and joke and do whatever other bollocks wedding guests enjoy. We also opened up the long gallery on the second floor to handle the overflow, considering how many MacTaggarts are in attendance.

The door to my office is closed and locked to deter anyone from sneaking into my sanctum. I don't want any randy couples using my office as a location for sexual encounters. Only my wife and I enjoy the privilege of shagging on my desk.

I'd meant to lock the office door, but suddenly, I can't remember if I did that or not. Too late to worry about it now. Besides, everyone is too busy having a good time to think about breaching my private space.

Time seems to crawl along one second at a time while I avoid my blethering relatives and try to make my stomach want food. I fail. Eating won't help the pain in my chest or the gaping hole deep inside me that nothing can fill. I excavated that hole myself, using the pain of three disastrous marriages as the shovel.

A flash of white draws my attention to the other end of the great hall and to my wife, who's hurrying away.

I want to rush after her and…do something. But I just stand here, immobilized by indecision. What if she wants to be alone for a wee while? I should give her that much. My feet decide for me, compelling me to race after her, down the stairs and out the vestibule door into the night air.

Emery stands near the outside wall of the vestibule—talking to Graham Oliver.

They're at an angle to me, so they don't notice I'm here, especially since I hover just inside the doorway with shadows concealing me.

Graham warps his mouth into a nasty smile. "Sorry I missed the ceremony. I predict the marriage willnae last a week more."

My wife bars her arms over her chest. "Your predictions don't mean diddly-squat to me."

Graham scratches his chin. "But my next article will."

I step out of the doorway into the moonlight.

"What the bloody hell are you doing here?" I snarl as I stalk up to Graham, seizing the man's collar. "Leave my wife alone."

The bastard sneers. "Ye donnae know your bride as well as ye think, MacTaggart. I've seen sides of her bound to make ye cringe."

"*Dùin do ghob*, ye scunner."

"I'll shut the fuck up when I see fit."

Fisting my hands in Graham's shirt, I hoist him off the ground. Then I growl through my clenched teeth, "Go home to your sewer and stay away from my wife."

I hurl Graham away.

He crumples to the ground, scrambles to his feet, and brushes grass off his trousers. "I'll be seeing ye both. Soon."

The slimy *cacan* runs for one of the vehicles parked in the vicinity of the drive. I glare at the black sedan until the shadows of the forest engulf it.

"Relax," Emery says. "Don't let him ruin this day for us."

I grunt.

She slips her hand into mine. "Let's go back inside."

My wife leads me back to the great hall, and we enter the reception hand in hand. Everyone we pass looks at us as if we're the king and queen of Dùndubhan, the perfect couple with the perfect relationship, but they have no idea about our arrangement. We aren't soul mates, or whatever rubbish they're all thinking. Five minutes after we reenter the fray, Lachlan and Aidan spirit me away to a far corner to talk about shinty and other meaningless topics. I want to know what Graham Oliver is plotting, and I can't stop thinking about what he said. *My next article.* The scunner plans to smear my wife with his lies, I'm sure. If he humiliates her with those pictures that Sebastian Zegers took, I will throttle the lying *bod ceann.*

While my brothers chat about sports, I scan the crowd until I see my wife. She's talking to her mother and her sister, at the opposite end of the great hall.

While I watch, Penny Granger inserts two fingers from each hand into her mouth and lets out a whistle so loud and piercing that everyone stops talking. All gazes veer to my mother-in-law.

"It's time for the bride and groom's first dance," she announces.

We've been married for several weeks, yet she talks as if we only tied the knot today.

Penny seizes her daughter's hand and waves her arm in the air, clearly gesturing to me. Since I doubt I have a choice in the matter, I let Penny herd us both upstairs to the long gallery where the final stage of the reception will take place. It's become the dance floor.

I must seem dazed, considering the way Emery scrutinizes me as I take her in my arms for our first dance, cradling her palm in mine in the best approximation of formal dancing I can achieve. While I settle my hand over the small of her back, and she places hers on my shoulder, I exhale the breath I hadn't realized I was holding in until my ears started to ring. The tension in me eases a touch as we move across the floor together, turning in slow circles, keeping pace with the almost waltz-like tempo of the music. I don't know the song, but it's quite nice.

Emery smiles in a soft, almost loving way while gazing into my eyes.

She can't love me. I've given her no reason to feel that way. What I see in her eyes must be relief that the wedding is almost over, and soon we'll get back to everyday life.

But I realize with a mental jolt that I'm gazing at her in the same way. I don't need to see my face to understand. I feel it. The gentle, lulling music has seeped inside me, and I can't help searching for something in her eyes that will tell me what to do, how to give her what she needs.

I startle out of my reverie, not quite jerking, but blinking several times in the space of a second or two, as if I've gotten grit in my eyes.

No, I can't give Emery anything that she needs—except for a divorce.

Since I can't look at my wife anymore, I focus on the people around us. Gavin Douglas and my sister Jamie are entertaining the twin daughters of Hadley and Cole Wilson.

Emery loops her arms around my neck. "Did you fly Gavin back here for the wedding? Last I heard, he'd gone home to America. Jamie was bummed."

"I offered," I tell her, while I link my arms behind her back, "and Gavin accepted the invitation to travel here on the jet."

"You wanted Jamie to be happy."

"For one day, if nothing else. What happens next is up to him."

"That was very sweet of you. And it was extra sweet to invite Pam, Sabri, and Luke."

"Your happiness is worth any cost."

She tickles the nape of my neck with her fingertips. "You want people to think you're a grumpy grizzly, but you're really a teddy bear."

"You have a strange opinion of me." I regard her with guarded curiosity. "How can you call me sweet and a teddy bear after the way I've treated you?"

"Sometimes you are cranky. On rare occasions, you're a jerk. I understand why you are the way you are, though, and I accept it."

I try to pull my head back, but her hands prevent it. "Why would you do that?"

"Accept you as-is? Because I also know you want to evolve." She lifts onto her toes to level our gazes, letting my arms hold her off the floor. "Your therapy isn't over yet. You have potential, and I'll help you realize it in whatever way I can."

We lapse into silence while she rests her cheek on my shoulder. Her feet touch down on the floor.

And I stare into a distance even I can't see, a place too far away to reach. Emery thinks I'm "on rare occasions" a bastard. She must have selective memory loss, because I've been an ersehole more times than I've been kind to her. Whatever potential she thinks she sees in me, it's an illusion.

Sometimes, though, I wish I could be the man she imagines I am.

Emery whispers in my ear, "You are the handsomest groom ever, very regal and sexy in your formal kilt-wear."

I glance down at her but can't think of a thing to say. Should I compliment her dress? Or her hair? I've never been good at knowing what a woman wants to hear.

"Would it be rude if we snuck out of here?" she asks. "You slept in the other bedroom last night to make our mothers happy, but I'm feeling seriously deprived of sex and cuddling."

Cuddling. She wants more than sex, and I'm not sure I can handle that tonight. I've felt raw in too many ways ever since I woke up this morning.

"What's the matter, baby?" my wife asks.

"Nothing."

"Baloney."

I loosen my hold on her and swerve my focus to the doorway. Anything to avoid her gaze.

"Hey." Emery snaps her fingers to regain my attention. "You haven't told me what you think of my dress, or whether I look pretty today."

"Well—I—The dress is fine. Rather flattering."

"Gee, don't gush like that. It's embarrassing."

I cough and stare at her shoulder. "You look pretty today."

"If you're resorting to repeating what I said near verbatim, something is definitely up with you. Spill, Rory. That means talk to me."

My gaze flits here, there, and everywhere as I struggle to come up with an excuse she might believe. But my movements begin to seem frantic even to me, until I spot my salvation—the wet bar. "I need a drink. Excuse me."

I push away from Emery so fast that she stumbles half a step, then I bolt for the wet bar where Lachlan and Aidan are sipping whisky and blethering. My brothers gossip almost as much as their wives do.

Emery gapes at me as I bark orders at the bartender. The man seems confused by my tone of voice, but he brings me a glass filled with two fingers of Ben Nevis.

I swig the contents in one mouthful and demand another, tossing it back in a single swallow.

Aye, whisky is the answer. If I drink too much, at least I won't need to engage in any more conversations with my wife about why I am the way I am, though she claims that she already knows the answer.

I see you.

Whatever Emery meant by that, I donnae care anymore. The whisky has made me feel looser, but not enough that I can stop thinking. I slap my glass down on the bar and shout, "Another."

The bartender gives me an odd look, but he pours two more fingers of whisky into my glass.

"More," I say.

His brows draw together, but he adds another measure to my glass.

My gaze wanders around the makeshift dance floor, where I see my wife taking a stroll or a twirl or whatever the fuck people call it when they dance. My cousin Iain is enjoying the company of my wife as they shuffle their feet across the floor. No, Iain shuffles. Emery floats like an angel.

I see you.

Why do I keep hearing her voice repeating that silly statement? Of course she can see me. Everyone can. I'm not invisible.

My glass is empty again, so I flap my hand at the bartender. He wears a pinched expression when he approaches me. "Ah, Mr. MacTaggart, sir, your brother said I shouldn't serve you anymore."

"This is my house, and I will drink whatever I want."

"Aye, but—" The lad swallows hard enough it shows in his throat. "Your brother said—"

"Which one? Aidan or Lachie?"

"Uh, that one." He points toward Lachie.

"Fine, do what he says." I lean over the bar to grab the bottle of Ben Nevis. "I'll serve myself."

If I want to get buckled, it's my business, not Lachie's.

While I watch my wife cavorting with every MacTaggart on earth, and probably some who flew in from Mars, I guzzle whisky straight from the bottle. Aye, I'm feeling much more relaxed now. Emery can't see me, I'm sure, since I can't see her either. She disappeared into the crowd of dancing puppets with my cousin Evan. Or maybe it was Jack.

Puppets? They're people, ye eejit.

I lift the bottle to my lips.

And someone snatches it away from me.

"Enough, Rory," Lachlan says. "We're taking you upstairs to sleep it off."

"Sleep what off?"

Aidan clamps a hand on my shoulder. "You'll thank us for this in the morning, sweetie-pie."

"Willnae do that, ye kitchen."

"Do ye mean *cacan*, Rory?"

Isn't that what I said?

Lachlan gestures to someone.

Gavin Douglas trots over here like a good puppy. "What's up?"

"Tell Emery her husband is buckled," Lachlan says, "and we're taking him upstairs to their bedroom."

"Sure thing." Gavin gives me a strange look, then hurries away.

My brothers each grasp one of my arms and half-drag me out of the long gallery and up the stairs to the third floor. By the time we reach the bedroom door, I'm only half-conscious. I hear Lachie and Aidan talking, but I cannae understand any of it.

"We thought to drop him on the bed," Aidan says.

Someone's shoe drums on the floor. "I'd say dump him on the floor, it's what he deserves for this. But put him on the bed."

Is that Emery?

With a bit of grunting and huffing, my brothers heft me onto the bed.

"Should we, ah… undress him?" Lachlan asks.

"Don't bother," my wife says. "You can go. Thank you."

Footsteps recede, and the door thunks shut.

And I pass out.

Chapter Thirty-One

My head feels like a very large man has sat on it, and my mouth seems to have grown a colony of fungus inside it. The clock on the night-stand ticks so loudly that I think someone must've put a megaphone in front of it. What did I do last night? I remember dancing with Emery, then...

Mhac na galla. I got drunk.

Though my head hurts, I know this pain will be nothing compared to what my wife will do to me. I deserve to be punished, but I can't imagine Emery doing that. No, she'll give me something worse.

Her misery.

I shift on the bed, making it creak and rustling my clothes. Grimacing with my eyes still shut, I rub my forehead.

"Good morning," my wife says with far too much cheerfulness.

Aye, she is upset with me. Very upset.

"Congratulations," she says. "You slept in for the first time ever."

I peek out at her between my fingers, since I have my hands clamped to my forehead. "What happened?"

"Are you serious? You don't remember?"

"Remember what?" I drop my hand and peer up at the bed's canopy. Her question confused me for a moment, but now I realize what she means. "*Bod an Donais.*"

She drops her erse onto the bed near my feet. "Yeah, you are a devil's dick."

"Emery..." My voice trails off while the import of what I did last night sinks into my brain. "I ruined our second wedding night, didn't I?"

"Yep."

I spew a string of Gaelic curses. "Christ, I'm an erse. Please believe me, I'm sorry for letting you down again. You have every right to be angry, so go on and shout at me. I deserve it."

She folds her arms over her belly and massages her wrist furiously. "Not interested in yelling. Doesn't fix anything. You keep doing stupid things and then saying you're sorry. An ass you might be, but your apologies are wearing thin."

"What can I do?"

"Don't know." She scrutinizes my face, and her lips pucker. "I've got a revolutionary idea. How about you stop doing stupid things, then you won't need to apologize for them."

Her wrist-rubbing escalates into scratching.

I push up onto my elbows, my attention drawn to her wrist. "You're not angry, are you?"

"No. Well, yes, but that's a minor issue at this point."

With my eyes squeezed shut, I let my shoulders cave in. "I hurt you, again. Last night you said you accept me as I am, but I donnae see how you can overlook this. I behaved—I'm a selfish bastard."

"I don't overlook your faults or your behavior. I forgive it, usually, but—" She bites down on her lower lip. "Not sure I can do it this time."

"Cannae blame ye." I wince as I shove up into a sitting position and swing my legs over the bed's edge. My boots thump on the floor, and I stab a hand into my hair, scrubbing my scalp with my fingernails. "I realize it isn't worth much, but I am so sorry, Em."

She watches me for a moment, then her shoulders flag, and her body angles toward me. In a gentler tone, she asks, "Why did you do it? I suggested we have sex, and you scurried to the bar to drown yourself in whisky."

"I wanted one drink, but it…escalated."

"Why? Something scared you yesterday. Why you chose to deal with it by getting soused is beyond me."

My chin drops to my chest. "I don't know why I did it."

"You mean you don't want to tell me." She slides off the bed. "Total honesty. You promised me that. Remember?"

"I remember."

"Honesty means no lies, no evasions, no secrets. Lately, I feel like I'm getting all three from you."

Aye, she's right. But I can't share all my selfish, idiotic fears with her. It won't change anything.

"Should I assume our honeymoon is off?" she asks.

I open my mouth, but no sounds come out.

"Right." Emery spins toward the bathroom door. "I'm taking a shower."

She crosses half the distance before I manage to speak.

"Wait," I say, heaving my body off the bed and ignoring the way my head throbs. "Have a bath instead."

"Why do you care if I take a shower or a bath?"

"Please, Emery." I shuffle toward her, grasping her upper arms. "Have a bath. Downstairs."

"Downstairs? Why?"

"The ground-floor bathroom. Please."

"Wh—"

"Ground-floor bathroom," I plead. "Will you do this for me, even though I bollocksed everything badly and haven't earned the right to ask anything of you?"

"Oooh-kay. I'll take a bath on the ground floor. Happy?"

"Not yet, but I am grateful." I touch my lips to her forehead. "Thank you."

"Sure, whatever."

As she leaves the room, Emery tosses confused glances back at me.

Maybe I don't deserve another chance, but after the way I behaved last night, I owe Emery something. It won't be enough, but it's all I can give her.

I approach the door to the ground-floor bathroom and knock twice. Emery moans, though it's not a sexy sound. "Who is it?"

"Your husband."

"Which one? I've got so many, you'll have to be more specific."

"Rory," I say, over-enunciating the syllables. "May I come in?"

"You may."

I throw the door open and walk into the bathroom, shedding my terry-cloth robe along the way. My cock is rising, though I'm amazed I can get an erection after the way I overindulged last night. Emery's body, naked and submerged in the warm water of the tub, provides all the motivation my *slat* needs.

She waves at her own body. "Your wish is my command. I'm bathing on the ground floor. Care to explain why?"

"This is the only tub large enough."

"For what? This thing swallows me—"

I leap into the bathtub.

Water sprays up around us, flooding over the rim and deluging the floor. I land with my feet straddling her legs, then fall to my knees amid the swirling water.

And I smirk.

Emery grins. "Rory baby, you're in the tub with me."

"Twice you asked me, and twice I said no."

I wrap my hands around her calves, exerting just enough pressure to encourage her to bend her knees and draw them toward her chest. I settle onto my erse, knees bent in front of me, our toes touching. "I wanted to join you in the jacuzzi that morning in New Orleans. I wanted it badly. And when you asked me to join you in this tub, I wanted it even more."

"Why didn't you?"

"It felt too intimate." I balance my wrists on my knees as I force myself to gaze into her eyes without flinching or looking away. "Yesterday, when I saw you walking toward me in that dress… You were more beautiful than anything I'd ever seen, more beautiful than any masterpiece of Renaissance art. With the sun on you and your hair a glowing halo, you looked like an angel come down from heaven to bless this world with your incandescent beauty and life."

She struggles to sit up straighter, her eyes alight and her lips parted. "That was almost poetry. But I'm still confused about why you went all deer-in-the-headlights instead of telling me how beautiful I was."

"*Are*, Emery. You are beautiful, always, on the inside and the outside."

She says nothing for a moment, but her mouth falls open a wee bit further. "That's the best compliment ever."

I slide forward until my feet are wedged between her hips and the tub wall. "I should've told you yesterday. But the enormity of the day—you, the ceremony, the guests—it overwhelmed me. I overreacted, for reasons I don't fully understand."

"Graham showing up didn't help."

"Never mind Graham." I clasp her around the waist and lift her half out of the water, then set her down astride my lap. "Let's have fun in the tub."

She drapes her arms around my neck. "Yes, please, let's."

I bury my face against her neck, showering feather-light kisses on her skin. "The honeymoon is not off. Once we've had a bath and a breakfast, we will get in the car and drive."

Emery straps her arms tighter around me. "Remember when I said your sister worships you?"

"Mm."

"I was wrong." She tunnels her fingers through my hair and crushes her breasts to my chest. "Worshiping you is my job, exclusively."

"You've got it backwards. Your body is my temple, and I worship inside you."

"Prove it."

For once, I don't think about it. I show her.

Chapter Thirty-Two

Today, I've taken the biggest risk of all in my efforts to give my wife what she wants. I'm laying my life in her hands, trusting Emery not to go too far. Aye, that means I've handed her the keys to her new car, the one I secretly bought for her. It wouldn't be a proper gift if I informed her in advance. Now, as the road unreels before us, I employ all my self-control and don't tense up every time Emery veers around a curve while grinning and laughing.

"Enjoying your wedding gift?" I ask.

My wife steers the red Jaguar F-Type convertible around a curve while the wind whips through her hair, thanks to the fact we have the top down. "I love-love-love it. And I'll give you a proper thank-you tonight."

"Amazed you're not violating the speed limit."

"Saving that for later."

Though I had wanted to craft an itinerary for our road trip, Emery vetoed the idea. She wants to "see where the road takes us" and "have a blast with no bullet-point lists." Maybe I had planned to type up a list that might possibly have included bullet points, but that doesn't make me uptight. I freely admit I don't do well "winging it." Despite that fact, I love watching my wife drive a sports car while I have no bloody idea where we're going—except that our final destination will be Skye.

Emery's expression changes from focused to dreamy, the way she often looks after I've shagged her. But we're in the car, and we're both fully clothed. Wherever her thoughts have taken her, she seems distracted.

"Emery," I say sharply, to wake her up. "Pay attention when you're driving, please."

She flutters her lashes, rousing from her daydream. "What's the matter? No bodies scattered on the asphalt, so I think I've done fine at multitasking."

"Not murdering innocent bystanders is hardly an endorsement of distracted driving."

"You're right. Sorry, I'll keep my mind on the road."

"Maybe I should drive. You've been at it for more than an hour."

Emery pulls over so we can switch places.

She gets that dreamy look on her face again, but this time, I don't need to snap her out of it. She can fantasize about whatever she likes when I'm in control of the vehicle. Before long, we reach Loch Linnhe and board a ferry that will take us to the next leg of our unscripted journey toward Skye. I'm starting to enjoy having no plan, but I did mark one destination ahead of time because I know Emery will want to see it.

"Where are we going?" she asks, leaning forward to watch the loch's waters go by.

"You wanted to see the ocean." I brace an elbow on the open window. "I'm taking you there."

She whoops.

And I give her a look she sees often from me, one that I'm sure mixes confusion and enchantment. Aye, my wife enchants me. She puts everyone under her spell, even my monosyllabic groundskeeper, Tavish.

I've brought Emery to a sandy beach rimmed by outcroppings of dark rock. Naturally, she rolls her jeans up to her knees and skips across the sand with her head tipped back and her arms thrown wide, soaking up the sun's heat while a bonnie smile curves her lips.

"Even the sun can't resist you," I say from my position at the beach's edge. "It shows its face more often since you came to Scotland."

Laughing, she twirls in circles as her bare feet sink into the sand.

My gaze remains riveted to her movements, and though I can't understand her need to do silly things, I revel in watching her enjoy the simplest acts with abandon and sheer delight. Rules don't seem important today, not when my wife is spinning and laughing.

Emery leaps into the air to splash down in a tidal pool. Her feet plunge in deep. Water splashes up her calves, and she fakes an exaggerated shiver, fooling me for two seconds until she laughs and resumes her spinning with both arms outstretched.

I march over to her, lashing my arms around her waist to halt her. Then I pin her to my body and lift her feet off the ground to level our faces.

She grips my biceps, her gaze glued to mine.

"The water's bloody cold," I say, casting a pointed glance at my shoe-covered feet submerged in the tidal pool. "You'll catch pneumonia out here."

My wife hugs me tighter. "Good thing I've got you to warm me up."

"Are you finished admiring the ocean? You'll see more of it when we make our way to Skye."

"Let's go. I want to see everything." She tickles my earlobe. "Absolutely everything."

"May not have time for everything in three days." I struggle to turn us around while my feet are hindered by wet sand. "But I'll do my best."

I cart my wife back to the car and dry her feet with a towel I'd brought because I knew she would want to see the ocean as soon as possible. And I knew she'd insist on prancing about in the sand and water.

Once I've taken care of my wife, I settle in behind the wheel of the Jaguar and rest my hands on it, drumming one finger. "Should we continue up the coast, or go back to Corran to take the ferry? We could drive the interior route to Skye, through Fort William and Invergarry."

"You're driving. You pick."

"This is your holiday, love. You choose."

Did I say… No, I didn't just call her "love." That was a thought in my head, not words I spoke.

"Um…" Emery trails off, her brows crinkled as she glances at me.

Mhac na galla. I did call her "love" out loud. I must've done, based on her expression.

She wriggles in her seat and clears her throat. "Back to Corran."

Another ferry trip takes us back to the road that leads northeast out of Fort William, past Loch Linnhe and Loch Lochy. My wife thinks that name is amusing.

"Loch Lochy?" she says, her smile bright and her laughter tickling my senses. "Is there a Mount Mountie too?"

"No."

Emery laughs again.

Our journey toward Skye includes multiple stops of varying types, everything from scenic views to historic places and monuments of interest. I know Emery loves any sort of destination, and I can't resist explaining the significance of each stop on our road trip. Not having a plan doesn't matter. I know the history and geography of this region almost as well as I know Emery's body. She's easy to please, and I love that about her. Sometimes I wish I could be as open and free as my wife, but that's not in my nature.

Sex in the kitchen, in the daytime, doesn't change that.

I'm driving down a straight stretch of road when my wife sneaks a hand onto my thigh, sliding it down between my legs. "I know you have a wild heart, so let it show. Violate the speed limit, baby. See how fast this Jag can run."

"I'd risk a fine and penalty points on my license."

She massages my inner thigh. "How many points have you got so far?"

"None." I clear my throat, trying not to grimace when she strokes my thigh. "Sixty isn't fast enough for you?"

"Kilometers are shorter than miles. You're not going as fast as it sounds."

"We use miles per hour here." I collar her wrist and set her hand on her lap. "We are going as fast as it sounds."

"Come on, break the speed limit for one minute. Floor it and see how it feels."

Glancing at her sideways, I twist my lips into a wry smile. "You are a sexy little devil whispering in my ear, luring me to sin."

"Is it working?"

Oh aye, my wicked angel can tempt me to do almost anything. I punch the accelerator, and the Jaguar rockets forward with its engine roaring.

"Wooo!" Emery shouts while thrusting her arms in the air. She locks her hands over the windscreen's top edge. "Go, Rory baby!"

I grin and laugh, exhilaration rushing through me like I've swallowed half a bottle of whisky. But it's not speed intoxicating me. It's Emery.

After precisely one minute, according to the dashboard clock, I decelerate to sixty miles per hour.

"How did it feel?" she asks.

"Good, but not as exciting as making love to you."

Since this holiday is my wedding gift to Emery—well, that and the Jaguar—I decide we should stop at as many destinations as possible, even though that means we won't make it to Skye tonight. By the time we reach Invergarry, we're both too jeeked to drive anymore. But we stumble onto a quaint bed-and-breakfast situated on a working farm and spend the night there. The meal our hosts serve us reinvigorates me, and my wife too. I make love to her for an hour, worshiping every millimeter of her body until she's come for me three times, then we fall asleep in each other's arms.

And I sleep so well that I feel like I could paddle our Jaguar across the Atlantic to America.

Day two proves even better than yesterday. Emery listens with rapt attention and a sweet expression while I show her points of interest and haver on and on about each one. I've discovered I enjoy being Emery's tour guide, and I grow more invested in that role as we go along. When I realize I've become quite animated, waving my hands and doing silly voices, I don't even mind that I'm acting like a numpty. Anything for my wife.

We stop for lunch, then resume our sightseeing.

And Emery gazes at me like I won the Battle of Bannockburn for her. Maybe I puff up a wee bit when my wife looks at me that way, but it doesn't mean anything.

The sun is sinking toward the horizon as we cross the Skye Bridge over Loch Alsh and land on Skye. Fifteen minutes later, I park our car in the circular drive of the two-story home I bought but never visited after the purchase was finalized. Not until today. With Emery.

I shut off the engine. "This is it."

Emery climbs out of the car, tilting her head back to survey the grey stone building. "It's a mansion."

"A manse," I correct, coming up beside her. "Not a mansion."

"What's the difference?"

"This was, at one time, the home of a clergyman. Houses like this are known as manses."

"Sure, whatever you say. I'm used to America. We have mansions and McMansions, but no manses I know of."

I pull her against my side. "You're Scottish now."

We wander into the house, and Emery delights at every aspect of the historical home, from its intricate woodwork on display in every room to the period-appropriate furnishings and decor. I inform her the house dates back to the eighteen hundreds, which she thinks is "so cool." Despite never having spent time here, I'd arranged for a contractor to install modern amenities that blend into the historic elements without overwhelming them. Emery loves the fully stocked kitchen and the bathroom upstairs.

My wife devours the dinner I prepare for her as if I haven't fed her in weeks. Must be excitement making her ravenous. I nibble on my food while observing her with amused fascination as she shoves half an enormous mouthful of tatties and neeps into her mouth.

Maybe it's not excitement. Could she be nervous? Emery hasn't spoken since I set the food on the table, which isn't like her.

After dinner, we retire to the sitting room. Emery curls up on the sofa with her knees folded and turned to the side. I recline beside her with my feet on the coffee table.

She angles her body toward me and starts wringing her hands on her lap. "I'm a hypocrite."

I move only my eyes to glance at her. "Why?"

"I need to tell you something." She clamps her hands over her knees. "Something I should've told you days ago when I realized it, but I've been afraid of how you might react. That's not like me, you know, to be afraid to speak my mind. I have to say this, even if you freak out."

Freak out? Now *I'm* getting anxious.

I swerve my head toward her, my lips pinched. "What is it?"

Emery's fingers dig into her knees, and she chews on her lip. "I'm in love with you."

A wave of icy coldness crashes through me, and my voice goes flat. "I understand."

"You understand? What does that mean?"

I face forward and clear my throat. "I need a drink."

Launching myself off the sofa, I rush to the drinks cabinet and grab a bottle of Ben Nevis. My hands tremble slightly, though not enough for Emery to notice, while I find a glass and pour precisely one inch of whisky into it.

Why did she have to say that...thing she just said?

My wife jumps up and stomps over to me, bumping her hip into the drinks cabinet. "I love you, Rory."

"Heard you the first time," I mutter between gulps of whisky.

"And your response is to get drunk again."

I slap the glass down on the cabinet, making the liquid inside it slosh. My heart thrashes in my chest, like it needs to climb out and run away. "If you're expecting me to—"

"I'm not expecting anything from you. I'm telling you how I feel because we both promised each other complete honesty." She eyes the whisky glass. "That's a lie. I do expect one thing from you—not to get wasted."

The corners of my mouth slant downward, and I can't inhale a full breath. "I am not getting drunk. I'm having one drink."

"Because I told you I love you."

"Stop saying it." I nab my glass and down the rest of its contents in one gulp. "Repeating the words ad nauseam won't make me say what you want."

Her mouth tightens, though her lips quiver.

Didn't I tell her from the start what I could offer her? Now she wants to rewrite our entire relationship.

"Do what you want," Emery says, whirling toward the doorway. "I'm going to bed."

My wife shambles out of the sitting room.

And I return the whisky bottle to the drinks cabinet.

Ten minutes later, I'm lying in bed while I wait for my wife to come out of the bathroom. Once again, I need to make amends and try to be kind to her without giving Emery the wrong impression. The parameters of our marriage haven't changed. I should simply remind her of the rules and leave it at that.

But I can't do that either. Just thinking about it reawakens the pain in my chest.

I cannot love her. She needs to accept that.

Emery walks out of the bathroom wearing a black satin nightie trimmed in black lace. She keeps her head down, her gaze fixated on the floor as she shuffles up to the bed. Only then does she lift her head and notice me, nudging the bed with her knees as if she can't decide whether she wants to sleep with me tonight.

I pinch the bridge of my nose. "I've been an erse again."

She snorts. "An eejit and an erse, I'd say."

"Aye." I give the covers a hesitant pat. "Should I sleep in another room?"

"No."

I prop myself up with one elbow. "I'm sorry, Emery. I reacted badly, again, and hurt you—again. But I am not drunk. I never intended to get drunk, please believe that."

No, I hadn't planned on it. Would I have stopped drinking if she hadn't gotten upset? Yes, I would have. My behavior on our second wedding night taught me the folly of using alcohol to avoid my problems.

Emery rocks back on her heels, then forward again until her knees meet the mattress. "I believe you."

"Thank you," I say with a sigh. My eyebrows rise. "You're wearing a nightie. Didn't think you owned one."

"I have a few, but I don't sleep in them very much. Bought this one for—" She runs her palms over the fabric. "Doesn't matter."

"What did you buy it for? I'd like to know."

She stares at the mattress. "For our wedding night."

I wince.

My wife raises a hand before I can speak. "You already said you're sorry."

"Will you sleep with me, then?"

Rather than responding, she crawls on her hands and knees until she's beside me, then she sits back on her heels.

I finger the hem of her nightie. "It's bonnie, but not as bonnie as you."

"What are you wearing?" She picks up the edge of the covers to peek beneath them. "Oh. You're not wearing anything. Does that mean…"

"Too tired for sex, I'm afraid."

"Me too." She lets the covers fall back over me. "Why the nudie show if we're not getting it on?"

"I like feeling your naked body beside me." I trail a finger along her nightie's hem, grazing her skin. "You've picked this night to wear clothing to bed, for the first time since I've known you."

"Not true. You made me wear your shirt on the second night we shared a bed."

"So I did. You complained then, but now you voluntarily cover your luscious body."

"A problem easily resolved." She whips the nightie off over her head, tossing it toward the foot of the bed. "See?"

I flip the covers up so she can crawl underneath and nestle against me.

The issues between us haven't evaporated, I know that. But for tonight, all I want is to sleep with my wife in my arms and forget about everything else in the world. Soon, I'll have to deal with what she told me in the sitting room. Not tonight, though.

At five o'clock, I rouse from a good night's rest. But Emery looks so peaceful lying here tucked against me that I don't want to disturb her yet. So I go back to sleep.

When I wake up again, Emery is sitting beside me, smiling.

I arch one brow. "What?"

She points at the clock on the nightstand. "You slept in, without being drunk. It's after eight thirty."

"I woke at five, but I couldn't bear to leave my wife lying here all alone, soft and warm and naked. I went back to sleep."

Her smile broadens. "That's what I call progress."

Aye, maybe it is. But that thing she said last night keeps echoing through my mind.

I love you, Rory.

Chapter Thirty-Three

Emery cooks breakfast for us, and after that, we explore the area around the manse, and further to other parts of Skye. Ever since last night, when she said that thing, my wife has seemed less energetic than usual. She doesn't say much either. Her reticence compels me to speak up, if only to stop the itch deep inside me that started up again this morning.

"You look pensive," I say.

"Guess the amazing view inspired deep thoughts."

"About what?"

"Whisky and men."

I pull her against me. "You do have the strangest thoughts. Here we are on the coast of Skye, on a beautifully sunny day, and you're musing about whisky."

That damn itch won't go away. Well, at least it's not a pain in my chest this time.

Emery sweeps her gaze over the loch in front of us, though I don't think she's watching the various craft that navigate its waters. Not even a sailboat can catch her attention. Emery had clutched my hand as we trudged across the stone-littered shore, just so she could get a better view of the loch and the craggy mountains. A tourist shop lies behind us, across the way, but on this side of the road large black stones thrust up from the earth.

Emery links her arms around my waist and rubs her cheek on my chest. "Don't you want to know what men I've been musing about?"

"I hope it's not Luke, or that *bod ceann* before him."

"Mm-mm. Your brothers."

"I see." The lass is having me on, I'm sure. "Aidan, I can understand. We used to call him Don Juan, after all. But Lachlan?"

I make a disgusted noise.

"Oh come on," she says, giving me a playful slug in the gut. "Lachlan's hot. As for Aidan…whew."

Without letting go of her, I twist around until we face each other. I bind her to me with both hands joined over her lower back, then tip my head down to narrow my gaze on her. "It won't work. Trying to make me jealous. I have no worries you want someone else more."

"More than you? Never."

"Last night—" I compress my lips, knowing I need to clarify the situation but wary of treading too close to what she said after dinner. "I warned you I can't give you what you need."

"You said you won't, not you can't." She rests her forehead on my chest, relaxing into me. "Don't worry, I'm not trying to make you love me. I told you how I feel to get it off my chest, that's all."

A breath gusts out of me, fluttering her hair. "Whenever you want to leave, I'll give you the money."

"I'm not leaving. The only way you're getting rid of me is if you give me the heave-ho."

"The heave-ho sounds terrible, as if I'm pitching you over the side of a ship in the middle of the ocean."

"How this ends is up to you, Rory."

We stand here for a while, holding each other but not speaking or moving. What can I say? Not the words I'm sure she hopes to hear. Waves lap against the rocky shore, and car engines grumble on the road. But nothing, not even the squawking of a seagull, can penetrate my mind as more than background noise. How did I allow things to spiral so far out of my control? A simple arrangement, that was all I wanted. A convenient wife to show off to my family so they'd stop harassing me.

Emery is not convenient. She challenges me at every turn, and her defiance makes me randy. But it's her sadness that triggers something far more disturbing than lust, something I cannot allow to take root inside me. Not again. Three times, I'd loved a woman and been destroyed by it. If Emery leaves me—No, when she leaves me, I won't survive it.

Unless I push her way. Right now.

I shrug away from Emery and gaze out at the dark loch. "You asked me once why I bought a house here."

My wife doesn't speak or move, though I swear I can feel her questions burning on my skin.

"Three years ago," I begin, "I came to Skye on business. Doesn't matter why. On my way home, I drove past the manse and saw the estate agent's sign. Something about the house made me pull into the drive and get out of my car. No one was living there at the time, and the grass and shrubs were overgrown. With sunset almost over, the house looked dark and forsaken in the twilight, and I stood there watching the shadows consume it."

A sideways glance shows me Emery is not only listening, but watching me too as if she hopes to glean secret information from my expression.

I rub a palm on my chest and close my eyes. "This was a few days after I learned Una had given birth to a baby girl. She and her partner had done in vitro with a sperm donor. I learned this from Lilias when I ran into her in Ballachulish. Somehow over the years, she and Una had become friends."

Should I tell Emery this? It doesn't matter, not when she'll leave me at the end of a year. But something compels me to go on.

"Lilias was excited," I continue. "She showed me pictures of Una's baby, and of the three children she had with the boy she'd—" I hesitate, waiting for the lump in my throat to soften. "The teenager she'd become involved with while she was married to me. He's an adult now, of course. They married and have a wonderful life together with their children. Una is equally blessed, Lilias said. She also mentioned Isobel, gossip she'd heard about her. Apparently, my first wife was never able to have children, but she's happily married."

"That must've been hard to hear."

I nod solemnly. "I'm pleased for them, of course. And I might not have minded hearing about their joyful lives if Lilias hadn't also said—She told me I looked sad. Lonely. She offered to arrange for me to meet a woman she knew."

"Your cheating ex-wife wanted to set you up on a blind date?"

"Aye." Peering out at the loch, I feel a strange longing rising from deep within me, a need borne of pain I've kept sequestered for years. "I thanked Lilias for the offer but politely declined, then I excused myself. Said I had an appointment to keep. For days after, I kept wondering why my ex-wives seem happy while I'm...not." I stare at the horizon, unable to glance at Emery for fear of what I might find in her eyes. "When I saw the manse, forsaken and unwanted, I felt a kinship with the house. Ridiculous, I know. But it spoke to me, and I thought I might like to come here once in a while to... I don't know. Wallow in seclusion. I bought the manse the next day, over the phone, without ever setting foot inside it. I paid people to renovate and furnish it. I still pay people to care for the place."

"You never visited the house until now."

Though I smile, it's rueful. "Wallowing in desolation isn't as appealing as it seemed at first."

She slips her hands into mine. "Why did you bring me here?"

"You wanted to see the ocean."

"Don't be deliberately obtuse. You know what I mean. Why did you bring me to Skye, to the house you bought because it looked as melancholy and forlorn as you felt?"

I try to back away, but she won't let me go. "What makes you think I felt melancholy and forlorn?"

"You just told me." She inches closer. "The house was forsaken, unwanted, consumed by shadows. You felt a kinship with it. Takes a real genius to figure out you were talking about yourself when you described the house."

My lips twitch upward. "You are the cleverest woman I've ever met."

"I was being facetious."

And suddenly, I'm smiling at my wife like I haven't just bared my bloody soul to her. "I know. But you're still the cleverest."

She hops up to give me a quick kiss. "Let's get off this depressing jaunt down memory lane. You've had fun with me, haven't you?"

"Cannae help it. You insist on making me do ridiculous things."

Emery taps my chest. "You say it's ridiculous, but I've figured out that's Rory code for 'thanks for showing me a great time.' And you're welcome, by the way."

I splay my hands over her back. "Never could fool you, could I?"

"Nope. Why don't we go back to that lonely, desolate house of yours and find ways to have fun there. Maybe we can turn its frown upside-down too."

"If anyone can make a house smile, it's you."

After a meal at a local restaurant, we amble back to the manse. I enjoy my wife's body in every room except for the bedroom because I want to save that for last. We do more than shag, though. I share stories about my family and their barmy antics while Emery makes me laugh with tales of her family. In the evening, I suggest we play an erotic version of hide-and-go-seek, so I can sneak up on my wife and surprise her, then have a poke. But Emery wins our game after three rounds. I have a wee bit of trouble finding a place to hide since this house clearly was not built for a large man. Maybe the clergyman who once lived here was a leprechaun. During our last round of the game, my wife discovers me while I'm attempting to hide in a closet. I couldn't shut the door, though, because my feet wouldn't fit.

I do manage to seduce Emery in that closet, with the door wide open.

By the time we finish our evening meal and retire to the bedroom, the bleak mood I'd experienced during my confessions on the beach has faded away. I expected Emery to interrogate me about that sometime during the day or in the evening, but she never did. I said too much, and now she probably thinks she's made a terrible mistake by marrying me. If three women couldn't stand to be with me, how can I expect Emery to be any different? I am the problem, not my wives.

Emery sashays out of the bathroom wearing her black nightie and twirls in front of me.

I'm relaxing on the bed, in the nude, with the covers thrown back, admiring the view.

"Here I am," she says. "You seemed to like this nightie the first time I wore it. Thought an encore might be in order."

"*Mo gaoloch*, you are a masterpiece of sensual beauty."

"You said that the night we met. I assumed it was a come-on line."

"It wasn't." My *slat* won't let me think about why I called her my darling in Gaelic. I raise onto one elbow, offering my hand to her. "Come, and let me show you what I mean."

She crawls across the bed to kneel beside me.

"Emery," I purr, skating my palms up her thighs, under the hem of her nightie, and moving them higher to cup her hips. "Even your name is sensual."

I slide my hands down to catch the edge of her nightie, then flip it up and over her head. She lifts her arms to let me pull the garment free of her body. I toss it aside.

She eyes my erection, running her teeth over her bottom lip.

Laying back, I raise my arms above my head. "Take me."

The surprise on her face melts into a sexy little smile.

"Please," I say, my chest swelling with every labored breath. "Take me, Emery."

She mounts me, straddling my hips, and clasps my cock with both hands. "Sure you can handle me being in control?"

"You've been in control since the night we met." I suck in a breath when she palms my sac. "I surrendered to you then, and I'm done pretending it's not true."

My wife relinquishes my *bagais* to place two fingers on my lips. "Shh, baby."

I capture her fingers with my mouth, suckling the tips.

She skims her thumb over the head of my cock.

"Ah," I hiss. "Stop torturing me, will ye? I need your soft, wet—"

"I know what you need." With another flick of her thumb, she cups my sac in her other hand, tugs, and grins when I make a strangled noise. "Trust me to give it to you."

"Hurry, love. Ahmno strong enough to withstand your teasing."

Towering over me, she closes her hand around my *slat* and lowers her body onto my length, inch by inch, her slick heat gliding down my flesh with such exquisite slowness that I start to breathe harder. A groan vibrates through me when she's taken me all the way inside her lush body. She lays her hands on my chest, delicately nibbling on her lower lip while she teases my skin with her fingertips.

I clutch her hips.

She rides me at a leisurely pace, lifting her body almost free of my cock and sliding back down, rocking her hips to make me gasp and grip her harder. I watch as her cream coats my *slat* and dribbles down her inner thighs to moisten my skin too. The scent of it drives me mad, and I want to feast on all that luscious cream, but not until after she fucks me. When I thrust a finger between her folds to tease her clit, she cries out.

I mutter in Gaelic, between panting breaths, not having a clue what I've said.

The pace quickens along with our mounting desire, and she seems as powerfully aroused as I am, slamming her body down on my cock while I pinch her nipples and rasp my finger over her clit. She moans and rides me harder, faster, our bodies pounding into each other while I arch my hips every time she sinks down on me. She moans my name over and over.

"Rory baby, yes, oh God, Rory baby, yes, Oh God."

"Emery, I love ye, Emery, I love ye."

She comes with such force and speed that she can't even cry out, her nails scraping my chest while her body clenches me fiercely enough that I can't hold back any longer. My body stiffens, then I thrust into her so hard that she bounces on the bed, and I shout her name, spending myself inside her.

I roll us onto our sides, running my hands over her body while we recover from the intense pleasure we just shared.

Did I say... No, I couldn't have. If I did say that, I hadn't meant to, and it was a reflex triggered by an impending orgasm. I don't—She can't believe—No, Emery understands my limitations.

She doesn't believe I love her.

Once our breathing normalizes, I ease Emery onto her back with my body covering hers and my arms framing her head. She opens her mouth, clearly about to speak.

I seal my lips over hers. No talking. Maybe by morning, she will have forgotten what I might or might not have said during sex. I kiss her slowly, using my lips and tongue to erase her memory of those words. Aye, I'm exactly the sort of eejit who thinks that will work.

When I finally give up her lips, I shift to the side so I can glide my hands over her entire body. First, I confessed on the beach. Now, I've inadvertently spoken three words I should never have spoken.

Bod a' chac.

Emery cradles my head in her hands and murmurs, "You're not alone anymore."

Weight. On my chest. Pressing me down until I feel like I'll punch through the floor and straight into the earth's core. No, I don't want to hear those words. Somehow, it's more terrifying than when she said she loves me. Because I don't feel alone when I'm with her.

And that means, when she leaves me, I will be ruined.

I hold her, my eyes closed, and let the whispers of her breaths lull me until the scent and feel of her wipes away the fear and pain. I fall asleep like that, sheltered in the arms of the only woman who has ever made me wish I could become someone else, not because she expects me to change, but because I would give anything to be what she needs.

No, I can't change. And I will lose her.

Chapter Thirty-Four

What does a selfish bastard do when his wife announces she loves him and sees him and says he's not alone anymore? I can't speak for all those other blokes, but I run away. Two days after Skye, I'm packing a suitcase while my wife lies sprawled across the foot of the bed watching me. I keep my head down, but still, I can see her peripherally and feel her gaze burning into me.

I've arranged to go on a business trip to Paris, for a conference I hadn't meant to attend—until we came home from Skye. This morning, I had quickly made my plans and announced them to Emery, who had stared blankly at me for a moment, then seemed to resign herself to my need to flee the country.

Anything to escape from my wife. From her questions. From her love.

The final day of our so-called honeymoon had turned into a tense and awkward affair. Even Emery couldn't muster any enthusiasm for sightseeing, despite my attempt to pretend nothing had happened the night before.

My wife supports her head with one hand, and with the other, she wiggles her fingers on her thigh. "We only got home yesterday, and this morning you announce you've got to leave the country on a sudden business trip to France."

"Thank you for the summary," I say without inflection, "but I recall what I said to you twenty minutes ago."

"Do you realize how it sounds?" She sits up and tucks her feet under her. "On Skye, you told me about a painful time in your life. And oh yes, I said I love you. Are you running away to avoid being around me?"

"Of course not." I lift my head to frown at her. "I am not a coward."

Am I? A few weeks ago, I would've denied it. Now, I'm not certain of anything.

"No," my wife says, "but you are freaked out. I can tell. You go all Robot Rory when you start to worry you've let me get too close."

"This is a business trip." I clap the suitcase shut and fasten the latch with a sharp click. "Two days at a conference, followed by two days working with a colleague to learn about the French legal system."

She clambers to her knees and waddles closer. "Take me with you."

"To a conference on international law? You would be bored."

"Have you noticed boredom being a problem for me? I know how to entertain myself." She leans across the closed suitcase to grasp the lapels of my suit jacket. "If you take me along, I can entertain you every night."

I pry her hands away. "Despite what you may think, I can survive four days without you."

Guiding her hands to her sides, I release them.

"Maybe that's true," she says, "but can you go four days without sex?"

"Yes."

"At least let me drive you to the airport, instead of making poor Tavish go all the way to Inverness."

"He'll be visiting his mother, who lives there."

I snatch up my suitcase and stride to the bedroom door. On the threshold, I pause to glance back at my wife. My beautiful, kind, wonderful wife. "I'll see you in four days. Goodbye."

Pivoting on my heels, I march out the door.

Did I honestly think that would stop her?

Though I hear her running after me, I have longer legs and take the stairs two at a time, reaching the Mercedes parked in the drive before my wife makes it through the vestibule door.

Tavish observes us from the driver's seat, seeming confused or perhaps worried.

"Rory!" my wife shouts, sprinting across the lawn to catch up to me.

I hesitate with my hand on the passenger door.

Emery hurtles her body through the air, colliding with me, and latches both arms around my neck. Her feet hang suspended above the ground while she mashes her mouth to mine. I can't respond, not the way she wants, not this time. I exercise every iota of my willpower to make my muscles go rigid and resist the siren call of her body. But my mouth didn't get the memo. My lips yield to hers without my permission, and I open them to her invasion.

My cock jerks.

Of course I want her. That's never been the issue.

Her lips tighten, as if she's smiling against my mouth. Then she severs the kiss. "Call me when you get to your hotel, okay?"

I nod.

She lets her body slide down mine, withdrawing her arms only when her toes touch the ground. "Have a safe trip, baby. I'll miss you."

With a grunt, I yank the car door open and toss my suitcase into the backseat. Once I've settled into the passenger seat, Tavish steers the Mercedes down the drive.

And I…turn around to wave my fingers at Emery in a hesitant gesture.

She blows me a kiss.

I stare at her until the trees obscure my view.

I miss my wife. Running away from her hasn't changed anything. I want to go home, but I can't do that. This business trip had been my idea, and rushing back to my wife will only prove that I used work as an excuse to escape her. Sticking to my plans is the only reasonable solution. But I don't want to stay in Paris for one minute longer.

Without Emery, I feel…adrift.

My need for her is my greatest weakness, and I must harden myself to her so that when she leaves me, I won't be ruined forever. As much as the distance hurts, I need to show my wife I can survive time away from her. Calling her three times a day—morning, lunchtime, and evening—serves proof that I'm fine without her. It's not desperation. My tactic makes perfect sense.

To a moron. Emery has stolen my common sense along with my self-control.

We talk about nothing of importance, and though she tries to engage me in teasing conversation, my lighter side has been swallowed by the darkness ever since we returned from Skye. Even Emery has trouble thinking of things to say, so we chat to each other as if we're acquaintances, not a married couple. Emery tells me all about her visit with Calli, Aidan's wife, who's teaching her about library cataloging. I have no idea what that is, but my wife seems to think it's fascinating.

Well, at least she isn't miserable without me. Maybe that means she accepts that I don't love her.

She also tells me how Lachlan begged for her help with his computer. Aye, that's no surprise. Lachlan never has had much technological acumen. I know more than he does, but I'm no expert either. Other members of my extended family ask for Emery's help too. Even my clients contact her.

"They act like I'm Steve Jobs," Emery says one evening. "I could make a career out of resuscitating hard drives in the western Highlands."

"Is that what you want?"

"Not sure. Finding your true calling in life is harder than it sounds."

"You'll figure it out. You're intelligent and determined." I try for a teasing tone when I add, "Stubborn, some might say."

"Says the pigheaded Scot."

"Taking my stubborn wife is my favorite pastime."

Aye, our phone conversations often turn into flirtation, though we usually change the topic as soon as that happens.

"Wanna have phone sex?" my wife asks.

I've just taken a sip of water and end up spluttering. "What did you say?"

"Oh, I think you heard me just fine."

"While I appreciate the offer, I prefer the real thing. Besides, I'm not the sort to…do that."

"You're exactly the sort." Her tone turns sensual. "You are an exciting, adventurous man."

"Emery, you are the only person on earth who would call me adventurous."

"Nobody else knows you like I do."

Her statement stops me for a second, then the truth of it penetrates me. "You may be right."

"So, phone sex. Yay or nay?"

"In a minute." I have another matter I want to discuss with her now. "Emery, I noticed you transferred money into our bank account."

"Closed out my account in America."

"You're meant to spend money, not add it. All you've paid for is petrol."

"And the wedding dress. That's all I've needed. Had to buy gas when I drove into town. If and when I need something else, I'll tap into our account."

Though I try for several minutes to convince my wife to spend our money, she attempts to rationalize her frugality as "being a good wife." I'm sure she still feels uncomfortable taking money from our joint account, and I won't talk her out of that over the phone.

So I concede the argument. For now.

After a long afternoon of listening to boring presentations about boring legal rubbish, I return to my hotel suite and order dinner. I used to love the law, but now all I can think about is my wife. Who cares about revolutionary new techniques for drafting contracts? It's not revolutionary, anyway. A contract is a contract, and I don't care about the opinions of a thirty-year-old "whiz kid" who thinks he's smarter than everyone else.

My meal consists of pancakes with maple syrup and whipped cream. I couldn't get praline pancakes here. Aye, I'm eating breakfast for dinner because it reminds me of my wife. Maybe I'll take Emery back to New Orleans, just so we can feed each other those pancakes while she sits on my lap in a suite overlooking the city.

A memory rushes through my mind, of Emery racing out of the house to kiss me goodbye, despite the fact we both know I was running away from her, not attending an important conference. Every time I hurt her, she forgives me, even if all I do is apologize. She can't keep excusing my behavior. Eventually, she will get tired of it—of me.

My mobile rings.

I swipe it off the table and see who's calling. "Emery, I was going to ring you in a bit."

"Yeah, well, something's happened," she says. "Trouble on the home front."

"What's happened?" The unsteadiness in her voice might not be noticeable to anyone else, but I heard it. And my tone sharpens into a knife's edge. "Are you all right?"

"Fine, physically." Her voice hitches and quivers. "This is all my fault. I'm so sorry, Rory. I wish—God, it's all my fault."

"Emery, whatever it is, I'm sure it was not your fault. Tell me, please."

"Graham, he published a story. About us." A wee sob hiccups out of her, and she sniffles. "About me. Everyone will see it, the things he said. It's not true, but that doesn't matter because he—"

"Hush, love. It's not as bad as it seems."

She sniffles again, then blows her nose.

Graham Oliver, that bastard, will have his reckoning—at my hand.

"I'm coming home," I say. "Immediately."

"No, please, I don't want to ruin your vacation from me. There's nothing you can do. I thought you should know, that's all."

Even I'm not enough of a *bod ceann* to leave my wife to deal with Graham's bollocks on her own. I should never have left her.

"There's nothing you can do," she repeats, sounding even more miserable.

My voice mutates into a growl. "There bloody well is."

"Rory—"

"I am coming home." While cradling the mobile on my shoulder, I hurry to gather my things and shove them into my suitcase. "I'll call when we're in the air."

"Okay," she says, her voice so weak I almost can't hear it.

"Try not to worry, love. I will handle this."

By the time I get home, it's after dark, too late to go confront the *cacan* who upset my wife so much she cried over the phone. Emery meets me at the car, rushing up as soon it stops moving, and flings her body at me the second I step out of the Mercedes. I cling to her as fiercely as she holds on to me.

She buries her face against my neck. "I missed you, baby."

I press my lips to her throat. "I missed you too."

Her arms clinch me tighter, but I don't care if I can't breathe.

"I will deal with Graham in the morning," I say, and my voice sounds the way everyone describes it when they're trying to annoy me. But the steel in my voice is not a joke.

Graham Oliver will pay for this.

Chapter Thirty-Five

I leave Emery sleeping in our bed and grab a quick piece on my way out of the house. Mrs. Darroch is in the kitchen, so I inform her of my plan because it is no secret. Everyone will soon know what I've done, and I don't care. Graham Oliver must pay. Last night, after Emery fell asleep, I did something I never dreamed I would do. I visited the website of Graham's filthy scandal sheet and read the article he wrote about my wife.

Lies. All lies.

The headline screams, "Local Solicitor Marries Prostitute: Rory MacTaggart Buys a Wife to Satisfy His Deviant Needs." I donnae give a damn what he says about me, but my wife is off-limits. His so-called expose describes Emery as my "prostitute wife" and paints me as a sexual deviant of the worst sort. Where does he get this rubbish? I have never used chains on a woman unless her car got stuck in the snow. And that's the tame part of Graham's outlandish fictional tale of a sadistic solicitor and his slag wife.

Emery's ex-lover makes an appearance too. Graham quotes Sebastian Zegers as saying, "Get her in front of a camera, and she'll preen like a porn star."

I will hunt that bawbag down in whatever corner of Alaska he's hiding in and wring his slimy neck.

Somehow, Graham knows about the marriage contract and the prenuptial agreement, but those documents are kept in my home office. How he found that information, I can't imagine, but I will find out. The article also includes the photos he took of Emery, of course. Graham's defamatory bullshit wouldn't be complete otherwise. No wonder she was crying on the phone last night. Her worst fear has come to pass, and I wasn't even there to support her when she found out what Graham had done.

After letting Mrs. Darroch know that I'm driving into the village to confront Graham, I jump in the Mercedes and violate the speed limit so egregiously that I will most likely be arrested as soon as I reach my destination. I swerve around corners too fast, almost slide off the road twice, and finally arrive at the offices of *The Loch Fairbairn World News*.

World news, my erse. No one in the village or elsewhere on earth cares about Graham's rubbish.

But I care—because he hurt Emery.

I storm into Graham's office, halting inches from his desk, where he hunches in front of his computer. "I should throttle you, ye bleeding ersehole. Defaming an innocent woman? You've sunk to a new level of the filthiest pond on the planet, but that hardly surprises me."

Aye, my voice is honed to an edge sharp enough to slit his throat.

Graham sits back in his chair, hands slack on its arms, and gives me a nonchalant shrug. "I report the facts, MacTaggart. Look it up in the dictionary. F-A-C-T."

I thrust an arm across the desk to seize his shirt and hoist him out of his chair.

Graham's eyes widen, but only for a moment. Then his arrogance takes hold again, and the *bod ceann* sneers at me. "No one forced her to pose for pornographic pictures. Should've researched your bit of stuff before you married her to satisfy your deviant cravings."

"My deviant cravings?" I almost laugh, but I'm too incensed. "How do you know about the marriage contract?"

He shrugs again, smiling with smug satisfaction.

"Ye fucking bawbag," I snarl. "Donnae give a toss what ye say about me, but you will suffer for what you've done to my wife." I shake him hard. "Do ye hear me, *Mr. Oliver*?"

His smirk falters briefly.

I bare my teeth as I growl, "Tell me how you know about the contract."

The dangerous edge in my voice seems to convince him to confess.

"You left the door to your home office unlocked," Graham says, "on the day of your second wedding. The contract and prenup were right there, for anyone to find. Thank you for leaving your investigator's report on your desk too. Made my job much easier."

My fault, of course. I've spent so much time protecting myself from Emery that I failed to keep my wife safe.

I release Graham but keep leaning over the desk, my glare so hot that I feel quite sure Graham will get a sunburn from it. "Retract the story and apologize to my wife."

"Donnae think I will."

Just as I'm about to explain to this *cacan* what I can do to him, legally and physically, the door bursts open.

And my wife barrels inside.

Graham still has that self-satisfied look on his shriveled, yellow face.

My eyes narrow to slits, and my nostrils flare with every blustering breath. I snarl through tightly clenched teeth, my lip curling. "Last chance."

"I stand by the truth," Graham declares, folding his arms over his chest and lifting his chin.

Wrong answer. I slam my fist into Graham's jaw.

His head snaps back. The crack of the blow fills the office, and droplets of blood spatter onto Graham and me. The bastard staggers backward. His eyes go wide, and his face takes on a greyish tone. He holds a palm to his jaw as he flails for his chair, grabs it with one hand, and topples onto it.

I pull my fist back, preparing for another blow.

Graham cringes.

Emery rushes forward to grasp my arm.

Startled, I stare at my wife.

"Stop," she says. "Please, Rory. He's not worth it."

"MacTaggart, you've lost your mind," Graham says, but his voice has developed a slight whine. "I should tell the police about this."

"Go on, then," I say. "I'm a solicitor, ye *bod ceann*. Do ye think I'll stay locked up?"

He slouches deeper into his chair.

"I'm the only witness," Emery tells Graham. "And I'll testify you started it."

The ball of human slime blinks once, slowly, his gaze on my wife. "You'd lie?"

"It's as truthful as your article," Emery says. "And you did instigate this with your made-up story about us."

I squint at Graham. "No one believes your article. Retract it and apologize, or I will file a defamation lawsuit that will divest you of any and all assets you have left after the divorce."

Graham's pallor deepens. "Aye, I'll print a retraction."

I open my mouth, about to remind him of my earlier demand.

"And an apology," Graham hastens to add.

I nod. "Good. You can start your apologies now."

Graham swallows hard, wriggling in his seat the way slimy worms always do. He studies the disordered papers on his desk and mutters, "I'm sorry for what I've done to you."

Glancing at Emery, I wait for her response.

She shrugs. "Great, he apologized. Can we go now?"

"If you're satisfied, I am."

Emery turns toward the door, and I usher her out of the office with a hand on her back. While the door shuts behind us, I stop to scan the street. "How did you get here?"

"In the Jag."

My voice sounded flat, almost cold, when I asked the question. I feel cold too, though it's probably the aftereffects of adrenaline. Shouldn't I be experiencing a sense of triumph? Instead, I feel numb.

I spot the Jaguar and hustle Emery down the block to where she parked. Without a word, I pull the driver's door open and wave for her to get inside.

Emery does not move.

I wave again.

She stares up at me, her brows wrinkled. "Are you okay?"

"Fine." I step away from the car. "Go home. I'll follow in the Mercedes."

I point over her shoulder to where the car is parked a few spaces away from the door to Graham's office.

"How did Graham know about our contract?" she asks. "How did he find the pictures?"

I turn my face away. "I was careless, left papers on my desk on our wedding day. Graham slunk into my office before he hounded you, before the ceremony even began. The papers included the contract and a report from the investigator about Sebastian."

"Not your fault. Why did you have the contract out?"

She doesn't need to know I've often taken the contract out and re-read it, perhaps to punish myself.

I jerk my head toward the Jaguar's open door. "Go."

Though I can tell she wants to argue, my cold demeanor seems to change her mind. She climbs into the car.

Shutting the door, I shuffle back to the Mercedes.

On the way home, I obey all traffic laws and stare straight ahead at the road. As soon as we've walked into the house, Emery sags against the wall in the ground-floor hallway.

She aims her bleak gaze at me. "I'm sorry about everything that's happened."

For a moment, I just stand here like the robot she called me on the day I left for Paris. "Go to bed."

"Shouldn't we talk? I mean—"

"Go to bed, Emery. It's been a trying day."

I accompany her as far as the first floor, then veer off in the direction of my office, leaving my wife to mount the last two flights alone. Though I shuffle into my office, I halt halfway to my desk. Why am I in here? My wife is upset, and I've come to my sanctum to hide. She needs me. Even if I can't give her what she wants the most, I can comfort her tonight.

When I walk into our bedroom, it's empty. I check the attached bathroom, but she's not there either. Where is my wife?

A chill shivers over my skin as the truth becomes obvious. No, she wouldn't do that.

I jog down the hall and ease the door to the other bedroom open partway. A wedge of light spills inside the room from the hall.

And my wife is curled up on the bed, still wearing her clothes and her shoes, hugging her knees to her chest.

Pain stabs into my heart like a knife blade.

I walk to the bed. "What are you doing in here?"

"Trying to sleep."

"Why aren't you in our bedroom?"

She stares blankly down at the floor and hunches her shoulders.

I slip my arms under her body and lift her off the bed. "This is not where you sleep."

Then I carry her down the hall and into our room, where I throw the covers aside, not caring where they land. I remove her clothes and shoes before I lay her down on the bed, with a pillow cushioning her head, and drag the covers over her to shield her naked body. Once I've undressed, I crawl under the covers too, nestling her against me.

"Sleep," I murmur.

I don't know which of us falls asleep first, but I wake again later, experiencing a powerful need to hold her close and feel her against me for as long as I can. What Graham did, it happened because of me. I should've guarded the house better, protected her better, treated her like my wife instead of a tool to end my family's meddling. Was that why I married her?

Doesn't matter. All I've brought her is pain.

And I can't even fix the mess I've made, because it's not about Graham or Sebastian or anyone else. The problem is inside me.

In the wee hours, while I listen to Emery's soft, even breaths and gaze down at her face, I finally understand. But it's too late. The best thing I can do for Emery is to let her go. Maybe I haven't ruined her, but I have ruined myself, and I love her too much to drag her down with me.

The time has come to set her free.

Chapter Thirty-Six

Mother Nature seems to grasp the solemnity of the mood inside Dùndubhan today, weaving clouds in the heavens to block the sun's light and cast deep shadows over the world. The lowering grey sky suits my mood. I feel as colorless and bleak as the world outside. Though I get up just after four a.m., I linger in the bedroom, sitting in the chair by the window to watch my wife sleep.

She's perfect, and I don't deserve her.

After a while, I dress and head downstairs. Mrs. Darroch isn't in the kitchen yet since I normally rise at six and it's not even five. I don't feel like eating, but I force myself to consume a large muffin I find in a basket on the counter. Mrs. Darroch likes to keep snacks on hand. I eat my meager breakfast, but it tastes bitter instead of sweet, tainted by the bile creeping into my throat.

My Emery, you are irreplaceable.

I'd spoken those words once, and then I chastised myself for it. Now, when I want to say them again, I know I shouldn't.

I see you, Rory. Not just the parts you show everyone, but the pieces you try to hide.

Perhaps my wife does have the ability to see into my soul, but if she looked closely, she would find bruises too deep to ever heal.

After choking down the muffin, I scuffle through the house like a ghost in chains and make my way into my office. But no, I don't want to be here. Not today. When Emery is gone, I imagine I'll sequester myself in here again to avoid…everything. An impulse grips me, and I grab the papers I'd left on my desk. Then I exit the office and walk downstairs, but my feet feel as heavy as concrete. With no conscious decision to do it, I take myself through the dining room and into the sitting room.

What am I doing here?

I drag myself over to one of the chairs by the windows and drop onto it hard enough that the legs thump on the floor. Glancing down at my lap, I realize I'm still holding the papers I picked up in my office. The marriage contract. I don't know why I brought it here. Maybe I want to punish myself with reminders of what a bloody stupid bastard I am. I set the papers on my thigh and stare numbly out the windows at the somber sky.

For years, possibly all my life, I'd kept my world in perfect order—until the night I walked into a bar in New Orleans and seduced an angel into tarnishing her halo for me. Emery shattered my rules with sweetness, humor, and love. But it's too late. I've destroyed us.

Someone enters the room. I can see the ghostly figure in my peripheral vision, but it's not a specter. My wife has found me. I might not be able to see her face, but I can feel her presence. Though I don't want to do it, I glance up at her.

"Good morning," she says, loitering near the doorway and swinging her hands in a nervous gesture. "How did you sleep?"

"Not well." I can't prevent my voice from sounding flat. "Did you sleep?"

"Uh, not much." She jams her hands in the pockets of her fleece trousers. "Could we talk?"

I avert my gaze to the window. "Nothing to discuss."

She edges a few steps closer. "Rory, come on. We need to talk about things. A lot of things."

I blow out a frustrated sigh. Why can't she just leave me and be done with it?

Emery adopts the firm tone she often uses with me. "Listen, we need—"

I erupt from the chair, and the papers fly off my lap to spill across the wood floor. She's given me no choice. Talking is the last thing we should do. I spin toward her, then freeze with my back straight and stiff, my face blank even as I drill my gaze into hers in a vain attempt to convince her to leave without speaking the words. I can't say it. *Get out of here, go home.* No, my voice won't work, and I couldn't order her to go, anyway. I'm too weak-willed to do what I know should be done.

"Talk," I say in a crisp monotone. "If you must."

Emery rubs her arms. "I'm sorry, this is all my fault. The scandal Graham cooked up, he invented a lot of it, but the truth gave him a head start. You were humiliated because of me, because of my past, because I was stupid enough to say yes when my boyfriend asked me to pose for nudie photos. And I foolishly believed him when he said the pictures would stay private, for his eyes only."

I can't move, frozen from my muscles down to the center of my being. Nothing that happened was her fault. It's my doing.

She keeps talking.

"I never imagined my mistakes would hurt you. I wish I could fix this, but those pictures may never go away." She scratches her arms while her eyes glisten with gathering tears. "I wish I could erase all of it, so you never have to go through that. You were so upset you punched Graham and made him apologize to you, but that's not enough. How could it be? I brought this shame on you. It's my fault."

Emery thinks I made Graham apologize to me? That's rot. I don't care if the *bod ceann* harasses me. I assaulted him for *her*. A man in his right mind would tell the lass that, but I can't form the words.

She approaches me, tips her head back, and aims her shimmering gaze at me. "Please know I never wanted you to be hurt because of me. I love you, Rory."

"I understand."

"Do you?" She searches my face, but seems not to find what she hoped to see there. "I love you, but do you even like me? Or do you put up with me for the sex? On Skye, you said you loved me, but we were having sex and I don't know if you meant it. Did you? Do you?"

Yes, I meant it. Yes, I love her.

But it doesn't matter.

Emery chews on the inside of her lip, sniffling faintly. "Do you want me? Or would you rather get rid of your annoying American wife? I'm in breach of that morality clause in our contract, for sure, what with naked pictures of me—" She chokes on the last word but gulps in a breath and keeps talking. "Naked pictures of me in a newspaper, for everyone to see. The contract says if I shame you in any way, then you can end this, and I won't get your money. Not that I want it, I never did, but I'm not sure if you really believe that, if you want me around anymore or what."

That infernal contract. I wish I'd never drafted it.

Pivoting on my heels, I stalk to the fireplace while keeping my back to her. I rest a hand on the mantel, though I have no idea why.

Neither of us speaks for a moment or two, or a thousand. I'd resolved to send her away, back to America, but now I can't even tell her that. My voice refuses to function. My muscles ignore my commands to move.

I hear shuffling noises at floor level, but my mind doesn't register it as meaningful.

"What is this?" Emery asks, her voice weak and almost pleading.

At first, I have no clue what she's asking me. Then I turn my head in her direction and see the papers I'd dumped on the floor, now clasped in her hands. She's holding up one sheet—the last sheet, where we were both meant to sign. Emery scrawled her signature on the day when I found her at Travellis Games and she agreed to marry me. I'd told her I would sign it later.

But I never did. So many times, I took out that contract and tried to sign my name. I couldn't do it.

"You didn't sign the contract?" she says, the words part question, part accusation.

I take three halting steps toward her, stretching one hand out as if I mean to rip the papers from her hand.

She flaps them in the air between us. "How could you not sign it? You said you would. You let me believe you had. The contract was a promise, you said that. A one-sided promise, turns out."

Aye, it was. I can't deny it, even if I could speak.

Her fingers crook into the papers, crumpling them. "Was this a big joke? Trick the stupid, silly American into marrying you. Is this your way of getting revenge on the gold digger? Except I don't give a damn about your money. I give a damn about you. The joke's on me, I guess."

My fingers twitch, curling toward my palms, then flex straight. I want to touch her, but that won't convince her to leave. She's doing that on her own. All I need to do is keep my mouth shut. Then it will be over, and I'll sink into oblivion. But at least she will have a chance at happiness.

"You promised to be honest with me," Emery says. "But you lied. You know how I feel about secrets, and still, you betrayed me. I poured everything I have into helping you because I believed you wanted my help, but you were just... What? Playing me? Using me? I don't understand what you hoped to gain from lying about the contract, I really don't."

Tears stream down her face, and her cheeks have turned bright red.

She'll give up any minute. Walk away in disgust.

But words keep tumbling out of her. "You don't love me, do you? I pushed you to do things you never wanted. I swore I didn't mean to change you, actually believed it too. But that's what I did, isn't it? I tried to turn you into something you're not. Maybe I deserved to be lied to and treated like a trophy wife."

Maybe it's best that she believes I never cared about her. That will make it easier for her to move on.

Emery mops at her eyes with the sleeve of her sweatshirt. "I never cared about the stupid contract, but you should've told me you didn't want to sign it. We could've talked about it and... God, I don't know. You should've told me why you didn't want to sign. Tell me now, please, you owe me that much."

No, I can't tell her. The answer, the one I've just realized in the last five seconds, is that I couldn't sign because I've loved her since the first moment I saw her.

"At least tell me one thing," Emery says. "What was Skye about? The things you told me there. We got closer, a hell of a lot closer, and I don't think that was all in my head. It meant something, didn't it?"

Aye, it meant everything.

The ticking of the grandfather clock counts down the minutes until she walks away from me.

She covers her eyes with the heels of her hands as breaths hiccup out of her. When she lowers her hands, they fall limp at her sides. She shakes her head slowly. "You don't trust me. Nothing I say will change that. I spent so long trying to help you, to give you what you need, that I stopped thinking about what I need."

Finally, she's thinking about herself instead of trying to save our marriage. It was doomed from the start—by me.

"Say something," Emery demands. When I don't speak, she shakes her head again as tears roll down her cheeks. "I'm exhausted. Fighting to get you to let me in, even a little bit, it's like trying to drill through a mountain with a plastic spoon. I can't do this anymore, I can't."

My fingers twitch.

She smacks her hands on my chest. "Say something, dammit, I'm begging you. Talk to me."

No, I can't do that. I must see this through to the end, by not saying a bloody word.

Her lips quiver, and her hands tremble. "I can't do this anymore."

My fingers bend into my palms. "You're leaving."

"I don't want to leave, but we can't go on like this. I need time to think. Time away from you."

A strange sort of anguished relief rushes through me, and my knees almost buckle. I take one step backward. "Leave, then."

Emery wraps her arms around herself. "If that's all you have to say… You've left me no choice, Rory. I'm sorry."

She trudges toward the doorway, her shoes scuffing across the wood floor.

"Where will you go?" I ask.

"I don't know. A hotel, I guess."

The clock ticks five times.

And then my wife walks out of the room, never looking back.

For a minute or more, I can't move. Though I wanted her to leave me, now that she's actually going, I need to make sure she will be taken care of by someone who will treat her like family. Her parents and sister have gone home. She has no one here, no one except my family. I make arrangements for her, performing the task like an automaton. Robot Rory. Emery was right to call me that.

I slog up the stairs and find her in our bedroom.

She startles when I enter the room, frozen in the middle of packing her suitcase.

"I called Lachlan," I tell her. "He and Erica have offered to let you stay with them."

She drops a half-folded shirt into the suitcase. "Thank you."

Her voice sounds as lifeless as mine. Christ, I never wanted to hurt her. I had no choice.

"Tavish will drive you," I say.

"Don't bother him. I can drive myself, unless you're taking back my wedding present."

My jaw clenches. "Tavish will drive you."

She doesn't argue anymore.

Ten minutes later, I stand in the driveway and watch the Mercedes disappear into the darkness of the forest. Then I shuffle back into the house, aimlessly wandering until I find myself back in the sitting room. The papers that comprise the marriage contract lie scattered on the floor. I kneel to collect the pages and carefully put them in numerical order.

She's gone.

I rise and start toward the chair I'd sat in earlier, but I stumble and pitch sideways, grabbing the arm for support. It holds me up for a second, but then my legs give out, and I crash onto the floor with my back against the chair. Gooseflesh prickles my skin, and the wave of cold that triggered it penetrates every cell in my body and straight down to my soul.

The papers slip out of my grasp, fanning out across the floor.

Emery is gone.

I shut my eyes and try to pull in a breath, but only manage to gasp a few times. My throat has constricted. My eyes burn. She hasn't gone far, only to Lachlan and Erica's home near Ballachulish, but I know this is the end. I'd wanted this, hadn't I? To spare her from a life of misery with me by chasing her away. Now that I've done it, though, I keep hearing four words in my mind, over and over, echoing deep inside me.

What have I done?

Chapter Thirty-Seven

A foot pokes me hard. "Get up, ye bloody stupid man. I have words for you, and they willnae be comforting ones, ye *cacan*, since your behavior does not warrant kindness. That sweet lass loves you. And what did you do? Throw her out with the rubbish." Mrs. Darroch issues a long string of Gaelic curses. "You're like a son to me, but I could batter you myself right now."

This is a dream, isn't it? A nightmare. My housekeeper wouldn't dare to speak to me that way.

Oh aye, of course she would.

I crack one lid open to peer up at Mrs. Darroch. "Good morning to you too."

My voice is rough, most likely because my throat is as dry as the Sahara Desert, my mouth too. Every muscle in my body aches from the slightest movement. Aye, that happens when a person falls asleep on the floor in the sitting room. Well, it's what happened when I did that. I remember slumping to the floor with my back against the chair. The rest is hazy, though not because I got drunk. I didn't do that. No, I was stone-cold sober when I rolled onto the floor on my back and lay here until I fell asleep. The numbness I'd experienced last night held on until after I dozed off, but I don't feel it making a resurgence now.

Numbness might be preferable to the other option—feeling the full brunt of what I've done.

"Ye deserve the pain, *ye gòrach pìos de cac.*" Aye, only a stupid piece of shit would behave the way I did yesterday. What *have* I done? I drove my wife away, broke her heart, acted like I don't care what happens to her. Robot Rory, that's me.

"Aye, go on and curse at yourself," Mrs. Darroch says. "Donnae expect me to kiss your cheek and tell ye it's all right, not this time."

No, I don't expect that. She's not likely to call me *mo luran* either.

Pushing up into a sitting position, I yawn and rub my neck. Though I had dozed intermittently all night, I feel nothing close to rested. Emery had warned me that if I didn't stop acting like a bastard, she would do whatever is necessary to protect herself. Of course she left me. We both knew from the start that's how this would end.

But she said she needs time, not that she wants a divorce.

Sometime between collapsing on the floor and waking up this morning, I'd realized Emery is giving me one last chance. Needing time doesn't mean she will never speak to me again, but I know my apologies have worn thin. To get her back, I'll need to do more than say I'm sorry.

I have no idea how to win back my wife. Never tried to keep a woman who wanted to leave me, not until today.

Mrs. Darroch kicks me between my shoulder blades. "Well? Are ye going over to Lachlan and Erica's house to beg that lovely lass to take you back? Or would ye rather sit there feeling sorry for yourself? That's not the Rory MacTaggart I know."

No one knows who I am deep down. No one except my wife. Even I didn't understand until Emery showed me.

I scramble to my feet and whirl around, ready to bolt for the Mercedes.

Mrs. Darroch holds up a hand, eying me with a pained expression. "Ye might want to shower, shave, and put on clothes that don't smell like ye rolled in the garden right after Tavish spread the fertilizer."

Why would I smell bad? I do recall sweating as I lay on the floor last night. Cold sweat, but I suppose even that turns into a rank smell after a while.

I rush upstairs to get myself ready to see Emery. Then I race out to the car and roar down the driveway, not caring that the Mercedes jounces over potholes with so much force that my head would smack into the ceiling if not for the seat belt pinning me down. Once I get out on the main road, I slow down to obey the speed limit. I want to drive a hundred miles an hour, but getting myself killed won't help me win my wife's heart again. I arrive at Lachlan and Erica's house alive and well. No, that's not true. I feel like I might vomit, and I'm alive only in that my heart still beats and my lungs still function.

I rap on the door twice. Then I wipe my clammy palms on my trousers.

The door flies open. Emery looks at me, her cheeks flushed—with excitement, I think. Or maybe that's what I desperately want it to be.

I take a breath. "Please come home. I love you."

Her mouth falls open, but she doesn't speak.

Maybe I shouldn't have spoken those words in a flat tone. Didn't mean to do that. But I'm…terrified that my wife will never forgive me.

"Told ye," Lachlan shouts from somewhere inside the house. "He doesn't waste time."

"Quiet," Erica chastises.

Emery shoos me away. "Outside. Please."

I shuffle backward, my brows tightening, and keep backing up until Emery shuts the door and stops us a wee ways from the house.

"That's it?" she says.

"I thought you'd want to hear—you said—" I cinch up my whole face into a warped grimace and rub the bridge of my nose. Though I want to hide my feelings, the way I always do, I can't hold back anymore, not if I mean to convince her to come home. So I let my desperation show, on my face and in my voice. "You wanted me to say it. I thought this would…fix things."

But it hasn't, because I'm a flaming ersehole.

"If you'd said that a few days ago," she says, "it would've fixed everything. But after yesterday…I don't know how we make this right. I'm sorry, I just don't know."

I grip the back of my neck. "Do you want to?"

"Want to what?"

"Do you want to work this out? Do you want me?"

"Rory." She clamps her hands under her arms. "I love you. I want to be with you. But saying you love me doesn't resolve any of the problems I tried to talk to you about so many times. It doesn't erase what happened between us yesterday. You hurt me more than ever."

I raise my hands, needing to touch her, but let them fall to my sides. A weak shake of my head is all I can manage. "I thought you'd be happy."

"That you're here? That you love me? It's all well and good but—" She winces, laying a hand over her belly as if it hurts. "You just stood there. Robot Rory staring at me like I was invisible."

"How could I stare if you're invisible?"

"Don't be obtuse on purpose. You know what I mean."

I hang my head. "Aye."

Despite having my head down, I can see Emery scrubbing her cheeks with her palms, and I notice she seems a touch pale now. "I told you every-thing—everything—I was feeling. I told you how much I love you. And you said nothing. I cried, and I said I had to leave. You said nothing. While I walked out the door, you stood there watching like it didn't matter to you at all."

I lift my head, resisting the urge to contradict her. It mattered, but I need to prove that to her.

She holds up a hand. "Even then, I knew you cared if I left. I'm not saying you don't love me. I'm saying you still don't understand how much it hurt me that you had no comment on the most emotional monologue I've ever delivered to anyone."

Her shoulders flag, and her face seems a shade paler. She stumbles to the wrought-iron bench beside the house, slumping onto it.

I kneel before her. "Emery, I wish I knew how to make things right, but this time, I have no bloody idea how. Please help me."

"I'm too tired, Rory."

"You said that yesterday. Taking care of me has drained you."

"Yeah." She shuts her eyes. "I'm sorry."

"I'm the one who needs to apologize. Again and again, for all eternity if that will help." I settle a hand on her knee. "I miss you, Emery. I can't sleep without you."

"Did you not sleep when you were in France?"

"Not well, but that was different. I knew I'd be coming home to you. Now..." I draw in a breath, my lips quivering. "I no longer have the luxury of assuming you'll be there when I wake up in the morning."

She gazes into my eyes, but I can't tell what she might be thinking.

I massage my jaw. "Not signing the contract was a mistake because I broke a promise to you. But I don't regret not signing it, which I suppose is a contradiction. Can't help that. I never wanted to break a promise to you, but I couldn't bring myself to sign the contract. You told me you didn't care about the money, you didn't marry me for it, and I believed you."

"But?"

I inch my hand closer to hers, a finger's width away. "Part of me couldn't accept that anyone, especially a woman as vibrant and passionate as you, could want me without the enticement of money. Isobel cared for money and status more than love. I tried to become what she needed, tried until it had eaten up a part of me I may never get back, but it wasn't enough."

She stares at me, but I can't tell if it's shock because she believes me or because she thinks I'm a hopeless bastard.

I long to touch her, really touch her, but I don't dare try.

Emery walks her fingers toward mine until the tips of hers slip between them.

Relief floods through me, making me feel weak for a moment.

"You are not Isobel," I say. "I know this. You never needed anything from me but love, and I couldn't believe I deserved that. Mentioning the contract every time we grew closer... You were right. I used it as a wedge. I also used it as a sort of insurance policy, to keep you around even after you got tired of me. Not signing the damn thing, that was a sign I should've recognized sooner if I weren't such an eejit. I couldn't do it because I didn't want you to stay for the money. I wanted you to stay for me."

"But I didn't know you never signed the contract." She shifts in place as if she can't find a comfortable position on the bench. "Besides, it was the other stuff that mattered more. You don't trust me."

"I do."

"Really? You thought you had to pay me to stay. You wouldn't explain why you got drunk on our wedding night, or a ton of other things."

I nod toward the empty space on the bench. "May I sit beside you?"

"Do what you want."

Though I settle onto the bench, I maintain a distance between us. "I've been a bastard, I know. You have no reason at all to come back to me, but you are wrong. I trust you. The things I said over the past few weeks, they came from my fears and had nothing to do with you."

"Nothing? Come on, Rory."

"Well, they had something to do with you." I angle toward her, laying an arm across the bench behind her shoulders. "The more time I spent with you, the harder it was to deny the truth. I fell in love with you, Emery. My behavior at the wedding, that was the day I realized how much you mean to me. When I saw you coming down the aisle toward me, in that fairy-tale dress with your hair gleaming in the sun like a halo. Your smile was so sweet and full of…love. And deep down I knew I loved you, more than I've loved anyone in my life."

Her focus remains on me, but I can't gauge her state of mind.

"Getting buckled was a mistake I'll regret forever," I tell her, my voice soft but imbued with all my tangled emotions. "You deserved a perfect wedding, particularly after the way I bulldozed you into marrying me in front of a magistrate. Realizing I love you, it turned me into a bampot of the worst sort. I knew if you left me, and I was certain you would, I would never feel this way again."

Emery says nothing for a moment that feels like an eternity, her gaze on me but her thoughts impossible to decipher. Then she straps her arms over her belly. "This is partly my fault, I'm sorry."

"How on earth is it your fault?"

"You told me, in your own way, you weren't ready for a real relationship. I agreed to a marriage of convenience, then I demanded you care about me." She sags against the bench with my arm supporting her shoulders. "I pushed you at every turn, tried to make you change. That's what Isobel did to you. I convinced myself I was your therapist." She snorts. "And that you needed my help—wanted it, even. I drove you to drink. That's my doing."

"Emery…" I slide a little closer. "Nothing is your fault. You put up with me no matter what I did, forgave me every time I acted like a bastard. Your love changed me, not because you forced me to do anything, but because I couldn't help loving you. I need you with me, and I have evolved."

"Just like that? It's been a day, Rory. Nobody changes overnight. You want me to come home, but that doesn't mean anything will be different if I do."

"I didn't change overnight." I brush a lock of hair away from her face. "You showed me how to love again. It took weeks. It took too much effort from you and not enough cooperation from me, but it happened. Last night without you, not knowing if you'll ever come home, I finally gave up being afraid of this. I will do anything for you. Please believe me, *m'eudail*."

She clutches her belly as sweat beads on her forehead.

"You're unwell, Emery."

When I reach out to touch her forehead, she bats my hand away.

"I've got the flu," she says. "Probably caught it from the chickens."

"Chickens?"

"You know, bird flu." She groans. "Never mind, dumb joke."

I scrutinize her, my lips tight. "Let me take you to a doctor."

"No, I'm fine, really." Emery heaves her body off the bench, and though she turns toward me, she doesn't meet my gaze. "I need a nap, that's all. And you need to do more thinking before you announce you've overcome your fears. Please, go home. I'll call you tomorrow."

"I don't need more time, Emery. I need you." I rise from the bench. "But I'm more concerned with your health today. You need a doctor."

"I need sleep." Her face is grey, and her lips are pale. "We'll talk more tomorrow, okay?"

Emery hurries into the house with a shuffling gait, as if her feet have become too heavy, and trips over the threshold. Though I sprint after her, she slams the door shut in my face.

"Emery!" I hear Erica shout from inside the house.

Though I hear more voices, I can't make out the words.

"Lachlan!" Erica shouts. "Hurry, something's wrong with Emery."

My heart thuds so hard I gasp. Emery. What's happened to her? I'm reaching for the knob when the door flies open.

Lachlan flaps his arm, urging me to go inside. "Rory, get in here, man. Your wife needs a doctor. Now."

I follow him down the hall to where Erica is holding Emery up with her arms around my wife. When I see the pool of vomit on the floor at Emery's feet, I fight to stay calm. She needs me to take care of her, for once, and I will not let her down this time.

Erica moves aside while I hoist my wife off her feet and clasp her to me.

I curse in Gaelic. "I'm taking you to the hospital."

She nods weakly.

And I barrel out the open door, heading straight for the Mercedes.

Lachlan sprints past us to open the rear door, and I lay Emery on the backseat as gently as I can. Sweeping hair away from her face, I kiss her forehead.

"Donnae worry, love," I whisper. "I'm taking care of you."

Emery lunges her head forward and throws up on the floor.

Chapter Thirty-Eight

The rest of the day becomes a long blur of actions and words, doctors and family, as everyone tries to help in whatever way they can. Only the medical professionals can fix my wife, though. She has appendicitis, a doctor informs me. Emery needs surgery, right away. This would be one time when cool calmness would benefit me, but though I remain even-tempered until my wife is wheeled away for surgery, after that I snap. Cannae control my emotions anymore, not with my wife being rushed into an operating room. I bark and snarl and glower at everyone, even my family, as I haunt the waiting room like an ogre.

Fuck what everyone else thinks. My wife is being cut open right now.

Hours go by, and gradually, I reassert the calmness I'd marshaled when I carried Emery into the hospital. Still, I lose track of time and feel like I'm floating in outer space where I have no bearings. I'm adrift without my wife. Eventually, I wind up sitting in an uncomfortable metal chair that doesn't quite fit my body while my wife sleeps in a bed beside me. After briefly waking, she sank back into sleep. I don't think she noticed I was here, too groggy to comprehend anything.

The hard seat makes my erse hurt, and I fidget, causing the chair to creak.

For half an hour, I've tried to concentrate on a magazine to distract myself, but the only one I could find is devoted to home decor. Aye, that's a topic of interest to me—if I'd suffered a severe brain injury. I shift in my seat again, and it creaks louder this time.

"Hey."

My wife's voice startles me, and I drop the magazine. "Emery, you're awake. How are you feeling?"

"Like I got sliced and diced." She manages a faint smile. "Thank you for coming with me."

"Of course I came." Dragging the chair closer, I fold my hands around hers, careful to avoid the IV line taped to the backside of her hand. "I haven't taken care of you, but that changes now."

She wriggles as if she can't get comfortable either.

"Easy," I say. "You've only just woken. Are you in pain?"

"Some."

Though I don't want to leave her, I hurry outside to track down someone who can ease Emery's pain. Then I return to my wife's side. "A nurse will bring medicine for you."

"Thanks."

"Stop thanking me. I have more than enough to make up to you to fill several lifetimes." I focus on her hand, cradled in mine. "Will you let me look after you while you recover? I have no expectations of what will happen once you're well. But I'd like to care for you."

"Rory, about what I said earlier. I was sick, and I didn't mean—"

"Hush." I skim the backs of my fingers over her cheek. "You're not to make major decisions for at least a week, two would be better. Anesthesia impairs your thinking."

"But I know what I—"

With one finger on her lips, I silence her. "No arguments this time. Wait two weeks. Then we can discuss things."

She seems to accept my command. I don't want her to vow she'll stay with me forever, only to have her realize later it was the aftereffects of anesthesia clouding her mind. If she still wants me, I can wait a few weeks to hear her say it.

I touch my lips to her forehead. "The surgeon says they'll release you later this evening. I can take you to Erica and Lachlan's, if you'd feel more comfortable there."

"Oh, Rory." She raises her free hand to touch my cheek. "I want to go home. With you."

A smile struggles to take hold of my lips, but they twitch and quiver from the effort. Then, at last, I muster a smile that must look pathetic. "No more secrets, Em. I promise."

She nods, her smile small but sweet.

I press my cheek to hers.

Everything will be different now. I will be different. Whatever Emery decides about us, at least I will know I've done everything I can to show my wife how much I love her.

Two weeks should feel like a long time, considering what I'm waiting to hear my wife say. But the time races by so fast that I hardly have a chance to worry about Emery's answer. I'd married her in a whirlwind, and now I await her decision as the days fly past us. Have I changed? I think so, but it's my wife's opinion that matters. For the first time in years, maybe in my entire life, work becomes a secondary concern. Spending time with my wife is all I care about, and my clients will need to wait a bit longer to regain my attention. If anyone has an urgent concern, I will speak to them. But I spend only a few minutes now and then in my office.

Every morning, I lounge in bed until Emery wakes up. Sometimes I fall back asleep while I'm waiting. And every day, I greet my wife in the same way when she rouses.

I smile, lean in to kiss her, and say, "Good morning, *mo gaoloch*."

Sometimes I call her *m'eudail* instead. She never asks me what those words mean. My tone of voice must reveal the fact they're endearments.

On the first morning after her surgery, I create a sumptuous breakfast for my wife. Blueberry pancakes with a mountain of butter as well as a loch's worth of maple syrup, not to mention both bacon and sausage with scrambled eggs too. She needs to regain her strength, doesn't she? I won't worry about feeding her healthy food until she has recovered fully. Blueberries are healthy, aren't they? And eggs have protein. Aye, I'm taking good care of my wife.

Emery needs to sleep downstairs for a while, until she's up to climbing three flights of stairs again. I offer to carry her to our bedroom every night, but she prefers to sleep in the guest wing. Though she tries to talk me into sleeping in our third-floor bedroom, I refuse to go upstairs until she can go with me, under her own power. Never again will I sleep in a separate room from my wife.

When I've laid our breakfast out for Emery on the dining room table, she grins and laughs. "Wow, you sure know how to treat a girl. Not sure I could eat this much in three days, but I'll give it a shot."

"You don't have to eat all of it." I scratch my jaw, eying the spread with a touch of embarrassment. "I may have overdone things."

But I intend to keep overdoing it for the rest of our lives. Emery deserves more than the best. She deserves everything, and I'll do whatever it takes to ensure she's happy, healthy, and satisfied.

I prove my determination to do that a few days later in the sitting room when I drag the sofa over to the windows just so Emery can enjoy the view while resting comfortably. I lay a fleece blanket over her legs and bring her a mug of hot cocoa. Then I sit in a chair nearby so she can stretch out on the sofa.

After a few minutes of silent contemplation, I decide it's time to explain myself to Emery.

I get up and perch on the sofa beside my wife's hip. "I love you, Emery. Do you believe me?"

"Yes, I believe you." She strokes my cheek, her hand warm from the cocoa mug. "I love you too."

I cover her hand with mine, fastening it to my cheek, and turn my face into her palm to kiss it. "About Graham... I didn't assault him for my sake. His ridiculous article didn't humiliate me, it humiliated you, and I could not stand for that. Before you walked into his office, I'd threatened him with everything I could think of to make him issue an apology—to you."

"That apology was aimed at me?"

"It was." I rub my thumb over the back of her hand. "Donnae care what the scunner says about me. But when he slandered you, I had to make it right. Would've skelped him bloody if necessary."

She wriggles her fingers on my cheek and smiles in her sweet way.

"Graham has moved to Liverpool to stay with his mother," I say. "As for Sebastian, he checked himself into a psychiatric clinic. The investigator determined Sebastian doesn't have the pictures of you anymore, and Graham admitted he found only the one image, on a website that archives other sites. The owners of that site complied with my demand they delete the image immediately. It's over, Emery."

"Saying thank-you doesn't seem like enough, Rory. No one's ever fought for me before." She leans forward to feather her lips over mine. "You are my knight in a kilt."

"I've made too many mistakes to earn that designation." I lace our fingers, absorbed by the movements. "You were right. All those rules, I invented them as a means of keeping you at a distance. Didn't work. I think about you even when you're miles away."

"Is that a bad thing?"

"No." For the first time in the history of us, I give her a smile of unrestrained joy. "It's wonderful."

The next day, Emery tries to walk outside—on her own, no less.

I spot her sneaking away and lunge between my wife and the vestibule door. "Where are you going?"

"For a walk."

"You can walk indoors. It's too soon to leave the house."

She bites her lip, but it seems like she's doing that to stave off laughter. "I can handle strolling around the front lawn. The doctor said I should get up and moving right away."

"He didn't say traipse into the wilds where you might break your stitches."

"It's staples, not stitches."

"That's worse. The staples might pop loose."

Emery takes my face in her hands, her mouth grazing mine. "Rory, you adorably silly man, I will be fine. Come with me. It'll make you feel better, and I'd love the company."

From that day forward, I accompany my wife on her daily walks and let her call me "cute" and "adorable" and even "snuggle-icious." She uses other silly terms too, and though I sometimes roll my eyes at them, we both know I love every ridiculous thing she calls me.

One afternoon, we're relaxing in the sitting room when Emery brings up a subject neither of us has broached before. Emery has stretched out on the sofa while I'm "kicking back," as she would say, in a chair by the windows while I enjoy the view.

"I think you've worked a total of three hours in the past four days," my wife says. "What happened to all that vital, important work that used to keep you busy sixteen hours a day?"

My lips pucker as I consider her statement. Then they twitch upward briefly before I let them spread into a broad smile. "Fuck work."

"I appreciate the sentiment, but that's not really an answer."

"You were right. I hid in my office to avoid spending time with you, to avoid loving you. It didn't work, and I'm done with that. I'll help people who need it, the ones who can't afford a solicitor, but otherwise, I'm retired."

She gapes at me. "Retired at almost-forty? Are you sure you're ready to join the ranks of the idle rich?"

"I have no intention of being idle. We can do whatever you want. Anything. Say it, and I'll make it happen."

"Anything?"

"Yes. You wanted a new career, a new mission in life. I'll support you in whatever way you need."

"Well, I was thinking—"

I hold up a hand. "Not yet. No decisions for two weeks."

My wife accepts my command, but I know she's only humoring me. Maybe I am acting like an overprotective eejit. I can live with that.

The next day, the MacTaggart clan descends on our home. When Lachlan had rung me yesterday to ask permission for a visit, I asked Emery if she was ready to be overrun by an army of Scots and the American Wives Club. Aye, those barmy women have officially adopted that name for their group that seems to revolve around interfering in everyone else's lives. Emery feels better every day, so we agreed she could handle a brief visit.

My family doesn't stay too long, but seeing them makes Emery happy. It makes me happy too. I've been sequestered at Dùndubhan with my wife for a week, and though I could spend the rest of my life with only Emery, I enjoy seeing my family. They all seem surprised when they see me, probably because I smile and joke with them and dote on my wife.

Neither my family nor Emery's cares about Graham Oliver's expose, despite the details it included about our marriage contract and the prenuptial agreement. They also don't care that I'd talked Emery into a marriage of convenience. Everyone else apparently realized we love each other before Emery and I recognized the truth. And my family wasn't surprised at all that I'd been reluctant to commit to a normal relationship, since they know my first three marriages ended badly. The Grangers don't care about any of that either. During a phone conversation, Penny and Ted both assure us that after meeting me, they'd trusted me to take care of their daughter.

I don't worry about why they feel that way. Emery has taught me that logic holds little sway over the human heart.

My wife has changed me in other ways too. We watch superhero films together, though I doubt I'll ever share her enthusiasm for them. I start to appreciate them more when Emery compares me to the men in the movies.

She squeezes my biceps and says, "Mm, yours are much firmer and sexier."

On another occasion, she slides her hand up my inner thigh and announces, "Your legs are so much more toned and powerful, perfect for driving a woman half-crazy in bed."

After that, I volunteer to watch as many of those films as she wants.

The deadline I'd set for Emery lands on my birthday, though I haven't mentioned that fact to her. Now she should be recovered enough to make rational decisions, unaffected by her surgery. I don't want to make this day about me, but my wife has other ideas.

In the evening, we're relaxing on the sitting room sofa. Emery sits in the corner with her legs bent under her, while I'm beside her with an arm on the sofa's back and my legs outstretched. I also have my feet on the coffee table, something I would never have done before Emery.

She rubs her cheek against my arm. "I have a surprise for you."

I turn sideways to lay an arm around her. "What sort of surprise?"

"One sec." Without disturbing my arm, she sneaks a hand behind her to pull out an object she'd hidden between the cushion and the sofa's arm. She offers the gift-wrapped package to me. "Happy birthday, Rory baby."

I glance at the package, then look at her. "You haven't called me that since before—since everyone found out about our arrangement."

She tips her head to the side. "Haven't I?"

"No. Is it a good sign?"

"Guess so." She thrusts the gift at me. "Open it."

I accept the package, tapping my fingers on it. "How did you know it's my birthday?"

"Oh please. I've got five sisters-in-law and two brothers-in-law, not to mention parents-in-law. Did you honestly think I couldn't find out when your birthday is?"

"I should never doubt your skills in uncovering my secrets."

"Yep, you should know better by now."

With a single swipe of my hand, I strip off the wrapping paper. The gift—a rectangular book with a smooth, hard cover—glistens in the subdued lighting within the sitting room.

"What is this?" I ask, turning the book over in my hand.

"Flip it open and you'll see."

I open the cover. A smirk tightens my lips as I regard my wife out of the corner of my eye. "Interesting title."

Emery wriggles closer and points at the words on the page as she recites them. "The evolution of Emery and Rory baby, a pictorial history."

"Yes, I can read." I pull her snug against my body. "Do I want to know what pictures you've got in here?"

"Be brave. Flip through it."

I trace my fingers over the lettering on the title page. "Did you write this by hand?"

"Yep. And I had every picture printed out, so I could stick it to the page with my own little fingers. I handwrote the captions too."

"Captions?" I turn to the first page of photos and smile as I read the headline. "Once upon a time, there was an uptight but very hot Scotsman who lived alone in his castle. Until, that is, he met a princess geek…"

I touch the first photo. It's the self-portrait she took in Pat O'Brien's on the night we met.

"That's me," she says, "right before you walked up and propositioned me. I left that part out of the caption."

"I see that." I move my finger down to the words beneath the photo. "Emery, thirty seconds before she met her solicitous solicitor."

My wife rests her cheek on my shoulder. "Why did you pick me that night? I've always wondered. You could've had your choice of hot babes, professional and unprofessional ones. Why pick the girl in faded jeans and a goofy T-shirt who hadn't showered or brushed her teeth?"

I hook a finger under her chin, tilting her head up so we're gazing into each other's eyes. "I saw you take this picture."

"I didn't see you."

"You wouldn't have. I was in the shadows near the doorway." I rub my thumb across her lower lip. "I saw you, and then I saw nothing else. The way you smiled when you posed for your self-portrait, the way your hair shimmered in the light, you were the most radiant woman I'd ever laid eyes on. I had to have you."

She licks at the pad of my thumb. "Good answer."

"The truth." I lower my hand. "I saw you rooting about in your bra as well. Hunting for cash, but I didn't know that. I thought you were a bit barmy, in the most adorable way, and I was enchanted."

"That answer's even better." She pokes me in the side with her finger. "Even if you did call me barmy."

"I love your unconventional nature." My gaze returns to the photo of her. "When I watched you fiddling with your bra, I had no idea you were hiding the crown jewels in there."

"A hundred bucks isn't a treasure trove."

I touch a finger to her breastbone, revealed by the low neckline of her blouse, and drag the tip down into the valley between her breasts. "I wasn't talking about your money."

Her breath hitches when I slip my finger under her breast. "And Aidan wonders why women like you. It's no mystery to me."

We browse the album together, laughing over the photo of me eating pancakes with "surgical precision," according to Emery, and we read aloud the captions that summarize our weeks together. Finally, we snuggle closer when we come to the wedding pictures.

I tap the photo of me at the altar, wearing a somewhat dazed look. "Who took this? Not you, unless you hid a camera in your bosom."

"Hadley took it. She said we needed to document how shocked you were by my effervescent beauty."

"You are effervescent, and beautiful. But I was stunned by how deeply I love you."

"Are you still stunned?"

"Every day." I whisk my lips across hers. "By your beauty, your intelligence, your never-ending positivity, your passion, everything about you."

"I adore you, Rory MacTaggart."

"And I worship you, Emery MacTaggart." I pick up the book and aim it at her. "The last photo isn't of us. It's the house on Skye."

"Because that's where I told you I love you, and it's where you shared your feelings with me for the first time."

I shut the book and set it on the table. "I shouldn't have said it during sex. I love you, and I should've told you the day I realized it. I can't blame you for wanting to leave me."

"I told you I needed time to think."

"Time away from me." I bow my head. "I used to believe I gave up on Isobel too soon, that I should've fought for her. Now I know I should've done the opposite and ended our marriage long before she left." I sag against the sofa. "My worst regret is that I let you walk away without saying a word. I wanted to fall to my knees and beg you to stay. Instead, I let you go without a fight. I will never repeat that mistake. If you want to leave me now, I'll run after you. I'll make a bloody fool of myself in any way necessary if it will keep you from going."

"I'm not going anywhere."

"You left me once, and I deserved it."

"Oh Rory, you've got it all wrong." She climbs onto my lap, straddling me with her hands on my shoulders. "I asked for time, not a divorce. I needed to think, but I never had any intention of leaving you."

I rest my hands on her hips. "You came back because of your illness."

"Wrong again." She glides her hands up my neck to cradle my nape. "I wanted to tell you then, but you insisted I shouldn't make decisions for two weeks. Well, it's been two weeks, and I can tell you. I came home because I love you and I need you, and I want to live with you for the rest of my life. I came home because this *is* my home. Anywhere you are is where I belong."

My fingers tense on her hips. "You mean it?"

"With all my heart." She spreads her legs wider, sinking into my lap. "I'm never walking out that door again unless it's with you."

"You weren't sure I'd changed."

"I was sure. You weren't." She frames my face with her hands. "Do you believe it now?"

"Aye. I believe in you, and I believe in us."

With her hands holding my face, she leans in until our lips skim each other and our breaths mingle. "I've meant to ask you. There was something you said on our first wedding night. It was Gaelic, I think. I'm dying to know what it meant. You probably don't remember."

"No, I remember." Lowering my voice to a rough whisper, I repeat the words I'd spoken on that night. "Yer so beautiful, ye make my *bagais* ache, *cho cinnteach is a tha bod's an each*. I want my face in your *camas*, my mouth on your *brillean*. The translation is you're so beautiful, you make my balls ache, as sure as a horse has a penis. I want my face between your thighs, my mouth on your clitoris."

"I'm on board for all of that." She grazes her tongue across my lips. "You haven't kissed me in weeks, not the way I want you to."

"Didnae want to overtax you."

"I'm fine, baby. Recovered and cleared for all activities." She sucks my bottom lip between her teeth and releases it slowly. "And I do mean all activities. But let's start with a real, bone-melting kiss."

Anything for my wife.

The following day, I convince Emery that we must visit Loch Fairbairn for the sole purpose of having "a ridiculous outing packed with frivolous behavior and even more frivolous spending." She laughs when I say that. But she is the woman who refused to spend our money, and I mean to talk her into buying things she doesn't need, just because she wants them. Emery deserves to be lavished with all the best things life has to offer.

I do have an ulterior motive, though.

We drive into the village in the Jaguar, and I commit a flagrant if brief violation of the speed laws strictly to make my wife smile. Before she can dash into a shop to browse the clothing selections, I catch her arm and inform her that I have an urgent task to complete at my office. It's a lie, but for a good cause. I instruct her to meet me in the village square in fifteen minutes.

Ten minutes later, I locate my wife. She has just set down two over-stuffed bags and walks toward the front windows of the only restaurant in the village. Most of the cafe's front is sequestered behind a wrought-iron railing, but one section of the windows extends past that.

I see my reflection in the window as I come up behind Emery.

She notices my reflection too and grins. Then she whirls around. "Rory baby, finally. Your wife needs feeding."

I halt in front of her with my fist closed around a small, square object. "Something to do first."

"What's that?"

I lunge backward two steps. Then I grasp the hem of my untucked T-shirt and strip it off, pitching it onto the stone sidewalk. Wearing only my jeans and shoes, I spread my arms wide and break into song, belting out "You Make Me Feel So Young."

Emery bursts into giggles and slaps a hand over her mouth. Her laughter grows louder and more enthusiastic, until her eyes begin to water.

Done with the first verse and chorus, I reach for the metal button on my jeans and start to unhook it.

My wife rushes forward to stay my hand with her own. Between lingering giggles, she says, "What on earth are you doing?"

"Told ye I'd make a bloody fool of myself for you anytime, anywhere."

"I thought that was a thing you say, not a thing you actually do." She pries my fingers away from the button. "Besides, your nakedness is exclusively for my viewing pleasure."

A wee crowd has gathered across the street. Men and women point, smile, and shake their heads in amused disbelief. One person calls out, "Never thought I'd see the day Rory MacTaggart goes barmy for a woman."

Heedless of the crowd, I drop to one knee and raise the wee velvet box I'd concealed in my hand. Flipping it open, I reveal the diamond ring. "Will you be my wife, Emery?"

"Uh, I am your wife. Married you twice. How many weddings do you need?"

"Not a wedding." I thrust the box up at her. "You never got a ring or a proper proposal."

She tries not to laugh, which results in a snort. "This is proper? You half-naked on the street?"

"For you, this is the most proper sort of proposal." I pluck the ring out of its velvet bed and lift it to her left hand. "Will you be my wife, my Emery baby?"

"Yes." She grins. "Forever."

I slip the ring onto her finger, in front of the gold wedding band, and kiss her knuckles. Then I surge to my feet and shout, "I love my wife!"

"I love my husband!" Emery shouts.

Sweeping her into my arms, I spin us round and round.

And the crowd cheers.

Epilogue

Two Months Later

If anyone had asked me three months ago what my life would look like today, I would've grunted and informed them nothing ever changes. Take another wife? No, never. Ease up on my work schedule? Donnae be daft. Fall in love? Not unless the earth starts revolving around the moon. Those would have been my typical, grumpy responses back then. But now, I have a vibrant, sexy, enchanting wife who adores me as much as I adore her.

The Ogre of Loch Fairbairn is happy. Contented. Whole.

Sunshine streams through the windows in my office, a pleasant respite from the cool fall weather we've been having. It's warm enough that I could shag my wife outdoors today, and I will do that later. I think I'll take her in the forest this time, up against a tree on the path we often follow on our walks. Aye, Emery would love that.

First, I need to finish a bit of work.

My wife sashays into my office, carrying a book, and sprawls on the chair in front of my desk with her feet on the desktop. The sunlight paints her in golden hues, like the angel she is.

My wicked little angel.

Though I see her, I don't let on that I do. Instead, I act as if I'm engrossed in my work. Why? Because I love the way she teases me about it. "I'll be finished in ten minutes, then we can play."

"That doesn't work for me. I want to play right now. To celebrate."

"Celebrate what?" I glance up, and my eyes widen. But they narrow swiftly as my mouth curves into a sensual smile. "It's a good thing we're the only ones in the house today."

Although we have welcomed a number of guests lately, including Emery's American mates, none of them got to see my wife dressed the way she is today. And they never will.

"Don't know what you mean," she says, feigning innocence.

I drop my pen, leaning back in my chair. "You are barely clothed, *mo gaoloch.*"

"Really? I hadn't noticed." She stretches languorously and rises from her chair.

Cannae resist drinking in her appearance, from her ComicCon T-shirt to the black lace of her tiny knickers, and down to the naked expanse of her legs and her bare feet. I exhale a deep groan, rife with the lust she purposely provoked in me. Not that I mind. Having a poke with Emery is my favorite pastime.

Then I notice the book she's holding.

"What are you doing with that?" I ask, caressing the desktop with my fingers, the way I want to touch her body.

Emery ambles to the desk and leans against it as she hands me our photo album. "I added something to it."

I accept the book and flip it open, smiling at the title page. "We're still evolving, then?"

"Absolutely. I hope we never stop."

"We won't." I thumb through the pages, past the pictures that represent every stage in our relationship. When I reach the final page, I freeze. "What..."

She taps her finger on the picture that stopped me, one she's shown me before—a photo of Emery as a baby. "A preview of what the next phase in our evolution might look like. Your little guys are strong swimmers."

"My what?"

"Your sperm, baby. They got the job done."

I stare at her for a moment, baffled by her statement. Then I finally grasp her meaning and break into the biggest smile I've ever given anyone. "It's true?"

"No, I thought it would be funny to trick you."

"We—" I haul in a shaky breath and exhale it as laughter. "We're having a baby?"

"Yes, my sweetie-pie, we are."

I leap out of my chair, throw my arms around her, and drag my wife across the desk. Her feet have just touched down on the floor when I lift her up, her feet swinging, and consume my wife with a kiss that verges on being indecent. When I pull away, I keep our lips close enough that they brush each other. "I love you, Emery."

"I love you too, Rory baby."

"You were right. We do need to celebrate." I set her down, then grip her around the waist and flip her to face the desk. "Donnae move."

She obeys, facing away from me.

Only when we're shagging does my wife do what I say without teasing me or demanding to know why. I wouldn't want her to be too biddable. Her fire, and that light inside her, drew me to Emery on the night we met. And they still draw me in.

I shed my clothes.

My wife glances over her shoulder at me. "Time to play?"

"Aye."

She gasps when I yank her lace knickers down to her ankles, then she kicks them off. My ravenous wife apparently can't wait to get started, and she rips her shirt off over her head before I have the chance to do that. Naturally, she isn't wearing a bra. My wife came here to fuck, and she always arrives prepared.

"Palms on the desk," I command.

"Yes, my lord." She slaps her hands on the desktop and wiggles her erse. "I live to serve."

"Like hell you do." I skate my lips over her rump and then glide my tongue along the upper curve of each cheek. "You're obstinate and independent, and I wouldn't have you any other way."

I drag my hands up her sides, around to her belly.

She spreads her legs.

"You are so beautiful, so perfect," I rumble, while my hands travel up her body to fondle her tits. As I palm those globes and knead them, scraping my thumbs over her nipples, I crush the hard length of my erection into her back. "You are the most precious gift I've ever received."

"You're so sweet." She moans when I slide my cock between her thighs. "But for heaven's sake, say something dirty."

I chuckle and shift one hand to her mound, diving two fingers between her folds. "Ahm going to fuck ye, Em, until my cock is slick with your cream and ye beg me to make ye come. Is that dirty enough?"

Her mouth opens, but she can't speak. I've plunged my fingers down her cleft and inside her opening, where all that luscious cream waits for me. When I stroke her clit, she moans again with more volume and hunger. I sweep my fingers up and down, settling the heel of my hand on her taut nub, and work her flesh until she bucks her hips forward, then back, in time with every stroke of my fingers. She rotates her hips in a frantic attempt to rub her *brillean* against my hand, but I make sure she can't quite get what she wants, not yet. Emery whimpers and digs her nails into the desktop. I keep her balanced on the edge of climax, teetering but unable to tumble over, because I know my wife loves it.

But *mhac na galla*, my cock feels ready to explode.

"Please, Rory, please."

I nip her shoulder. "Cannae resist a warm, wet lass who begs."

Clutching her hips, I thrust deep inside her.

"OhGodyesohyesthankyou," she cries out, the syllables coming so fast that they blend into one word.

Her climax convulses her entire body as her inner muscles clench my cock in waves that seem like they'll never end. I grit my teeth against the need to come, because I won't do it until she's done. Her strangled scream echoes in the room just as her spasms wane.

I pump in and out of her body, my *bagais* slapping on her erse with every inward thrust and her slickness creating a sucking sound with every withdrawal. She rocks her hips backward to meet my thrusts, crying out every time I penetrate her. Faster, deeper, harder, I punch into her while she throws her head back and plasters her backside to my front, lashing her arms around my neck while I grunt and groan and shout.

She comes again.

"Oh God, Em!" I shout, plowing into her twice more, holding the last thrust while I come deep inside her body. As I gasp for breath, I wrap my arms around her with my hands over her belly. "I hope our bairn is just like you."

"I hope our baby's like you."

Reluctantly, I peel my body away from hers and turn my wife toward me. "Our baby will be the best of both of us, and better than either of us because our love made this bairn."

"This is one lucky baby." She loops her arms around my waist. "And the first of several, I hope."

"Several? Best keep practicing for the next one, then."

By the time we finish practicing, we've made our way up to the third floor and collapsed on our bed. My wife lies sprawled across my body, tracing lazy circles on my chest. "In a couple months, we'll have our first Christmas together."

"Can't think of a blessed thing I need or want." I kiss the top of her head. "You've given me the two best gifts—your love, and our baby."

"I think we should throw a big holiday party."

"Anything you want, *m'eudail*. This will be the first Christmas in years where I've had something to be grateful for."

She lifts her head to gaze at me, her eyes full of a love I know she sees in my gaze too. "Our life is amazing. Now, if I could just help Jamie and Gavin…"

"Matchmaking?" I groan. "What can I do to dissuade you from that course?"

"It might be hard…" She skims her hand down to my groin. "But I'm sure you'll think of something."

I don't mind as much as I act like I do if my wife and sisters-in-law conspire to meddle in the lives of Jamie and Gavin. Maybe they will find the kind of joy Emery gives me every day. But if Gavin breaks my sister's heart…

"Oh no," Emery says, "there will be no plotting to assassinate Gavin."

"What? I didn't say a word."

"I can read your mind, baby."

"Then read this." I roll on top of her, drilling my gaze into hers, and think the filthiest thing I can imagine. "What am I thinking, *mo leannan?*"

"Can't quite hear it. Better show me."

I demonstrate my thoughts for her, and I mean to keep showing her every day how grateful I am to have her in my life. She is the only true wife I've ever had, and the only woman I'll ever need. One night in New Orleans changed my life, but the love of one determined woman saved my soul.

**Want more of Gavin and Jamie? Experience their story
in *Gift-Wrapped in a Kilt* (Hot Scots, Book Four).**

**Did you miss the original version of this story told from Emery's
viewpoint? *Scandalous in a Kilt* is available now everywhere.**

*A*nna Durand is a bestselling, multi-award-winning author of contemporary and paranormal romance. Her books have earned bestseller status on every major retailer and wonderful reviews from readers around the world. But that's the boring spiel. Here are the really cool things you want to know about Anna!

Born on Lackland Air Force Base in Texas, Anna grew up moving here, there, and everywhere thanks to her dad's job as an instructor pilot. She's lived in Texas (twice), Mississippi, California (twice), Michigan (twice), and Alaska—and now Ohio.

As for her writing, Anna has always made up stories in her head, but she didn't write them down until her teen years. Those first awful books went into the trash can a few years later, though she learned a lot from those stories. Eventually, she would pen her first romance novel, the paranormal romance *Willpower*, and she's never looked back since.

Want even more details about Anna? Get access to her extended bio when you subscribe to her newsletter and download the free bonus ebook, *Hot Scots Confidential*. You'll also get hot deleted scenes, character interviews, fun facts, and more! Plus you'll receive the short story *Tempted by a Kiss* and mutliple bonus chapters in both ebook and audiobook formats.

Visit AnnaDurand.com to sign up.